THE RIGHTFUL HEIR.

I. "THE EARL OF MONTREVILLE DASHED INTO THE ROOM."
II. "ON THE ROCKS—DEAD."

No. 1.

THE RIGHTFUL HEIR;

A ROMANCE OF

THE DAYS OF GOOD QUEEN BESS.

BY THE AUTHOR OF "THE NIGHT GUARD," &c.

CHAPTER I.

THE CHAPEL ON ST. KINIAN'S CLIFF.

"WHITHER go you so fast, Master Walter?" cried the armed sentinel at the gate of Montreville Castle, as young Walter Tracy burst hurriedly from the inner door of the western tower, and crossed the court-yard.

It was a dark night, and the grand old castle frowned like a grim watcher over the surrounding country; while around the battlements, which many a stout heart had defended against rebellious foes, the wind howled dismally and warningly, seeming to bring up wild messages of danger from the great restless sea, which rolled but a short distance off beneath the rugged cliffs.

Not heeding at first the challenge of the sentinel, young Walter, the page to my Lord of Montreville, sprang upon the raised stonework and gazed over the battlements.

No shadow of coming evil overclouded his heart then, as he gazed out over the dark country, and down upon the jagged rocks upon which the grand old castle of Montreville was built.

He took one sweeping glance over the scene, and then, tossing back the dark chestnut curls that waved down from beneath his plumed cap, approached the sentinel who had accosted him.

"What said you but now, good Hubert?" he asked.

"I asked whither went you so fast?" repeated the sentinel; "but since you have stopped to speak, I presume you go not at all.

As the man spoke, the page, whose eager eyes were fixed upon the castle, started and gazed up more earnestly still.

In one of the large windows—the window of a room which looked out not upon the battlements, but down over the sheer deep walls—a light suddenly appeared, casting a gentle flickering beam upon the surrounding darkness.

It remained a moment, and was then extinguished.

"I go at once, good Hubert," cried the page, excitedly; "tell no one you have seen me. No matter who demands my presence, say you know nought of me. I may be hours absent, and none must know of my being without the castle. Hubert, I saved your life once, when the savage wrath of the Lord of Montreville would have hurled you from these battlements. Do me this simple service."

"I will, and would do more for you," said the man; "but," he added, lowering his voice, as if the very wind might whisper echoes of treason, "is it true that you visit yonder castle of Lanfornette? The deadliest foe of the heirs of Montreville has been seen in converse with you. Are you sure you go not there?"

"I swear it. Let me pass, good Hubert," exclaimed Walter; "there is no treason to my lord in *this* heart, you may swear. Ha! who comes? The change of guard. Quick, open the gate."

Infected by the eager manner of the young page, whose eyes seemed to dart fire as he waited, the sentinel quickly unlocked the gate, and in a few moments the youth had fled over the clattering drawbridge, and was lost amid the gloom and the darkness.

As the door re-closed upon him the guard reached it.

At their head was a man of some thirty years, clad in the clothes of a gentleman, but scarcely of a man of high degree.

"For whom did you open the gate, Hubert?" said he. "For one who went in hot haste it seemed to me."

"It was my brother who quitted me so quickly, Sir Grey," returned Hubert, unhesitatingly; "he came to bring a message to my lord."

"What message?"

"A message for his private ear, Sir Grey de Malpas," returned the man, "and that you *must* be aware, Sir Grey, cannot be for you."

"Insolent!" exclaimed Sir Grey, as his hand flew to his sword; but in a moment he turned away with an impatient gesture, saying to the men, "Relieve the guard yourselves. I have other things to think of."

Then he walked away that he might stifle the passion which was evidently fast rising in his breast, rendered none the less potent and tumultuous by the smothered titter of the men he left behind him.

"Curses on the varlets," he muttered, as he leaned over the battlements where young Walter Tracy had leaned but a few moments before. "Curses on them, and on the fortune which has placed me at their mercy! Poverty! poverty! another word for crime! The servants laugh at it, the masters pity and scorn it; the sea yonder seems to raise its hoarse voice in jeers when I gaze out upon its majestic waters; and yet I—cousin to my lord—I Sir Grey de Malpas, young, brave and——. But of what use is this? I must be doing. Revenge is my only hope now, and that shall descend swift and sure as the falcon's swoop."

He stood shuddering in the gusty wind for another moment, and then turned to re-enter the castle.

At the door he was met by a retainer.

"My lord has need of you to write to London, Sir Grey," said he, respectfully.

The poor noble started.

"Ah! Jacques," he said, "your voice seems strange to me. Amid all these insults you alone are faithful. Take this piece of gold; it is the poor kinsman's mite; but," he added, lowering his voice, "some day *I* shall be Lord of Montreville, and *you* shall be my first henchman. Mark well the Lady Margaret and the boy Walter. Watch them, I say! watch them!"

And, as he hissed out these words, with an intonation of fearful hate, he passed away and entered presently—bowing and respectful—the study of the Lord of Montreville.

Meanwhile the young page, when he left the castle, walked rapidly up the sloping ground to a spot overshadowed by lofty trees, and out of range of any of the sentinels on that dark stormy night.

Here he halted, and, leaning his back against a tree, folded his arms, and gazed back at the castle.

His eyes beamed brightly—eagerly, as he gazed, and his bosom seemed to swell with a strong emotion.

Each moment, indeed, appeared to add to his agitation.

He had not long, however, to wait.

Presently a light appeared in the turret window.

"The second signal," he murmured, his heart beating wildly in his bosom—"dear, dearest Margaret! loved of my youth, sole idol of my heart, ere morning to be mine—mine, mine for ever."

The surging sea that boiled and roared beneath the cliffs appeared to echo back his speech, but to fashion words of far different meaning—"never—never."

But the youth saw not this interpretation of their hushing warning.

His heart was full to overflowing with joyous yearning.

Margaret de Montreville, sole heiress of an honoured race, and future mistress of the castle and rich domains, had promised on that evening to become, by a secret marriage, the wife of him—the poor page—the owner of an unspotted name and nothing more.

Young hearts, full of life's first passion, reckless of all consequences, dreaming only of the wellspring of unquenchable love springing up in their hearts, they had long loved in secret; and, in the face of a dread union with one she hated, the Lady Margaret de Montreville had consented to fulfil on that night the promise which she was well aware could never be fulfilled in public and with her father's consent.

Little did the grey-haired Lord of Montreville, sitting in his study, dictating to his poor kinsman, Sir Grey de Malpas, a letter to the Court in London, dream that young Walter Tracy, his favourite page, was waiting beneath the elm trees to snatch from him the brightest jewel in his coronet.

But so it was; and as the third signal light beamed out upon the darkness the youth's impatience displayed itself in his eager strides to and fro.

Presently two white figures gleamed for an instant on the battlements, then the gate was once more opened, hurrying steps made for the shadowy wood, and in another moment a tall, stately, lovely maiden — the heiress of Montreville—was clasped to her page-lover's heart.

"Oh! rapture—rapture! sweet, sweet Margaret," he exclaimed, as he held her from him after a moment, and gazed into her face, "am I awake or dreaming? Can it be true, bright flower, that you have torn yourself from the sunshine of yonder pleasant pathways to share the dark and chequered path with me?"

"Yes, dear Walter," she murmured, tremulously; "yes, I am here—yours, yours for ever—true as yonder sea to the shore—true as the bright sun to the earth."

"Come, let us hasten then, love," said Walter, drawing her gently towards the path beneath the rocks, "the priest awaits us, and your absence must not be so long as to be noticeable. Do you, Agnes," he added to the maid who had accompanied her mistress, "follow us closely, for the way, as you know, is steep."

In a few moments more they had descended the steep path, and were making their way along the dark and shingly shore.

It was on this wild dark night, in the year 15—, when St. Kinian's Cliff was enveloped in haze and gloom, that an old man stood upon its summit and gazed down upon the rocky path below.

St. Kinian's Cliff was a bold and rugged promontory, thrusting its head out daringly over the moaning waves, and sheltering by its shadow deep ravines and echoing caves, where man's vengeance upon man had been wreaked full oft in secret.

Far away on one side, looking from its ragged topmost rocks you could see vast woodlands, whose summits seemed to kiss the sky, and cottages of herdsmen dotted here and there, and loftier mansions on the edge of pleasant meads, and nearest of all the Castle of Montreville towering up—grim and gaunt sentinel—over the surrounding country.

On the cliff itself, though not upon its topmost summit, was a little structure which boasted the name of chapel—a little place where pilgrims came to pray, where the poor came for comfort, and the rich for absolution.

This was the chapel of Alton, the priest to whom the young people, full of love and hope, were wending their way in the darkness.

He had several times warned the passionate and impetuous youth.

But all in vain.

He had resolved to secure his bride; the bride had consented, what more had he to wait for?

The priest had urged to deeds of daring; to the winning of knightly spurs; to the bold claiming of his bride, when he had fought his way to distinction.

But Walter Tracy's desires were different.

"No, no," he cried, "let me secure my beloved—let her be mine—mine only for no man to wrest from me—no father's cruel will to force into a hated and unnatural marriage. Then I will away to the Golden West, whose rivers run with riches, and in those perfumed bowers of wealth and wonders fight for the treasures that shall make me the equal of the Lord of Montreville. But I tell thee, old man, I must have something to give me hope and earnest in such a combat, and that hope and earnest is a fair and loving bride."

So the priest consented, and, as we have seen, was now anxiously awaiting them.

Presently he beheld them stepping carefully yet rapidly in and out the rocky obstructions, and ascending the winding pathway towards St. Kinian's Cliff.

"Ah!" he cried, "they hurry eagerly towards me as to one who can make them happy for ever! They little reck the quicksands and whirlpools against which their barque of life will have to make its way!"

In a few moments more the young lovers had scaled the battlements which Nature had set up in its own defence, and stood beneath the little porch of the chapel.

"We are to our time, holy father," said Walter Tracy, as he led forward the trembling girl who clung to his arm.

"Yes, my son," replied the priest, "yes, and the chapel is ready. Enter."

Passing over the threshold—from Man's Free Ground into God's Holy Temple—they reverently approached the altar.

The little chapel had been made light and pleasant, as far as it could be, by the priest's own hands.

Candles burned in niches, showing out dim old figures of saints and quaint picturings on the dark walls, and casting a strange lightness over the chill abode of peace, sanctified by use and age.

I need not pause to describe the ceremony that made one in love and by right the humble page, Walter Tracy, and the Lady Margaret, sole Heiress of Montreville.

A trembling tongue murmured forth words on one side, and a tender bosom trembled forth deep sighs; while on the other a manly face beamed with rapturous joy, and a manly breast swelled with a pride which was prouder even than that of birth.

At length the service was over, the papers signed, and the young lovers were made one till death.

"Bless you, thrice bless you," said the priest as they departed. "Till the day you absolve me from the vow I have made you, your secret is safe. Be wise, loving, prudent, and, when the time comes, be not afraid to tell all."

The young page wrung the hand of the kind counsellor, and in a few moments the trio had taken their way once more towards the Castle of Montreville.

As the clock struck twelve the two white figures—the mistress and the maid—entered by the large gate.

Half an hour after a man was seen dimly, uncertainly in the darkness, scaling the low wall of the private court of the castle.

The sentinel challenged the intruder, and, receiving no answer, fired; but, on a search being made, no one was found, and the superstitious guards set it down at once as a visit from some unearthly guest, whose presence boded no good to the Lord of Montreville.

CHAPTER II.

ON THE ROCKS—DEAD!

SIR GREY DE MALPAS—deadly as was his hate of the family whose poor kinsman he was, and nothing else—had little chance within the year which followed the secret marriage of the page and the rich heiress to perpetrate any of his schemes of vengeance.

The young bride and bridegroom often and often met in secret; but though, from the manner of Lady Margaret, Sir Grey had some suspicion, he had nothing upon which to base a practical plan of malevolence.

So a year passed.

A year of secret happiness for Margaret, and yet of grave sorrow.

Being now nineteen years of age, she was considered by her father to be eligible for marriage, and a suitor appeared in the person of Lord Ronald de Spenser, a man some twenty years her senior, yet hallowed in the eyes of the Lord of Montreville by the fact that he had a large rent-roll, and could trace his ancestory to the buccaneers who accompanied William the Conqueror to England.

Forced thus to dissemble, compelled to show a smiling face to her new suitor, while her heart was weeping, she passed a sad and dreary time when her young husband was sent, on the eleventh month of their marriage, upon a special mission to London.

It was Sir Grey de Malpas who planned and effected this journey; but he failed in his endeavour.

With her young husband absent, the Lady Margaret was more careful than before.

Watch as Sir Grey might, he could discover nothing against her fair name, and when, at length, a child was born, during the young husband's absence, a temporary plea of illness shrouded her from all observation.

Oh! she longed for him then!

Oh! how she pleaded to Heaven for his quick return when the first infant smile broke out upon her like a sunbeam. Oh! how little of the pride of Montreville was in her when she heard its first crowing welcome, and saw its joy as it nestled upon her breast!

To say that Sir Grey de Malpas was quite off the scent would be wrong.

He was not.

He had seen an interchange of smiles between page and lady; he had seen the frown settle upon the face of Walter Tracy as Ronald de Spenser led the Lady Margaret to her seat; he had guessed love and love's recklessness and treason, but he had never dreamed of secret marriage.

More and more, while the young page was absent, did he close in his toils, yet in vain.

The bright-faced, joyous, impetuous youth who had taken Lord Montreville's letter to London, was as light and joyous, and impetuous when he returned as when he went, and as he quitted my lord's presence, and hurried out upon the battlements, there was a gleam of intense happiness upon his features, which smote Sir Grey to the very soul.

"You have done well in London, my young sir, I reckon?" said Sir Grey; "the king doubtless received you at court?"

The page despised the speaker, not for his poverty or his words, but the spirit that spoke through them.

"Were it so, I should keep the knowledge to myself," he said; "it might be dangerous for a page to soar too high."

They were at the door of the guard room as they spoke; and Walter, nodding somewhat superciliously and significantly, quitted his side and passed out into the court yard.

The night was bright and clear, and one glance sufficed to show to Walter Tracy that his faithful friend Hubert kept the gate.

"Not a word that you have seen me," he said; "I scale yonder wall. If they by chance ask for me, say—"

"What?" asked a voice behind him.

It was the voice of Sir Grey de Malpas.

"Say," cried Walter, eying him scornfully and angrily, "that I made a jest to lead astray a beggarly buffoon, who ought to be *kicked* and *scourged* from Montreville!"

And with these angry words he turned and re-entered the castle.

But it was not in Sir Grey de Malpas's power to prevent the visit of young Walter Tracy to his wife that night.

He knew how anxiously she hoped for his coming; he knew that within there a son had been born to him, *sole heir of Montreville*, the pledge of his heart's great love; and this knowledge, dangerous, as it was in itself, made him laugh to scorn all warnings of a further peril.

When thick night, therefore, had fallen over the castle, he once more stole forth, and made his way cautiously towards the wall of the private court.

This time no one interrupted his progress towards his wife's chamber.

Everything was very still.

Hubert, the friendly sentinel, was not there, but the hush of the sea, and the gentle sighing of the wind round the old turrets, and the darkness and loneliness, had lulled the watchers off to sleep, and, though the bright moonlight lay upon the broad courtyard, the young page made his way unperceived, and leaping the wall was soon beneath the window of the bride that eagerly expected him.

A long, low whistle was the signal given, and in a few moments the casement above was thrown open, and a rope-ladder was cast down to him.

Without this assistance it was impossible to reach the window; for directly below it was a sheer fall of some fifty feet upon jagged rocks, upon which the castle was built.

Fastening the end of the rope-ladder

to a large nail, the young page, regardless of the giddy height over which he had to trust himself, hurried up the frail support, and in a few moments had entered the room and clasped his young bride in his arms.

"Oh! Walter," she cried, "what have I not suffered in your absence! Insult —secrecy—dread worse than death!"

"I am here now, then," he cried, "here to defend you and love you. But, tell me, where is my child?"

The nurse, a faithful old domestic, who had seen the Lady Margaret's eyes first beam out upon the world, advanced as he spoke, and brought to him his child.

Oh! how the young father's heart leaped, as the helpless babe nestled in his arms.

Some unseen angel figure seemed to hover over him—some angel voice seemed to whisper to him, as he stood holding the helpless babe on one arm, while with the other he clasped his young and beautiful wife.

"Oh! when will your father be able to claim you and your beloved mother?" exclaimed he, "Oh, Margaret," he added, as he replaced the child tenderly in its mother's arms, "how terrible is this secrecy—this creeping of honourable love by back ways! Yet I had a vision last night, Margaret—a vision of great things to come. We were acknowledged husband and wife before the world—nobles were our friends, and then——"

As he spoke, there was the tramp of soldiery without, the clinking of swords, and the grounding of muskets.

Then came a whispered command from un-recognised lips, and a loud knocking at the door.

The pale bride glanced eagerly and fearfully at the door, while Walter, to whose breast she clung, as to a tower of strength, glared desperately, also, in that direction.

"Who is there?" asked Margaret timidly.

"Say, rather, who is in your room, Lady Margaret," shouted the angry voice of the Lord of Montreville. "Open, wretched girl!—open to your father's command, if you would not have me burst through the door, and my soldiers look upon your shame!"

"Oh, merciful God! Walter!" mur-mured Margaret. "Oh, mad that we have been—to risk a union that might come to this! Oh, fly, my husband—fly! One kiss on my brow, one blessing on your babe, then go—and God be with you!"

"Open, I say, rash girl!" shouted the Earl of Montreville, again.

"Thus, then, I bless thee, poor helpless pledge of love, too rashly gratified!" cried Walter. "Oh, Margaret, I go! Tell me, in this hour, you regret not the marriage which has given us yonder bade!"

"Hark—hark, Walter, they are bursting open the door! Quick! quick to the window—quick! I regret nothing! I love you—I love you! Go!"

Heavy fell the blows of the retainers upon the stout oaken door as Walter dashed open the casement.

In an instant he recoiled.

"Ah! what villian has done this?" he cried aloud. "The ladder is gone! But it matters not. To save you and mine I fly, though death is in the leap!"

"Oh, no, in mercy, no!" cried Margaret, clinging to him, and clasping him to her wildly beating heart. "Not that horrid leap—anything, anything but that! Face my father. Plead to him for me and our child, but do not risk that terrible leap, where death awaits your coming!"

He kissed her passionately, and put her from him by gentle force.

"No, no, dear one," he cried, "one kiss of my child—so; one embrace from you! 'tis well. I go not to death but honour! Look down below there where yon gnarled and stunted tree clings to the jagged rocks. That will break my fall, and, quitting for years, if need be, the precincts of the castle, I will return to you noble and your equal. Adieu, adieu, Margaret. See, the door yields. Now for death or glory!"

Then, ere she could restrain him, he sprang from the window into the dark void.

An instant after a crashing sound and a wailing cry rang out on the night air, and the dark shadows of great frightened birds flew across the window.

"Oh! good and merciful God!" exclaimed Margaret, sinking on her knees, as the nurse fled into the adjoining room. "Grant that he lives. Poor Walter!"

" As she wailed out the name, with a tender moaning, the door was burst open, and the Earl of Montreville dashed into the room, followed by Sir Grey de Malpas, and a crowd of armed retainers.

" Was I wrong, was I wrong, my lord," cried Sir Grey, vindictively, as he pointed to the kneeling girl. " Behold your daughter on her knees; see yon open window! He has fled; but he *has* been here. Let your retainers——"

" Peace!" exclaimed the earl, sternly. " If he be gone, this is no subject to make gossip of among my servants. Look to your lady!" he added fiercely to the maid, Agnes, as Margaret fell senseless on the floor. " And you, fellows, can go. I and Sir Grey can fathom this mystery ourselves."

" A child's cry yonder," said Sir Grey, as the retainers drew back wondering, and passed away along the echoing corridor. " Will you see it, and be sure?"

" Accursed be my sight if ever I blight it with such a shame as that," cried the earl. " That they were married I believe; but, mark me well, the child this night I give up to your care. Place it where *she* will never again behold it. Now come with me. We will first explore the rocks below where no man, save one held up by a miracle, could fall and live. Oh! that my eyes should gaze upon a scene like this! But, come; first for the proof, then for the child—away with it for ever!"

Alone, the stern earl and the poor kinsman left the postern-gate of the castle, and, with a flaming torch, hurried along the jagged rocks which formed the foundation of the grim old castle.

They guessed at once, ere they started, what sight would meet their eyes.

The old fortress, built years, long years before, to brave not only the tempest but the storm of man's anger also, was founded, as I have just said, upon sharp and rugged boulders, and towered a terrible height above the surrounding country.

The spot where the young page had taken his fearful leap was about the deepest fall of all, and here they hurried with eager steps, expecting full well that, if alive, he could not have crawled far.

Not far had they to search.

Beneath the window, where he had snatched the last kiss from his child and its young mother, lay the form of the noble youth, hurled to his early and inevitable death.

The old earl gazed sternly upon the mangled form for some moments.

" A noble and a handsome youth he muttered. " Presumptuous boy! Why did you not mate with your equal, whose tender, quiet love might have taken the place of the stormy passion which has disgraced a father and ruined thee.

" You pity him?" said Sir Grey, glancing up vindictively.

" I pity most myself," returned the earl. " See that he is buried secretly, within the hour, and then to Margaret's chamber, and secure the child. Heed no cries—no entreaties, but bring it away. No violence I desire, but mark well that I hear not of it again."

" Your will shall be done, my lord," replied Sir Grey, " most willingly."

Within an hour a grave had been dug beneath the battlements of the castle—wondering men digging it—wondering men holding torches—the poor kinsman looking on with a grim smile, and thinking in his own treacherous heart—

" One less between me and Montreville!"

The stormy wind howled the only requiem that poor Walter Tracy was honoured with, save the hoarse song of the restless waves; and when the body had been laid in its narrow bed, and the earth had been trampled down, there was no sign to show where the brave heart, grand in its death, had been hidden from the gaze of prying mortals.

The wind had increased, and the rain had begun to descend in torrents, as Sir Grey de Malpas issued once more from the castle, with the babe he had wrested from the arms of its terrified nurse.

He held it beneath his cloak with a savage firmness, as he would have clutched a prize; for was not this another life between him and Montreville, and was it not in his power to destroy this also?

The wind howled, and the rain drove in his face, and the thunder boomed, and the lightning dashed its forked tongues from one horizon to another; but Sir Grey de Malpas faltered not in his terrible purpose.

At length he arrived at the spot where he had resolved to consummate his villany.

" Now," he cried, as he stood on the

verge of St. Kinian's Cliff—two hundred feet above the boiling waves—"now, as his father died on the jagged rocks, so shall the young heir of Montreville die also. 'Never let me behold it,' said my most gracious kinsman; I will do his bidding to the letter."

While he spoke, however, and raised the babe to cast it to its doom, a hand was placed upon his shoulder, and as he started round in dismay a flash of lightning revealed to him the stern and angry features of 'Alton, the hermit-priest.

CHAPTER III.

SAVED FROM THE TOILS.

FOR some moments Sir Grey de Malpas and the priest stood upon the cliffs above that stormy sea, striving to see each other's features through the gloom.

But they strove in vain.

The lightning, as if to mock them, had ceased its vivid flashings, and the sea, and the land, and the sky, were all enveloped in deep darkness.

"By what right do you stop my path, old man?" cried Sir Grey de Malpas, savagely, furious in his black heart that anything should step between him and his vengeance.

"By the right which Heaven gives to every man to protect the innocent," returned the priest sternly. "I heard your muttered words. I guessed full well their import. Yonder—if you have with you there a child, as I suspect—is a poor fisher's cottage, where it can receive the kindness it so much lacks. Give it to me. I will take it thither, and, depend upon it, my Lord of Montreville will never be troubled by the sight of it."

Sir Grey muttered a low curse, and, for an instant, debated in his own mind whether it would not be as well to solve the difficulty by hurling the old priest from the summits of the rocks, as well as the child, so that below there in the deep and well-nigh inaccessible ravines, the Heir and the Holder of the Secret might lie and moulder away unseen together.

But second thoughts convinced him of the folly of such a course.

The child, truly, might be sacrificed, but the witness and the avenger might live.

At this moment, too, a light was seen streaming out from the door of the cottage indicated by the priest, and the fisherman, attracted by the sound of voices, stood upon the threshold and held above his head a large lantern.

Cursing in his heart the interference of the priest, Sir Grey de Malpas was about to hurry forward, when Alton stopped him.

"Stay," he cried; "if this is a secret you desire kept, let me take the child and see to its being placed yonder in proper care. The sight of your face, well known in this vicinity, will turn suspicion towards Montreville. Come, quick, ere the man accosts us. Give me the infant, and your purse, and await me in yonder chapel. I will be with you anon."

Tenderly clasping to his breast the helpless babe that Sir Grey de Malpas relinquished with such reluctance, the priest hurried towards the cottage and addressed the fisherman.

"God be with you, Master Stanforth," he said. "I bring to you a strange charge, but yet one that will bring money with it. Can I enter?"

"Aye, Mr. Alton, enter and welcome," returned the man; "it's not a night for men to tarry without when there's warmth and shelter within. But where's your friend? I thought I heard two voices."

"You did, but he is gone," returned the priest, hurriedly.

Then entering, he approached the fireplace, and sat down close beside the chair of the fisher's bonnie wife.

Both Robert Stanforth and his spouse had a good reputation in the vicinity for honesty and kindliness of heart, and they broke forth into exclamations of pity and surprise when they beheld the face of the poor, unfortunate child who had come so secretly into the stormy and unfriendly world.

"Poor, helpless babe," said the woman, as she pressed it to her breast; "how could a mother give up to strangers the care of such a child as this?"

"Alas!" murmured the priest, "the mother had no alternative! The parting was forced upon her; this child, though he is the offspring of a lawful marriage solemnised by me, must yet remain secret and unknown. His own safety depends on our silence. His mother, doubtless, will visit him; but the veil of her silent sorrow must not be raised. Here is money; tend it well, and Heaven's blessing rest upon you."

With this blessing the priest rose, and, quitting the hut, hurried to his own humble dwelling near the chapel on St. Kinian's Cliff.

Here he found Sir Grey de Malpas anxiously awaiting him.

"Is all right?" asked the poor kinsman; "have they received the child?"

"Yes, and will tend it well. Go, tell my Lord of Montreville that I accept the post of foster-father to its weak life. While he lives he need not fear that he will see it; but tell him also I will guard its welfare as should be guarded the welfare of one whose blood is that of an ancient line.

"Small thanks from the earl for that," thought Sir Grey de Malpas; but he said aloud, "'Tis well; the child is guiltless, but wide seas must part him and his kindred for ever ere he is old enough to question much."

"Of that his mother will be best judge," said Alton; "maybe when years have ripened him into youth his mother would wish to recognise one who, spite of all, is yet the Heir of Montreville."

"Madman!" cried Sir Grey, fiercely, "his mother at this moment is a trembling prisoner; his father—dashed to pieces on the jagged rocks—lies in a secret grave beneath the battlements. Look to it, priest; think not to rear in him a rival to the true Heir of yonder castle. Thy wiles and cunning may be great, but the tide of events will prove their uselessness. Farewell!"

"Stay!" cried the priest, "whom call you the true heir of Montreville?"

"The Lord de Beaufort, mine and my lord's first cousin, who is to marry the Lady Margaret."

"And should they have sons, Sir Grey de Malpas might yet miss the earldom."

"True," said Sir Grey; but death is all powerful and all uncertain, and might step in to stop such dire injustice."

With these words, he inclined his head slightly, and passed away over the dark cliffs.

"That man means murder if ever man meant it," muttered the priest, as he retired to his humble dwelling; "but come what may, I will protect the child of the noble youth who here, on his marriage night, received my blessing on his future."

It was on the third night after this—a calmer night be it said—that a gentle knock was heard at the priest's door. and upon his opening it he beheld two females veiled and dressed in black.

These were Lady Margaret de Montreville and her maid, Agnes.

The priest removed his hat, and bowed reverently—respectful to her rank and her sorrow.

"Lady," he said, "what seek you?"

"To see my child; to see if it be well housed, well cared for. They must not see my face, but my little one must look on me and smile. I have but little time, take me to it at once."

"This way, my lady," said the priest, as he locked the door, and in a few moments he was leading the way towards the hut of the fisherman, Robert Stanforth.

We hurry over this scene.

The more stirring incidents of our tale demand it.

The mother, veiled from the prying eyes of those who stood silent and respectful as she passed through them, went eagerly towards the little chamber where her baby lay fast asleep.

One glance she threw around her, to see if any one but the priest and the maid were there, then she eagerly threw up her veil.

"I must wake him!—I must kiss him!" she cried, as she bent in the fulness of her motherly love over the little cot where the discarded Heir of Montreville lay in its sweet unconsciousness of sorrow.

Then she raised him from his soft pillow, and straining the little form to her breast, kissed its closed eyes until they opened and smiled upon her.

If any one, no matter who, had entered the room at this moment she would not have observed them, for she had eyes only for the child, which she strained to her heaving bosom, and gazed with intense love into the pleasant baby-face.

Presently her maid touched her on the shoulder.

"A saintly face, my lady," she murmured; "but the time presses; we must go, or we shall be suspected."

"True, true, Agnes," she answered, "true, true. But, is he not lovely; is he not his father's portrait? Oh, bless you, bless you!"

"The clock has struck ten, my lady," again urged the maid, "we will come again."

"You are right, Agnes," answered Lady Margaret, with a sigh, as she placed her babe down gently upon its pillow, "I must go. Dear child, adieu, adieu!"

Then she kissed it passionately, and after one long, lingering look, she drew down her veil and passed out once more into the night.

Thus it went on for some time—month after month, year after year.

Secret meetings between mother and son; with eager watching eyes, seeking to discover the truth.

Many a time did Sir Grey de Malpas strive by bribes and even menaces to persuade the fisherman to betray his trust.

But Robert Stanforth was a man of staunch metal.

His heart was in the right place: he was, in fact, a true son of Britain; and even when the visits of the mother of the child unaccountably ceased, he took upon himself more than ever the responsibility of guarding the nameless one.

So Time rolled on.

Many times during the seven years which passed so drearily away for Lady Margaret, did Sir Grey de Malpas renew his efforts to draw Stanforth into a scheme of treachery.

But it was all in vain, and Sir Grey, like many other villains of his stamp, was compelled *to bide his time.*

CHAPTER IV.

WRECKLYFFE, THE BUCCANEER.

NINE years more passed.

During these years strange things had happened.

One dark night, Sir Grey de Malpas had followed Lady Margaret, and returned eagerly to the castle to betray her to her father.

Sir Grey had hoped that she would after this be forced into a convent, and that thus another obstacle would be removed from his path.

But it was not so.

A stormy scene ensued, deadly threats were uttered, and to save her honour, her husband's memory, and her child's life, she consented to become the wife of Lord Beaufort, and to unite thus the two branches of the family.

Another son had been born to her— Clarence Beaufort—the recognised heir of Montreville; her father was dead, and she was mistress of the castle.

Yet she was not mistress of her actions.

Secret visits to the bedside of her first-born were now impossible, and, at length, when Sir Grey de Malpas brought her the news that her boy had sailed to far-off seas, and that news had reached England of his death, she kept her sorrow closed up in her aching heart, and only pressed more warmly to her bosom the one that was spared to her—the one who could take its life from her breast—the one that could be caressed openly—the now acknowledged Heir of the ancient line of Beaufort.

Threats and entreaties from Sir Grey and the old earl, had succeeded in quieting the priest, and he swore that until the death of the old earl *and* Lord

Beaufort, he would never reveal the secret.

More they asked not.

Was it likely that so old and frail a life would survive a strong and healthy one such as Beaufort's, albeit he was twenty years older than the bride who was forced to his arms?

Yet Sir Grey de Malpas lied.

The boy was *not* dead, nor yet from England's shores had he stepped one mile, save in the fishing-smack of his protector and friend, Stanforth.

Oftentimes, when standing on the high cliffs, his gaze wandered towards Montreville, and he saw walking on the battlements a tall, stately figure, clad in dark garments.

Little did he dream that this was his mother; little did she imagine that the tall and vigorous youth, whom she often beheld aiding the men in launching their boats, was her own first-born, and the offspring of her forbidden love!

It was on a pleasant summer evening, some hour or two ere the fisher's time came for putting off to sea, that the priest, Alton, surprised the youth gazing in melancholy reverie towards the Castle of Montreville.

"You are in a brown study, Vyvyan," said the priest. "Of what are you thinking?"

The youth started round.

A wild gleam shot from his eye, as if he had deemed it possible that on the moment some one of the beings created by his fancy had sprung unbidden into life.

He seemed disappointed when his eyes fell upon the priest.

"What am I thinking of ask you, good father?" he cried. "Thinking of a home which I know not—of kindred I never saw. I am verging upon manhood now; tell me, why have I not a mother and a home? How grand it must be to be born in yonder castle like the young heir yonder, to own a mother, whom all love and honour, to be nurtured in the lap of luxury, and have men's reverence by right. Yet, if one cannot own *these* blessings, one can at least boast a mother and a home. Tell me, then, priest, who was my mother? where was my home? why am I nameless, that *you*, my foster-father, should christen me Vyvyan?"

He seized Alton's arm as he spoke, and gazed earnestly into his face.

"Boy, to thy questions I can answer nothing," returned the priest. "I am bound to preserve a secret—a strange and terrible secret—bound by an oath which I dare not, cannot break. When time absolves me I will declare it, but not till then will tears or entreaties, or menaces force me to break my vow. This much I will say, however, you are nobly born, and, mark me, the cloud which dims the dawning sun often foretells its splendour at the noon."

"Yet, I remember something," said Vyvyan. "Sweet memories of bygone times struggle to my brain. I have seen (not always in my dreams, I swear it) a lovely face, sweet with a stately sorrow, and I have heard lips murmur words that only mothers murmur. But, who and what she was, and where I saw her, my brain does not reveal to me. Oh, priest, think of your own dear mother—think of the want I feel."

"Have I not been kind and gentle to you, Vyvyan?"

"Oh, kind and gentle—yes! But chide me not that deep and restless thoughts are stirred within me. Something seems wanting in this world; in the bright face of Nature there appears one void. Oft have I thought in secret on calm nights, when the still heaven watched o'er the slumbering sea, and soft stars danced on every crested wave, and this thought had but one reading—'Why am I motherless?'"

Tears stood in Alton's eyes as the impulsive boy pleaded to him thus, still grasping his arm, and looking up into his face earnestly—anxiously, as to one who held in his hand the Fate of his Future.

"Ask me no more, Vyvyan, I entreat," he cried. "I cannot break my vow. You must abroad to peril and adventure: with your own hand win distinction and glory, and return to England to shame those who will not own you, and bring back joy to the breast of the one—the only one whose heart beats still for you!"

The youth's eyes flashed fire.

"Aye, you speak right, Alton, I *will* win distinction. You know the stranger, Wrecklyffe, him you have seen of late wandering in the village, and gathering to him a crew of brave, bright spirits?

I will join them; he is a poor, but honourable man, and, in these days of wild, adventurous sea-fights, I'll win my road to fame. He has spoken to me once; at yonder tavern he awaits me and others. I go to him, Alton; nay, detain me not. Your words have fired me; I *will* go; upon the sea I'll tread the path of glory, and, with *your* blessing, return to find a mother."

So saying, he raised the priest's hand to his lips, and darted impatiently along the rocky road towards the inn.

"Heaven save me as I well discharge my trust!" murmured Alton. "Yet how to avoid this end? He is bold, impetuous, and, if his life is granted, will win his way to greatness. His mother might fear for him; I should, *never*."

Nor would anyone have feared for him, who gazed upon his dauntless bearing—his firm tread—his whole air of noble courage, as he walked onwards along the rugged path towards the "Mariner's Rest," which, as I have before said, was placed on the summit of a rocky shelf overlooking the sea.

As he approached the ancient house of entertainment, he could hear the sounds of wild laughter and singing, and loud above all a voice which he recognised as that of the strange looking man whom he had met so often in the village and its vicinity.

Again and again he had encountered this stranger, near Alton's cottage, and on the rocks, and a simple " good morrow" had led to discourse of a wild and romantic nature, which had fired the soul of the young hero, and made him long for action.

A shout welcomed him now as he rounded the corner and came suddenly upon a scene of reckless carouse.

On the corner of a table, in front of the inn, was seated a man, upon whose face Time and the Storms of Nature and Passion had stamped their indelible seals.

His eyes were fierce and stern, his features bold and prominent, while his attire, ragged, yet cast upon him with a kind of wild grace, showed that he still had memories of a past which had been one of wealth and honour.

"Ha, Vyvyan!" cried he, as our hero approached. "Welcome — thrice welcome! We expected you. Ho! there, wench," he added, turning towards the pretty maid of the inn, who was standing by; "more ale—good ale, for our young friend—So you have chosen at length to join us?"

"Softly, good master," said Vyvyan, smiling. "My heart yearns truly for adventure, but one night is but small space for deep thought."

"Oh! if you can stay to think, young sir, you are not of such stuff as sea-rovers are made of. Why, at your age, I would have cast aside love, fortune, everything, to have roamed o'er the wild blue seas with Drake or Frobisher. Think of the glory that awaits thee—think of the proud Spaniards whose galleons filled with gold, sail insolently over the Spanish main! Fancy the glow of the heart as your swift ship rushes down upon them; think of the wild cries, as your first broadside pours in! Think of the cheers that rise from English throats as your boarders dash on the deck of the enemy, and sweep them yelling into the sea! Then, as the flag is hauled down, and the English ensign runs up to the mast-head, think of the rush of manly pride into your bosom when you remember what souls will glow in England when they hear of your deeds of glory. See yonder flag," he added, pointing to the British ensign, which one of the men had unrolled, and was trailing on the ground; " that is your beacon—that is the fortress you have to defend. Reflect that the brave Island Queen has blessed it and given it to *us*— the mariners in whom she confides—as a sacred trust to guard for her!"

"Your words are wild and brave," said Vyvyan. "I have dreamed of scenes like these, and the sea seems to call me nightly with its many voices. You have seen these things?"

"Seen them! aye, truly," cried Wrecklyffe, as he drained his goblet, and brought it down with a clatter on the rough table.

Then, as he saw how Vyvyan's eyes flashed and his bosom heaved as he listened, he proceeded still more glowingly, telling wild stories of enchanted isles, whose rivers ran with gold; of brave Walter Raleigh, of daring Drake, of Columbus, whose prophetic eyes peered into unseen places, to discover worlds and treasures for all mankind.

Vyvyan gazed and gazed, and trembled

with excitement as he did so, while even the maid of the inn stood behind the enthusiastic youth and listened with open mouth to the words of the wild seaman, who, as he raised his glass aloft and poured forth his stories of the sea, seemed fired himself, as he wished to fire others.

Even the rough men round him, whose forms and faces told of many an encounter with the storm, listened eagerly as he spoke, gazing upon him, wrecked and ragged as he was, as the impersonation of a master mind, and raising a loud and hearty cheer as he ended his speech, and quaffed his foaming ale to his mouth, hot and dry with speaking.

" You speak like one who loved adventure truly," said Vyvyan ; " when do you start ?"

" To-night, at twelve, we leave these shores," said Wrecklyffe. " Come, sit by me, and drink to England's Queen. I have much more to tell you yet. We have commission to sail at once, and pursue, with others, the ships that will in a week leave Cadiz, laden with armed men for the Western Isles. There is special honour waiting us, and," he added, sinking his voice, " if *you*, like *me*, have fortune to retrieve ; if you have hopes of glory and suspicions of a birth (aye, start not, I know all), a birth, a right unrecognised, come with me and win your way, with your bright sword, to what you deem your own !"

More we need not repeat of Wrecklyffe's words.

His pleadings were those most likely to fire a young man's heart, and when he had drank with his new companions awhile, and pledged his word to join them, Vyvyan passed away, full of strange excitement, towards the priest's house, from which he was about to take, in his own person, the only comfort and the only pleasure which the hermit had known for long, long years.

Towards nightfall, the wildly-attired men who had caroused with Wrecklyffe till they were nearly mad with drink, left him, and he remained alone in the dark-pannelled chamber in the inn to which they had adjourned.

As soon as they had all departed, a man who had been concealing himself behind some bushes near, advanced, looked cautiously around him, as if suspecting the presence of enemies, and then hurriedly entered the inn.

This man was Sir Grey de Malpas.

CHAPTER V.

ALONE WITH TRAITORS.

" I HAVE waited long, Wrecklyffe," said Sir Grey, as he sat down by the fire, near which the sea-rover had located himself ; " and the night is cold."

" True, true, I have kept you," said Wrecklyffe, " but my men were indulging in their last carouse ere sailing. But enough of that ; I have good news for you."

" You have trapped the boy ?" asked Sir Grey, eagerly.

" Aye, truly trapped him ; yet my heart is somewhat taken with him I confess. He is as bold and brave a lad as ever wore a sword or trod a deck. He would make a famous buccaneer."

" Aye, truly," said Sir Grey de Malpas, " he would, but he must not live to court that fate. Listen to me," he added, in a lower voice ; " you, who are ruined, should have sympathy with me, who, as years go by, see nothing but plodding, plodding serfdom. It is better to be a pirate, a robber, than a poor kinsman, whose sword is used as that of a head-retainer."

" I do sympathise with you — what then ?" cried Wrecklyffe. " I cannot, nevertheless, understand you. Were I in your position, I would be Earl of Montreville *without* the sympathy of any. You have a sword—what more can you desire *

Sir Grey de Malpas smiled—an unpleasant, ghastly smile.

"Aye, aye," he said, "each to his own ideas. This boy stands between me and Montreville—he is one. The old earl will die; doubtless the Lord Beaufort will die, too. They are both carpet knights, men of no thews and sinews. Look at me. I shall outlive them all. Then this Vyvyan disposed of, there are but a weak woman and an infant between me and honour. Say, good Wrecklyffe, will you swear this boy returns no more?"

"He knows not his kindred—fear him not," said Wrecklyffe; "he will learn manners in my school."

Sir Grey glanced round him with the swift glance of cunning cowardice.

"Wrecklyffe, you have sworn to aid me; have you not."

"I have."

"Here is the gold I proffered," said Sir Grey, in a half whisper, as he placed in his hand a purse; "you need not disdain it. It is from the old earl, and contains two hundred golden pieces. This is your reward for taking him away, nameless, and in secret to the far Western Isles, where none can know his story."

"Good," said Wrecklyffe, as he placed it with a laugh in his broad belt; "good, this is the beginning of my fortune."

"And here is another containing a like amount. What think you this is for?" said Sir Grey. "They are the last gold pieces of the poor despised kinsman; for what think you I would give them."

"I know not," laughed the buccaneer loudly again; "for the Earldom of Montreville, doubtless?"

"Aye, truly," hissed Sir Grey, through his clenched teeth; "then for *his* death who stands first between me and Montreville, I will give you this money. Take it, and let to-morrow's sun see but his drifting corpse upon the wild, wide ocean."

Wrecklyffe weighed the second purse in his hand, as if thinking both of its weight and his companion's words.

Then, after a moment, he said—

"Well, well, this boy shall trouble you ro more. Look on it as done already. I accept the task."

"Good Wrecklyffe!" exclaimed Sir Grey, with fiendish pleasure, grasping the buccaneer by the arm, "you are my best friend."

"And my own worst enemy," said the other, as he shook off the hand of the poor kinsman; "I like the boy, and would have saved him for better things, but——"

"But," interrupted Sir Grey, with a sickly laugh, "you take the money and prefer it to his glory!"

"You lie!" cried Wrecklyffe, fiercely. "I do *not*. Once you saved me from disgrace, and I swore to do your bidding. I have done it; it is well. The score is quit between us. Vyvyan shall trouble you no more. And now, since you have kept your word as regards the money, let us part. It will not do for Vyvyan to see us here together; he would suspect me, and refuse to come aboard."

"True, true; I will go now," said Sir Grey, rising; "and when at Cadiz, and you sight some English vessel returning swiftly homewards, send word to England, 'Vyvyan breathes no more.' I go now, but on the battlements of Montreville I shall wait and watch, and when the red light from your ship ascends into Heaven, and falls into the sea, I shall walk more proudly and erectly into the Castle, for one life less will live to baulk the purpose of my existence. Farewell, good Wrecklyffe, farewell."

"A cunning and a desperate traitor," muttered the buccaneer, as Sir Grey de Malpas passed out; "yet I have sworn, and will perform my vow. Poor Vyvyan, he is a brave and noble youth, and might make a man of whom England could be justly proud. But, ha! I see the light upon the beach, my men are gathering. Two hours more of secrecy, and then, ho! for the Raven flag!"

He buckled on his sword as he spoke, and strode from the room down to the sea-shore, now busy with a hundred workers.

The men had now somewhat recovered from their carouse, and were eagerly employed rolling up strange-looking barrels from inland, and carrying, moreover, numerous large chests of strong, dark wood.

No one interrupted their work.

The "Black Vulture"—so was named the ship of Wrecklyffe—was regarded by all as one commissioned by the Government to sail after the Spanish galleons; and the coast-guard (a shadowy crew in

No. 2.

"THE NEXT MOMENT THE BUCCANEER WAS HURLED TO THE DECK."

those days) would not have interfered had they been there.

As it was, nearly all their number had been draughted into the army, for wild rumours of war had been long afloat, and great boasts of coming armaments had been wafted across the seas from Spain.

"You are busy, Lancaster," said Wrecklyffe, after a while, addressing one who had temporary command of the men; "have you seen anything of our new friend, Vyvyan?"

"Yonder he stands, by the rock, captain," cried Lancaster; "he is thoughtful and silent to-night, unlike himself of the morning; but he's a brave and generous youth I'll be sworn, and one who will live to command."

Unheeding this remark, which somewhat jarred upon his feelings, Wrecklyffe strode towards Vyvyan.

"You are here betimes, good Vyvyan," he said, "are you glad your word is pledged?"

"Oh, yes, kind sir!" returned the Heir of Montreville, eagerly. "Yonder, across the ocean, where the bright moon in trembling beauty sports on the crested waves, there seems to stand a Form—a MOTHER'S FORM—beckoning me on to glory! I have no mother—have seen no mother, mind you; but that sweet face which smiled upon the sea, was such as man, seeing it in his sleep, would swear to be his mother's! There's glory yonder, o'er those mighty billows, or I'm no prophet for the future."

"Poor youth!" muttered Wrecklyffe, "he little recks the glory which his kindred wish for him. True, Vyvyan," he added, aloud, "where Drake and Raleigh beckon us to follow, there can be but little doubt of fame and fortune! Let us aboard at once."

A small boat, manned by two rowers, was lying near, and stepping into this, the buccaneer and the Heir of Montreville were soon being rowed rapidly towards the ship.

The dark hull of the vessel soon loomed above them, and they scrambled aboard.

For a few moments Vyvyan was allowed to roam at will over the deck of the ship, which he regarded as his first stepping stone to fortune, to gaze on the moonlit sea and the dark line of land far behind him, and the grand old castle towering high above all, even over St. Kinian's Cliff, where he had so lately taken a tender adieu of his foster-father Alton.

After a few minutes, however, he was rejoined by Wrecklyffe, who led him down below, without speaking, into a chamber which was pitch dark, and smelt as if it was in the lowest part of the ship.

Here he was about to address his captain, and demanded the reason of this strange accommodation, when he was pushed violently forward, a door was closed on him, and he heard the voice of Wrecklyffe saying, in a hoarse whisper,—

"It must be done before the men come on board. I do not like to slay him; but I have sworn it, and it must be accomplished."

Then Vyvyan knew that he was out on the wide sea, helpless, in the hands of traitors!

CHAPTER VI.

OUT AT SEA—THE "BLACK VULTURE" ON THE TRACK OF PLUNDER.

DOWN in the dank and dismal hold of the "Black Vulture," Vyvyan could see nothing but a wall, as it were, of dark night, and hear nothing but the plashing of the boisterous waves against the side of the hull, and the rattle of gun-carriages, and the tramp, tramp, tramp of heavy feet.

The voices of those who had so coolly and calmly spoken of and planned his murder, had died away, and he was alone with his thoughts—thoughts which had long since lost their pleasurable character.

Out on the blue sea he had gone to find

a mother. It seemed now that he was to find a grave.

Not knowing to what great family he belonged—not knowing, of course, to what estate he was the rightful, though discarded, heir, he could not understand thoroughly his position.

But that he was the victim of some preconceived villany he could see well.

What he heard from Alton, the priest, had for the first time set his mind wondering and soaring above the level which might have been thought to have been his.

The hints of the priest; the mystery about his mother; the knowledge that he was of noble lineage, convinced him now that *some one*, in whose path he stood, must have paid for his destruction.

For why else should Wrecklyffe, an *utter* stranger, desire to effect to his doom?

For a long time as he pursued this course of disconnected dreamings, the ship remained quite stationary.

Presently it gave a lurch to one side, and then its position and its rushing motion told him they had started on their voyage.

There was a short reprieve at least, then, and the last words spoken by Wrecklyffe rather gave him hope than otherwise that he might yet escape the hands of his foes.

He was not in error in this surmise, however inaccurately formed.

Wrecklyffe, in fact, as soon as he had gone on deck, was so thoroughly occupied by the charge of the preparations necessary before starting, that he was compelled for awhile to postpone the crime of which he had undertaken the commission, and the short delay changed thoroughly the course of his thoughts.

Bad man as he was, he did not care to dye his hands in the blood of an innocent being at this, the first starting of the expedition.

"Let him follow the course of Nature," said he to himself, as the anchor was weighed, and the "Black Vulture" yielded to the influence of the rising wind. "In some of our desperate battles on the sea he will surely find his doom, and, if *not*, why, then, the far-off Western Isles will be his home. Sir Grey de Malpas does not pay well enough for me to cast a bad omen on my journey."

It would be difficult to analyse the feelings of this man at that moment.

His life was wrecked truly, but with the wreck had not yet sank the remnant of his hate for murder!

Plunder and rapine he had no distaste for.

Plunder, in fact, was now his natural desire; since, in addition to the losses which were the result of wild extravagance, he had been robbed again and again by pretended friends.

He went cheerfully upon his wild and savage voyage, justified by the past for wickedness in the future—at least, in his own judgment.

So the "Black Vulture" danced over the waters, plunging merrily along over the crested waves towards the Spanish Main.

It was a week after the night on which they weighed anchor that the door of Vyvyan's place of confinement was opened, and he was permitted to proceed on deck.

During the week provisions in plenty had been given to him, and a light whereby to eat them, but he had not the privilege of moving from his dark and damp prison.

When he now emerged upon deck it was a bright and moonlight night.

The rays of the silver goddess were lying in quivering lines of light upon the tremulous waves, illumining also the deck of the "Black Vulture," where everything was in intense excitement.

Some of the wild-looking sailors were busy spreading every available stitch of canvas, though a stiff breeze was blowing; while others again were quickly removing from the guns the coverings which had concealed them.

They were evidently preparing for the chase of some enemy.

Once on deck, Vyvyan was allowed to roam whither he listed, and wondering in his own mind what had so suddenly changed the mind of the desperate buccaneer, he walked hither and thither, examining with an eager curiosity the various preparations which were being made with such anxiety and rapidity.

Presently, as he was leaning over the bulwarks, a hand was placed upon his shoulder, and turning quickly, he saw Wrecklyffe standing beside him.

The desperate man knew not that the young discarded Heir of Montreville had overheard his words, and assuming, therefore, a friendly demeanour, he said—

"Well, my young friend, how fares it with you now?"

"As well as it can fare with one who is promised safety and a path to glory, and who is cast into a dungeon," replied Vyvyan, with some sternness.

"You misunderstand my motives," replied the buccaneer. "I placed you there that you might be in safety. There was one on board this vessel to whom I resolved your presence should not be known. He is no longer here, so you are free once more. Here are your weapons, see you use them well as becomes one whose heart is set on glory."

With a glad heart, Vyvyan buckled on his sword and placed his pistols in his belt.

For an instant he felt, as his hand once more held that with which to defend his life and honour, as if he could have struck his foe to the ground.

But prudence restrained him.

It was best to dissemble, best to conceal from Wrecklyffe, at any rate for the present, his knowledge of his treacherous words.

"Many thanks for these," he said. "But tell me why these preparations for battle? I see no enemy."

Wrecklyffe turned swiftly and pointed to a speck which broke the long belt of quivering moonlight.

"Yonder," he said, "is the vessel I pursue. She is a merchant vessel, armed truly, but laden with goodly treasures."

"A Spaniard, of course?"

"Yes, yes," returned Wrecklyffe, turning his head for a moment. "They are our natural foes."

The young man glanced hurriedly round to catch a glimpse of the face of the speaker, but for some reason or another, not then understood, but comprehended to the full afterwards, Wrecklyffe veiled his features.

"Comes that ship then from Spain with treasure?" asked Vyvyan. "That seems strange."

"No, no; you have been below, and have not observed the course we have steered," replied the buccaneer, hastily. "That ship is making for Cadiz, and ere morning dawns we must be alongside and aboard of her. See well to your laurels, Vyvyan."

So saying, he turned away, and proceeded to give further orders to his men, leaving Vyvyan a prey to strange doubts and fears.

The "Black Vulture" was now plunging along like a racehorse, the sea flying in white dazzling spray from the bows, and the canvas bellying out famously before the strong and steady wind.

The vessel, which had at first appeared so small in the distance, was now growing visibly larger, showing that the space between the two ships was rapidly diminishing.

Vyvyan watched eagerly.

Though overcome by a vague fear, he could not nevertheless avoid a feeling of excitement, and standing there on the poop he was lost in eager anticipation.

Hour after hour went by, and at length the first streaks of dawn became visible in the western horizon.

As they did so—as the first grey light fell over the ocean—Vyvyan beheld the large hull of a merchant vessel not a quarter of a mile distant from them.

All was excitement now.

Rapid orders were given by Wrecklyffe, and obeyed with lightning speed.

The men stood to their guns, and all was, in a few moments, ready for action.

At this time, Vyvyan, who was standing near the buccaneer, shouted in a loud voice,

"Stay—stay your hands! Yonder ship is English! See the flag they hoist."

Wrecklyffe burst out into loud, discordant laughter.

"Ha, ha!" he cried. "Run up the Raven Flag! What matters it to me whether yonder vessel be English or Spanish? We, the Wild Rovers of the Sea, are masters of the wave, and permit none others to cross our path. Now, then, give them a warning!"

They were not now more than three hundred yards from the strange vessel, and the captain of the "Black Vulture" might easily have hailed it, and demanded surrender.

But, before doing this, he was resolved to cast terror into the minds of the ill-fated crew, and the "warning" he had ordered with such glee was soon given.

A long carronade was run out from the bows, there was a loud report that rang across the ocean waves, and a ball crashed through the rigging of the merchantman.

"Heave to!" shouted Wrecklyffe through the speaking trumpet.

"What do you want?"

"A quick surrender of treasure."

"We are English; we hail from Southampton!" was the astonished answer.

"It matters not," returned Wrecklyffe, with an oath. "Surrender, madmen, or I shall sink you!"

There was no reply from the trader, only a sudden commotion and bustle showed that the crew were actively making preparations for some defence or flight.

This activity was soon explained.

In a few minutes, just as the "Black Vulture" was rushing hand-over-hand upon its quarry, the merchantman careered round suddenly on another tack, trembled a moment as if about to founder, and then plunged away in an opposite direction.

"Hurrah!" cried Vyvyan, impetuously. "Villains, they will escape you now!"

❧

CHAPTER VII.

THE CHASE OF THE "OCEAN QUEEN"—THE SEA FIGHT.

SCARCELY had the words left the lips of Vyvyan when Wrecklyffe was by his side.

"Rash youth, beware!" he cried; "remember, I am master here."

"Too well I know it," exclaimed the youth, "and yet I fear not. I will fight with my good sword to aid yonder innocents against you."

"Away with him!" exclaimed the pirate-captain, furiously. "We can waste no time in babbling to children and idiots. Bind him to yonder mast, and mayhap some friendly bullet will save me the task that I was paid by his friends to do."

In a moment, before Vyvyan could make any real efforts at resistance, he was seized from behind by powerful hands, and carried away to the stern of the vessel, where he was bound securely to the mast.

Here he was left to the mercy of the battle, while Wrecklyffe proceeded to give orders for the pursuit of the fugitive.

The English vessel, on whose bows appeared the name of the "Ocean Queen," had gained considerably by its manœuvre, and, by the time the pirate-vessel turned, it had forged greatly ahead.

Before, not understanding the character of its pursuer, the captain had made no effort to escape.

He had been deceived at first by the sight of the English flag; but now that he knew the character of his foe, he crowded all sail, and went rapidly onwards.

The pirate had not now so great an advantage as he had imagined; but still his craft was more lightly made, and was, moreover, long and slender in the build.

Its high raking masts, moreover, could carry more sail, and when its head was once turned in the direction of the enemy, and every stitch of canvas was set, the "Black Vulture" soon began to lessen the intervening distance.

As soon as this fact began to be apparent, renewed activity was observable on board the merchant ship, and they evidently were making preparations for a fight.

Like brave men, they were resolved to try the strength of courage and despair against the brute force of those whose very villany seemed to speak of cowardice.

Vyvyan gazed at the chase with straining eyes, his heart beating with a terrible excitement as he thought of the awful scenes so soon to be enacted.

In about half an hour the vessels were at close quarters, and Wrecklyffe, springing on the forecastle, began issuing his commands with fierce vigour and resolution.

"Now, then, boarders there! prepare!" he shouted, "Now, then, gunners, ready! Give it them with a will!"

As he spoke, there was a tremendous report.

The pirate vessel appeared to shiver in every timber, and a crashing, rending sound told that the heavy broadside had taken terrible effect upon the "Ocean Queen."

A loud scream, as from dying and maimed beings, was answered by a loud shout of savage triumph from the pirates, and then came a second report—a second broadside, but this time from the brave foe!

Then the ships rushed together with a crash, the grappling irons were thrown out, and the real, stern, terrible fight began.

"Boarders there to the fore!" shouted Wrecklyffe, as he sprang first on to the deck of the enemy. "At them, brave Vultures! Hew them down! No mercy now! Hurrah!"

With loud shouts and imprecations, the savage crew leaped into the thick of the foe,

The clash, clash, clash of swords—the rapid firing of pistols—the groans of the dying—the yells of the brutal buccaneers and the brave cheers of the merchant crew—the smoke—the constant flashes of light and the crashing of timber, made up a scene of furious noise and confusion and terror which can scarcely be described in the pages of romance.

Men gripped each other's throats in savage fury, and rolled in their death agonies on the deck slippery with gore.

Others hacked and hewed at the wretches who clung wounded and maimed to the balwarks, over which they had been flung.

Others took aim at poor struggling souls in the water, and savagely ended their sufferings in mere wantonness.

Some hacked at the rigging, some at the masts, some at the dead bodies, attacking every one and everything in their mad rage.

It seemed truly as if demons had been let loose from the infernal regions.

And all this time Vyvyan was bound and helpless!

Then there came a mighty crash, louder than all before, and the main-mast of the merchant vessel came rushing down, striking down several of both crews, and entangling many in the rigging.

It was at this moment that the captain of the merchantman determined to make one more effort, and endeavour, in the confusion, to retrieve the fortune of the day.

He was a fine specimen of an old sea captain; tall, with broad shoulders and an eye of fire.

A loud cheer responded to his appeal as he shouted out at the top of his voice—

"On, boys, to the rescue! On, on for England's glory!"

The crew of the "Ocean Queen," wounded, almost decimated as they were, dashed forward bravely, but at this moment Wrecklyffe, who had just struck down an enemy, advanced furiously and attacked the captain with savage rapidity.

This was no time for indulging in admiration, or some even of the villainous crew might have paused to view this combat.

Both were good swordsmen, and the contest might have lasted a long time had not treachery been used to close it.

One of the pirates, who was rushing forward with red-stained hands and blood-shot eyes, seeking some fresh victim, and seeing the old captain parrying Wrecklyffe's brilliant strokes, raised aloft a sharp-bladed axe.

In another instant it descended, and the old man sunk, with his skull cloven in two, down among the dead and dying on the slippery deck.

The crew of the merchantman now lost all courage, and though they still made feeble efforts at resistance, they were soon driven up in a corner, and when thus huddled up they were fired upon mercilessly.

Then followed a terrible scene.

The pirates, maddened by the prospect of victory, cut the throats of the poor creatures as they lay upon the deck and flung them into the sea.

Those who were only wounded shared the same fate, and as Vyvyan watched and watched with straining eyes, he could see the circling wavelets crested with red foam—the life-blood of the conquered!

After an hour's hideous work, the pirate crew, having disposed of all their enemies, transferred the treasures from one ship to the other, and placing on deck the spirit barrels, which they found in plenty, they prepared to destroy all evidences of their dreadful crime!

Placing a slow match in the magazine room, they hurried back on board their own ship, and in a few minutes the "Black Vulture" had careered back on another tack, and was darting away from the prize.

With starting eyes Vyvyan watched the doomed ship as they hurried away.

Not for long did he have to watch.

There was a rush of smoke and flame, and then there was a loud crashing of timbers and the fragments of the "Ocean Queen" rushed up towards the silent Heavens.

All that was left of the ship and its crew was now the floating corpses and the charred and misshapen timbers.

CHAPTER VIII.

ALONE—WITH HEAVEN!

WRECKLYFFE, maddened, as it were, by the first success in his wild and desperate career, drank deeply and rapidly that day, and would have left Vyvyan still tied to the mast had it not been that his lieutenant on his own responsibility released him.

All that day and half the next, the vessel went driving before the wind with scarcely one to guide it.

In the afternoon of the second day Vyvyan was summoned on deck.

It was a horrid deck to stand on, still slippery with the blood of the slain, which the men, tired with their hideous work of the day before, had not attempted to clear away.

Wrecklyffe was standing near the mainmast, while around him were gathered a band of as ill-looking ruffians as ever trod a deck.

"Vyvyan," cried the buccaneer, "you have been preserved as if by a miracle. I admire your desperate courage. Be one of us."

"Never!" exclaimed the youth, firmly. "Never! I have already said this."

"Have a care, mad boy," responded the pirate; "have a care. I, like thee, cast off, and disinherited, and desperate, had but one choice—the pirate's flag or death! Choose thou. I am more gracious than thy kindred. I offer thee life. The gold *they* gave me paid for thy ocean grave."

"Demon, thou liest!" cried Vyvyan, loudly.

In an instant the pirate's sword leaped from its scabbard, his eyes grew red with anger, and with a desperate oath he sprang towards his foe.

But the instinct of self defence told Vyvyan what to do.

Snatching a sword from one of the pirates near him, he whirled it round his head, and, in another moment, the buccaneer fell to the ground with a deep wide gash in his cheek and brow.

Then came a deadly scene.

Furious at this treatment of their chief the pirates rushed at Vyvyan.

Terrible curses rang out upon the still air, swords flashed in the sunlight, and the youth, driven inch by inch along the deck, saw before him no alternative but death by their hands, or a self-inflicted doom in the cold, quiet sea below.

Certainly the chill ocean seemed to offer a quieter resting-place and a quieter death than the howling, yelling fiends who were seeking his life.

For a long time Vyvyan, with the supernatural strength given to him by the instinct of self-preservation, contrived to keep them back.

But presently his arm grew tired, a dizziness invaded his brain, and he was just staggering under a heavy blow when a tall, commanding form, which Vyvyan recognised as the pirates' lieutenant, dashed through the savage crew.

"Hold!" he cried; "stand back!"

"TWO DARK, CRUEL FACES WERE PEERING UP AT THEM FROM BELOW."

"This is but murder—this youth shall not die thus. Remember ye not that such a deed as this—the life of one taken by many in unfair fight—will bring a curse upon our ship, and stay our hand in the hour of victory?"

The pirates fell back at once, though some still murmured angrily.

"He has murdered our captain," growled one.

"He *must* die!" cried another.

"Our captain is not dead," returned the lieutenant; "but this youth *shall* die, though not by your swords. Tied to a plank, and cast upon the angry waves, he shall float away from us to find his doom by starvation and the cold. Seize him, my men. Now, all together."

It was quite useless for Vyvyan to attempt further resistance.

Feebly now his sword flashed hither and thither, and at length overpowered and faint, he fell senseless on the deck.

The next few moments sufficed to complete the pirates' vengeance.

A broad, stout plank was brought on deck, a kind of sail was fixed at one end, and upon this the unfortunate prisoner was bound in a half-sitting posture, with his back leaning against the miniature mast.

Then six of the strongest pirates lowered themselves by ropes, and launched him upon the waves.

A loud and derisive cheer broke from the lips of the savage crew as the wind caught the little sail, and the frail barrier between life and death began to run before the breeze.

"Take our kind wishes to our friends in England!" shouted they, as he departed, and then they laughed in terrible glee at their own hideous jesting.

Vyvyan closed his eyes that he might not see their faces, and soon the dusk of the night closed in and veiled him fully from the eyes of his desperate foes.

That was an awful night.

All stillness—darkness—cold!

Nothing around but the heaving, monotonous sea; nothing above but the moon and the silent stars!

Yet his frail bark went safely, rapidly onwards.

Wrecklyffe had said that he was more gracious than the youth's own kindred.

"Truly now," murmured Vyvyan, as he gazed with a shudder around him; "the very sea is more kind than my friends!"

How he longed for morning!

The blessed light of day would, at least, bring warmth to his numbed limbs.

It brought him more—it brought him companionship.

Hideous companionship it was.

Below, in the clear trembling waves, he beheld a dark, swift-moving, shapeless thing, with watchful, glassy eyes.

It was the ghastly shark hungrily swimming round his prey.

Before this he had prayed for death.

Before this he had sought to wrench his limbs from the stiff cords that gnawed into his flesh, that he might drop into the sea and seek oblivion.

But now life grew once more sweet, and he scanned eagerly the horizon.

For a long time he did so in vain.

He seemed to be absolutely alone, with death flapping his raven wings above him.

The shark kept him company, and great birds flew by, and stared at him as they circled round his head.

But this was all.

At length came the scorching noon, and the burning sun poured in unabated glory upon his bare head, parching his tongue with unappeasable thirst, and making his brain reel.

Then, as the noon passed, a few drops of rain fell, and, thrusting out his tongue, he eagerly caught some of the refreshing drops, and scanned again the heavens with eyes that he had hitherto kept close in fear of the blazing sun.

What was that on the dim horizon far —far away?

A sail?

Yes—yes, it was a sail, that grew larger and larger as it advanced towards him.

Oh, how his heart beat then!

Oh! how his prayers went up to Heaven, that he might be again cast into the companionship of men!

No matter to him then if it were Spaniard or English, so that he could speak again to human beings — hear human voices—see human faces.

Onward the vessel came, and, as the hours passed, and the ship came nearer and nearer, Vyvyan's heart rose, and his pulses beat high with hope.

But he was again doomed to a heart-rending disappointment.

The wind veered round, and, catching the small sail of the tiny raft, it drove it in a straight line, while, as the large vessel was on another tack, they soon parted company. Tears of anguish started to the shipwrecked youth's straining eyes.

Wild visions crowded into his maddened brain.

Loud, shrill cries for "Help!" rang helplessly from his parched lips over the wide and voiceless ocean.

Then sweet dreams of the mother he so longed to find overcame all else, and an angel form appeared to float over the waters as the dusky mantle of night fell upon them.

Then, as the darkness of night came over him, his senses left him.

He shrieked aloud, clutched at imaginary beings, and then his weary head drooped upon his breast, and all was blank!

*   *   *   *   *   *

The dawn was just breaking in golden glory over the dancing waves as a noble ship, on whose bows could be read the "Elizabeth," was running along before a strong wind.

The night had been a somewhat still one, but with the sun had risen a good breeze, and the "Elizabeth" had hoisted every stitch of canvas to make headway while it lasted.

On the deck very little was doing.

Two officers were leaning against the bulwarks smoking leisurely some small and delicately rolled cigars.

The man was at the helm, and he and the two officers seemed the only persons who had any kind of occupation.

The rest of the crew were lying listlessly about on the deck, some asleep, and some indulging apparently in silent enjoyment of the sunshine that flooded the scrupulously clean deck.

Sea-captains, versed well in England's latest victories, would have known well both of these men, and most pre-eminently one of them.

Few who had been in desperate sea-fights of late could fail to recognise those sunburnt, weather-beaten features—those bright, piercing eyes, which had watched so many tempests and eagerly followed the movements of strange and fiercely-fighting enemies.

"Well, Kemersham," said one of these officers, a tall, somewhat spare, but handsome man, addressing his companion, who was a little shorter and younger, "if this breeze lasts we shall soon near our destination."

"Yes, indeed, Sir Francis," returned the other. "Yet I hope that ere we *do* reach our destination, we shall meet some treasure ship whose golden treasure will recompense us for this long inaction."

"Aye, truly," replied the first speaker; "yet fear not. My men know me well, and will not grumble, even if they reach the West Indies without one single brush with the foe. When we *do* reach those golden regions, we will fill our cabins with the glittering metal, or my name is not Sir Francis Drake. But it is strange, Kemersham, that we do not see a sail."

Kemersham smiled.

"Mayhap our enemies have heard of our coming this way," he said, "and have kept scrupulously out of our path. The last meeting the Spaniards had with us has given them, I doubt not, a sickener."

"True," replied Sir Francis Drake, joining in his companion's smile. "True. The Spaniards have now lost all power to boast since I and you and brave Essex and kingly Raleigh have ridden the seas with them. Yet I care not to rest upon my laurels. *I'd* gladly see something of a fleet, even if instead of golden treasure it contained but good guns and brave men."

As he spoke, he glanced with his long glass on all sides.

But on the monotonous ocean there seemed no sign of such a sight.

Presently, however, Kemersham uttered an exclamation of wonder.

"By St. George!" he cried, "am I dreaming, or is that a tiny craft yonder?"

Sir Francis Drake, the terror of the Spanish freebooters, hurriedly turned his glass in the direction pointed out by his lieutenant.

"By my faith!" he exclaimed, after a few moments' earnest scrutiny, "by my faith, if I were as superstitious as my mariners, I should swear it was some strange spirit of the deep steering away towards some enchanted island. Look you again. It seems to me like some unshapely boat with a sail, and within it a man, or some such being."

CHAPTER IX.

THE STRANGE SAILS.

KEMERSHAM, the lieutenant of the "Elizabeth," gazed long and earnestly over the waters.

In those days of superstition, a strange sight at sea roused in the seaman's breast a thousand doubts if not fears.

Wild tales were then rife of wondrous sea-serpents, that rolled madly over the foaming waters, and could with one stroke of their mighty tails annihilate the largest ships.

Mermen and mermaids, and the fabulous dolphins too, were said by travellers to disport in the merry sunlight, and syrens still led men on to destruction.

Much, therefore, as both Sir Francis Drake and his lieutenant might have laughed at each other's fears, they watched with unusual interest the curious object approaching them; and even though they affected to despise superstition, they would not have been astonished if they had met with some unheard-of creature of the deep.

"You are right, Sir Francis," said Kemersham, "you are right. We will launch the cutter, and pull towards it. Ho! there, Thomas and Martingale, and you lazy fellows that lie yonder, get ready the cutter."

The men addressed at once sprang up, and glanced eagerly round the horizon, as if expecting to see a vessel in sight.

But, though evidently disappointed at not perceiving anything, they quickly obeyed orders, and the boat was soon launched.

It was then that the wondering crew beheld the strange object which had attracted the attention of their officer, and pulled eagerly towards it.

It was a long pull and a strong one, but the little raft was quickly advancing towards them, though in a diagonal line, and they were soon alongside.

"A man bound to a plank!" exclaimed Kemersham, the lieutenant, in amazement; "see to him at once."

The men quickly severed the cords, and dragged him into the boat.

When once here Kemersham poured down his throat some strong spirit, but the youth still remained motionless.

"Pull quickly to the ship," said the lieutenant, "that our brave captain may see him. But he is dead, I fear."

The men, who were full of the superstition that their masters despised, obeyed orders nevertheless with a will.

But they scarcely liked their task.

Their hands, which would have eagerly wielded a sword, had trembled as they undid the fastenings that had bound the poor captive to the mast, and as they rowed back, they glanced ever and anon at their mysterious companion, as if to assure themselves he had not flown away suddenly from among them.

Sir Francis Drake was eagerly watching them from the bulwarks of the "Elizabeth" as they neared it, and when they had gently lifted the wrecked and senseless waif of the ocean on board, he started in surprise.

"A noble and a kingly youth, in truth!" he exclaimed; "yet he is dead, I fear. Take him to my cabin—let him be clothed in dry and warm things—let the leech see him. It would be a great and good action to rescue such a one as this from death's long, chill journey."

Vyvyan had dreamed of strange wild forms, and the livid orbs of the ghastly shark had followed him in his last vision; but when at last he opened his eyes, kindly faces smiled upon him, kind voices spoke to him in his native tongue.

He was saved, for God had watched him on the deep!

The first thought of Vyvyan, when he awoke to consciousness, was—

"Where am I? and how came these kindly faces around me?"

Then he closed his eyes that he might re-open them and convince himself that it was not all a dream.

"Where am I? and how came I here?" he asked, as Sir Francis Drake bent over the couch upon which they had placed him. "I see I am with friends, and that Providence has by some miracle saved me from the deep; but how, good gentlemen, I cannot well conceive."

Drake smiled.

"To you who fainted on that frail raft your safety must indeed appear a miracle. You were faint and well-nigh dead when by chance our vessel sighted your tiny sail. My lieutenant, Kemersham, here took out a boat at once, and pulled eagerly to your rescue."

"And who, kind sir, are you?" asked Vyvyan, scanning curiously the tall and commanding figure of Sir Francis Drake.

"I am Sir Francis Drake," replied the great circumnavigator of the world. "Rumour, per chance, has brought my name to your ears; but tell me by what marvellous adventure we found you, as we did, cast on the wild waste of waters alone?"

"It is truly marvellous that my mishap should cast me into such glorious company," said Vyvyan. "I will tell my story from the commencement, it it will not fatigue you."

"Indeed, no," said Drake; "but finish first the repast that is laid before you. Your strength, however great, must have suffered by such a terrible journey. Your story will enliven us, for, during the whole voyage, we have encountered not a Spanish vessel, and our time, therefore, has lain heavily on our hands."

With wondering interest, Drake and Kemersham, together with other officers of the "Elizabeth," listened to the tale of the young disinherited, who, receiving fresh strength from the food which he had not tasted for days, was once more able to speak with all his old passionate energy.

"Well," said Drake, as Vyvyan concluded his narration, "well, in all my many adventures, I have never met so strange a one as this. Thank heaven, you are saved."

"Thank Heaven, and you, its most worthy instrument, Sir Francis," cried Vyvyan, as he pressed to his lips the hands of the noble sailor; "and, now that to you I owe my life, I dedicate to you my sword. Of whatever value it is, it is at your service, and Heaven grant that in our wanderings over these mighty waters, I may meet the one who so unworthily sought my life."

"I gladly accept the proffer of the sword of one so brave yet so unfortunate," said Drake. "If Heaven grants you life, you will yet be able to realise your dreams of glory, and return home with such renown that those who may have paid to send you far away, will be proud to own you as one of their kindred."

"I doubt it much," said Vyvyan; "but, at any rate, I will make them wish that they had acted better. In their own hearts they shall at least acknowledge it, if they refuse to acknowledge it to me."

That evening, some two hours after the finding of Vyvyan on the lonely raft, the man at the mast-head sang out—

"A sail! a sail!"

"By St. George, Sir Francis, the stranger has brought to us good fortune," exclaimed Kemersham, as he raised his glass and glanced over the wide ocean; "there is a sail at last."

Sir Francis drew near and gazed wistfully over the sea, in the direction indicated by his lieutenant.

"By St. Andrew," he cried, "you are right; but it is no foe. To my mind, it is an English vessel under full canvas. We must bear towards it."

In a few minutes the necessary orders were given, and the "Elizabeth" flew merrily along before the wind in the direction of the strange sail. Night, however, advanced apace, and there was no chance of meeting the vessel they so much desired to speak with.

There seemed, indeed, to be no inclination on the part of the other commander to approach an unknown vessel in the darkness; and so, until the grey of the morning, nothing more was seen of the stranger.

It was then that Vyvyan, leaning over the bulwarks, descried once more the vessel in the distance, and hastened to communicate the knowledge to his captain, as he now considered Sir Francis Drake.

"The ship's in sight again, noble captain," he said; "and, as far as my knowledge of the sea enables me to judge, it is an English vessel of some size."

"Aye, and bearing down upon us," cried Sir Francis, as he ascended to the deck. "Hoist the flag there, and let them see from whence we hail."

In a few moments both vessels were running towards each other with pennants flying, and as they neared, Drake saw, to his surprise and pleasure, that it was the "El Dorado," the new ship of Sir Walter Raleigh.

As soon as the ships came side by side, Sir Walter came on board the "Elizabeth" to greet his friend in arms and exchange news for news.

When they had greeted each other, and Sir Walter had been introduced to Vyvyan, he gave the gratifying information that two Spanish ships of suspicious appearance had shown near the island of Uterbo, and that he was on their track.

"This meeting," he said, "could not have been more opportune, Sir Francis, for we can now attack both. I expect ere noon if we keep on this tack we shall come up with them."

The commanders dined together; mutual pledges of friendship were given, and then Sir Walter Raleigh regained his own ship.

An hour after the looks-out on board both vessels sang out—

"A sail! a sail!"

And as they glanced, telescope in hand, over the wild waste of waters, the dark hulls of two strange vessels rose distinctly against the far-off horizon.

"Make all sail," was the order on both the "El Dorado" and the "Elizabeth."

But they soon had to part company.

The Spaniards, for such they appeared to be, suddenly veered away on separate tacks, and after an interchange of good wishes, through the speaking trumpet, the two English commanders sailed away after their enemies.

The strange vessels, upon seeing their approach, made all sail away, and night closed in again upon a stern and desperate chase, in which, however, each hour the English were gaining the advantage.

Although night closed in thus, however, morning found the "Elizabeth" still in view of her foe, who, indeed, in the utter darkness which fell over the ocean, was unable to watch the movements of its enemy.

The "El Dorado" and the other strange ship had disappeared.

The Spaniard gold ship, or pirate, as it might be, resolved at any rate to avoid coming into collision with the Englishman; and as the breeze freshened it sped away with every stitch of canvas spread until the ends of the yard-arms almost touched the water.

But as the bright glorious sun approached its noon-day splendour, a visible advantage was gained by the "Elizabeth," and as evening approached the English crew could see plainly on to the deck of the enemy.

The crew of the stranger seemed composed of men from all quarters of the globe; dark-faced, swarthy-looking fellows all of them, and armed to the teeth.

For some reason or another, however, they seemed to avoid all collision with the foe, for they strained every nerve to make for a dark long line of coast, which could now be distinguished in the distance.

"If we let him make much more headway before the night descends," said Kemersham, "we may find ourselves by morning in a nest of these villains, from which our brave crew may find it difficult to escape."

"True," said Sir Francis, "yonder coast no doubt conceals some Spanish forts; but never mind, our duty is before us, and we must not shirk it. By St. George, I would we had more sail, I would crowd it on at once at all hazards, even though we fled sideways along the waves."

In spite of everything, however, the Spaniard could not be overhauled.

The dark line changed to an uncertain coast, the coast presently was seen edged by trees that hung over the salt sea waves.

But still on they went.

There appeared no sign of harbour or refuge, yet on in a straight line went the Spaniard.

"They are rushing to certain death," cried Sir Francis. "What can it mean?"

"I know not," said Kemersham, as he strove to pierce the thick darkness which had enveloped everything, "but, by Heaven! we must tack, or we shall follow their example."

As he rushed to the man at the helm to give his eager orders, the Spaniard darted forward, and, in the mist and the gloom, where no inlet could be distinguished, disappeared from their gaze just as the "Elizabeth" swung round on another tack in time to save herself from being dashed in among the boiling surf.

"This is some phantom ship," said Kemersham. "By Heaven! Sir Francis, it was a close run."

"Aye, and a narrow escape from destruction," cried Drake; "but, phantom or no phantom, I'll wait here to meet it when it comes again. Reef all, and let go the anchor, Kemersham. I will await the judgment of the morning."

In a very short time the "Elizabeth" was under bare poles, and anchored nearly opposite the spot where the mysterious vessel had disappeared.

CHAPTER X.

THE PIRATE ENCAMPMENT.

"SIR FRANCIS," said Vyvyan, respectfully approaching the great commander, as he leaned over the bulwarks thoughtfully, "the moon will presently be up, and yonder island should be explored. I will volunteer this service, if one more will go with me."

"You are right, brave youth," cried Drake, warmly. "The thought occurred to me. Who will go with him?" he added, turning to two or three who stood near.

"I will," said Kemersham. "He is a brave youth, and with such a companion I fear no one."

"Good," replied Drake. "To better hands I could not commit my fortunes. Be careful, however, and do not risk your lives unnecessarily. What you must do is to take the cutter with four men, who will row beneath yonder trees. Try there whether you can effect a landing; if so land, and endeavour to discover where this ship has disappeared. I believe in no phantoms. There is some trickery here."

"Whatever it is, we will discover it," said Vyvyan, "and that, too, quickly."

It was not long before the cutter was launched, and the four men were pulling the two adventurers towards shore.

On reaching it, they were soon able to comprehend the mystery which had appeared so utterly unintelligible.

In the darkness of the dusky evening the look-outs had been completely deceived.

A rocky headland truly jutted out into the sea; but the other side, where the trees hung over the water, was distant some three hundred yards from it, the two forming a kind of bay quite hidden from view.

In this bay the pirate-vessel was now snugly ensconced.

"A daring run, by Heaven," whispered Kemersham, as they lay upon their oars to reconnoitre. "One false move—one tremor of the helmsman's hand, and they would have been dashed to pieces against the rocks."

"Yes, but no doubt they know the locality well," replied Vyvyan, "and have repeatedly tried the same trick. But see, yonder, on the opposite shore, there is a light; it seems like a camp-fire. Let us proceed thither and reconnoitre. Pull gently," he said to the men, "slowly and noiselessly towards yonder point, where the large tree hangs nearly to the water's edge."

The men, eager for adventure after their long inaction, readily obeyed, and it was not long before the boat rustled in among the strange, long, trailing plants which fringed the dark beach.

They had no sooner leaped ashore, when they heard the murmur of men's voices near them, and towards the point whence this issued, the two friends cautiously made their way.

Behind trees and rugged piles of rock they crept nearer and nearer, until, on

"'BACK COWARDS!' SHOUTED VYVYAN, 'LET ME COMPLETE THE WORK.'"

No. 3.

reaching a point where the ground rose suddenly, they stopped to gaze in wonder at the scene before them.

Below, in a deep hollow, were collected some hundred men, clad in varied habits, most of them of fantastic shape and colour, and many ornamented with costly embroidery of gold or silver.

Richly decorated were the handles of their knives and pistols, rich in hue and texture the sashes in which their weapons were stuck, splendid were the gold-tasseled caps of their leaders, and their jewelled vestments.

But there was no variety in the expression of the faces, however much there might be in feature.

All were ferocious, uncompromising, brutal ruffians, ready for any enormity.

In the centre of this encampment was an immense fire, at which a variety of things were being cooked, while a fat fellow, who looked like a French cook, was engaged in attending to them.

But neither the pirates nor the fire attracted the gaze of the two English adventurers.

It was to a group near the blazing flames that their glances were entirely directed — a group consisting of an English gentleman, about forty-five, and a young girl of some fifteen years.

The former was a fine stalwart, handsome specimen of the British nation— the latter was exquisitely beautiful.

Golden hair fell in glittering wavelets over faultless shoulders; blue eyes gazed tenderly, sorrowfully at the flames; little white hands lay listlessly on her lap.

The two were evidently prisoners.

"By Heaven!" cried Vyvyan, "this is infamous, that such innocence and loveliness should be in the hands of villains like these. Quick! let us return and apprise Sir Francis of our discovery."

Kemersham uttered a low laugh.

"What, have you lost your heart, my young friend," he said, "before even you have won honourable distinctions, which a life on the Spanish Main promises to every brave and adventurous heart?"

"Speak not so," said Vyvyan, in a low but stern voice, "speak not so! Our duty is to succour the weak and helpless, as well as to attack our enemies. Should yonder girl continue in the hands of those bloodthirsty villains, who knows what terrible fate may be hers? Let us away while yet we have a fair chance to retreat, and give to Sir Francis Drake a true knowledge of this place."

"You speak rightly, Master Vyvyan," said Kemersham, "I did but jest. Let us away."

With these words he turned from the scene, followed swiftly, though noiselessly, by Vyvyan, who could not refrain from casting a last lingering look at the vision of beauty which had taken possession of his youthful heart.

They had scarcely reached their boat and settled to the oars when the wind lulled, a hot air seemed to surround them and, as if by magic, a thick fog rolled from off the land out over the quiet sea.

It was one of those pestilential death-mists which appear to bear a mortal taint for Europeans; but it carried no dismay to the hearts of Kemersham or Vyvyan.

Their hearts were too full of their strange discovery.

Yet their haste and eagerness availed them nothing.

When they succeeded with difficulty in reaching the "Elizabeth," they were enveloped everywhere in the death-mist.

They could see nothing—hear nothing.

The sea was as still as a lake, and the atmosphere so dense as to be almost suffocating.

Eagerly they told their story to Sir Francis Drake.

But his answer only confirmed their own suspicions.

It was simple madness to make any attempt, for a boat manned by rowers who could not see a compass would never find a landing place, and might drift out into an endless ocean.

"We must wait till the morning," said Sir Francis, "till then all idea of giving aid is out of the question."

But the morning came and the fog still hung over the sea and the mysterious island.

CHAPTER XI.

EVELINE.

LITTLE rest came to Vyvyan on that night, but what *did* come was blessed by dreams of beauty.

The sweet face and form he had beheld amid the throng of wretches on the island—like a fairy form among a host of demons—haunted his couch and made him sorry rather when creaking timbers or an unsteady walker burst in upon his blissful slumbers.

For the first time love was awakened in his breast—love at first sight—the truest, best of all.

This is the love that crumbles empires, and defies the world!

Seas may flow between, mountains may frown, armies may show their threatening phalanxes, kings may threaten, storms may rage, but that face once seen—once graven on the heart, must and will be seen again, unless the one against whom no one can battle—the grim destroyer, Death, steps in to forbid an advance!

The next morning, as I have said, the fog lay heavy—thick as before, over land and sea.

There was no possibility of moving off, and, therefore, Drake, irritated as he might be by this compulsory inaction, was compelled to remain as he was.

Listlessly apparently, but in reality eagerly watching the spot where they hoped to see the shore, the sailors leaned while the officers sought refuge from the foggy atmosphere in the cabin below.

Hours went by, and then a slightly more chilly atmosphere became perceptible.

The captain of the " Elizabeth " immediately unfurled all sails, and weighed anchor.

Then gradually the fog lifted, and little by little the island became visible.

And with it there became visible also another thing.

While the " Elizabeth " was wearing round to the wind, a great shadow seemed suddenly to loom out of the darkness, and the Spanish vessel, which had first got under weigh, darted by.

" Now comes the chase in earnest," cried Sir Francis Drake. " Give it to her, Kemersham."

In an instant a long carronade was run out of the poop, and a loud report, followed by a crash of timber, told that the shot had taken good effect upon the enemy.

The Spaniards, meanwhile, were not idle.

They were no cowards.

No sooner had the echo of the gun fired by Vyvyan's own hands died away upon the increasing breeze than there was a loud report again, and one of the " Elizabeth's " men fell dead—overboard.

The combat had now begun, and Vyvyan's heart beat high in his breast.

Oh! how he prayed that the terrible weapons might avoid the fair bosom of the one he already loved.

Yet he did not flinch from his duty.

Again and again the deadly hail poured in, and no shots were better directed or did more terrible effect than those fired by Vyvyan himself.

It soon became evident, however, that the Spaniards had accomplished some strange *ruse* upon the preceding day.

It was clear, after half an hour's sailing, that the enemy were gradually but surely winning the race, and that on the day before they had only sailed along at moderate speed in order to lure their English foes to destruction.

" We must cripple her," cried Sir Francis, as he beheld his enemy making such evident strides away from him. " Now, then, Vyvyan and Kemersham, run out the long carronades, and aim at the main-mast. If that goes by the board, they are ours!"

Vyvyan and the lieutenant proceeded, with wildly beating hearts, to obey the orders of the daring seaman.

They knew well that upon their steadiness of aim depended the fate of their enemy.

To Vyvyan there were two incentives —a desire to look well in the eyes of his new commander, and a wish also to be instrumental in the saving of the one who now acted like a talisman to his newly-aroused feelings.

Steadily, coolly, they sighted the cannons when the gunners had run them out at the poop.

"We will fire together," said Kemersham.

"Aye, and we must not fail!" added Vyvyan, resolutely.

A moment passed.

"I am ready," said the young adventurer.

"And I," said Kemersham. "Fire!"

The men, who had the flaming tow in readiness, at once acted upon orders.

The red flames belched forth, the blue smoke curled and sped away upon the wings of the breeze, and a yell of agony, mingled with a terrific crash, told how truly the balls had sped.

It was easy to see when they could gaze over the waters what execution had been made on board the enemy.

The main-mast, struck in two places, lay a hopeless wreck over the side of the vessel, and the wide sails dragging in the water impeded the progress of the vessel.

"Now, then," cried Sir Francis Drake, his eyes gleaming with enthusiasm, "now, then, boarders, prepare. Gunners, be ready. One broadside, and then at them!"

The Spanish pirate, seeing now that all hope was gone of avoiding a hand to hand conflict, prepared to act on the defensive.

A black flag, with a death's head upon it, was run up, the wreck of the main-mast was cut away and cast into the sea, and a crowd of armed men rushed upon deck from the cabins.

Meanwhile, the "Elizabeth" forged quickly ahead, and was soon broadside on to the enemy.

"Now, then, my lads, give it them," shouted Drake, and in an instant the terrible broadside of the English ship was poured in upon the desperate crew of the nameless vessel.

The Spaniards were not idle.

They had resolved to fight till the last, and an answering rattle of heavy metal, which pierced the bulwarks of the "Elizabeth," and killed four of the English crew, told they were in earnest, and had goodly weapons to fight with.

Nearer, nearer—hearts beating wildly —eyes gleaming brightly—steel glittering everywhere—the two ships came.

Another broadside from both, timbers crashing and men falling with the shock, and then the two monsters of the deep grappled with one another and the fierce fight began.

"Surrender!" cried Sir Francis Drake, as they approached closely.

"Never!" was the reply.

They gave no quarter—no mercy to their own opponents.

They believed the English to be the same.

So the stern men resolved to do battle to the death.

Not a moment was lost.

The instant the two ships grated one against the other and the irons fixed them one to the other, the two sets of boarders met on the bulwarks.

"St. George for Merry England!" cried Sir Francis Drake, as at the head of his own boarders he leaped upon the swaying timbers. "Now, my men, on, on to victory!"

"Death to the English! Spain and the West for ever!" was the answering rallying cry, and for a long time no progress was made by either.

Standing on the bulwarks both crews fought with equal ardour.

The Spaniards in those days were tall, stalwart, brave fellows, and no insignificant enemies, and brave and resolute as the English might be, they found themselves quite matched in heroism for a time.

Indeed, for a long while, each man could only take care of himself.

Orders were issued, but could not be obeyed.

It became a fierce conflict of man to man.

At length the "staying" qualities, for which Englishmen have alway been celebrated, began to have their effect.

The Spaniards commenced yielding a little.

This was enough.

The moment an enemy yields there is a turn in the tide of battle, no matter how insignificant it may be.

The English sailors at once saw the advantage and took it.

With a loud and hearty cheer they crowded still more thickly upon the bulwarks, forced their way over, and began the fight upon the deck of the Spanish vessel itself.

It was now that Vyvyan, who in the midst of the stern fight, could not avoid thinking of the fair face and lovely form of the young English girl whom he had seen sitting pale and in dread near the fire of the pirate's encampment, resolved to make an attempt to reach the cabin, where, he doubted not, the captives were.

Telling Kemersham of his wish, he shouted to the men—

"This way—this way, my boys. Now, then, to free the captives."

The Spaniards, who had no suspicion in regard to the knowledge which Vyvyan had obtained on the island, took this movement as a kind of diversion in the battle.

Though, therefore, they made a vigorous effort to repel them, they knew not upon what errand they were bent.

The young girl and her father were seated in the cabin; the latter calm, pale, and stern, the former trembling, and nearly senseless.

Ever and anon the old man endeavoured to calm her by gentle, soothing words.

But it was in vain.

She was, as I have said, very young, and such a scene was far too much for her tender nerves.

Just as her father was imprinting a kiss upon her cold and marble forehead, a loud voice was heard without, crying,

"This way, Kemersham! Cut them down—hew them down! St. George for England!"

"English voices! Heaven be praised, Eveline," cried the old man, starting up.

The shock was too much for the young girl, who sank exhausted and fainting in his arms.

At this moment the cabin door was burst open and Vyvyan sprang in.

"Give me your daughter, old man, and take this," he cried, thrusting into his hand a sword which he had snatched from a dying Spaniard, "we come to save you. Quick, and follow me."

So saying he flung the insensible girl over his left shoulder, planted his right foot firmly on the ladder, and struggled upon deck, followed by the old man, who, though bewildered, was yet roused to action by the hope of escape.

In a few moments they had gained the deck, when, with his precious burden still in his arms, Vyvyan found himself face to face with a wall of fierce and blood-stained marauders.

"On, my men, for England and for glory!" cried he, as the father of his precious burden stood, sword in hand, ready to support him.

But their hopes seemed now at an end.

The rush of battle had separated them from their companions, and they were left almost alone to face their desperate foes.

"Cut down the young upstart," shouted the Spanish chief. "On them, my brave fellows!"

And, with a yell which sounded scarcely human, the pirates dashed upon their prey.

CHAPTER XII.

THE RESCUE.

IT would have appeared to any one an act of madness for Vyvyan and the father of the fair stranger to attempt to stem the tide of wild marauders, who dashed with headlong fury towards them.

But it takes but a small breakwater to turn aside an angry wave, and before the impetuous valor—the desperate, determined courage of the young sailor, and his companion, the pirates for some moments were kept at bay.

These few moments sufficed to bring them aid.

Kemersham, who, in the wild tide of battle, had been swept to another part of the deck, suddenly dashed in to the assistance of his friends, followed by a score of English sailors flushed with the victory that was already dawning on them.

Little by little now Vyvyan, in spite of his heavy burden, forced his way through the opposing ranks towards his own vessel.

The eyes of the pirate chief had gleamed with furious rage as he saw his fair captive borne from him by an English foeman.

He had resolved in his own black heart that this lily of the North should live to grace his wild and lawless home in the Grecian isles.

For this reason he had spared her father, hoping that his clemency towards him might beget a feeling of clemency also in her breast; and now that he saw the one whom his villanous heart loved carried away in the arms of another, his rage knew no bounds.

Again and again his furious sword flashed and gleamed as he struck with savage rage at the head of his young foeman.

But again and again the eagle eye of Vyvyan enabled him to dash aside the impending danger, and to hurl his opponent back, wounded and maddened, among his men.

The young adventurer had nearly reached the bulwarks of the " Elizabeth," when a fearful resolve took possession of the pirate's mind.

He took one eager glance around him to ascertain the state of the battle.

Everywhere now the Spaniards were yielding ground before the impetuous order of the British.

There was no hope but in surrender, and that surrender signified the quiet giving up, not only of the ship and whatever it might contain, but the girl he loved.

" It shall not be," he yelled. " Never does Don Pedro de Mendoza yield a prize such as that! Take her, since fortune favours you, but take her in death."

As he spoke he snatched a pistol from one of the men near him, pointed it at the senseless form of the young girl, and fired.

Vyvyan was powerless to aid her, but another hand was near—the hand which had so ably seconded him in all his efforts.

Rushing forward, the father dashed up the murderous weapon just as the bullet sped, and the leaden messenger of death rushed whizzing into empty air.

One look of horror and desperate hate the pirate gave, and that was all.

In another moment the old man had drawn back a pace, and the sword of the father had avenged the attempted murder of his only daughter.

In an instant there was a scene of wild and indescribable confusion.

The Spaniards, deprived of a leader, upon whom, in spite of his villany, they could depend for courage and discretion, were at a loss what to do.

They could not conceive that, after such a desperate fight, and after the death of so many brave men, the English would consent to give quarter, and they fought on, therefore, in wild desperation, some of them even flinging themselves into the sea to avoid what they deemed inevitable death at the hands of their natural enemies.

Vyvyan, however, experienced now but little resistance.

Those whom he found in his way made but a feeble effort to impede his progress, and in a few minutes after the death of the pirate chief, he found himself on the deck of his own ship, whence he rushed below and placed his lovely, but still insensible burden in the commander's cabin.

He had scarcely done so when there was a sudden lull in the fight.

The loud and sonorous voice of Sir Francis Drake had been heard far above the tempest of the battle, and in a few moments the Spaniards saw a scene which wrapped them in amazement.

They—huddled up at one end of the deck—beheld the brave English sailors collected at the other, with their weapons lowered, and the fight over at the very moment they had expected death!

"Spaniards!" exclaimed Sir Francis Drake, advancing, and addressing them in their own language, "Spaniards, your captain is dead; the victory is ours; further resistance would simply result in useless bloodshed. Yield, then, to necessity, and throw down your weapons. You will find in us a generous foe, and we will set you down at any port on this coast that you choose to name. Speak. Give up your arms and it is done."

The Spaniards, who were perfectly astounded by the words of the great commander, conferred earnestly and rapidly together.

The conference did not last long.

It would, as Sir Francis Drake said, have been utter madness, and wilful waste of human life, to have carried on the contest any further against such odds.

With angry, sullen faces, therefore, they laid down their arms, and a few minutes more saw them stowed away as prisoners of war in the hold of the "Elizabeth."

Copious provisions were given them, and the doctor attended to their wounds, and though angry at first at being compelled to yield to their detested enemies, they were soon obliged to admit that they had not fallen into bad hands.

Meanwhile Vyvyan had not returned to the scene of conflict.

He had seen enough to convince him that the tide of battle had set in inevitably in favour of the English, and he had not moved, therefore, from the side of his fair divinity.

Restoratives were quickly applied to the young girl, and presently she opened upon her preserver as lovely a pair of blue, bright eyes as ever opened upon the world!

The deafening din of battle was still to be heard overhead, but she could see at one glance around her that she had been saved, and was with friends.

"Dear father," she said, as the old man, pale from loss of blood, bent over her and kissed her, while her warm, young arms encircled his neck, "dear father, thank God you, too, are safe from those hideous men!"

"Yes, I am safe, and you, too, thanks to this brave youth," replied her father, as he pressed Vyvyan's hands, "who rescued us from the grasp of unrelenting foes."

"Oh! how can we repay such unasked for—such brave devotion?" cried the young girl, as she took his hand and strove to raise it to her pretty lips.

Vyvyan prevented her, and lifting her little hand he impressed upon it a long and fervent kiss.

"I am sufficiently rewarded," he answered, "by a smile from the loveliest eyes in Christendom."

A deep blush mantled upon the cheek of the young girl, as the young man's eager, admiring glance fell upon her.

"We will reward you right royally, if we can but find the chance," said the father of Eveline; "the De Courcys have ever been favorites at court, and I as the last of the race can claim a royal favor."

Vyvyan pressed warmly the hand extended to him.

"I need no reward," he said, "save the honour of your friendship. It is enough for me to have saved you: to be permitted to defend you and your fair daughter. My own sword must win my way to fortune, or my vow, long since registered, will be forfeited for ever."

At this moment Kemersham entered the captain's cabin.

"The battle is over, fair lady," he said,

bowing with deep reverence to Eveline de Courcy; "there is no longer danger to apprehend. Vyvyan, Sir Francis Drake has need of you at once."

Vyvyan turned towards the friend who had aided him to save the young and tender being who was now all in all to him.

"I will come immediately," he said. "Lady, and you, sir," he added, glancing towards Eveline and her father, "I will be with you anon."

And with a smile at Eveline, he passed away with Kemersham.

When he entered the cabin of Sir Francis the brave commander advanced to meet him with outstretched hands.

"Vyvyan, noble youth," he said, "to you I owe most of the honour and glory of this enterprise; and if now your spirit yearns for adventure and renown, there is a chance of its immediate fulfilment."

"My bright sword longs for further battle, Sir Francis," cried Vyvyan; "show me but the path to renown and I will follow it."

"The way is clear," said Sir Francis Drake; "I have now an opportunity of proving to you how highly I estimate your worth. Kemersham, my lieutenant, has truly the first claim upon me—you have the second. The "Alfonso" is a noble ship, and worthy to be re-named and manned. I intend to send her to England with a few brave spirits on board, to obtain a fresh crew, and rejoin me at Telbago. I have appointed Kemersham the captain, and to you, Vyvyan, I give the post of lieutenant."

"Can this be true?" cried Vyvyan, as a bright flush of pride mantled upon his cheek. "You over-rate my services, kind sir."

"Not in the least. Then you accept the office?"

"I do, most noble captain," exclaimed "and should you grant me one you would redouble my gra-"

"And what is that?" asked Sir Francis, with a smile.

"The boon I ask, is to be permitted to convey to England the captives we saved from the Spanish pirates."

"I guessed as much, good Vyvyan," said Drake. "The boon is granted, since such is their desire. To-night we shall part company; I make westward, to place on shore the Spaniards whose lives we spared, while you will make all haste for England. Between this and midnight I will get ready a letter for her most gracious Majesty Elizabeth, which I wish you to give to her yourself; 'twill aid you in your path to glory, should fortune ever frown. Go now, and tell the lady how things are ordered, and at midnight I expect to come aboard the prize and find all right for sailing."

The night fell dark and heavy over the sea; but, long ere midnight, all had been prepared according to order.

The masts and sails were repaired sufficiently to commence the voyage; spare spars were taken from the "Elizabeth" on board the "Alfonso," ready to repair the mainmast on the morrow, and the two rescued captives were placed in the cabin so lately the abode of a fierce and unrelenting wretch, to whom human life was as naught compared with gold.

About a quarter of an hour before midnight a boat put off from the "Elizabeth," and Sir Francis Drake came on board.

In the cabin of the "Alfonso," he formally named the prize the "Dreadnought," and installed Kemersham and Vyvyan as captain and lieutenant.

Then, having given them their dispatches for England, and taken leave of them, and Courcy and his daughter, he quitted them, and, wishing them "God speed," returned once more to his own ship.

Then the two vessels parted company; the lights of the "Elizabeth" faded away in the distance, and the "Dreadnought," under but half canvas, made its way towards the north.

CHAPTER XIII.

A CHASE BY AN OLD ENEMY.

WHEN the morning dawned, the men on board the newly-christened vessel commenced eagerly their work, and while Vyvyan and Eveline stood indolently by the bulwarks, gazing at them while they laboured, or out over the wide, rolling sea, the mainmast was once more placed in position, and ere evening fell over the ocean all sails were spread, and the "Dreadnought" was making impetuously towards the shores of Old England.

For a long time that voyage was a dream of love.

There was little to do in the way of command, for the weather kept calm and bright, and the vessel sped quietly though rapidly on its way, and so hour by hour, being together and unchecked, these two hearts expanded in mutual love, and Vyvyan's dreams of glory and renown were now mingled with sweet visions of youthful passion.

There was nothing in Eveline to dispel these visions.

It was evident to all that Vyvyan's love was not unrequited.

The brave devotion which had resulted in saving her from a general fate had at first begotten admiration, but constant and daily intercourse had changed this admiration into a tender love.

And so they went on, floating over a summer sea, which in its peace and calmness was typical of their first romance!

But this was not destined to last long.

They had met on their way several strange sails, but, as yet, all had been friendly, and exchanged mutual good wishes.

But when they were within two hundred miles of England, just as the day dawned, the look-out sang out—

"A sail! a sail!"

Kemersham and his lieutenant at once hurried to their point of observation, and gazed at the stranger through their glasses.

Vyvyan glanced long and earnestly as it expanded upon the horizon and took by degrees more definite shape.

It seemed familiar to his eyes, and as hour by hour passed by, and it drew nearer, he was certain that he recognised an old enemy.

"If my eyes do not deceive me, captain," he said, turning to Kemersham, "that ship is well known to me."

"What ship, then, do you make it out to be?" asked the captain.

"I believe it to be the 'Black Vulture,' commanded by Wrecklyffe, my old pirate foe," returned Vyvyan; "its peculiar build assures me of it. If he overhauls us it will be a terrible massacre, for nothing but a miracle could save us."

"We have a swift and well-trimmed ship," replied Kemersham, boldly; they shall have a stern chase for it. Besides, we have plenty of guns—plenty of ammunition, and we would try the issue of a battle, at any rate. Never shall he say that Englishmen surrendered at discretion."

"Trust me, captain," cried Vyvyan, "I would gladly aid you; but still with such precious burdens on board as we have, it behoves us to be careful."

"Truly it does," said Kemersham; "but with such a sea and such a wind as this, we have a chance of avoiding an encounter."

He was right.

The breeze was freshening rapidly, and the sails of the "Dreadnought" bellied out bravely before it.

Still the dark hull of the stranger became larger and larger, and Vyvyan's heart beat swiftly and more swiftly as it came onwards.

It was a new sensation this for him.

He was used to battles now—used to scenes of bloodshed—careless of the events of the hour, and full of trust in his own destiny, as men of those times were.

But to see an enemy and fly from him was an unaccustomed and unwelcome change in the programme of his life.

Still, what could be done?

He had but a handful of men; his ship was in sad need of repair, and he had with him not only important despatches, but a sacred charge in the persons of De Courcy and his daughter.

So on sped the "Dreadnought" on the blue ocean in one steady course until night closed in.

When the first dark shadow took the place of the sun, there was no longer a doubt about the identity of the pursuer.

It was the "Black Vulture."

To say that Vyvyan's heart sank within him at the thought, would be wrong.

It was not so.

He knew that Wrecklyffe would most certainly attempt a deadly revenge; he knew that rage must have filled his heart when he discovered how the next in command had disposed of the one who had struck him down before his own men; he knew that now everything was in favour of disaster and ruin, and nothing in favour of success and safety.

Yet he did not despair.

For Eveline it might mean peril—for him, with Heaven above, and brave hearts and bright swords below, there was hope and strength remaining. The whole of the night was occupied by Kemersham and Vyvyan in separate watches, and morning found them both eagerly scanning the horizon.

The "Black Vulture" was still nearing them gradually.

They had made now considerable progress, and were already in hopes of seeing the white cliffs of England.

What could it mean?

Was Wrecklyffe about to attempt an attack upon an English ship in English waters?

So, indeed, it seemed, for, as the day again went by, preparations for action were rapidly made on board the "Black Vulture," and the Raven Flag fluttered from the mast.

The first shot was fired as the heavy shades of evening fell.

But it did no injury.

"A reckless and a desperate villain, truly," exclaimed Kemersham; "but, if this wind will but last, he will still be defeated, for we shall be within the certain safeguard of an English port."

There was no chance of further battle that night, for the wind fell, and a heavy mist obscured everything that was not comparatively near.

It was Vyvyan's first watch that night, and as he leaned over the bulwarks and gazed towards white-cliffed England, he could not but think of the hermit-priest who had reared him, the unknown mother who had hovered over him in dreams, and the hopes which an unknown future appeared to offer to him.

It was in the middle of a reverie that he was startled by a sudden apparition.

A great shadow seemed to loom above the ship, then a sudden rush was made by an unsightly object whose identity he could not make out; then there was a shock—a collision—and the bulwarks of the two ships grazed against one another.

At this moment a man, holding a lantern in his hand, leaned over the side of the pirate vessel and held the light aloft.

As he did so, Vyvyan saw his face plainly.

He knew too well that hard and villanous face.

It was Wrecklyffe.

The recognition was mutual, but there was no time for words.

A muttered curse was wafted on the air, then a huge wave parted the ships, and the mist separated the sworn enemies once more!

CHAPTER XIV.

DEATH WAITING!

ENGLAND'S shores at length loomed out, white and bright in the leaden-hued morning, and with many a cheer the seamen who had run a long and perilous voyage greeted the first glimpse of their island home.

Penraven Bay, in Cornwall, was the port towards which they made—a small refuge from the tempest, fenced in from the wild wind by rugged and precipitous rocks—a harbour of refuge, half natural, half artificial, and capable of containing only three or four large ships at a time.

As they approached its welcome mouth they could see that one vessel was already there, and in a moment Vyvyan's mind instinctively formed a notion as to its name and character.

As they entered the quiet basin no further doubt existed.

It was the " Black Vulture !"

"A daring villain, truly," exclaimed Kemersham, as the young adventurer pointed out to him the name painted in red letters on a black ground : " and yet he is safe. We have no proofs against him."

"None but our own words, and they will avail but little," said Vyvyan; " the traitor bears letters of marque which protect him from all English vessels, and see ! he hoists the British ensign. But why is he here ? There in some fresh trickery and villainy afloat, I'll be sworn !"

"No doubt of it," said Kemersham, " no doubt of it. But I will keep strict watch upon him. No movement shall escape—so fear nothing for your fair charge or for yourself."

For the present, however, there seemed no peril for either.

The men on board the pirate ship were all engaged busily : some repairing the injuries received during the collision of the previous night ; others scrubbing the decks ; others seeing to the rigging, and others again engaged in some mysterious labour connected with heavy bales of goods, which were evidently some of the plunder taken from the ill-fated merchant vessel whose destruction by the pirates Vyvyan had been a helpless witness of.

Of the pirate, Wrecklyffe himself, nothing was seen.

For some reason or another he kept himself below, and he who seemed in command of the vessel was the man who had committed the young adventurer to the mercy of the waves to save the vessel from the curse of blood.

About midday, therefore, Vyvyan accompanied De Courcy and his daughter to their home.

It was near Penraven Bay that the mansion of Sir Leonard de Courcy was situated—a fine, old house, just such as might have been thought to be the residence of a Cornish gentleman, in the days when battlemented walls protected nobles from the wrath of kings.

I need but briefly describe it.

High-turreted, moated, covered with ivy, its grey old towers o'er-looked the wrathful billows, and the lights in its topmost windows many times had guided lost mariners far out at sea towards the little harbour of refuge.

Sir Leonard de Courcy and his daughter had been long absent from their quiet home, led out to the west as Vyvyan had been by dreams of golden store, and, now that they returned, robbed of the treasure that they had gained, the domestics welcomed them like beings risen from the dead.

It was necessary for the "Dreadnought" to remain some considerable time in harbour to undergo repairs, fit out, and obtain a crew before proceeding upon their voyage to the West Indies, and Vyvyan, therefore, gladly accepted the proffer of hospitality made him by Sir Leonard.

"One night's rest, Sir Leonard," he said, " and then I must away to London, with the despatch entrusted to me by Sir Francis Drake; but I shall soon return, glad indeed to rest before I start afresh upon the road to fortune."

It was evening time when Vyvyan and Eveline parted on the terrace.

He had that evening received a note from Kemersham:—

"*Go not till evening. Enemies dog your steps. Go secretly and suddenly under cover of the darkness.*

This warning he took care to abide by, and, at the postern-gate of the mansion, at the extremity of the grounds, a saddled horse awaited him.

"Eveline—sweet Eveline," said Vyvyan, as he took her hand in his and pressed it, "I go to-night upon a long, and, maybe, perilous journey. Have I your blessing on it?"

The young girl blushed and hung her head, her light curls shimmering like molten gold in the moonlight.

"My blessing always, sir," she answered, tremulously. "Have we not a debt of deep, deep gratitude to you? Have you not saved my life, and that, too, of my father?"

"Oh, speak not of that, sweet Eveline," he cried, "speak not of that! It is not gratitude I wish for. See yonder ocean, on whose trembling bosom the moonlight dances merrily. There are times, as *you* know well, when those still waves are raised aloft like mountains, on whose jagged and foam-crested summits the lightning springs in leaps of vivid fire! There are times when the wind howls and raves among the rigging, and all seems lost and ruined! It is at times like these that sailors watch and long for some bright light—some friendly star to guide them on their way, and give them promise of fair weather. Be thou that light to me, sweet Eveline; be thou that star! Oh! let me think, dear girl, that in this stormy world I have, at least, one boon which none can rob me of—the priceless treasure of your love!"

Any one who had beheld the flutter of her bosom, and the delicate blush upon her cheek, and the magic smile in her eyes, could at once have known where her young love was set.

"You have known me so short a time," she said; "you have spent your time upon the sea. You may yet behold queenly beauties who will enthral your heart and cast my image in the shade. Wait awhile ere you rashly link yourself to one whom Time may change in your eyes."

Vyvyan knelt before her.

"Oh! Eveline, Time will not change me save he takes me hence. My Eveline, I love you—I love you. Be mine!"

The answer came very softly and tenderly as she placed her hand upon his head.

"Yes, Vyvyan. God bless you. I am yours."

Oh! the pleasure, the joy of that first embrace as Vyvyan sprang to his feet, and folded her fluttering form to his breast.

"Oh! this is happiness," he said, as he pointed towards the sea. "What care I now for storms or foemen—the raving wind or the fierce sea robbers? I have a shield in your love—an instinct of preservation. "Oh! Eveline, you have torn the thorns from off my path and sown it thick with roses."

If he had but glanced back he would have seen two stealthy forms creep in among the bushes at the bottom of the terrace—dark-looking, well-armed men, whose faces showed truly the character of their minds.

"We have him safe enough," muttered one, as he glared up at the loving pair.

"Aye, he's caged," replied the other. "This will be his first and last love dream."

It was quite evident that the warning sent to him by Kemersham was no needless one.

The men who thus spoke, glorying in their own villany and rejoicing in the misery it would cause, were of that class who would shirk no horrid deed to obtain possession of gold or to work out the vengeance of a superior.

Little did those lovers, wrapped in their sweet dream of youth, imagine that near to them were the merciless agents of a cruel foe.

Little did they dream that while they were indulging in visions of a blissful future, death was fluttering his wings above their heads, and waiting eagerly to end for ever their hopes.

"Are you compelled to leave me, Vyvyan?" again urged Eveline." "A sad presentiment oppresses me, and makes me dread this long journey in another's interest."

"I *must* go, dearest Eveline," murmured Vyvyan, after another warm embrace. "My duty calls me to London, or I would not leave you. Fear not, however, that I shall long delay. My beacon light will light me on my return, and bring me to you on the wings of love. Adieu, Eveline, adieu."

"Adieu, dear Vyvyan," she answered, as she received his last kiss. "Heaven shield you on your journey—and remember, that if danger threatens and disaster falls, there will live *here* one to avenge you."

"Heaven bless and guard you," exclaimed Vyvyan, as loth to leave her at this blissful hour, he pressed her again warmly to his heart; "your love will give me power against a thousand foes. Adieu —once more—adieu."

Then he sprang from her embrace and was gone.

The hired ruffians who waited below watched his departure eagerly.

Then as he made his way towards the postern, they rushed away through the bushes and made all speed towards a place in the wall, where they knew it was easy to escape.

Here they quickly clambered over, and in a few minutes they were standing in the shadow of the high battlements with their pistols ready for use.

"We must fire at him as he comes up," said one of them, "you remember Wrecklyffe's orders were strict."

"To kill without mercy."

"You are right," said the other; "but be ready. He is coming."

As he spoke the clatter of horse's hoofs was heard approaching, and Vyvyan and his horse emerged from the shadows of the dark road.

"A welcome from Wrecklyffe," shouted one of the ruffians, as he fired at the rider's head.

The echo of the shot rang loudly through the clear air, and Eveline, as she entered the house started in instinctive terror.

"Fly, fly, Gerard!" she cried, as the retainers were about to close the door. "Some ill has befallen Lieutenant Vyvyan, I feel sure; fly, while there is yet time."

The retainers, at all times eager to do the bidding of their beloved young mistress, hastily seized some weapons hanging in the hall, and rushed through the gloomy garden towards the postern gate.

On passing through this the groans of an animal in distress guided them to the spot where the pistol shot had been fired; but when they arrived there they saw nothing but a horse struggling in its last agony, and the dead body of a man lying on its face in the road.

CHAPTER XV.

BAFFLED TREACHERY.

SEEING the dying horse and the still form lying on its face in the road, the retainers of Sir Leonard de Courcy at first almost feared to raise it up.

In the darkness it was quite impossible to distinguish the clothes of the dead man; and knowing the terrible blow it would be to their young mistress if they took back to her evil tidings of Vyvyan,

it was with trembling hands that they at last turned over the senseless clay and examined the pale features.

One glance sufficed.

The swarthy, ferocious, brutal countenance which met their eyes was little like the bright, handsome face of Eveline's betrothed.

"He has settled *his* account at any

rate," cried Gerard, one of the retainers; "but where is the lieutenant? Let us search."

And so they did; but for a long time no trace of combat could be seen, or evidence, indeed, of flight.

Presently, however, dark spots upon the chalky road attracted their attention, and on casting upon them the bright light of the lantern, they saw that the red marks led from the high road towards a dense mass of brushwood that skirted that part of the highway.

They had scarcely reached the spot when there was a loud crashing and crackling of bushes at some distance, while near them they distinctly heard a low groan of mortal agony.

"Here's another in distress," said the foremost of the retainers. "Pray Heaven it is not the young lieutenant that has dragged himself here to die. It is here somewhere among these low bushes," he continued, as he searched eagerly among the dank undergrowth. "Ah! what is this? A man's foot! Quick, Gerard, the light!"

The other domestic at once knelt down, and threw the glare of the lantern full on the face of a dying man.

One glance, as before, was enough.

It was not Vyvyan, but another of the ferocious ruffians who had watched with bloodthirsty coolness the love scene on the terrace..

"'Tis well," said the man, "'tis well. Master Vyvyan has escaped, and left the mark of his strong arm upon these wretches. Speak, sirrah! what means this scene on our quiet highway?"

There was no reply.

The man was too far gone to make any.

His lips moved in an ineffectual effort at speech, his eyes glared wildly an instant, his nostrils dilated, and then a convulsive movement passed through his form, and all was over.

There was no use in further seeking now, and so after a few glances round to see if danger threatened them, the two retainers made their way back to the castellated mansion.

The absence of Vyvyan may be easily explained.

The man who had so insolently proclaimed a welcome from Wrecklyffe fired unsteadily in his great haste, and the horse of the young lieutenant fell instead of his master.

In an instant after there was another flash and a report, and the insolent boaster fell to the earth.

Then Vyvyan, seeing that his animal was entirely beyond use, rushed at the second man, who, on beholding the rapid and disastrous fate of his comrade, lost all courage and fled.

The young adventurer, who might now have pursued his way undisturbed, resolved nevertheless to punish the would-be assassin, and caught him as he reached the wood.

The fellow, seeing Vyvyan so close behind him, was compelled to turn and defend himself.

But the contest did not last long.

The cowardly villain was no match for the practised swordmanship and eager courage of the young lieutenant of the "Dreadnought," and he soon fell headlong in the agonies of dissolution among the tangled brushwood, where the retainers of the old mansion had found him.

Hearing the rush of feet along the road, and naturally supposing that fresh enemies were after him, Vyvyan had waited no longer to see if they were friends or foes, but darting away through the trees made all haste towards a twinkling light which seemed like that of an inn.

Here he resolved to take horse to London, deeming it better to obtain a fresh steed from strangers than to risk a return to the stables of Sir Leonard de Courcy.

The light which led him on proved no *ignis fatuus;* and after partaking of a goodly draught of ale to cool his thirst after the combat, he found a horse ready saddled and bridled for him, and away he dashed upon the road to London.

Wrecklyffe, meanwhile, who had waited the issue of the treacherous enterprise in a low inn close to the little harbour, became impatient as time went on and he saw nothing of his messengers.

They had strict injunctions to meet him at the inn the moment the deed was done, and when at length midnight came and still no tidings reached him, he rose from his seat near the blazing fire, drank off another tankard of ale, and without acquainting anyone of his intention quitted the inn and made his way towards the spot where he expected to fall in with his associates.

The retainers of Sir Leonard had dragged away the second corpse and laid it by the side of the first, and when, therefore, the buccaneer stealthily and slowly approached the postern he fell prostrate upon the ground over one of his friends, so that the cold, clammy face of the dead pressed against his cheek.

"What have we here?" he cried, savagely, as he turned the light of his lantern upon their faces and beheld their rigid features. "What, Markham and Ewin dead! Curses on the young hound! he has escaped me once more."

When he rose to his feet he stood for a moment with his arms folded, gazing down upon the senseless dead.

"Strange, strange!" he muttered, "when first Sir Grey de Malpas gave me the task of slaying Vyvyan for him I shuddered at the deed, and would have saved him at the peril of my life. I liked not murder done in cold blood as he would have had me do it, but now his blood alone will satisfy my vengeance. Now that he has thwarted me, and risen from the grave as it were to confront me, I hate him with as deadly a hatred as ever did Sir Grey."

He paused a moment, and then moved away towards the harbour.

"My men must fetch yonder carrion," he muttered, as he went, "and cast them into the sea, for it will not do to have them found here in the road. Ah! good thought," he added, as a sudden idea flashed across his brain; "good thought. I will away to-morrow to Sir Grey de Malpas, and let him know that this stripling is still living. For art and cunning I know no one better, and where open warfare fails, treachery often opens the road to success."

With these words, which gave a kind of comfort to his villanous heart, he hurried on with quickened steps towards the inn where he had left his comrades.

CHAPTER XVI.

THE QUEEN RECEIVES VYVYAN—OLD MEMORIES—OUT TO SEA ONCE MORE.

VYVYAN, meanwhile, rode safely on to London, and, putting up at the "Mitre Tavern" in the Fleet Street, proceeded within the hour to the queen's palace.

It would not suit my story to describe in detail the reception given him by the virgin queen.

Elizabeth, who almost worshipped her brave commanders, and thought nothing too great an honour for Raleigh, Drake, and Essex, had, it may well be imagined, a bright smile and lavish thanks to bestow upon a young, brave, and handsome adventurer like Vyvyan; and when, after two days spent amid a splendour which fairly dazzled the protegé of the hermit priest, he turned his horse's head once more towards Cornwall, a bright diamond star glistened on his breast, placed there by the queen's own hands.

Lonely vigils were those of Eveline de Courcy, watching and waiting for her betrothed lover.

Happy, indeed, was she in the knowledge of his devoted affection, and in the thorough consent of her father to their ultimate union; but that there was danger abroad for her heart's chosen one was too evidently proved by the desperate attack made upon him the night of his departure.

What still greater perils might not threaten him now, in the heart of a strange city, with no friends near to cheer or aid him, and with a desperate foe (such as she knew Wrecklyffe, from Vyvyan, now to be) ever on his track to destroy him?

Still there was in her heart a kind of presentiment of good.

"VYVYAN RELATING HIS ADVENTURES TO THE QUEEN."

She could not bring herself to believe that one so noble, so generous, and, above all, one she loved so dearly, could be permitted by Heaven to fall a victim to base treachery.

Glad as she was to see him, no matter under what circumstances, she uttered a cry of horror and astonishment as he sprang one evening into her room, with his face bloodstained, and his clothes torn as if in a desperate struggle.

His sword, too, was grasped firmly in his hand, and his hat gone.

"Great Heavens! What means this, Vyvyan?" she cried, as she sprang forward, and threw herself into his arms.

Vyvyan's breast was panting with excitement, as he answered her.

"I have been beset again, Eveline," he cried. "You know the bridge across the Devil's Causeway; there three men were lurking, and as my steed, plunging onward through the darkness, as if impelled by the same eager desire as his master, these three hidden traitors fired upon me. They missed me."

"Thank Heaven!" murmured Eveline.

"There was still more to come, my sweet one," murmured Vyvyan. "I glanced back as I rode, and in the light their carbines gave I saw the face of Wrecklyffe. I know too well his fierce and brutal features to have mistaken him even on such a night as this."

"But you escaped him!"

"Yes, to find, at the bend of the road, six men on horseback, drawn up ready to receive me. It was how I got this sabre cut on my face, for against such odds it was scarcely possible to contend, and I was too far from any human habitation to have the slightest hope of assistance. There was nothing for it, therefore, but to dash headlong upon them, and either cut through their ranks, or perish in the attempt."

"Oh, would that my father and his retainers had been there to face this coward band."

"Aye, so thought I," said Vyvyan, smiling, as she nestled up closer to his bosom. "But Heaven gave my arm the strength of all my wished-for friends combined; my horse, too, though hired, was a good one, and with one plunge, one sabre cut right and left, I was clear of my enemies, and am here safe with you, dear Eveline."

"Did you recognize none of them?" asked the young girl.

"It may be fancy," said Vyvyan, "but among the voices I seemed to recognize one that was familiar to me—the voice of Sir Grey de Malpas, the poor kinsman of my Lord of Montreville, whom I have seen often in my village home. I am not certain."

"Yet with this uncertainty," said Eveline, "you will not surely venture to the village either at night or alone. Send for Alton hither; both I and my father would gladly welcome the preserver of our preserver."

The hint thus given was acted upon on the morrow, and if Wrecklyffe or his cowardly employer Sir Grey had for one moment imagined that the opportunity would be given them of destroying him in secret, they were miserably mistaken.

Alton, the priest, gladly obeyed the summons of his foster son, but even now the seal of silence was upon his lips.

He still refused to explain anything in regard to the mysterious story of Vyvyan's birth.

In vain the young and enthusiastic adventurer spoke to him of the mother who still haunted his dreams—of the glory he had already gained at his sword's point—of the renown in store for him—of the rapture with which his mother would greet him coming to her self-crowned with honour.

The old priest shook his head.

"No, no," he said, "the time is not yet come. When it does come, I shall be but too glad to give you the benefit of my absolution from my vow. Between this and me stands yet another life, and until that life is passed away I cannot and dare not reveal the secret which you so burn to hear. Go on, nevertheless, steadily in your path of glory, and win distinction, that when your mother does welcome you she may welcome a hero."

This was all he could be induced to say, and Vyvyan at length abandoned as hopeless the task of endeavouring to sound him.

Meanwhile, busy days went by.

The "Dreadnought," placed in the hands of able shipwrights, was soon transformed into a splendid vessel.

New spars, new rigging, new sails, and new paint, performed, as it were, a miracle of change; and as Vyvyan, with pride and pleasure walked with Eveline over its clean, white decks, he could searcely bring himself to believe that it was the same vessel from which he had rescued his beloved companion, and which he had but lately seen deluged with the blood of the slain.

These pleasant times, full of love and hope, soon passed away, and at length the dreaded hour of parting came for them, as it will come for all sooner or later.

It may be imagined that the young adventurer lingered till the last.

Much as he longed to finish his education on the sea: to visit new lands, and wrest golden treasures from the hands of England's natural foes, he could not but feel a pang of bitter regret at leaving the one he loved more than life.

While her gentle form leaned confidingly against his breast—while her little hand pressed his—while her tender eyes beamed up in to his, and her soft voice murmured words of love and hope, he felt as if death itself could have no greater sting in store for him than this hour of parting.

"Oh, Eveline!" he said, as he kissed her warm lips, upturned to him, as she listened, "when I quitted your side to go to London, I went almost gladly, because I knew I was to return to you, but now——"

She gazed up at him in terror.

"Oh, sad presentiment, Vyvyan!" she cried, "you will still return?"

He embraced her again fervently.

"I meant, sweet love, that I was *soon* to return to you," he said, "whereas wild winds and waves will separate us, perhaps, for years. But through those years, one beacon star will guide me—one hope will keep me happy—that star will be you, sweet heart—that hope will be the hope of being reunited to you, never more to part."

Thus in tender converse the hours sped away until the last moment came.

Then the last embrace was taken, the last kiss given, the last farewell spoken, and Vyvyan was rowed away under cover of the darkness towards his own ship, which was to set sail at daybreak.

Two feelings were now struggling for supremacy within his breast.

The one was regret at quitting the side of the one whom he loved better than life itself.

The other was the desire to win renown that he might claim her—and his mother!

During the whole time that had been expended in manning and renovating the "Dreadnought," the "Black Vulture" had been in harbour also, apparently for the purpose of watching the proceedings of the other vessel more than of obtaining any reinforcements or aid for itself.

Its dark hull loomed gloomily over the waters on that night when Vyvyan went on board the "Dreadnought," but when the first rays of the morning sun broke over the rolling billows, it was gone!

Wrecklyffe's treachery had failed on land; it behoved them to watch what it might effect at sea!

CHAPTER XVII.

BY NIGHT AT PORTO LAGOS.

WHATEVER Wrecklyffe's intention might have been, it was, nevertheless, certain that he would not so easily and so readily give up all designs against one whose success had caused his hatred to be doubled, and who had laughed his power to scorn.

A good look-out was kept, therefore; but although the "Black Vulture" had sailed so short a time before the "Dreadnought," not a glimpse of the pirate vessel could anywhere be seen.

Kemersham, who had in a great measure shared the hospitality of Sir Leonard de Courcy with Vyvyan, had been on board hours before his lieutenant, but he had seen no sign of any extraordinary activity on the part of the enemy, nor had any of the sailors seen her move out of harbour.

She had passed away like a thing of air, as silently and as suddenly as if she had sunk down in a summer sea, without an effort on the part of the crew to save her.

Time went on.

Scarcely a vessel passed them on their journey.

A strong and steady wind bore them on rapidly towards the West Indies, where, at Telbago it will be remembered, Sir Francis Drake had appointed to meet them.

Being instructed not to attack any vessel on the way, but to hurry out with the reply of Queen Elizabeth to Drake's despatches, they were not sorry that the necessity for battle and flight was alike saved them.

Sir Francis Drake, whose ship was lying in Telbago Bay, was scarcely certain when he saw the elegant vessel approaching him that it was the "Dreadnought"—that battered and battle-beaten hull which he had dispatched to England for repairs.

The well-known faces of Kemersham and Vyvyan, however, soon dispelled the illusion, and he received with eager gladness the letter from the English queen.

"She approves my choice, and gives me joy of my young commanders," he said. "You will soon now have to try your mettle. Strange vessels have been hovering about this island, and when to-morrow we make for Porto Lagos we shall fall in with one or two craft of most suspicious build and appearance. There is one in particular which carries an English flag, and shows letters of marque. I like not its look, nor the look of those who man it. In my mind it is a pirate in disguise."

"What is its appearance?" asked Vyvyan, in whose mind a suspicion at once arose. "Has it a black hull with a red line around it?"

"It has."

"The 'Black Vulture,' I will be sworn!" cried Vyvyan, enthusiastically. "Oh, that I could now have one fair fight with Wrecklyffe and end this lengthened feud!"

"He carries letters of marque, you for-get that," said Sir Francis. "Of such an artful villain we must beware. "But should you find him trespassing on our ground you have my warranty to attack him at once. Meanwhile, what comes yonder?"

"As he spoke he pointed with some eagerness towards a spot in the water at some distance from them.

Far away stretched the coast of Telbago, its high hills fringed with plenteous greenery, its low beach lined with numerous houses, and here and along its perfumed shores round white forts, showing how Spain, even in her first hour of conquest, had feared that the West was but a dream for her.

Between these forts—which now were full of English soldiers, if so we may term the wild though well-armed adventurers taken thither by Sir Walter Raleigh and others of his class—between these forts and the spot where the English shops rode at anchor there was a dark spot which presently developed itself into the shape of a boat.

"It is a boat," cried Vyvyan, "pulling from the shore. Mayhap they bring us news."

Drake's eyes sparkled.

This was what he expected.

During Vyvyan's absence, he had cruised about these seas, meeting with enemies, and twice attacking and subduing them; going inland on long and dangerous journeys, and picking up, as history gravely tells us, gold in bars and nuggets as he went.

But he had heard of late of five large Spanish galleons, laden and staggering with their golden freight, and for these his eyes had for many a long day past eagerly scanned the horizon. He had left word with those who manned the Spanish forts to send him word at once if any news reached them from the opposite side of the island, and it may be imagined, therefore, that he anxiously awaited the coming of the strange boat.

The news they brought him was exactly in accordance with his wishes.

The Spanish galleons had already appeared some fifty miles east of Porto Lagos.

Sir Francis Drake, although intensely excited by the golden prospect before him, gave his orders with calmness and despatch.

To Kemersham he assigned the duty of proceeding to the Harbour of Porto Lagos, and remaining there until the Spaniards had entered, had obtained water, and had sailed away once more.

The "Elizabeth" would then descend upon them from the sea, and the "Dreadnought" from the land.

"If the 'Black Vulture' is there before us," said Vyvyan, "we shall have tough work of it. Wrecklyffe is not the man to allow the capture of such a rich booty before his very eyes."

"Fear not," said Drake; "in such a matter as this he will fight with us. Five galleons laden with gold are certainly prize enough for three English vessels."

Within the hour the "Dreadnought" was speeding away under all sail towards Porto Lagos, which they reached just as the shades of evening had fallen over the island.

About an hour after their arrival another vessel glided noiselessly in before the steady wind, and took up its position on the opposite side of the bay.

Nothing could be done that night, and it needed, therefore, but little persuasion on the part of Vyvyan to induce Kemersham to leave the ship and take a stroll along the rugged streets of the half-built town.

Night, as I have said, had fallen over Porto Lagos, but still they could see as they went the ruins of old forts and houses, and tall trees nodding over them, and great shadowy hills filling up the background.

Here and there lights were visible, and from some of the larger houses came the sounds of revelry and mirth.

But with all this, even with the ships in the harbour, speaking of commerce with other countries, it was but a caricature upon civilized communities.

The young captain and his lieutenant paused at the door of one of the houses whose doors were open invitingly, and after a moment's hesitation entered.

Drinking, and the smoking, too, of the newly-found weed, tobacco, was proceeding madly, as was also gambling, and the faces of those around were flushed and excited.

They had imagined, as they entered, that they had heard familiar voices.

They were not mistaken.

Among those who gambled highest, whose voice was loudest, but who drank least, was Wrecklyffe, the buccaneer.

He cast a glance of wonder, mingled with hatred, at Vyvyan as he entered.

Then he rose from his seat, and approaching him said, with a genial smile—

"Well met, young sir; the sea, it seems, was kinder than your friends or I, and granted you your life."

A bitter and insulting answer was on Vyvyan's tongue at once.

But Kemersham restrained him.

"Not here," he whispered; "choose another time. Within this den of thieves who knows what foes may lurk? Be calm—be prudent—remember the words of Drake."

"We are strangely met in every truth," returned Vyvyan; "but, we may yet meet again on a better field. For the present, converse is scarce the order of the hour. We have disturbed your play. Proceed."

Wrecklyffe hesitated but a moment.

He knew that Vyvyan was right.

Any quarrel provoked by him now would bring down upon him the anger of all present, who, busy in their games, would not care to be interrupted by a quarrel.

So, much as he would have liked the opportunity, he returned to his seat, and sullenly resumed his play.

In spite of the tempting offers made by those around, both Kemersham and Vyvyan resolutely refused to join the circle of gamblers, and, indeed, the main object of the young captain was now to induce his friend to leave the scene of drunken revelry before there was the chance of a quarrel with his old enemy.

Of this fact Wrecklyffe seemed perfectly aware, for no sooner had the two young adventurers quitted the room than he rose up, flung down his cards, and, after whispering a few words to some of the men, quitted the house also with one of his companions, and followed the two friends.

The night was very dark.

The sickly moon was obscured behind, and only the pale light of the stars illumined the scene.

But still he could see the forms of Kemersham and Vyvyan, as they walked on in eager converse.

As they neared the quay, his resolution seemed suddenly taken.

"Halt there!" he cried, "I desire a word with you."

Kemersham and Vyvyan started and turned round.

"What want you with us?" cried Kemersham, haughtily, though not insolently.

Not so impetuous as his younger companion he did not forget Sir Francis Drake's injunction to pick no quarrel with the foe.

"A word only with the braggart at your side," cried Wrecklyffe. "I bear no insolence from boys. What if the sea has cast you up as it casts up its foulest weeds, am I to suffer taunts from you? Have a care, young sir; we are not in England. In these wild lands might and a good sword are the only arbiters, and pretty arms and strong stone walls cannot hide you from my vengeance."

"Insolent assassin!" shouted Vyvyan, and, ere Kemersham could restrain him, he had drawn his sword and dashed upon the bold buccaneer.

Indeed, had Kemersham wished to interfere, the opportunity would not have been given him, for the pirate's friend, seeing the turn affairs had taken, at once drew his weapon and attacked him furiously.

The young captain of the "Dreadnought" was a good swordsman, but in this contest he had at last found his match.

His antagonist, whoever he was, was a brilliant fencer, and gradually but surely the captain found himself driven back—wounded and faint—towards the edge of the quay.

Not so Vyvyan.

Wrecklyffe was a good swordsman, but the young lieutenant, besides having been schooled by severe practice, was fired by the memory of old wrongs, and burning with desire to avenge also the last insult offered to him.

The buccaneer, therefore, found his match; though, if anything prolonged the contest and gave Wrecklyffe a chance, it was the sight of Kemersham wounded and giving ground without a friend to aid him.

The clash of steel rang strangely out over the still ocean, and echoed among the far-off silent hills, and soon the gamblers left their cards and stood at their doors, and people glanced out of windows to look and wonder at the unaccustomed sight.

At this moment Kemersham, in making a lunge, missed his footing, staggered and fell—weakened with loss of blood—on one knee.

The sword of the pirate glistened in the moonlight, which now burst forth, and then, oh, horror to Vyvyan, who could not rush to aid him, the bright blade buried itself in the heart of the brave young captain.

At this moment a number of dark figures scrambled up from a boat which had rowed ashore hastily from the "Dreadnought," but they came too late.

Wrecklyffe, however, suffered for his friend's success.

Glancing round to see whence arose the smothered groan of agony, he lost a point; Vyvyan's blade sparkled and trembled aloft and then plunging forward as if sharing its master's eagerness, it ran through the pirate's body.

He staggered back and would have fallen into the water had not a crowd of men rushed up at this moment and caught him in their arms.

"Back, cowards!" shouted Vyvyan, "let me complete my work."

And, in his fury at the fate of his friend, he would have dashed into the midst of the pirate host had not friendly arms restrained him.

"Where is the 'Dreadnought's' captain, if Kemersham and you be dead?" exclaimed a voice near him—the voice of the third lieutenant. "Think of Drake's orders—of those who wait at home. For this outrage Drake himself will grant you leave to track the 'Black Vulture,' and avenge the death of one of our bravest officers. See, you have already given him room for thought; wounded and senseless, they bear him on board his vessel. Let us go on board at once."

Within a few minutes they stood on the deck of the "Dreadnought."

"Sir Francis is at anchor within three miles," said Vyvyan. "Man the pinnace, and, with sail and oar, go with all speed to *him*. This evening's work may alter all his plans. I will now to Kemersham. Where *is* he ?"

" He is in your cabin, lieutenant," said a sailor; " but, see yonder. There is another matter that will change your plans. The pirate is preparing for sea."

The man was right.

On board the "Vulture" all was activity; the anchor was being weighed, the sails unfurled.

With Wrecklyffe desperately wounded, and no Spanish ships in sight, what could this mean ?

CHAPTER XVIII.

THE WRECK OF A YOUNG LIFE.

SIR FRANCIS DRAKE was, as I have said, at no great distance from Porto Lagos, and it was not very long before the dark hull of the " Elizabeth " was seen approaching the harbour.

When he came on board the " Dreadnought," a dark frown was upon his face.

" Where is your first-lieutenant ?" he said, sternly, to one of the sailors. " Why is he not here to receive me ?"

" He is by the side of Captain Kemersham," returned the man, " who we fear is dying of his wounds."

Drake had a generous heart.

He felt inwardly persuaded that there must have been some quarrel with the members of the " Black Vulture's " crew; and yet, when he thought of the youth of Kemersham, and the bright life cut short so suddenly just in the midst of its glory, his sterner feelings fled.

Kemersham was lying helplessly in his bed, very pale and ghastly, his eyes wild and piercing, pain giving them a lustre they had never worn before.

He brightened as he beheld Sir Francis Drake enter.

" Kemersham," said the brave commander, as he took his captain's hand, " I fear you have disobeyed my orders."

" Indeed—no," replied the dying man. in a weak voice; " Vyvyan will tell you how it happened."

" We broke no orders, Sir Francis," returned Vyvyan. " We were on shore walking quietly along the quay when we were attacked by Wrecklyffe and one of his villanous comrades. He sought the quarrel, and has gained his reward, for my good sword has pierced the ruffian's breast. Even now he intends some base, mean trickery against us."

" And what is that ?"

" I know not, except he is aware that the Spanish galleons are near us. When I left deck his men were weighing anchor, and by this time no doubt his vessel is standing out to sea."

As Vyvyan spoke there was a loud knock at the door of the cabin.

" Enter," cried Drake, and a rough mariner came in at the summons.

" The ' Black Vulture ' is making out of port, captain," he said; " she's over the bar by this time."

" Just as I said," cried Vyvyan, excitedly, " some villany is afloat."

" And yet," said Drake, " he bears letters of marque, and cannot be touched by us. He, doubtless, has some double game in view. We will watch him, and if he gives us but a chance, fear not that I shall let him escape."

Their attention was at this moment attracted once more to Kemersham.

He had remained silent during the conversation, and now, when he addressed them, his faint and trembling voice showed too plainly the approach of dissolution.

The surgeon of the vessel had from the first given no hopes whatever of his recovery.

The sword had passed through the lungs, and the violent inward bleeding left no chance of cure.

"Think not of me, kind friends," he said, "let not my dying hours stay you in the path of duty. Follow this villain, who has been the cause of my death, and stay his treacherous plans. Besides, since I am to die, I would rather be received into the wide bosom of the fresh blue ocean, than be buried in yonder strange land where wild beasts might dig up my body, or savages mockingly scatter my dust to the winds."

"Give not up to despondency," cried Vyvyan, who, young and enthusiastic, could scarcely believe that his friend — young, enthusiastic, and brave like himself—was leaving him for ever. "Cheer up, you may yet be better."

Kemersham smiled so sad a smile, that it brought a tear into the young lieutenant's eye, and caused a quiver of the lip, which was not lost upon the dying man.

"Do not grieve," he cried; "this hour must come for all, and some must die young. I should not regret life, were it not that one in England waits in eagerness my return—a sweet, gentle being, who was to have been my bride. But, as it is, she knew my constant peril, and was aware that a mourning heart might be her lot as surely as that of a happy wife."

"Can I take your last words to her, dear friend?" murmured the young adventurer, as he bent over the couch of the dying captain.

"No," said he, "no. Let her not know it. 'Twill do her no good to learn that I am dead. Let me still live in her memory, and her hope. She is all I have in England to remember and to mourn for me."

This strange request was almost the last he made.

His strength quickly failed him; his eyes glazed; his mouth grew rigid; his voice failed him, and he lay very still, holding Drake's hand, and gazing up at him and Vyvyan as long as he could with looks of tender thankfulness.

It was soon all over.

The poor eyes closed; the body shivered; the brave—the young—the good, was senseless clay!

I shall not speak of the funeral.

Funerals at sea have been so often described, that my account would be but the repetition of many others; but there was something specially mournful in this one, which spoke of the extinction of a young life in its prime.

"Vyvyan," said Drake, when the body had sunk into the waves, and all was over, "there is now no captain of the 'Dreadnought.' Accept the command at my hands, and think less of the fact that you have stepped into your friend's place than that you have power given you to punish those who have pursued you and him so long with treacherous hatred."

Vyvyan accepted the post in this spirit, and as he trod the deck for the first time as captain, he swore that Kemersham should be terribly avenged.

⁘

CHAPTER XIX.

WRECKLYFFE'S STRATAGEM.

THAT same day the "Elizabeth" and the "Dreadnought" stood rapidly away to sea.

The waves had closed over the body of the young commander, but there was no time for the indulgence of vain regrets.

He had fallen in the discharge of his duty, as they might all do, and the men, after the first gloom had passed away, resumed at once their ordinary duties, and were as eager as ever in the chase.

Not a trace could be seen anywhere of the "Black Vulture," but after about two hours' sailing they beheld the dark hulls of some strange ships looming in the distance. Sir Francis Drake at once brought the "Elizabeth" close up to the "Dread-nought," and spoke to Vyvyan through his speaking trumpet.

"The enemy are in sight," he said. "We will keep to our original plan; I will stand out to sea, and you must enter the harbour of Porto Lagos."

"How many Spanish vessels did you expect to meet?" asked Vyvyan, as he carefully scanned the horizon with his telescope.

"Five."

"There are six yonder."

Sir Francis Drake glanced again with his glass over the quiet sea.

"True," he answered; "and one appears to be entirely different in appearance to the others. This may portend some trickery on the part of our foes. We must be on our guard."

"Shall I await your orders, then," asked Vyvyan, "before proceeding to the harbour?"

"Yes," replied Drake, "we must watch them carefully, and regulate our movements by theirs."

His mind seemed certainly to be possessed by a strange presentiment.

If he had heard Wrecklyffe's conversation with his lieutenant on the previous night he could not have acted more in accordance with coming events.

Wrecklyffe's wound, as our readers may imagine, was a terrible one.

Vyvyan's sword, driven home by the spirit of hate, had plunged through his chest, beneath the shoulder, and though it had avoided a mortal part, it had inflicted a fearful gash, from which at first the life blood flowed in an unceasing torrent.

Under skilful treatment, however, this at length ceased, and, weak and exhausted, the buccaneer could yet issue his orders.

He had an artful plan in view.

He had special confidence in his prestige, and knew well that his crew, unless led on by himself, would be liable to checks, and even defeats, and he determined, therefore, that no conflict should take place until strength was given him to wield his sword and lead them on to victory.

"Landford," he said to his lieutenant, when his wounds had been bound up, "let the men weigh the anchor, and make at once for the open sea."

"Why so, captain?"

"Because, in my present condition, to fight would be madness. The men will never show their natural courage if I am here in my cabin, helpless. We must win by stratagem what we have lost by misfortune."

"Good, captain," replied the lieutenant, "you have but to give your orders, and I will immediately obey."

"In the first place, then, let the men weigh anchor. Give that command at once."

Landford immediately quitted the cabin and went on deck.

When he returned the movement of the ship showed that the order had been given and attended to.

"Now," said Wrecklyffe, "my wounds may keep me prisoner here for some time. At any rate, in open battle, I am no match for the young villain who has winged me. We must sail towards the Spanish galleons, give them information that Drake and his ships are watching them, and then assist them to some harbour of refuge. When Drake and Raleigh and Vyvyan are gone, sailed away discomfited and disappointed, we'll fall upon them ourselves, and take their treasures."

"A hazard, truly; five to one," said the lieutenant "'twould have been better had we been able to join with our enemies."

"Yes; but that chance is gone," replied Wrecklyffe. "Well, if that arrangement fails we will still prevent their success, and make a good haul for ourselves. We will take them to the harbour of San Josef, arm them with our own weapons, and aid them in fighting their way. For this we claim, and will receive beforehand, a good reward."

Landford smiled.

"You are a brave, as well as a cunning foe," replied he; "the plan is good, and the night favours its accomplishment. Everything is dark and dismal, and they will not perceive us. I will now go on deck and give the necessary orders. Meanwhile, captain, sleep and rest may enable you, before you imagine it possible, to take the command once more."

So the "Black Vulture," impelled by the steady breeze, made rapidly towards the Spaniards, who, on seeing her approach, at once made ready for action.

Their alarm, however, was of very short duration.

The " Black Vulture " hove to.

" A friend !" said Landford, through his speaking-trumpet. " We have important news for you."

The captain of the nearest vessel hesitated only a moment.

There was no preparation for action on board the pirate ; men were lounging on the deck ; the guns even were not unmasked.

" Come alongside," was the reply of the captain of the merchant ship. What news have you ?"

" Not far hence," cried Landford, " are two English privateers, while a third, commanded by Sir Walter Raleigh, hovers at no great distance. Have you arms and men wherewith to defend yourselves against them ?"

There was a pause.

Again the Spanish captain hesitated. Was this a *ruse?*

Was this Englishman striving to lead them into a trap?

" Well, well," he thought, " we are five to one. If he attacks us we can surely hold our own."

" No," he said; " against three armed ships we should have little chance. Is there no harbour of refuge where we could conceal ourselves and escape them ?"

" Yes," said Landford, " we can take you to San Josef; and afterwards mayhap assist you against them. But we shall, of course, claim a handsome reward."

" We shall be right willing to pay you," returned the Spaniard. " As soon as morning dawns we will proceed under your guidance. At San Josef we can arrange the amount and nature of the reward."

It was thus that in the early morning Vyvyan and Drake, glancing out over the sea, saw six ships under sail in place of five.

CHAPTER XX.

SAN JOSEF—THE CHASE OF THE SPANISH GALLEONS.

IT was indeed a puzzle to Sir Francis Drake when he saw the rich prizes he had longed to grapple with, veer round and stand away upon an entirely opposite tack.

Nevertheless he resolved to watch ; and seeing that the strange sail which had created so much surprise in the mind of the young lieutenant was leading them on, he gave orders to Vyvyan to accompany him in pursuit.

Night fell over the sea as they neared the harbour of San Josef, and the eager foe was separated from his quarry.

To our minds, in these quiet, civilized days, it may seem strange that a man like Sir Francis Drake should have lain in wait for plunder.

In those days it was different.

The wealth wrested from the West by Spain was regarded as the rightful prey of other nations.

Spain then was the natural foe of England, and it was against her navy and her merchant vessels that the queen of England granted letters of marque to all bold and wreckless adventurers.

Treasures taken represented also in those times conquest made.

Wherever a successful cruiser, after destroying a Spanish ship, descended upon the thinly-colonised coast, and drove the Spaniards inland, the flag of England's queen was at once planted upon the soil.

It was on the evening of the second day after the sudden change in the course of the Spanish galleon that the look-out shouted out—

"Sail, on the lee-quarter!"

Vyvyan, who had not parted company with Drake since the alteration in orders, heard the words, and looked out anxiously.

In the distance, under full sail, a ship was making straight towards them; and, as it came nearer and nearer, and at length pulled up alongside, they recognised it as their old friend, the "El Dorado," manned by brave British seamen, and commanded by the Conqueror of the West, Sir Walter Raleigh.

With this accession of force there was little hesitation on Drake's part.

The prizes were well worth their trying for, and so, keeping carefully under shadow, as it were, of the shore, they waited.

The harbour of San Josef was a fine natural one; and here the English privateers had for a long time kept a repository of arms.

It was to this that Wrecklyffe alluded in speaking to the Spanish captain; and, seeing that his foes were resolved to wait for their prey, and that he himself was unable to keep them to himself, he struck a heavy bargain with the Spanish captains.

It was a bright moonlight night when the Spaniards left their place of refuge, and sailed out before a gentle breeze with canvas bellying out to the full.

The "Black Vulture" passed out of harbour with them.

Three weeks had passed, and Wrecklyffe's wound had healed.

Once more, though gaunt and pale, and robbed of half his strength, he was able to move among his men, and wield his bright sword, whose flashing blade seemed to inspire his men with hope and resolution for victory.

His heart was full of terrible visions of revenge, and as he walked the deck his fiercely gleaming eyes wandered savagely over the heaving, restless sea.

Silently and quietly the three English vessels followed.

Six to three were great odds, even with ill-armed men; but they never once allowed their thoughts to drift in that direction. All they saw was a rich freight of gold, which by right of conquest would belong to them, and this they resolved should be theirs.

There was also an amount of glory to be won, for in those days no thought was given to the injustice of this wholesale plunder of hard-won wealth.

Brought up to believe the Spaniards England's mortal foes, they looked upon them as beings whom it was their proper aim to destroy and rob.

It was a solemn, beautiful sight, as the white sails of the pursuers and the pursued flashed in the bright moonlight, and the dark hulls rolled on the white crested waves.

In those days of sailing progression was necessarily slow, but still as time went by it could easily be seen that Vyvyan and his friends were rapidly overhauling their foes.

I will not pause to describe the incident of the chase.

I have described others, and this was but a repetition of them.

It was dusk, twilight was just verging upon night, when the combatants came up to one another.

In an instant Raleigh, who took the command of the small fleet, issued his orders, and a demand of surrender was shouted through the speaking-trumpet.

It was Wrecklyffe's voice that was heard laughing a grim laugh of derision as the demand was made.

"Never!" returned the Spanish captain; "we are no cowards, and this night's battle will prove to you that Spain's prowess is nothing of the past."

This reply was enough.

Drake made it an invariable rule to give the enemy a chance of yielding; but it was very rarely that such a thing was thought of until the last moment.

The dark gloom of night was soon illumined by bright flashes.

Canons roared, rockets flew upwards towards the blue vault of Heaven, and each English vessel engaged with two Spaniards.

As luck would have it, Vyvyan found himself engaged with one of the largest galleons, and Wrecklyffe's vessel.

Of course in the darkness nothing could be attempted but firing at a distance, but as morning dawned, the combat began hand-to-hand.

The English ships, manned with brave and well-armed crews, found themselves between two Spanish ones, so that the boarders had to be divided into double companies.

It was a brave and desperate fight.

Again men grappled fiercely—again they dashed like wild beasts at each other—the one side striving to reach the wished-for treasure, the other to defend it.

Boats were run out from both sides, and met midway in savage fight on the rolling waves, which everywhere began to be covered with pieces of wreck, and torn sail-cloth, and tangled masses of rigging, and ghastly corpses, which ever and anon disappeared beneath the waves, as the ravenous shark plunged for its ready prey.

Wrecklyffe, in this wild fight, seemed to avoid his old enemy,

Perhaps, conscious of his weakness, he declined giving the chance to his younger and stronger enemy of gaining over him an easy victory.

Vyvyan sought him everywhere, choosing the personal command of that boarding party which would lead him to the deck of his old pirate foe, whose death would clear from his path the vilest and most inveterate of those who hungered for his blood.

The battle was a long, terrible, and well-contested one.

Hour after hour passed by, and still the report of fire-arms resounded over the wide waste of waters; still men fought and strove; still the sea was tinged with blood; still oaths and execrations, and shouts to flagging spirits rose into the air.

Night at length separated them, and, by a kind of mutual consent, the grappling-irons were cast off for the time, and all waited for morning.

Then a most unexpected event happened.

All day heavy clouds had covered the sky—heavy, grey, storm clouds.

No one had paid special attention to their appearance, however, for the storm of man's passion truly occupied all attention.

Now, however, it was far different, and both English and Spanish saw, as the sun went down, that a sudden and violent change in the weather was about to take place.

All was black, lowering, threatening, for a time, a stillness and heat in the air which foreboded a tempest.

Then suddenly the wind rose, the sails flapped angrily against the mast, and as quick orders were given by the different commanders, the violent lightning began to play afar, and dash with terrible rapidity and brightness from one horizon to the other.

It was now a scene of dismay and terror.

Except when Heaven's bright fire lit up the ocean, it was quite impossible to see one vessel from the other, and each commander expected every moment that some terrible collision would consign treasure-ships and all to the bosom of the angry deep.

So it went on for hours.

Flashing lightning, booming thunder, waves rolling mountains high, officers roaring out commands in the intervals of the fearful tempest, men rushing wildly, bravely, to execute orders, and some in their zeal losing footing and being plunged into the white-crested waves that swept them away like helpless atoms into the utter darkness.

Vyvyan was standing near the bulwarks, striving to peer through the terrible darkness, when a loud cry arose.

It was such a cry as would haunt a man until his dying day.

It was the spontaneous yell of despair from a hundred human beings, who, amid the impenetrable darkness, could expect nothing but instant destruction.

The wind and the wild waves had been driving the vessels towards land, a coast bristling, as it were, with sharp and jagged rocks, and upon one of these it was evident that one of the vessels—friend or foe—had struck.

It was a terrible thing, standing there in the darkness, listening to the wild yells of agony, yet unable to proffer the slightest aid.

The lightning again and again shot forth its lurid flames. But it was of no avail.

Nothing could be seen but black, mountainous waves, seeming to join the sky, which lowered threateningly over all.

The black hulls of the ships could not have been distinguished in such a sea and in such darkness.

Vyvyan leaned over the bulwarks and peered out in vain over the ocean.

Then again came the wild despairing cries of lost and hopeless souls.

His head reeled.

Who were they who thus cried out in fearful agony? Were they his foes—sent headlong to their account?

Or were they the noble hearts whose example had fired him on his road to glory?

He was thinking thus when something appalling happened.

A sailor, by his orders, had run up to the extremity of the yard-arm to steady a sail which had escaped its ropes, and was fluttering wildly with the breeze, when there was a sudden gust of wind, a terrible crash, and a man's body came dashing down upon the deck.

Not thinking of the havoc which the tempest was making near him, Vyvyan dashed forward, and was in the act of raising the stunned and wounded mariner, when a fearful weight fell upon the bulwarks. Splinters flew hither and thither; groaning voices told that lives had sped to eternity, and, ere he knew what fearful thing had happened, he felt himself hurled from the deck of his own ship down into the boiling waves!

To Heaven he prayed as he rose to the foam-crested bosom of the mighty ocean, and seized a large float of timber—part of the riven mast.

But it was Eveline's face he saw!

Eveline, angel-like, floating above him in the air, smiling like Hope, telling him of a love to live for—a future to strive for; beating back despair; commanding him, amid this storm and wreck of Nature, to fight for life and laugh at disaster!

Bravely he clutched his frail support, dashed hither and thither by the billows.

But he could see nothing.

No land—no ships—no friends.

Even the lightning had ceased, and the thunder, and he was amid a mass of darkness; waves above him—waves below him—nothing to grasp at—nothing to do but cling to his straw and hope!

And hope he did, thinking of the affianced who awaited him and the unknown mother whom he had yet to claim. And so hours went on.

Then at length the lightning played out once more, and he saw not far from him the dark hull of a ship.

Whose ship it was impossible to say.

Neither was it possible to approach it in any case.

He had no means whatever of progression.

He was, in fact, entirely at the mercy of the waves and wind

Presently the lightning began to play incessantly, and vividly lighting up the ocean and showing Vyvyan all objects around him.

The Spanish galleons, and Raleigh, and Drake, and the "Dreadnought," had all disappeared.

The dark line of coast was still distinguishable, and now and then a flash—a tiny, twinkling flash of light—showed where the harbour of San Josef lay.

Life was there—secure on *terra firma.* Men could kneel and pray there, and hear the whisperings of tender voices, thanking God that they were safe at home; while he——

But despair was not for him, when Eveline was in England waiting!

It was as these thoughts passed through his mind that the lightning showed him a dark mass in the water, which he recognised as the hull of a vessel lying broken and fixed upon a rock.

It was the "Black Vulture."

Full well—too well he knew it!

What could he do now?

He was drifting fast towards it.

How could he ask or expect help from them? Would, indeed, the angry waves be more bitterly cruel to him than they?

Suddenly, as he thought, a loud shout rang over the waters; a bright light shone on the poop of the pirate vessel, and then, as the lightning once more burst forth, he saw Wrecklyffe standing near the bulwarks—triumphant and erect.

In his hand was a pistol.

His fiendish laugh was heard clearly by Vyvyan as it rang over the waves.

"Ha, ha!" he shouted, through his speaking-trumpet, "Providence delivers you into my hands. Wait till the lightning plays once more over the ocean, then you'll see how I remember you."

To say that a sensation of dread did not invade the brave heart of the young adventurer, would be false.

It was not a coward's fear.

It was thorough consciousness of helpless loneliness.

He was on one side at the mercy of the storm, on the other at the mercy of his ruthless pirate foe.

So near land, too, whither the drifting sea was consigning him!

He had not long to wait for a consummation of his worst fears.

A blinding succession of flashes illumined the sea, and then a smaller flash burst forth upon the night.

The report of a pistol echoed over the surging waves; a sharp pain invaded Vyvyan's body; Heaven, earth, and ocean seemed blended in one undistinguishable mass, and then all was oblivion.

* * * * *

Calm fell over all as morning dawned; but, as Wrecklyffe gazed anxiously from the deck of the "Black Vulture," which still was firmly wedged upon the rock, he saw neither friends nor foes; no Spanish galleons—no English vessels—no spars with floating men.

A grim smile broke over his dark and cruel countenance.

"'Tis well, Landford," he said, turning to his lieutenant; "they have all gone to their account. The sea has swallowed up treasures and treasure-seekers together. Get out the boats, and let us hasten on shore."

Within an hour the remnant of the pirate crew had landed at the harbour of San Josef.

Wrecklyffe's first question to the inhabitants who crowded around was—

"Have any bodies been cast on shore?"

"Only one, master," said a rough English sailor; "it was the body of a young Englishman fastened to a mast."

"Vyvyan, by all that is holy! cried the buccaneer. "Where have they placed him?"

"He lies in yonder hut," replied the man, pointing to a wooden house beneath the shade of some trees.

"Good," said, Wrecklyffe, smiling. "Landford, accompany me. We will see how the rejected Heir of Montreville looks in death."

❧

CHAPTER XXI.

LOST TO VIEW.

If Wrecklyffe had imagined for a moment that the one who had so often escaped him would be left by Providence at his tender mercies, he was wrong.

Vyvyan seemed truly watched over by a special guardianship.

When the fierce and cruel pirate made his way with his comrade into the little hut which stood beneath the shade of the trees, he found no one there.

There were evidences that some one had been there, and that very recently.

But that was all.

"Curses on him!" cried the buccaneer, "where can he have gone?"

As he spoke, a tall, thin man, with a roll of tobacco-leaves in his mouth, sauntered up and leaned in at the door.

"Who are you in search of?" asked he.

"The shipwrecked Englishman, returned Wrecklyffe, as he gazed at the swarthy countenance of the stranger, who seemed, from the color of his skin, to be of half-black, half-white extraction.

"He is gone," said the man; "his comrades took him away."

"His comrades!" exclaimed the pirate. "Why, none were saved but he!"

"None from the wreck," cried the man; "but a large vessel came in early in the morning, and a band of several men carried him off."

"He was dead?" said Wrecklyffe, inquiringly.

"Not he," replied the other; "he was not only alive, but he was able to walk away. By the way, is your name Wrecklyffe?"

" It is."

" Then I have something for you."

As he spoke, he handed him a letter.

It was in Vyvyan's handwriting, and ran as follows :—

" PIRATE AND MURDERER,—You once said that my kidnred paid you for my destruction. I am going now to prove it. With Drake and Raleigh to back the 'Dreadnought,' the Spanish treasure-ships will be ours, and, with riches and honour, I go to seek my home and friends. The sea may not again cast us in each other's company. Mayhap England's shores may prove more charitable to my eager thirst for revenge ; and we may meet upon the firm land, where no wild waves can separate us, and where your treacherous shots in the dark will be more difficult to you. Till then remember that Heaven has again preserved me, and that I am your deadly foe. " VYVYAN."

" You don't appear to admire the letter," said the swarthy stranger, as he saw the hot blood mount to Wrecklyffe's cheek.

" I do not," returned Wrecklyffe, " and the boaster who penned it will right soon regret the day he wrote it."

The stranger laughed.

His Spanish and Indian blood revelled in the idea of the fierce vendetta.

" The younger mariner is a brave and genial youth," he said, " with a bright, eagle eye, and a strong arm, and I should doubt, in any contest, whether he would be one to laugh at."

" He is brave, no doubt ; but brave as he may be, his courage shall have a right good test," said the pirate. " Tell me, how did he escape ? The last I saw of him was when the lightning, playing wildly over the ocean, revealed him to me, clinging to a broken mast."

" I know it. It was then that you drew your pistol and fired at him."

" How heard you that ?"

" From his own lips. The shot took effect, and fainting and wounded he was left at the mercy of the wild waves. He lost his senses at first when the shot struck him, but the kindly waves rescued him from oblivion, and when the cold water had restored him to consciousness he was nearing the shore. Weak and helpless he could not make for land, but the wind and waves aided him in his endeavour, and flung him high and dry upon the sands. The shock stunned him, and he was carried away for dead. But he is not dead, he lives to be——"

The stranger stopped.

" What ?" asked Wrecklyffe, eagerly.

" What you will find him on your return to England."

And with these words, he moved off in the direction of the sea-shore.

Wrecklyffe looked after him, as if for the moment he was inclined to follow, and then returned moodily to his companions.

CHAPTER XXII.

IN WHICH THE READER IS TRANSPORTED TO ENGLAND, AND IS CARRIED TO OLD SCENES ONCE MORE.

NEAR the grand old Castle of Montreville, nestling like a dwarf beneath the protecting wing of a giant, stood a small house.

It was a desolate-looking place.

Facing the wild sea-waves, it had had to face many a storm wind ; and sun, and air, and time, had made sad havoc with its appearance.

Its walls were grey and overgrown with straggling parasites—its windows were broken—its doors rusty—and its gardens covered with stunted undergrowth.

Where bright flowers had been were now all weeds, in mockery as it were of former beauty ; and all around—the dilapidated casements—the neglect everywhere visible, and the ruins near (grey,

"ANOTHER, AND AN ELDER BEAUFORT LIVES,' CRIED SIR GREY DE MALPAS."

mossy, and straggling, as if the present house were but the remains of some more stately and antique edifice) gave sign of a chequered life—of baffled hopes—of disappointment and despair.

How terribly mean and poor looked the house—how grand and stately the castle towering above it !

So thought he, who, leaning on his spade, gazed distractedly around him upon the wild, neglected scene.

His hair was blanched, his form was bent, yet you could see in the features the memory of former days. You could read in the cruel eyes, the bitterly hard mouth, the whole air and mien, the character of Sir Grey de Malpas, the poor kinsman of my Lord of Montreville.

He had been for some hours at work upon the neglected garden ground in front of his house, but, as if defeated in this struggle with nature, he now leaned upon his spade, and gazed around him.

His eyes wandered from the sea to Montreville, and from Montreville to the sea.

His desires led his gaze in one direction, his hopes in another.

Montreville, its wealth and title, the dream of his youth; the object of his fierce ambition as a man; the cause of his villany and the misfortunes of others, lay upon the one side; and upon the other was the wide ocean, upon which he had cast the Rightful Heir of riches and honour, and which was wafting him home steadily—safely after many days.

Suddenly, as if angry with himself for attempting the unthankful task of rescuing the hard and unfertile soil from its inutility, he flung his spade upon the ground.

"I cannot dig," said Grey, contemptuously. "Oh, what a helpless thing is the white hand of well-born poverty! And yet between all this squalor and desolation which surrounds me, and the pomp and grandeur of Montreville, stand but two lives, two frail lives—a woman's and a boy's. I may outlive them both."

As he uttered these words—words containing the evidence of hope struggling against despair—a man, brown and weatherbeaten, was seen suddenly advancing along the road.

Long time before, full of daring courage and expectation of riches plundered from the Golden West, he had sailed from England a reckless buccaneer, tied by no bonds of kindred or humanity, but pledged to a war with the world.

Disappointed in his hopes, deserted by his men, the bronzed and tempest-tossed mariner who approached the ruined tenement of Sir Grey de Malpas, was Wrecklyffe the pirate.

"Good day," he said, as he caught sight of the grey-haired man leaning over the little gateway of the garden. "He sees me not, or else he does not know me. He is changed, but less changed than I am. Winter has crept on *him;* the lightning has stricken *me.* Good day, Sir Grey de Malpas."

Sir Grey started in anger.

"Pass on," he cried. "I am no spendthrift fool that I should offer hospitality to strangers. Pass on."

Wrecklyffe smiled.

"Have years so dimmed eyes which were once so keen, De Malpas, that you do not recognise me ?"

Sir Grey started, and eyed the speaker narrowly.

One earnest look convinced him.

"Ah, Wrecklyffe, is it you ?" he cried. "What brings you here after so many years?"

Wrecklyffe laughed loudly.

"Brings me," he cried. "Say, rather, what hurls me back? Pestilence, famine, and unequal battle have been my lot, and England has welcomed me, lastly with a terrible storm that swept the decks from stem to stern. One wreck, stranded yonder, is rotting now in the golden sunlight; the other stands before you."

"Well, well," said Sir Grey, "I am not so poor that I cannot share a crust with you and give you shelter. Time has dealt harshly with both of us, since first we made friendship. I can remember well how strong you were, how straight-limbed, well-favoured, yet stern-hearted. Yet I, my lord's poor cousin, could twist and turn thee at pleasure with these slight hands. That is the use of brains."

"Still gibes and stings; but why boast brains and starve ?"

"The first are poor cousin's weapons, the second is the poor cousin's fate. It is a sad change since the day when the village maidens sighed and wondered why heaven should make men so wicked and so comely. But come, we will leave the past and speak of the present. That scar upon your front speaks of grim service."

" It was in your cause, De Malpas, that I received that wound. The boy, whom at your bidding I enticed on board my vessel, left me this brand of Cain."

" And that boy," cried De Malpas, seizing him eagerly by the arm, and looking him earnestly in the face——

" He is now a man, and on these very shores," eturned the pirate. " This morning, as I gazed from out my hiding place, amid the rocks, I saw his face; my sword trembled in its scabbard as he advanced. If you need his death, revenge stands before you in me."

Sir Grey staggered back with a ghastly pallor on his convulsed features.

" He lives ! he lives !" he cried. " There is a third, then, between the beggar and the earldom."

" Hush, hush !" cried Wrecklyffe; " at this moment I hear steps and voices. When shall we meet alone ? It is he who comes."

" He with the plume ?" asked De Malpas.

" Yes, yes ; that is Vyvyan."

" Quick, then, within," said De Malpas, " I will remain and listen."

As Wrecklyffe hastily entered the ruined tenement, Harding, the second-lieutenant of the " Dreadnought," approached, followed by several sailors, while Vyvyan stepped gaily up on the other side.

Time and travel had but changed him in making him more manly and more handsome, bronzing his face and lighting up his dark eyes with the brightness of courage and success.

" Well, captain," cried Harding, " what tidings of the Spanish Armada."

" Bad news," said Vyvyan, " they say the fighting is put off, and a storm on the Bay of Biscay has driven the Spaniards back. This is but rumour, but we shall soon learn the truth. Harding, these lines are for Drake; take horse, quickly, and bear them to him. If our country needs stout hearts to guard her, he'll not forget the men on board the ' Dreadnought.' You can be back before sunset with his answer."

" And where shall I find you, good captain ?"

" In yonder towers of Montreville.

Meanwhile," he added, turning to the sailors as Harding passed off, " make merry at yonder hostelry ; here is money for you, and the toast I give you is, ' no foes be tall enough to wade the moat which guards the fort whose only walls are men.' "

With a loud cheer for their young captain, the men moved away, just as Falkner, the first lieutenant of the " Dreadnought," came hurriedly up the road.

" Ah, Falkner," exclaimed Vyvyan, " you are soon returned. Your smile seems fresh from home. Is all well there ?"

" Yes," returned he, all's well. I was but just in time. My poor, old father ! bailiffs at his door. His crops had failed, and he was compelled to till the lands of others. I poured gold into his lap, and, as he smiled, I cried, ' Now, father, you will forgive the son who went to sea against your will !' "

" And he forgave you," said Vyvyan. " Now tell me of your mother. I never knew one, but I love to mark the quiver of a strong man's lip when his voice lingers on the name of mother. She blessed you ?"

" Ah, yes, a blessing worth the praise of all," said Falkner, while the bright dew glistened in his eyes. " But enough of me. Now for yourself. What news ? Your fair betrothed—the maid we rescued from the Spaniards, with her brave father —is she found, and still faithful ?"

" I'll swear she's faithful," returned Vyvyan, " but not yet found. Her father is dead; the stranger sits at his hearth, and with her next of kin near her. In yonder sunlit towers of Montreville my Eveline dwells."

" And your foster father, Alton ; have you seen him ?"

" Not yet," said the young captain; " and now you speak of it, you can do me good service. His house is scarcely an hour's journey' and in the village you will find a guide. Seek him, and tell him of my return, and bid him expect me before nightfall. We ad venturers are judged harshly by the world, so tell him that no battle storms have changed me. In the far seas his foster son remembered the prayers of his childhood, and invoked blessings on his grey head. Farewell, and now for Eveline, my long wished-for betrothed !"

With a joyous mien, he then turned and made his way hurriedly towards Montreville.

He would scarcely have been so joyous or so certain of happiness had he beheld the thin form of Sir Grey de Malpas emerge from his hiding-place.

A look of ghastly treachery and villany was upon the features of the poor cousin.

"Ha! ha!" he muttered; "you seek the towers of Montreville; I will meet you there. And yet he must not see the priest. The hour has come when Alton is absolved from his vow of secresy. Since the boy left, the father and the husband are dead. He must *not* see the priest! But how shall I prevent it? Ah! Wrecklyffe! he will aid me, and he is within there ready!"

With these words he turned again, and with tottering gait passed into his ruined house.

CHAPTER XXIII.

IN WHICH THE READER IS INTRODUCED TO THE YOUNGER SON.

WALKING in the gardens of the Castle of Montreville about the time of Wrecklyffe's interview with Sir Grey de Malpas, was a lady with whom my readers are already familiar, and upon whose brow time had passed lightly enough.

This was Lady Montreville, mother of Vyvyan, widow of my Lord of Beaufort.

She was changed of course, by time, but her eyes were still bright and beautiful, her form still graceful, her step still queenly.

Above her towered the stately Castle which had seen the birth of her eldest son —around her were bright flowers in pleasant gardens looking out over the rolling seas.

But her heart itself was darkness.

Memory was busy there.

"This would be his birthday were he living still," she said, in a tender voice of sadness, as she pressed her hand over her throbbing bosom and looked out over the sea. "Alas! the ocean has been his grave long since! I dreamed of him last night. But away ye thoughts of the past! With the death of him my first born, died shame and slander. I have yet a world of hope in the son that is left me, and for him I must live and smile. Ah, here he comes."

As she spoke, a youth entered the grounds, a youth of noble mien, fair-haired, handsome, seeming one who could live bravely through an existence of joy; but not framed like Vyvyan for war and desperate conflicts.

"See that my gallant roan is ready," he cried, addressing Marsden, the seneschal of the castle, who accompanied him; "and be sure to bring the falcon which my Lord of Leicester gave me. I should like to try its mettle."

"Clarence, you see me not," said Lady Montreville, advancing as the old servant retired.

"Ah! dear mother, welcome," said Clarence, glancing round. "Where is my soft-eyed cousin?"

"Ah! Clarence," said his mother, "I do not like to see this growing intimacy with Eveline. I see you haunt her steps, and whisper sweet words in her ear. She is fair, no doubt, but she is no mate for you."

"Mate! that is an awful word, sweet mother," exclaimed the young Lord Beaufort. "Cannot youth gaze on beauty save by the torch of Hymen? I mean no marriage. Eveline is fair, but I fear that another holds the first place in her heart."

"Of whom speak you?"

"The one who saved her life. Eveline's is sweet companionship; but at present the chase and the sweet woods and waves are my loved haunts. Hark! even now I hear my steed neighing with impatience, and my falcon shaking its silver bells. Now, remember, mother, no kiss or smile from me when I return, unless my fair-faced cousin Eveline stands beside you, blushing my reward for courage. Adieu !"

And in these words, which betrayed his love, and belied his former speeches, he sped gaily away.

As he did so, Eveline herself, taller, more graceful, more beautiful, yet still the Eveline of old, entered the garden.

She was so engaged with her own thoughts, and the mournful rhyme she was singing, that she did not observe Lady Montreville, but advanced towards the parapet that overhung the sea; still weaving flowers into a garland, which presently she cast over into the rolling waves.

Plaintively the words came from her rosy lips :—

> "Bud from the blossom
> 　And leaf from the tree,
> Guess why in weaving
> 　I sing 'Woe is me!'
> 'Tis that I mean you
> 　To drift on the sea,
> And say when you find him,
> 　Who sang, 'Woe is me!'"

"A quaint, but mournful rhyme," said Lady Montreville, advancing.

Eveline started.

"You ! Madam—pardon !"

"What tells that tale, Eveline ?"

"It is but a simple village tale," replied Eveline, "speaking of a lost seaman, and a crazed girl, who was his plighted bride. Good Marsden, your seneschal, knew her well, and often marked her singing on the beach as she launched her flowers smilingly over the sea, hoping that they might reach her long-wrecked lover. I know not why they should, but both the rhyme and the tale haunt me."

"Sad thoughts should not haunt young hearts, senseless child."

"Am I not an orphan ?"

"Ah, there is another reason for your quiet sorrow, methinks," said Lady Montreville. "I fear your eye roams towards Beaufort. You must beware, vain girl. The flattery of the great, like the swoop of the eagle upon the dove, in its descent destroys."

The tears stood in Eveline's eyes as she turned away.

"You speak thus, and yet you bid me to grieve not that I am an orphan."

Lady Montreville noticed her not as she passed away.

"I have high dreams for Beaufort," she murmured, "and bright desires. He is the one bright spot in the darkness of my thoughts. He is to me like the hope that dims the lonely captive's cell. He will be first among those who surround England's throne. Kings shall revere his mother."

As she spoke thus, Sir Grey de Malpas, followed by a servant, entered the grounds.

A cloud of anger was hovering on his brow.

"What say you ?" he cried, as he leaned upon his staff.

"Sir Grey ! ha, ha !" said the servant, with an insolent jeer. "Lord Beaufort begs your pardon. He shot your hound; it's bark disturbed the deer."

Sir Grey shook his head mournfully.

"The only voice that welcomed me ! A dog, too ; did he begrudge me that?"

The servant laughed again.

"Oh ! it was done in kindness, sir," he answered; "kindness to him and you. The dog was wondrous lean."

"I thank my lord," replied the poor cousin, as the servant quitted the scene. "So my poor hound is dead. Yet he but barked ; this dog can bite. Ah ! there is my Lady Montreville."

"He gazed at her a moment.

Then, with the stealthy crawl of a venomous snake, he approached the countess.

"He lives !" he cried.

"He ! Who !" exclaimed she, starting back in terror and dismay.

"THE HEIR OF MONTREVILLE ! Another and an elder Beaufort lives. So," he added to himself, "so ; the fang fixes fast. Good, good !"

For a moment there was silence.

Then, with her hand pressed over her heaving breast, Lady Montreville spoke.

"You said, ten years ago, 'Your first-born is no more,' and bade me believe he died in far-off seas."

"So swore my false informant," said Sir Grey. "But now the deep which took from this shore the harmless boy has cast from it the bold-eyed, daring man."

" Clarence — poor, proud Clarence," murmured the countess.

" True, poor Clarence, indeed," said De Malpas, with cruel triumph, " poor as his poor cousin. Ah! the air is keen, and Poverty is thinly clad, subject to rheums and agues, and leans upon a crutch like your poor cousin. If Poverty begs, Law sets in the stocks; if it is ill, the doctors mangle it; if it is dying, the priests scold at it, and when 'tis dead, rich kinsman cry, ' Thank Heaven!' Ah, if your elder prove his rights to Fortune, your younger son will know this Poverty."

" Peace, malignant man," cried Lady Montreville. " Why do you torture me? The priest, who alone shares with us the secret, has sworn to keep it."

" Only while your father and second husband survived. Yet what avails his tale unbacked by your confession?"

" All—all," said the countess, with white lips; " he has proofs—clear proofs. Thrice woe to Clarence!"

" Proofs—written proofs?"

" Yes, both of the marriage and the birth."

" And why was this so long concealed from me?" asked Sir Grey, who now saw before him another obstacle to his villanous plans.

Lady Montreville glanced at him contemptuously.

De Malpas did not lose the look.

" You were my father's agent, Grey de Malpas," cried she, proudly; " not my familiar."

A look of hatred shot from his gleaming eyes.

" Here, then, ends my errand," he said, and, with a mocking bow, he turned to go.

He knew well in his own dark mind how thoroughly she was in his power.

Lady Montreville, pale, bitterly resentful, yet hesitated but a moment.

She recognised the villany of the man, but she also knew how useful he might be to her.

" Stay, Sir Grey!" she cried. " Forgive my rash and eager temper. Stay, stay! and counsel me. What! are you sullen still?—Are you in want of gold? If so, befriend me, and you will find me most grateful."

Sir Grey de Malpas raised himself to his full height, and eyed her severely.

" Lady of Montreville," he said, with something of dignity in his manner, " I once was young, and longed for gold that I might wed the maid I loved. Your father said, ' Poor cousins should not marry;' and gave me this sage advice in place of the gold I sought. I yielded; yet as years went on other ideas filled my soul. I longed for wars, and fame, and honours—foolish you may call them, yet still what men all love. Then once more I asked the Lord of Montreville for gold to join the knights, my equals, as should become a Malpas and his kinsman. What answered he? He had need of his poor cousin at home to be his huntsman and his falconer!"

" You forget favours as easily as you remember injuries," answered the countess. " After my fatal nuptials and their sad fruit, do you but count as nothing—"

" Stay," interrupted Sir Grey, that was but hire for service and for silence, not a gift."

" Aye, and spent in riot, waste, and wild debauch."

" True," replied Sir Grey, raising his hand towards heaven, " true; in the grand inebriate wish of the pauper to know what wealth is, if but for an hour."

" Blame me not that those wild revelries have drained your purse," said Lady Montreville. My halls are open to you, my Beaufort spurns you not; you have been welcomed—"

" Aye," he said bitterly, " at your second table, and as the butt of lacqueys, while your kind son, in pity for my want, has this day killed the faithful dog who shared my poverty. Well, well, let it be so; you want my aid as your father wanted it before you, and you tempt like him with gold. I accept the service, and when the task is done, we will talk of payment. Ah! I hear a rustling in the bushes. It will be safer to continue our conference within. Vouchsafe your hand, fair lady."

" Well might I dream," said the countess, as they passed up the steps, " well might I dream last night a fearful dream."

It was Eveline, whose dress had rustled amid the bushes, and disturbed the schemers, and as they mounted the steps, she emerged from among the trees.

" Oh! could I find some talisman," she murmured, " to conjure up before my eyes the form they pine for. Yet in love there is no real absence. The loved one glides beside our steps for ever. Oh! where art thou, my unforgotten Vyvyan?"

There was a rush of feet as she murmured these gentle words, and then a well-remembered voice broke the silence of the garden.

"Here at thy feet!" cried Vyvyan. "Look up, look up; these are the arms that sheltered you when the storm howled around you; these the lips where till this hour the sad and holy kiss of parting has lingered like the fragrance left by angels. Look up, my soul, and brighten all things with your glances."

"Oh joy! oh joy! my Vyvyan," murmured Eveline, as she lay in rest and rapture on his breast.

"What, weeping still, when leaning on my bosom!" he cried, as he kissed her lips in fervent love, "has my sailor's bride no other voice but blushes?"

"Oh, I had treasured words that would take a life to tell," said Eveline, "and now we meet again my memory seems at fault."

"You can recall them at another time." replied Vyvyan; "when life with life blends into one we shall have time enough. But why do you start and tremble thus?"

"Methought I heard her slow and solemn footfall," she said.

"Speak you of the Lady of Montreville? Is she then so stern?"

"Not stern, but haughty."

"Haughty to *you!*"

"To all, even when kindest. No, I wrong her," said Eveline: "she is never haughty to her son. When her proud eyes moisten as she greets him, hearts that may have been lately stung by her manner yearn towards one so full of human love! Alas! how shelterless seems life when the love of parents is lost."

He clasped her more closely to his heart, as she spoke with faltering accents.

"Like you, perchance," he said, "looking round earth for this same parent shel-

ter, I may find nought but tombs! But come, let us wander towards the sea, and gazing out over its heaving bosom, forget that we are orphans."

As their departing forms glided through the trees, Sir Grey de Malpas and my Lady of Montreville quitted the house, and once more descended into the grounds.

They were continuing a conversation.

"Yet, still," said Lady Montreville, "if Alton sees——"

"Without the proofs," returned Sir Grey, "the priest's story would be like idle wind. The man I am about to send is swift and strong, and, ere this Vyvyan (who would have been here before me but that I took the shorter path) departs from your castle to the priest's dwelling our agent will gain the solitary hut, and——"

"Remember, no violence."

"No, none but fear. Fear will force from the aged man your safety and your Beaufort's birthright."

"Let me not hear the ignominious means," replied the countess. "Gain you the end. Quick—quick."

"And, in the meantime," said De Malpas, "if the sailor comes, be nerved to meet him as a stranger and to detain him here as a guest."

"Fear not, my heart is wax, but my will is iron. Go."

"Now—now," said Sir Grey, as he passed from her presence, "now for Wrecklyffe's revenge and my earldom!"

"Nay, Vyvyan," murmured the gentle voice of Eveline, as, leaning on her lover's arm, she neared the spot where Lady Montreville still stood, "nay, you cannot fathom her imperious temper!"

"I care not for her pride," he answered; "a king upon the deck is every subject's equal in the hall. I will advance. God save you, gentle madam."

Lady Montreville started; and, as her eyes fell on Vyvyan, she clasped her hand to her bosom, and uttered a low faint cry.

"Avenging angels! Spare me," she murmured to herself, "it is he, my first-born!"

"'BACK, BOY! I COMMAND YOU!' CRIED THE COUNTESS, WITH PALE LIPS."

CHAPTER XXIV.

THE FIRST RECOGNITION.

So occupied was Vyvyan with the fair and gentle being at his side, that he did not observe the start of wonder and dismay which his sudden appearance had caused Lady Montreville.

She had therefore time given her to collect her thoughts and compose her voice: and turning towards him, she asked in a quiet tone which strangely belied the pallor of her face—

" Whom do I address, gentle sir ?"

" The name I bear, noble lady," he replied, is Vyvyan."

" You are most welcome, sir," said the countess. " Walk within and regard my castle as your home while you please. We have heard of you from Eveline."

Vyvyan's heart beat loudly at her voice. Yet why ?

This question his heart failed to answer, but, bowing lowly, he exclaimed as he placed his hand upon his heart—

" Madam, I shall be prouder throughout my life for having been your guest."

The smile with which Lady Montreville greeted his words meant far more than it conveyed.

Though in her own heart knowing that he was her son, she had consented in her mad love for Clarence, her younger-born, to conceal the fact from him, to destroy all proofs, to rob him of his birthright!

Drawn on by the specious words of the arch-schemer, Grey de Malpas, she had learned in a few hours to look with calmness upon a deed from which her heart would have shrunk in more reasonable moments.

Yet now she saw him, now his eyes had once more met hers, her bosom swelled with an unaccustomed feeling, and she longed to clasp him to her breast.

Yet she knew well if she *did* so, Clarence—her pride, her nursling—would lose all, and fall into that abject, bitter poverty which Sir Grey de Malpas had so eloquently and so cunningly described.

" Oh," she exclaimed, as she moved off to re-enter the castle, " how love and dread make tempest in my heart !"

" A most majestic lady," said Vyvyan, as he neared the house, bending over the fragile form of his young love. " Her fair face made me tremble, and called back old dreams. You said she had a son ?"

" She has ; a comely youth."

" He is a happy man then to have such a mother."

" Yet he might envy thee."

Vyvyan passed his hand gently round her waist and smiled—a world of tenderness in the smile.

" Yes, most arch reprover," he said, " as kings might envy one whose arm entwines his all."

And so, lovingly embracing, they passed up the wide steps which led to the Castle of his Ancestors.

CHAPTER XXV.

IN WHICH THE SEA CAPTAIN TELLS HIS TALE OF SHIPWRECK.

" In truth we made but a scurvy figure after our shipwreck," said Vyvyan, laughingly, as an hour after he sat with Eveline and Lady Montreville at a table heavy with fruit and wine.

It was a Gothic chamber, lofty, massive

in its carving and its ornamentation, with a huge hearth surmounted by armorial bearings, and walls covered with old portraits, taking you back into the far-off recesses of the past, and telling mutely tales of bygone battles and of love.

And through an open door you could view the quiet cloisters and the alleys of the courtyard, where years before Walter Tracy, the ill-fated page, had met and strolled with the stately lady who was now sitting by her first-born's side, like a stranger and an alien.

"You jest merrily over your misfortune," said she, as she gazed upon his noble features.

"It is the way with sailors," said Vyvyan, who had been narrating his adventures; "always in extremes. I can be sad sometimes."

"Your sigh speaks of sadness," said the countess; "if ever I can serve you depend on me."

"Trust her, Vyvyan," said Eveline; "the mournful tale of your young years would raise you up a friend wherever pity lives in the heart of woman."

Vyvyan, whose noble heart was utterly entranced by love for his gentle betrothed, did not observe the pallor which overspread the countess' face at these words, which set her mother's heart beating wildly in her overcharged breast.

So yielding to some secret feeling, the young adventurer spoke :—

"Gentle lady," he said, "there is a charm in your voice that unlocks a haunted chamber in my soul; and I will briefly tell you the sad story of an outcast, because I know full well that you will listen and pity me. Until my seventeenth year my hours passed away beneath the roof of a poor village priest, who taught me all I know, but refused all else—all secrets of the past. Throughout this time my mind was filled with restless thoughts. Something was absent—something was missing in harmonious Nature, until at length one night the truth flashed to my mind, and I asked the priest why was I motherless."

"And he?" asked the countess, avoiding his gaze, yet speaking eagerly.

"He replied that I was nobly born; and as he spoke of clouds and future sunlight, faint memories stole upon me."

"Of what?" said the countess.

"Of a face sweet with stately sorrow, and a mother's words murmured gently over a sleeping child."

The tears swelled up into Lady Montreville's eyes, and fell upon her heaving bosom, as he spoke.

But she drove them back resolutely.

Foolish mother! Loving both, yet sacrificing all for one!

Vyvyan spoke once more.

"About this time a stranger came to our hamlet. He was rough and wild, and a roysterer, but some said well-born. He called himself a sailor, and his talk was of El Dorado and Enchanted Isles; of hardy Raleigh, and of fearless Drake, and of great Columbus. His stories fired my soul; the sea seemed to beckon me to its breast, and so I left my home with that wild seaman."

"And still the priest revealed no more?" said Lady Montreville, leaning on the table, and eyeing him intently.

"No," returned Vyvyan, "he told no more, neither did he rebuke my ardour. 'Go,' he said; 'the noblest of all nobles are the men in whom their country feels herself ennobled.' Scarce had the brisk sea-winds filled our sails, when the man who had lured me to the ocean showed his treachery. I was cast into the dark hold of the vessel, and left there alone for long hours, when one day I was called on deck, and there, amid a scowl of swarthy brows—amid a crowd composed of the refuse of all countries—the pirate stood revealed. A peaceful merchant vessel was in sight, and presently upon this a merciless attack was made. To be brief, I refused to join in the massacre of helpless people, and, bound to the mast, I witnessed scenes that would freeze your blood to hear.

"When all was over I was unbound, and grimly he listened to my boyish upbraidings.

"'I, like thee,' he said, 'cast off, and desperate, and disinherited, had but one choice, death or the pirate's flag. Choose, *thou*. I am more gracious than thy kindred. *I* offer you life; the gold *they* gave me paid for thy ocean grave.'"

"Hold! the fiend but lied!" cried Lady Montreville, seizing him by the wrist, and forgetting all but her horror at the words.

"I cast the lie into his teeth, gentle madam," said Vyvyan, who in her manner recognised nothing beyond interest excited by his tale, " and on the instant he drew his weapon on me. My fate was not to die. I plucked a sword from one who stood beside me, and smote the slanderer to my feet. I should have been sacrificed in the hell of rage that then burst forth, but Heaven gave me unexpected aid. The pirate next in rank forced back the storm, and led by the strange superstition of the seas, forbade my death by blood-shed. I was then bound and fastened to a plank, a little sail was fastened to the end, and amid the gibes and sneers of those bloodthirsty traitors, I was set afloat, and left alone with God !"

" Oh! let my hand take thine," cried Eveline, gliding closer to her lover, " let me feel its warm life, and thank Him whose eye was over you."

" That day and all that night I was tossed upon the waves, and then I wept as I recalled the wretch's words, and murmured to myself, ' Even winds and waves are kinder than my kindred !"

A sob escaped from Lady Montreville's bosom.

" Nay, then, sweet lady, if my story saddens you—"

" Heed me not," said the countess. " Night passed——"

" Day dawned, and there, in the golden sunlight of the morning, I saw a sail. Like my dreams of happiness, it vanished, and I was left to face the scorching noon-tide. With this came thirst and famine! and with my parched lips I called on death, and sought to wrench my limbs from the stiff cords that gnawed into my flesh and drop into the deep. But just as I thought and prayed, the clear wave trembled, and below I saw a dark, swift-moving, shape-less thing—a ghastly shark, with glassy eyes. Then life once more grew sweet,

and on I floated until oblivion came, and——"

" Quick, quick !" said Eveline.

" I awoke to hear my native tongue—to see kind looks—to find myself saved."

" Oh !" exclaimed Eveline, again. " Such memories as these make life for ever after nearer Heaven."

" Break not the tale," said Lady Montreville. " I burn to hear the rest."

" Little remains to be told," continued Vyvyan. I fought my way to victory and manhood. At the death of my captain, the noble Drake—true lion of the ocean —named me captain. I have had since then numberless adventures and faced numberless dangers ; but here I am alive from out of them all. My tale is done, and each past sorrow, like a wave on shore, dies on this golden hour."

Lady Montreville watched with interest the affectionate, tender manner with which he turned to Eveline.

" Oh, how he loves my ward," she murmured. " Whom Clarence also loves. That thought piles fear on fear. Yet stay, this very rivalship gives hope of safety. It gives me a pretext to urge on secret nuptials, and a prompt parting ere he meet with Alton. Oh, could I act more bravely ; but here, in my mother's bosom, is that which chokes all reason. Captain Vyvyan," she added, turning to him, " the summer air is cool and pleasant in yonder shadowy alleys. If you will taste it, I will join you presently."

So saying she passed out followed slowly by Vyvyan and Eveline.

" A most compassionate and courteous lady," said he; " how could you call her proud ?"

" Nay; evermore," said Eveline, " I will love her as a mother for the soft pity she has shown to you."

CHAPTER XXVI.

THE FIRST QUARREL.

THE afternoon twilight was gathering over the Castle of Montreville when Sir Grey de Malpas and Lord Beaufort entered the spacious court-yard.

" Hood him gently, Marsden," cried Clarence; " it is indeed, a noble falcon. Ah! old knight, good-day. You have a lowering look as if still ruffled by some dire affray with lawless mice at riot in thy larder."

Sir Grey de Malpas laughed grimly.

"Mice in *my* house!" he cried. "Magnificent dreamer! The last was found three years ago last Christmas stretched out beside a bone! It was so lean and worn it was piteous to behold it. I canonized its corpse in spirits of wine and set it in the porch, a solemn warning—to its poor cousins! Oh!" he murmured to himself, "he killed my dog, too. When shall I be avenged?"

At this moment Eveline and Vyvyan, engaged in eager converse, were seen lingering in an alley in the back ground.

Lord Beaufort's jealous eye was the first to single them out.

"Ah! knight," he cried, "look there. A stranger, and whispering to my cousin."

"He is jealous," thought Sir Grey. "Something should come of this!"

Then he added aloud—

"Let us withdraw. Though old, I *have been* young. The whispered talk of lovers should be sacred."

"Lovers!" cried Clarence Beaufort, in angry surprise.

"Ah! lovers truly," cried De Malpas. "Did you not know that in your absence your mother has received a welcome guest in your fair cousin's wooer? He is a stalwart and a handsome gallant."

"You are not serious!" exclaimed the young lord, impatiently. "A wooer to Eveline! Quick! What is his name?"

A strange and baleful light beamed in the eyes of De Malpas.

"His name!" he said, doubtingly. "My memory begins to fail me. Seek your mother; ask *her; she* will tell you."

The last words of Sir Grey scarcely reached the ears of Lord Beaufort.

He had, while the old knight was speaking, advanced towards Vyvyan in a threatening manner.

"Whom have we here?" he cried. "Familiar sir, I do not see the Golden Spurs of Knighthood."

Vyvyan desired no quarrel with the son of his reputed hostess, and turned round therefore with no anger in his look.

There would have been less haughtiness still could he have known that Clarence, Lord Beaufort, was his brother.

"Alas!" he said, "we sailors have not so much gold that we should waste it on our heels. The steeds we ride to battle need no spurs, Sir Landsman."

"They seem to overleap all laws. It appears you are one of those wild Sea Rovers——"

"Yes," interrupted Vyvyan, "who refuse to yield to Spain the right to treat as thieves and pirates all who cross the line upon the ocean which her finger draws across it. We, the Sea Rovers, on our wandering decks carry our land, its language, laws and freedom; we wrest from Spain the sceptre of the seas, and in the New World build up a New England. For this high task the Old and New World shall bless the names of Walter Raleigh and his bold Sea Rovers."

"And of these names," said Beaufort, "yours is——"

"Vyvyan."

"Master Vyvyan, our rank scarcely warrants us in entering in the lists with blustering mariners. We bar you not our hospitality, but we desire no converse with you. Go to the seneschal and tell him to lodge you with your equals."

This was too much.

Vyvyan's face flushed crimson and his hand wandered involuntarily to his sword.

"Equals, stripling!" he cried; "my equals in very truth should be bearded men, nobles with titles that mere carpet knights should bow to — memories of dangers, and scars on bosoms that have bled for England."

"He has you there, cousin," whispered De Grey, as he made a feint to draw Lord Beauford back. "You shall not strike him, Clarence. Strike me, I'm weak and safe, but *he* is dangerous."

Lord Beaufort, however, was not thus to be restrained.

Breaking easily from the grasp of the feeble old knight, and rushing towards Vyvyan, he drew his sword fiercely from its scabbard.

Before, however, any engagement could take place between the lovers, Lady Montreville entered the courtyard, and rushed between them.

"Oh, madam!" cried Eveline; "protect your guest from your rash son!"

"How's this, Clarence?" exclaimed the countess, with pale lips. "Your sword drawn on your—— Back, boy, I command you, back! And you, my guest, have I failed in anything that you should rebuke the mother through the son?"

Vyvyan bowed respectfully.

"Madam, forgive me," he said. "My sole offence is this. Being treated as a slave, I spoke like a man!"

"Why these unseemly humours, Clarence?" cried his mother, whose bosom was torn with varied emotions.

"Wherefore!" exclaimed the impetuous youth, as he drew her aside, "you ask me wherefore, and while we speak his touch profanes her. Who is this man? Do you approve his suit? Beware, mother, or—"

"You would not threaten your—Oh! hear me, I implore you!" cried the wretched countess, as she suddenly stopped the words which rushed to her lips. "Oh, Clarence, stay your anger!"

"Mother," said Clarence Beaufort, almost fiercely, "I was taught in childhood, by you, to brook no rival, curb no passion. Will you aid this unknown sea adventurer against your own son where most his heart is set?"

"Your heart, Clarence! 'Tis but a few short hours since you said it was *not* love."

"That, mother," he answered, "was before a rival's presence made it so. Fear nothing if you dismiss this insolent unknown; but, by my honour, I swear, mother, that if he be not dismissed straightway, blood will be shed."

"Thrice miserable boy," exclaimed Lady Montreville, whose face depicted the agony of her mind, "may Heaven hear you not."

Beaufort, who was inflamed with mad rage against his unknown brother, paid no heed to her words, but, sheathing his sword, strode fiercely from the scene.

As he passed Vyvyan he whispered sternly,

"We will meet again, and soon."

Lady Montreville at this moment caught sight of Sir Grey de Malpas leaning on his stick and eyeing the scene with a countenance which he in vain strove to render unimpassioned.

"Villain!" she murmured; "but no, I dare not yet upbraid. After him; quick, Sir Grey, appease, soothe, humour him."

Sir Grey bowed sneeringly.

"Aye, madam," he said, as he hurried from the scene as fast as his infirmities would permit, "aye, trust to your poor cousin."

The countess watched his departure, and then spoke in a hurried tone to her cousin.

"Eveline," she said, "you love this Vyvyan."

"Lady," answered the young girl, with a blushing hesitation, "Lady—I—he saved my life and honour."

"Leave us then, gentle child," said Lady Montreville, in whispering accents. "I would confer with him. May both of you be happy."

Eveline, in the sweet modesty of her gentle nature, looked up in Vyvyan's face, and smiled as she turned away.

"She consents," she said. "Well may you bid me love her."

"Captain," said Lady Montreville, as soon as Eveline had departed, "if I can tell rightly from your speech, you do not mean long sojourn on these shores."

"My errand was twofold, gentle lady," said Vyvyan; "first to behold my affianced, and see if you would ratify her father's promise that she should be mine. My most earnest wish, however, was to learn if I could find my mother."

"And you have as yet heard nothing?" asked Lady Montreville, glancing down.

"Nothing; but hope still lives within me. When I gained these shores, I heard of war and danger; the long threatened invasion of this country by Spain was spoken of as certain. I have despatched a messenger to Sir Francis Drake to ask sure tidings. Even now I wait a reply. If England be in peril, she has the first claim upon me. If, as rumour says, the cloud is already disappearing without a storm, then, when I have gained my bride and discovered my birth, I shall sail back to the Indian seas, and revel once more in that wild adventure that realizes for man the wild dreams of his youth."

"You speak like a frank and brave soldier," said Lady Montreville; "I will reply as frankly. First, as regards England's danger. For five long years we have heard the vain boastings of the Spaniards, backed by the mutterings of monkish traitors; well, we live still, and all the promised deluge dies like harmless spray on England's scornful cliffs. Believe me, sir, she needs no aid from *you*. If she be in danger small use is *one* man's valour. If she lacked soldiers, the women and their babes, methinks, would rise in arms to save her!"

The eagerness with which she spoke, which arose ot necessity from her anxious wish for his peaceful departure ere he could learn the secret of his birth, Vyvyan mistook for the fiery glow of patriotism.

"Stately matron!" he cried, "you speak as England herself would speak, could she take visible image."

"You have my free consent to claim Eveline as your bride," continued the countess. "She shall not go to your arms undowered; but, for her sake and your own, I beg of you to let the marriage and your departure take place at once. You have seen my son—you have marked his fiery temper—he is your rival; I would not have you meet. Indulge a mother's impatient terrors and quit these shores to-night."

"This night—with her—my bride!" cried Vyvyan, taking her hand.

"On one condition, that upon the moment that sees you one you will set sail from England, and place the wide ocean between my son and you."

"This night—with Eveline—dream of rapture!" exclaimed the impassioned lover.

Then he checked himself.

"Yet," he added, "my birth untracked——"

"Oh!" said the countess, pleadingly, "do not delay bliss when assured to you, for the sake of a wild doubt. Leave all to me. I have wealth and power. *I* will explore the mazes of this mystery. *I* will track your parents."

"Oh! blessed lady," said he, "find me a mother that has eyes like thine, and were she the lowliest born of all yonder hamlet I would not change my lot with monarchs."

His beaming eyes were full upon her face as he spoke; and a tremor and a deathly shudder passed through her frame, while a strange, wild yearning filled her bosom.

Oh! how she longed to press him to her breast, and take from Alton's hand the task of unveiling the one great secret of his mournful life.

But Clarence!

Would she not then destroy him?

"Oh! can I bear this?" she murmured to herself. "Good sir, your Eveline is well-nigh my daughter; you are her plighted spouse. I pray you one kiss upon thy brow. Oh! sweet!" she sighed, as he knelt before her and her lips touched his face.

Vyvyan remained kneeling, gazing up into her sad eyes with infinite wonder.

"Oh, as I kneel, sweet lady," he cried, "and you bend over me, methinks an angel's hand lifts up the veil of time, and I see hovering over my infant couch a face like thine."

"Mine, stranger!" exclaimed Lady Montreville, withdrawing her hand as he rose.

"Oh, pardon me, madam," he said, "I know it is a vain wild thought; but on my faith I think my mother was like *you*."

The countess, whose agitation was beyond all control, and whose eyes were moistening with bitter tell-tale tears, turned now to go.

"Peace, peace," she said, "we are talking serious time away. Inform your bride, and then prepare your crew. I will meanwhile give orders to the chaplain. Beside the altar we shall meet once more, and then—and then," she added, in a faltering voice of tenderness and sorrow, "Heaven's blessing, and farewell."

Vyvyan gazed after her as she waved her hand and departed.

"Most feeling heart," he murmured, "her softness melts me too! This night away with Eveline! And yet, amid this dream of happiness, a chill and ominous dread creeps through my veins! Away with vague forebodings; at the thought of Eveline the glad future breaks like land upon the sea when the bright golden morn dispels the rain-mist. Ah! here comes my messenger from Alton, breathless with speed. Well, what news, brave Faulkner?"

"Captain, your foster-sire has proofs that clear all shadows from your birth," said the first-lieutenant of the "Dreadnought," as he hurried upon the scene. "Go; he awaits you near St. Kinian's Cliff."

"And do my parents live?" asked Vyvyan, with impatience.

"I know no more. Ah, look you!

"'SEE,' CRIED DE MALPAS, TO THE COUNTESS, 'YOUR FIRST-BORN EDMOND COMES.'"

here is Harding; he brings news from Drake."

It was in truth the second-lieutenant of the "Dreadnought" who followed so soon at the heels of his comrades.

His face betrayed the fact that he had great news to tell.

"Captain," he said, "the rumour lied."

"The foeman comes, then!" exclaimed Vyvyan.

Harding drew forth a letter from the breast of his doublet and handed it to the young adventurer.

"These lines will tell you all," he said; "they are in Drake's own hand."

Vyvyan took the paper eagerly, and read aloud:

"'The Armada has left the Groyne, and we are preparing for battle. Come at once. I have left a place for you in the front of all.'"

"Brave words! and yet—poor Eveline."

"There is time," said Faulkner, "to see her, and keep your appointment with the priest. Leave me to call the crews and arm the decks. The tide will not be up until the moon rises, in the second hour after the sunset. Before that hour be past our ship will wait you by St. Kinian's Cliff. I know there is no need to pray you not to miss the moment whose loss would lose your honour."

Vyvyan grasped his friend firmly by the hand.

"If I do not come," he said, "ere your third signal gun reverberates over the waves, slip into my post, be captain of the 'Dreadnought,' for death alone would keep me from my duty."

"Your rebuke is just, captain," said Faulkner; "but could so great a misfortune happen as that you could not join us, I shall deem that signal as your funeral knell, crowd every sail, and know that your soul—"

"Was with my country still," said Vyvyan. "But hark, what shouts are those?"

"They seem to tell of fresh tidings from the enemy," said Faulkner, as he passed towards the battlements.

The terrace, as we have before seen, hung over the rocks on which the Castle was built, and from its embattled parapet a glimpse could be caught of the scene below.

"There is a crowd entering the Castle," said the first-lieutenant of the "Dreadnought," as he returned towards his captain, "and they seem in some great excitement. Ha, here they come."

As he spoke there entered the courtyard a confused and motly crowd.

Retainers in their stiff attire, sailors bronzed and weather-beaten, village maidens with rosy dimpled cheeks, and dressed in gay dresses of every hue, labourers and wandering loiterers, all followed the sub-officer of the "Dreadnought," who advanced towards Vyvyan with a broad-sheet in his hand.

Spain was now the great bugbear of England.

The Armada was the dream of all, and each morning the people on the coast rose early from their beds to scan the horizon, expecting to behold the long fluttering line of canvas which was to bring destruction on their island home.

No wonder then, that they watched with eager eyes the sub-officer as he passed forward and placed the paper in the hands of the friend of Raleigh and of Drake, two household words in every English home!

"Captain, look here," cried the man; "this is but just arrived."

Vyvyan received it eagerly.

"Ah!" exclaimed he, "this is the Queen's Address to her soldiers at Tilbury."

"Read it aloud, sir," said the sub-officer; "the crowd that now surrounds you waits for it with impatience."

Vyvyan raised his hand to call for silence, and then began:

"'Loving people, let tyrants fear! I, under Heaven, have placed in the loyal hearts that surround my throne my chief strength and safe guard, being resolved, in the midst and the heat of the battle, to live and die among you all. For my God and my people I am content to lay in the dust my honour and my life's blood. I am aware that I have but the body of a feeble woman; but I have a king's heart—a King of England's, too, and laugh to scorn the threat that Spain, aye, if all Europe backed her, would dare invade the borders of my realm. Where England fights with concord in the camp, trust in the commander, and valour in the ranks, swift will be her victory over every foe that dares menace her crown, her altar, and her people.' "

"The noble woman-king!" cried Vyvyan, lifting his hat as he concluded reading the address. "These words of fire will send warm blood through all the veins of freedom till England is a dream of the past. Uncover all! God and St. George! Hurrah for England's Queen!"

A loud shout—a shout that would have gladdened the heart of Good Queen Bess, rent the air as he spoke, and went echoing away among the rocks.

Ere it had died away, Vyvyan passed rapidly from among them, and took his way towards St. Kinian's Cliff.

No bride for him was there now, till England's enemies had been scattered to the winds; but before he rushed into the wild tide of battle he longed to know the truth—to claim his mother if she lived, to weep her loss if dead.

Little did he dream that his mother had already kissed him—little did he dream his mother had disowned him!

CHAPTER XXVII.

THE PRIEST'S SECRET.

I HAVE before described St. Kinian's Cliff, the wild, precipitous headland, near which Vyvyan spent the whole of his early days.

It had not changed now.

There were still there the wild peaks, and the craggy paths, and the stunted brushwood; still there the dizzy precipices and the rushing echoes of the wild, monotonous sea.

What attracted the notice of the young adventurer, however, were the little chapel and the cottage in which he had learned so much from the kind and diligent priest.

He hastened eagerly to the cottage, and knocked at the door.

The priest answered his summons.

"Ah!" he cried, "time has not so dimmed my eyes, or so changed you, that I do not recognise you. Welcome, my foster son."

He drew Vyvyan within as he spoke, and closing the door, passed into the room, where a bright and cheerful fire blazed up the ample chimney.

"And I believed them," he said, "when they told me you had died in far-off seas."

Vyvyan smiled as he pressed the old man's hand.

"Did I not bid you hope when last I saw you?" he cried. "Did I not tell you how the waves had saved me, and how superstition had stepped in to stay the pirate's murderous purpose? I said I would live to know the secret of my birth. Speak on, good Alton, for the sun sets fast."

"Listen—sit so," continued the priest, "for thy warm hand awakes me from one long night of desolate sorrow. The story is a brief one, though full of grand and unexpected meaning for you. There was a page, fair, brave, well-born, but poor, and in that bright morning of life when disparity of position is as nothing, he loved the heiress of a lordly house.

"She, in the first blush of maidenhood —scarcely, indeed, out of childhood— listened to his honeyed words, and loved him in return.

"After awhile a secret marriage took place, and for a year all went happily, though one, it seems, suspected after a time.

"At length the page, dispatched to a distance by his lordly master, returned to find his wife a mother.

"Then came the terrible crisis.

"While the young father was caressing with rapture the mother and her babe, a traitor was at work within the Castle, and bitter words of terrible meaning were whispered in her sire's ears.

"It was a kinsman who did this—one who, if she died childless, would be next heir to the estates.

"He had kept good watch; had tracked the bridegroom to the bridal bower, and aroused her father, who, mad with fury, seized his sword, and sought his daughter's chamber.

"He was ready for a fearful crime; but when the portal was burst open he escaped guiltless.

"Cold and tremulous with fear, on her bended knees, with hands upraised, she knelt upon the floor—alone!"

"And where was the page—her husband?" asked Vyvyan, breathless with impatience.

"Through the open casement the noble youth had sped to certain death, to save her life or honour," replied Alton.

"A terrible and cruel end to a young and bright existence," murmured Vyvyan, "and yet a happy death if it saved her he loved. Well, and then?"

"A midnight grave concealed the mangled clay, and buried the bride's secret," returned Alton, "while stern hands, by orders of her father, conveyed the babe to me, who to your lofty kindred owned the mean roof that shelters me."

"Oh! say," cried Vyvyan, impatiently, "have I a mother still?"

"Yes," said the priest, "she survived, and her vows and your birth were unguessed by the world. Then followed a long time of misery and vain resistance, and she was forced, at length, to the arms of a lordlier husband."

Tears stood in Vyvyan's eyes.

"As I have said," he murmured, "it is a mournful face I recall to mind—a patient, sad brow, and tears that rained on me from mild and sorrowing eyes. These, then, were my mother's!"

"In stealth a wife—in stealth a mother," said Alton. "Yes—then she indeed loved you."

"And despised not my birth?"

"No, no; in those days things were different. She looked forward with delight to the day when she could claim you as her own; and bade me hoard these proofs for that blessed time."

"You speak now of her love as a thing of the past," said Vyvyan; "what mean you?"

"Alas," returned Alton, "with her new ties came new affections. To her second husband she bore a son. She nursed this one herself in open day. She loved him better than life—better than thee—better than her own soul!"

"Poor mother!" said Vyvyan, "and I blame her not!"

"Haughtier thoughts came with her riper life," resumed Alton, who scarcely seemed to share in the young adventurer's enthusiasm, "and wordly greatness made her dread the world's shame. She forsook then her visits to her pillow. Her father threatened, your kinsman prayed, until, urged by terror for your safety, I—though Heaven knows how reluctantly—took vows to mask the truth and keep secret your rights while your mother's sire and her husband lived. You were nameless when you left my roof, because they both lived; but since your second voyage they both are dead. You live—you have returned—I am freed from my oath. Here are the papers that attest my tale and prove your birthright. HAIL, THEN, LORD OF BEAUFORT!" cried Alton, rising, "HEIR OF MONTREVILLE!"

Vyvyan sprang to his feet, and clasping his hands, looked fervently towards Heaven.

"'Tis she! 'tis she!" he exclaimed. "At the first glance I loved her, and when I told my woes she wept. This is *her* writing. Oh, see here, where she calls me 'Edmond—her child!' Old man, how you have wronged her sweet and gentle nature! Joy, joy! Adieu, good Alton, I go to claim and find a mother!"

So saying, he waved his hand to Alton, and without another word rushed to the door and passed out into the deepening twilight.

The priest with quick steps followed him to the door, and gazed at him as he sped down the mountain pathway.

"Just Heaven," he murmured, as he saw him rush eagerly along the craggy path, "grant that his mother may hear with pitying ears his tale, and grant him safety, too, from his many enemies."

CHAPTER XXVIII.

BEAUFORT'S TRIAL.

It was sunset, and the twilight was just creeping over the scene, when Sir Grey de Malpas and Wrecklyffe made their appearance in the courtyard of the Castle.

The look on the features of the poor cousin showed anger and disappointment, while that on the face of the pirate chief was expressive of sullen determination.

"The priest, say you, had left his home with but one man," cried Grey, as he stopped and faced his companion.

"The hour I reached it," returned Wrecklyffe.

"And yet you did not follow?"

"I did."

"And yet the prey escaped!" cried De Malpas, savagely. "I have done with you for ever! Your soul's wish was revenge—revenge on Vyvyan—I gave it you, yet you leave his way clear to a height as far removed from thy desire as yonder watch-tower is removed from a pirate's gibbet!"

"Silence! you——" began the pirate.

"Sir! do you dare?" interrupted Sir Grey.

Wrecklyffe's manner changed at once. He became cowed and subdued, and raised his hand deprecatingly.

"Along the moors I tracked them," he said, "but only came in sight of them just as they gained the broad and thronging road, where crowds were gathering and talking eagerly of Spain and its threatened thunders."

"What matters their wild talk to you and me?" said Grey. "The beggar has no country."

"I know it," answered the pirate; "but deeds such as these you desire me to execute are not to be risked madly in the open day and among an excited throng. I came to you for safer orders."

"I must have time to think," said De Malpas. "Hark! the door jars; she comes. Skulk yonder; hide well, but remain within call. A moment sometimes makes or mars a fortune."

As he spoke he pointed to a clump of thickly-clustering trees, behind which Wrecklyffe passed quickly just as Lady Montreville issued from the cloisters.

She started and flushed as her eyes fell upon the form of the poor cousin.

"What!" she cried as she advanced towards him, "what! can you look on me and not tremble? Could you pretend that the gold my father gave you paid for my son's murder! that he wished to be sold to pirates and cast out friendless upon the wide seas?"

"How?" exclaimed Sir Grey, in feigned astonishment. "I knew not of this! If such, indeed, be the truth, peace to your father's sins, for this is his sin and not mine. But let the past sleep; think not of that but of present evils. The priest has left his home with Vyvyan's comrade, and our scheme is foiled."

"I will see Alton myself to-morrow, then," said Lady Montreville. "Edmond can scarcely forestall me now. This very night all fear for me vanishes, for he sets sail from England for the far Indian main."

"Let me do homage to your genius, sorceress," said Sir Grey, bowing with mock humility. "What magic did you use?"

"My terror for Clarence, and Edmond's love for Eveline, were enough to rouse my brain, and give me the chance I desired," replied Lady Montreville.

"I see it all," thought Sir Grey, "bribed by the prize of which she robs his rival he goes this very night. So soon? this night?" he added inquiringly, aloud.

"Yes, this night," said the countess, "this night I save my Clarence. Till then keep close, close to his side. You have already contrived to soothe him slightly, have you not?"

"Fear not; these sudden tidings of the foe have thrown love for the time, at least, into the shade. But where is Vyvyan?"

"No doubt," said Lady Montreville, "he is with his crew, preparing for departure. But hark ! there is the voice of Clarence. How sweetly it falls upon my ear ! "

" This way, Marsden ! " exclaimed Lord Beaufort, as he entered. " See here ; repair these broken parapets at dawn ; place the culverins yonder ; delve down more sharply that bank, and see that the moat is cleared. And here, Marsden, these trees should fall ; they would serve to screen the foe. Ah, mother ! I did not see you there."

" I have but just arrived, " said Lady Montreville, with a fond smile.

"Will you then promise, mother, to make me a scarf to wear above the armour in which thy father, amid the shouts of kings, shivered French lances at the Cloth of Gold ? "

" Nay, my young lord," said Marsden, " that armour is too vast for you."

Lord Beaufort smiled.

" You forget, good Marsden, " he said, " that the breast swells in danger, and honour adds a cubit to the stature."

"Embrace me, Clarence ! " cried Lady Montreville. " I myself will arm you. Look at him, Marsden ; yet they say I spoil him."

Sir Grey de Malpas, during this conversation, had been leaning over the low parapet, and he now advanced and drew Lady Montreville aside.

" See in the distance, " he whispered, "who comes with swift disordered strides and the light bound of an impatient spirit. It is Vyvyan—Edmond, your first-born, who speeds hither, and the speed seems joy. He has doubtless sought his crew. Alton might there await him."

"His speed is to a bride, " said Lady Montreville with a smile.

" Aye, true, " replied Sir Grey with one of his sinister bows. " Old age forgets that love is as eager as ambition ; yet if you be guided by me, hold yourself prepared."

" And if it were so, " she murmured to herself, "I will sound the depths of Beaufort's heart. As he answers me will I hush or yield to conscience. Lead off these men," she added, to Sir Grey, "and you, Marsden, go and meet my guest of to-day. See that he enters through the garden postern. You, Clarence, come back."

"What now ? " asked Lord Beaufort, with some peevishness of manner, for he was anxious to follow his retainers.

" Speak kindly to me, Clarence, " replied Lady Montreville, as she placed her hand gently upon his arm. Speak kindly to me. Alas ! you little know, and never will know till the grave closes over me, how much I need this kindness."

"Pardon me, my mother," replied Beaufort, remorsefully pressing his lips to her forehead, "my blunt speech but now, and my froward heat this morning."

" Such follies are things of the past," said Lady Montreville, " and I do not remember them. Hidden honour has dawned upon you, and one hero more has sprung up from the soil. Ah, Clarence, had I too, an elder-born, as your father had by his former nuptials—could your sword carve out fortune ? "

"Oh ! yes, my mother." ·

" Well the bold answer rushes to your lips ! " cried the proud mother. " Yet tell me frankly, do you not prize greatly the outward show of things ? Tell me truly, Clarence ; you are rich with valour, health, and beauty, and hope, which is youth's. Could you descend from this proud heart ? Could you consent to live less grandly—to abandon the idea that you were heir to an earldom, and retire to the state of a simple gentleman ? "

Lord Beaufort eyed his mother curiously.

"If reared to it," he answered, "perhaps I might have been so contented ; but now—no, never ! Such as I am you have made me—ambitous, haughty, prodigal—and pomp a part of my very life. If I could fall from my high position, mother, it would be as Romans fell—on their sword's point. Why is your cheek so pale ? Why do you tremble at airy fantasies ? Who can deprive me of my title and my fortune ? The titles borne at Palestine and Cressy —the seignory, ancient as the throne it guards, will be mine in trust for unborn sons when the time arrives—pray Heaven it may be far distant, mother— which will transfer the circlet on that stately brow to one who will, I trust, be no unworthy heir."

"My proud soul," murmured Lady

Montreville, " speaks in his, and stills remorse. I'll know no other son. " Now go, Lord Beaufort."

" Why so formal, gentle mother? Have I so offended?"

" Offended, Clarence! No, no, " said Lady Montreville, " resume your noble duties, sole heir of Montreville."

" My choice is made, " she added, to herself, as Lord Beaufort raised his plumed hat and quitted the courtyard. " I will guard my heart for Clarence, as I would guard a fortress for my king. I will close its gates against the stranger. Let him come."

She had scarcely passed away among the rapidly-darkening cloisters, when Vyvyan and Evelyn came slowly along under the shadowy trees.

There was a lovely scene around them; the gentle moon still hiding its face, and only a few stars beginning to glint over the hushing sea, above which the dark, old towers of Montreville stood frowningly, as if defying the vain boastings of the Spanish foemen.

" I cannot bid you stay, " said Eveline, as they leaned upon a parapet, and looked down upon the ocean, which Vyvyan had called his second mother. " Your country calls you but you have stricken me to my very heart in the midst of joy by this sudden announcement of our parting."

" Live not so much in the present, sweet one," said Vyvyan; " think of the future. Would you not have me still worthier of your love?"

" You cannot be so, Vyvyan," said the young girl, gazing fondly up in his manly face.

" Sweet Eveline," said Vyvyan, " I am poor and nameless. Would it not suit my proud heart better? would it not please you, too, if I could lay at your feet rank and fortune won by my own bright sword?"

" These could give me no further happiness," said the young girl, " save in so far as they made you happy. Into the life of him whom she loves a woman's life blends and flows, and never more should she have a wish apart. If his lot be great, she loves greatness for *his* sake. If his lot be humble, for him she is content and happy. You are ambitious, Vyvyan; you wish to leave me that you may fight England's foes, and give your strong arm to your country's cause. It is well. Fame for your sake fires me too, and without a tear, without a murmur, I bid you go where glory will be yours. Win the honour that you seek, and I shall rejoice. If you fail to win it, then it will be joy to think I can console you."

" Oh! that I could give full vent to this full heart," murmured the Rightful Heir. " Time speeds away apace. Ha! there is the countess yonder. This way — come!"

And seeing approaching Lord Beaufort and Sir Grey, whose coming might delay his longed-for interview with the countess, he drew her away amid the trees.

Sir Grey de Malpas had, meanwhile, been at work.

The time was now so short, that he had not a moment to lose, and insidiously, even at the moment when he had promised the countess to soothe her youngest born, he had used the fleeting hours in breathing into Beaufort's ears a tale which would rouse his deadly jealousy.

He had done this in such a manner however, that it should not appear to Clarence that he had told him, but rather that the secret had been wrung from him.

" Leave England, say you, " cried Clarence, furiously, as he advanced with angry strides upon the scene, " and with *her?*"

" You have wrung the secret from me," said Sir Grey de Malpas. " Remember, I have your promise not to betray me to your mother!"

" Ah! then," said Clarence, " she thought to deceive me with her ambitious imaginings, while she in very truth rendered my life less to be coveted than that of a beggar. No, by Heaven! she *shall* not thus befool me!"

" Be patient," said Sir Grey. " Had I guessed that my words would have so galled you, I would have been dumb."

" Stand from the light, old man," cried Beaufort. " Distraction! she hangs upon his breast."

Hurrying after the loving couple, he seized Vyvyan unceremoniously by the wrist, and dragged him from Eveline, while Wrecklyffe, gliding partly from his hiding place, looked on with grim satisfaction.

There was a terrible fire in Lord Beaufort's eyes as he spoke.

"Sir, one word with you," he said; "this very day looks and words have passed between us such as those who wear swords and fear not to use them, cancel with deeds."

"The brave boy!" thought Vyvyan; "how I love him."

"What said you, sir?" exclaimed Lord Beaufort, impatiently.

"Oh, Clarence," cried Eveline, deprecatingly, as she approached the brothers, unknown yet to each other.

"Fear not, cousin," said Lord Beaufort, gently. "I am but making excuse to this fair gentleman for my rudeness at noon to-day."

"If so," said Sir Grey de Malpas, "let us not interfere with his courtesy."

"But——" said Eveline.

"Nay, then, you are too timid," answered the old man.

And he drew her with gentle force from the spot.

As soon as she was gone Lord Beaufort turned once more to Vyvyan.

"Let us be brief, sir," he said. "You quit these parts to-night?"

"I do!"

"Well, then, this place suits not the only conference we should hold; I pray you to name a spot and hour in which to meet again. We need no witness but the broad, early moon."

"Meet you again—oh, yes!" said Vyvyan, with a smile.

Lord Beaufort, in his eager haste, noticed not the tender look which Vyvyan cast upon him, his yet unclaimed brother.

He took the words simply as implying that he consented to the duel.

"There speaks a soldier," he cried, "and now I own my equal. What hour and place?"

"Wait here," said Vyvyan, "till I have——"

"No—no—upon your road," interrupted Clarence, "here we are watched by spies."

"On the very spot," thought Vyvyan, "where I learned the glad tidings that Heaven had given me a brother, there shall be our first embrace."

"So be it, then," he said aloud, "let it be on my road. Within the hour I pass St. Kinian's Cliff."

"Alone?"

"Aye, alone."

"Farewell, then, until we meet!" said Clarence, and, waving his hand, he turned to leave the courtyard.

Sir Grey de Malpas caught at his arm as he was passing away.

"I heard you, Lord Beaufort," he said. "St. Kinian's Cliff. I'll warn the countess."

"Do it and famish!" shouted Clarence.

"Thy warning strikes home," said the poor cousin, bowing.

"Aye, and my hand is firm," said the young man. "Within the hour I'll know what strength lies hidden in these arms."

So saying, he strode with eager steps from the courtyard.

Throughout the scene Eveline's heart had beat wildly in her bosom.

It was of little use what Vyvyan said.

She feared something, she knew not what, but a dread presentiment was in her heart.

"On your honour, Vyvyan," she said, as she beheld Clarence Beaufort quitting her lover's presence with rapid strides, "on your honour, I demand to know—has he forced a quarrel on you?"

"A quarrel, Eveline! It would be beyond his power. No, on my honour, thrice no."

"I scarce dare believe you."

"Why, then, Eveline, I thus defy your further trembling. Away I cast this weapon," cried he, drawing his sword, and casting it over the parapet into the sea. "If I now meet your cousin, both must be safe, for one will be unarmed."

"My own frank hero-lover, pardon me," said Eveline, as she gazed up fondly into his handsome face; "yet will you not need it?"

He laughed lightly.

"As against the Spaniards," he said, "there will be swords enough on board the 'Dreadnought.' But tell me, sweet one, are you sure his heart is touched so lightly?"

"What, are you jealous of me, Vyvyan, in such an hour as this?"

"No, no. I am not. I should be sorry for your sake and his that such a feeling should rise within my breast. Ha! here is Marsden."

The old man bowed lowly as he advanced.

"My lady, sir," he said, "invites you to her presence."

"Remember, oh, remember!" exclaimed Eveline, clinging to the young adventurer, "once more before we part. God speed you on your journey."

"Heaven bless you, Eveline," said he, as he kissed her sweet, red lips, "so I will take the echo from your lips as a good omen. Adieu, my own. Now, then, Marsden, lead me to your lady. How my heart beats within me."

Then with a wave of the hand, he followed the seneschal into the Castle.

"Gone, gone," murmured Eveline, as she followed with slow steps. "Oh, how black and drear seems all the world to me!"

Sir Grey de Malpas and Wrecklyffe had been silent spectators of all this scene.

Vyvyan's conduct fairly puzzled and troubled the dark, designing mind of the poor cousin.

"Why does Vyvyan accept this challenge," he muttered, "and yet cast off his weapon? Perhaps he desires no harm to the son of the guest who honours him, or maybe that in his absence he has met with Alton. Well, we must be ready to meet all changes. It matters not. What ho! there, Wrecklyffe, man without a hope."

"Save that of vengeance," said the pirate, as he strode towards his master.

"Were you near when Beaufort spoke with Vyvyan? Did you hear their conversation?

"I know that within the hour," replied the pirate, "the man who first wrote 'felon' on my brow hastens to St. Kinian's Cliff."

Sir Grey de Malpas clutched him by the arm, and, peering round him to make sure there were no listeners, said, in a hoarse whisper:

"Mark you, Wrecklyffe, what I ask is harder than to strike—'tis to forbear; but you will have your revenge in safety. Let Vyvyan first meet Clarence Beaufort. Watch what passes, and if the boy, whose hand is ever guided by his passion, should forestall your vengeance, and slay thy foe, remember, neither prevent nor assist."

Wrecklyffe laughed.

"That boy slay Vyvyan!" he cried, in a voice of utter contempt.

"You forget that Vyvyan is unarmed," said Grey de Malpas.

"Law calls that murder," said the pirate.

"Aye, and that murder, backed by proof, and by your witness, would give the murderer to the headsman's axe, and leave Sir Grey de Malpas Heir of Montreville, and you the richest squire in all his train."

"I understand your scheme," said Wrecklyffe, as the poor cousin clutched his arm eagerly; "but if the youth should fail or relent?"

"Then I baulk not your revenge," said De Malpas; "and if the corpse of Beaufort's rival be found where Beaufort, armed and angry, encountered him, to whom would justice track the death-blow?—Beaufort!"

"No further words," said Wrecklyffe; "or his hand or mine shall do the deed. Count one life less on earth, and weave thy schemes accordingly."

With these words the pirate turned and passed away quickly.

Sir Grey looked up at the stern old towers, the possession of which he so much coveted.

"One death avails as three," he muttered; "since for the mother conscience and shame will be sharper than the steel. So I shall overleap the gulf nor gaze below. On this side is desolate ruin; bread begrudged, and ribald scorn heaped upon impotent grey hairs; on that side bended knees and fawning smiles. No longer the poor cousin, whose very dog is butchered if it bark; no, no. Ho, there! room for my lord's knights and pages! Room at the Court! room there beside the throne! Ah! the new Earl of Montreville! His lands cover two shires; such men should rule the state! A gracious lord in truth! Some men may call him old; not so—the coronet conceals grey hairs. He limped, they say, when he wore hose of serge. Pooh! the slow march well becomes the robe of ermine. Back, conscience, back, taunting Fiend! Scowl on, ye boors and beggars! Room, smiling flatterers, room for the new earl."

And so, with an inward laugh and a quickened gait, the poor cousin hurried from the courtyard.

Agitated as may have been his feelings, they were no more wild than those that filled the bosom of Lady Montreville, as she sat at her casement watching the dark, rolling sea, and expecting each moment the arrival of her first-born.

Her eyes truly glanced at the wild waves, but in very truth, the grim old portraits on the walls saw as much as they did.

Her thoughts were busy with the past and future.

At length an impatient step was heard approaching along the echoing corridor, and Vyvyan entered the room.

"Already come to claim your bride?" she asked, with a smile.

"Alas!" said Vyvyan, "my nuptials are deferred. This very night the invader summons me. My sole altar now is England; my sole bride, Honour."

"Oh!" he murmured, "how shall I break it to her?"

"My Clarence on the land," said Lady Montreville, "and you on the sea, both armed in defence of your country; Heaven shield you both!"

"Say you that, gentle lady, both!" cried Vyvyan; "you who so love your son?"

"Better than life I love him."

"Oh!" thought Vyvyan, "time goads me on; I must rush into the thick. Had you not, madam," he exclaimed, aloud, "had you not another son—a first-born?"

"Sir!" cried Lady Montreville, starting back, pale as death.

"A son," pursued he, "on whom your eyes dwelt first—whose infant cry broke first on that divine and holy chord in the deep heart of woman which awakens all Nature's tenderest music? Oh, turn not from me! I know the mystery of your mournful life. Will it displease you to hear—to know—that son is living still?"

"Sir—sir!" exclaimed the wretched countess, "such license on your part will compel me to leave you."

"No," cried Vyvyan, casting himself on his knees; "no—no, you *will* not leave me—on my knees I say you *shall* not leave me."

"Loose your hold," cried Lady Montreville, striving to break from him.

"Oh," he went on, "I am your son—your Edmond—your own child—saved from the deep, the storm, the battle, rising from Death to thee—the source of life, flung by kind Heaven once more upon your breast, kissing your robe and clinging to your knees. Do you reject your son?"

The countess gazed at him for an instant in silence.

Then, with her hands clasped to her heaving breast, she said, slowly, sternly:

"I have *no* son save Clarence Beaufort!"

CHAPTER XXIX.

DISCARDED!

IT was a look of bitter anguish that Vyvyan cast upon Lady Montreville as she uttered the cold words which claimed Clarence Beaufort for her only child.

It was a searching look, too, striving to discover whether pride alone caused her speech, or whether, after all, there was a real belief in her own words.

He raised his eyes to Heaven.

"Oh! do not—do not hear her?" he cried. "Oh! God of my existence! You have no other son, lady! Oh, cruel one!

Look on these letters to the priest who reared me. See where you call me 'Edmond' 'child' 'life's all.' Can the words be so fresh on this frail record, yet have faded from your undying soul? Oh! by these, by all the solemn past, by your youth's lover, by his secret grave, by every kiss upon your infant's cheek, by every tear you wept when you heard his death, grieve not now that your first-born lives to call you—'mother!'"

With an imperious gesture, ill-assorted

with her trembling hands and faltering voice, she bade him rise from his knees—for there, during the last few moments he had remained, still gazing up lovingly into her face.

"Rise, sir," she said. "If these papers prove that such a son once lived, where are your proofs that you are he?"

Vyvyan sprang to his feet, and pointed towards her, as he exclaimed, excitedly:

"There—in your heart, in your eyes, that dare not face mine; in your trembling limbs, in every sense, which quivers and pulses at my voice, there are my proofs! Let pride encase you in adamantine armour; it is of no avail against the call of Nature when it cries, 'Parent, come forth!'"

The countess trembled now more violently than ever, and averted her eyes from the gleaming, eager, half-despairing half-hopeful eyes of her first-born.

What was she to do?

If she now gave way, Clarence must fall from the proud height where her own foolish teaching had placed him.

How wrongly she judged Vyvyan!

Although yearning naturally towards him as the offspring of her first and only love, she regarded him as a despoiler—one who came to wrest from his brother his title and his lands, and proclaim to the world her long-kept secret of youth; whereas, in very truth, her love and kindness were all he sought.

"My resolution gives way," she murmured to herself. "Lost Clarence! But no! what did he say? 'If told of lost estates and titles he would fall, as the Roman heroes of old fell, on his sword's point.' No, no. Impostor!" she added, turning fiercely towards Vyvyan. "If by employing most unworthy spies you have found some basis in my mournful life whereon to build up this fable, the law shall laugh it to scorn. Quit my presence!"

"No, I will not," exclaimed Vyvyan, with respectful sternness.

"Will not, say you," cried Lady Montreville, starting, and approaching the door. "Ho! there!"

Vyvyan, whose face had turned of an ashen paleness, strode to the hearth, and stood there—upright, stern—with folded arms.

"Call your hirelings!" he cried "and let them hear me. Lo! beneath my roof, and on the sacred hearth of those who have been sires to both of us, under their escutcheons, and before their ghostly portraits which look at me from yonder canvas, I take my dauntless stand armed with my rights. Now bid your menials thrust from his own hearth the Rightful Heir of Montreville!"

As he spoke the door was flung open and some armed retainers entered.

"Seize on him!" began the countess.

Then she broke down and clasped her hands before her face.

"Oh, I cannot, I cannot!" she murmured; "his father stands before me again in him. No, I *dare* not!"

The servants glanced in wonder and some alarm, moreover, at the scene before them.

What could it mean?

The countess, pale, trembling, weeping in the presence of her guest! What did this forebode?

"Madam," said the foremost of them, "did you not summon us?"

"They await your commands, Lady of Montreville," said Vyvyan, haughtily.

"I called you not—go," cried the countess.

Then, when they had bowed and quitted the chamber, she turned once more towards Vyvyan.

Not now haughty and imperiously, but imploringly—appealingly.

"Are you my son?" she said. "If so, have mercy, Edmond. Oh! Heaven knows with what remorse I yeilded to the will of my ruthless father, and took upon me a second vow of marriage. I *had* a child, I confess it. It was exiled from me, however, as *you* know. Where was my joy in its being—where was my pride, my triumph? There was none of this. Your couch was sought by me with the step of a felon; and every wind that rustled as I climbed the lonely mountain path from Montreville to St. Kinian's Cliff roused fearful dread within my breast. Oh! it was misery—cruel, bitter misery—to live in one eternal lie; yet in spite of all how dear you *were*!"

"I *was*," said Vyvyan. "Is, then, the time past for ever? What is my sin? In what have I offended that you should speak of your affection for me as a thing of the past?"

"I loved you, Edmond," continued the wretched mother, "until another child was born, like a blossom amid the snows! You were far distant from me, seen rarely, an alien, as it were, leaning for life, as it were, upon a stranger's breast. But this thrice-blessed one smiled in my eyes, took being from my bosom, slept in my arms. In his case love asked no concealment; here I could smile and kiss my babe; here I could put on my royalty of woman; and be its guardian and protector. It clung to me for everything—food, health, life. Mother and child were all to one another."

"And among all this wealth of love for him, murmured Vyvyan, "there was nothing—nothing to spare for me?"

Lady Montreville sighed, but continued her story—her pleading to her first-born.

"My boy, my Clarence grew up. As men looked on him they respected his mother the more, so fair and gracious was he, and heir to such high state. Years passed away. They told me that by Nature's death you had in boyhood passed away to Heaven. I wept your fate, and long ere my tears were dried the thought that all danger died also for my Clarence, softened the thought of my bereavement."

Vyvyan glanced at her in agony.

"Oh, mother!" he cried, "can you wish now that I were dead? Can you wish now that I were still what once you wept to believe me?"

Lady Montreville drew herself up by a strong and powerful effort, and gazed full into his eyes.

"Edmond," she said, "I did rejoice when my lip kissed your brow; I rejoiced to give your heart its bride; I would have drained my coffers for her dowry. But can you ask me if I rejoice because one rises suddenly, as it were, from the grave to doom to desolation the life I cradled, reared, and wrapped from every breeze? No!"

Vyvyan seized her hand.

"What would you have me do, mother?" he said, gently.

"Accept the dowry," said Lady Montreville, "and, blessed in the warm young love of Eveline, renounce your mother!"

"Renounce you?" he cried; "no; these lips belie not Nature. Never!"

"Enough," said the countess, bitterly;

"I can resist no more. Go, destroy his life!"

"Why must my life destroy my brother's, madam?"

"Since," pursued Lady Montreville, "his life was meant to soar to power, not grovel to dependence, it does destroy it. I seal his death warrant when I say, 'Down to the dust, usurper; bow the knee and sue for alms to the true Lord of Beaufort.' These words shall not be said; I'll find some nobler. Your rights are clear, and yet the law might long delay them. I forestall the law. Let these lands be thine. Wait not for my death to lord it in my hall. So I shall not say to Clarence, 'Be dependent,' but 'Share poverty with me.' I go to seek him, and at his side I will depart. My Clarence spurns your arms. I wronged you in the past, take now your vengeance!"

Vyvyan's face, as she spoke, was convulsed by agony and despair.

Could this be his mother?

Could this be the one whose angel form had beckoned him on to glory—whose angelic face had in his dreams floated over the midnight sea, and called to him to win honour and renown for *her* sake?

Was this the Guardian Spirit which had watched over him in battle—which had nerved his arm, and made him laugh to scorn the efforts of countless foes?

Oh! how his heart sank within him!

"Merciless! hold and hear me," he cried, in a voice solemn in its very sorrow. "Why speak to *me* of alms and vengeance? A mother truly never cradled my heart, or she had known it better!"

"Edmond!" murmured Lady Montreville, reproachfully.

He waved her back.

"Hush!" he cried. "Call me that name no more—it dies for ever! Nay, do not plead to me. I do not renounce *you*, for to do so would be treason in a child; I call on you, my mother, to renounce *me*. As for these nothings," added the noble sailor, handing her the proofs of his name and birth, "take them. If you dread to see again fond words you are now ashamed of uttering, they are blurred already with my tears—tears of joy that I had found a mother. I did not think of lands and halls, pale countess, I only thought these arms at length would clasp a mother, these ears at length would hear a mother's voice. The papers now are worthless. Keep them; put your arms about me—so. Let me remember in the days to come that I have lived to hear a mother bless me!"

"Oh, Edmond, Edmond!" moaned the unhappy woman, "*you* have conquered. His father's voice, his father's eyes! Look down from Heaven, Bridegroom, and pardon me. I bless your child."

"Oh, Heaven! she has blessed me!" said Vyvyan, rapturously; "the blessing mounts to the skies! Dear mother! how that name thrills through me! Place your hand upon my heart. Now you have felt it beat will you again misjudge me? Ah! what is this? Do you still recoil from me?"

The wretched countess, overcome—torn by conflicting emotions, broke from him again.

"Oh! what have I done," she cried, deliriously; "betrayed, condemned my Clarence!"

"Condemned your Clarence!" exclamed Vyvyan. "By your blessing, no! That blessing was my birthright. I have won *all* I claimed—give him the rest. Silent as sacred be the memory of this atoning hour. Look—evermore," he added as he leaned forward and kissed her brow, "thus then, dear mother, I seal the secret of your first-born! Now only Clarence lives! Heaven guard him well! Now I am dead to you for ever! Farewell—farewell!"

With a wave of the hand, Vyvyan then broke from her, and rushed from the room ere she could make an effort to stay him.

"Hold, hold, Edmond!" she cried, as she hurried to the door, "too generous son! Come back, my Edmond—come back!"

But as she passed out into the shadowy cloisters there was *no* answer, save from the echoes, for Vyvyan's form had disappeared.

The dark night prevented her seeing anything distinctly, but as she hurried to the parapet and leaned over, she fancied she saw a dark figure bounding up the mountain path.

Vainly she wailed out, "Edmond, Edmond!"

Vainly she cried "Come back! Come back!"

The hoarse waves rolled beneath and drowned her moanings; and the wild sea wind caught away the echoes and carried them up amid the lofty crags.

Oh! what bitter tears she shed, as she leaned her bosom upon the cold stonework, and gazed out into the fathomless darkness.

What would she not then have given to have been able to recall the generous noble spirit who had sacrificed himself for her and his brother, as his father had sacrificed himself for her before!

Little did she imagine that at this very moment Clarence was thirsting for his blood, and that even in the event of *his* sword failing, other and more desperate spirits were lying in wait to destroy him!

It was in vain now, of course, to think of following his steps, or sending in pursuit of him, for she knew not which road he had taken; so all that remained to her was to wait in patience, and pray to Heaven to shield him and restore him some day in the far future to his home.

While still leaning over the parapet, with her eyes turned towards the far-off jagged summit of St. Kinian's Cliff, where her second son, even then, was waiting with loosened sword the coming of his brother, she felt a gentle arm passed around her waist.

Turning round, she saw Eveline's pale and tearful face.

"He is gone?" said the young girl, half inquiringly.

"Yes, Eveline, he is gone," answered Lady Montreville, with much emotion; "we have now but to weep for him together."

With these words, which were full of mystery for Eveline, she drew the young girl away with her, and passed into the Castle.

CHAPTER XXX.

ST. KINIAN'S CLIFF BY NIGHT.

THE men who saw Wrecklyffe enter the "Mariners' Rest" that night might well, indeed, be pardoned if they did not recognise in the tattered weather-beaten man the brave roysterer who had told his tale of El Dorados and Spanish treasure long years before.

Who that had seen him sitting on the edge of the table, with cup foaming and uplifted, telling wild stories of the sea, and pointing out to Vyvyan the glorious flag of England as his incentive to glory would have believed in such a return?

Then he was a bold, bad man—a reckless plunderer, a pirate.

Now he was a hang-dog ruffian, seeking men's lives for greed, a famished wreck, a servile assassin.

The gold he had wrested from Spaniards and from English by open plunder he had squandered in wild debauchery.

The men he had feasted had deserted him, and he was compelled to return to his old employer, Sir Grey de Malpas.

He had resolved, however, to have one more venture.

A pirate's life, even its bloodthirsty and desperate phases, had something of pleasure and happiness in it for his wild nature, and, compared with his present poverty and degradation, it seemed to him a paradise.

As may be imagined, Sir Grey de Malpas had promised him a rich reward if he succeeded in fixing the guilt of Vyvyan's murder on Lord Beaufort, and with this the wretched man of guilt had resolved to attempt a new campaign.

A ship he had, such as it was—a small, quickly sailing schooner—which, with the aid of a few desperate men, he had stolen from its moorings, but at present had neither men sufficient to man her, nor riches sufficient to fit her out with provisions and other necessaries.

For these he depended on Sir Grey de Malpas.

For the aid of Sir Grey de Malpas he depended on murder or perjury.

There was a look of intense thought—deadly, racking thought—upon his face as he strode into the tavern where once the boors had admired his stalwart frame and blustering boldness.

The night was far from a fair one, and the inn was crowded; and as this wreck of former daring entered, the throng drew back, half grinning, half afraid. The tavern-keeper whispered to his wife: "Look at that hang-dog!" and the girl, who once had listened—wrapped—to his wondrous tales, trembled as his loud voice called for ale.

"Troublous times these, master," said one of the rustics, bolder than the rest, as the scarred and fierce-looking pirate raised the tankard to his lips and drained it at one draught.

Wrecklyffe glanced quickly round to see if the men were jeering him; and as his cruel eyes fell upon the rustic, the speaker almost regretted his impetuosity.

"Aye, troublous times truly, fair sir," said Wrecklyffe, "that casts a man back so scarred and battered on his native shore that the tavern-keeper who once called him 'Gentle sir,' whispers of 'hang-dogs' to his wife, as he enters; and men, who were wont to talk of him and courage—of stalwart forms and bright swords—now jeer and scoff at his torn clothes. Mind ye! these rags cover the same limbs—this sword is the same—this wrist can parry as it did years long since—this eye is as keen. Nature's unkindness has only spoiled the raiment; it has not touched the *man!*"

As the bold, bad man stood erect before them uttering his boastful words, there was a murmur of admiration and approval; but the fickle crowd—ever ready, moreover, to side with a landlord, in expectancy of future favours—were soon turned in a contrary direction by Boniface, saying:

"Come, come! We want no tavern brawlers here! This is a place to drink and pay the reckoning."

The last words created a slight laugh at Wrecklyffe's expense, for no one expected that such a ragged wretch could afford to pay.

The pirate, with a fearful oath, threw down a piece of gold.

"Curses on you!" he cried, as he loosened his sword, "is there one among you who dares face me singly?"

There was no response, but a great deal of whispering, while the landlord's wife plucked him by the arm and entreated him to be quiet.

"Oh! fear not," added the pirate, laughing, as his eyes fell on the face of the girl, who, years before, had served him with his ale, "I come to do no harm. I come as you say, to drink and pay my reckoning; but I have learned too much in my wild journeyings to suffer gibes and jeers from idle dogs. Some more ale, landlord."

The Boniface who had been considerably mollified by the sight of the gold in the hands of one who had every disposition to spend it, at once served him, saying in a low tone:

"Take no notice. They mean no insult."

"Perhaps not," cried Wrecklyffe, in a loud voice; "but are there any of these blustering braggarts who feel warmed by the chance of a close tussle with the Spanish foe? Rough as I may be, a gallant ship that calls me captain rides not a mile away. In three days I sail hence if my crew is complete, with letters of marque from Her Majesty the Queen of England. I need but ten brave hearts to fill my number. What say you? Fear not, what the wrecked *mariner* receives as an insult the *captain* will forgive."

He paused a moment, but though his auditors listened, and the jeering laughs died away, there was no one there who seemed disposed to accept his offer.

"What!" he cried, "no reply? Know ye not that the West teems with gold—that Spain's proud ships are stalking, unchecked, over the ocean, when their rich treasures might be poured into our laps? Think what stores you can bring home for sweethearts and wives; and cast in your lot with me, who knows the Spanish Isles better than you know your own coast. I can give you till to-morrow to consider, and if any of ye are brave men ye will come."

A faint murmur of applause followed his speech.

But it was very faint.

Not that all there were faint-hearted; but as they gazed at the strange, wild, roughly-accoutred man, they wondered to themselves why—if he knew so well the store-houses of Spanish gold—he had not used some of it to stay the wreck and desolation of his own fortunes.

"Well, good-night, comrades," he added, as he quaffed his ale, and strode towards the door. "To-morrow I will return. Mayhap some of ye may fancy to cast in your lot with me. If so, there's room for ye, and plenty of good cheer; and the Spaniards shall pay the piper."

"A wild and storm-beaten man," muttered the landlord, as he leaned his fat arms upon the bar, and looked after the guest he had courted in days gone by. "His is a sad story, if he be the man I deem him."

A sad heart, too, and an anger-rent one was Wrecklyffe's, as he passed out into the night, and made his way towards the cliff.

"Curses on yon rubicund idiot, and his coward crew of flatterers!" he muttered, as he went. "To call me hang-dog, too! My men would laugh at me and pitch me headlong from my own deck into the seething ocean did they but know I heard the words and bore them. S'death! 'twas a painful task to smother such feelings; but revenge—revenge like mine—must not be baulked by the mean necessities of a tavern brawl. Ha! who comes? As I live, Sir Grey de Malpas!"

It was, indeed, the poor cousin who approached along the road and suddenly confronted him.

"How, now, Wrecklyffe?" he cried; "why are you not at your post?"

The pirate laughed.

"Your thirst for your kinsman's blood misleads you, De Malpas," he said; "it wants yet an hour, a full hour, to the time when Vyvyan meets Lord Beaufort. Remember how little use your bounty is to me if I cannot take immediate advantage of it."

"IN AN INSTANT MORE THE WITHERED BOUGH GAVE WAY."

"True, true; but taverns are not places to steady the hand or sharpen the wits," said Sir Grey, spitefully.

"I have need of strong drink to make me equal in bloodthirstiness to you," returned Wrecklyffe, tauntingly; "however, tell me what brings you here at this hour?"

"To tell you his death is more needed now than ever," said De Malpas, excitedly, not even noticing the taunt of the pirate. "He has seen his mother, and, from what I heard, she is relenting. I left the Castle before the conference was ended, but I believe that ere he quits her presence to join his ship he will be received as the Rightful Heir of Montreville. For my sake and yours, be certain of this night's work."

"Aye, be not afraid," said Wrecklyffe; "my sword is as keen as your haste."

"But whither go you now? Even at this moment Lord Beaufort waits on the cliff to slay his brother, eager to plant the brand of Cain on his own brow, while you——"

"More prudent than in the days of yore," replied Wrecklyffe, "am proceeding to make sure that in the future I may reap the fruits of this night's deadly vengeance. Farewell."

"Farewell. And remember," said Sir Grey, eagerly, "as soon as the deed is done, either by your hand or Beaufort's, hasten to my dwelling and apprise me of it.. Gold shall be yours, if my lady's coffers are drained to their last coin."

"Expect me within the hour," cried the pirate; "time presses now. Farewell."

And wresting himself from the grasp of his enemy, he plunged away amid the darkness, and hurried down the gloomy mountain path which led to the beach.

There had been on this beach for the last hour a scene of dismal gaiety.

The crew of the "Isabella," as the little schooner was called, were collected on the sands round an immense fire, whereon they were cooking various kinds of eatables.

They were a wretched lot.

Collected from among the very scum of the earth, they were attired in all varieties of costume, or rather every variety of rags, and looked, as they sat or walked round about the fire, the very picture of desolate misery.

But they were fine, stalwart fellows, although the stamp of wretchedness and poverty was upon them; and Wrecklyffe knew well that on their desperate hearts he could depend in ill-matched fights.

Growlings of evil import were the order of the night before he approached, for the provisions they had were only obtained by plunder, and not a cupful of any drink was to be obtained to cheer them.

Some of the more blustering among them had begun to inveigh against their captain, when Wrecklyffe's heavy step was heard, and in another moment he strode into their midst.

"You seem cold, my men," he cried cheerily.

"Aye, aye, captain," cried one, "it is cold, and it's thirsty work too, eating without drink."

"That's soon remedied," exclaimed the pirate, with a laugh; "as soon as you have finished your meal, go up to the tavern on the cliffs and spend this money. It's hardly got—wormed out of a poor miser; but it will serve to cheer your spirits till I am ready for you."

With these words, he drew from his pocket a handful of silver, and gave it to the spokesman of the crew.

A cheer—the first cheer that had risen from their lips for a long day, rose into the air.

Wrecklyffe's black heart swelled with a strange kind of pride as he listened.

It reminded him of the days of fierce and reckless battle—of the boarding parties—of the shouts of victory—of treasures won and wild revelry afterwards; but he soon checked it.

"Silence! my men," he cried, waving his hand; "ye know not who may be watching us. In three days we sail hence. Get on board ere morning, however, and make all ready, for I know not what may betide this night. If I come not in three days, sail without me."

He said this half boastingly, yet the words sent a chill to his heart.

Why should he doubt that he could come?

"If danger threatens you, captain,' said one of the crew, "why not take us with you?"

Wrecklyffe laughed.

"Oh, there is no danger," he said; "I did but jest. In three days my ship will be full of men, and of provisions, and we will sail under cover of the night towards those Spanish treasuries that make the

West so pleasant to our English palates. Farewell, my men, for the present—yet stay, here are two pieces of gold, the last I have. Use them for provisions."

With these he waved his hand to them, and passed away quickly along the sands.

After a few minutes he reached a rugged path, which led up towards the summit of St. Kinian's Cliff; and springing up lightly as one to whom joy gives speed, he was not long ere he reached the spot where he had resolved to watch the meeting of the two brothers.

Standing under the shadow of a broken rock, the pirate could see the jagged summit of the cliff, and out at sea the "Dreadnought" at anchor, awaiting its commander.

"The time approaches," he muttered, as he gazed dissatisfied on the quiet scene around; "what can delay him? Ah! I hear a step: who comes first? Ah! It is Lord Beaufort."

It was indeed Clarence Beaufort who approached, and gazed impatiently around him.

"Ah!" he cried, "still not here. The hour has long since passed. I will climb yonder highest peak, and see if I can behold any traces of his coming."

As he spoke, there was a flash across the sea, and a loud report gave the first signal of the "Dreadnought's" departure.

At the same moment Vyvyan, breathless with haste, rushed upwards towards the dark, frowning cliff.

Wrecklyffe's fierce blood boiled as he saw the one who had first insulted him—first struck him down in the presence of his men—and drawing his long knife he was about to rush upon him, regardless of all the injunctions of Sir Grey de Malpas, when Lord Beaufort approached.

"Hot lordling," he muttered, "I had nearly forestalled thee. Patience, patience !"

Then he crept under the shadow of the rock and stole out of sight of the brothers, though in a position where he could see all.

"Good," said Lord Beaufort, as he advanced towards Vyvyan; "from crag to crag he bounds. My doubts belied him; his haste is eager as my own. Welcome, good sir."

"Stay me not, stay me not !" exclaimed the young adventurer, as he pushed Lord Beaufort aside. "You have all. I have but honour, rob me not of that. Unhand me !"

"Unhand you, yes," cried Lord Beaufort, in astonishment, "to take your place and draw."

"You know not what you say," said Vyvyan, impatiently, "let me go."

"Why, you yourself named the place and hour," answered Clarence.

"Ah, yes, for here I thought to clasp—alas," murmured Vyvyan, interrupting himself, "I have no brother now."

"He thought to clasp his Eveline !" exclaimed Beaufort, fiercely. "Death and madness."

"Eveline," said Vyvyan sadly, "you love not Eveline. Be consoled. You have not known affliction—have not stood without the porch of the sweet home of men —you have never leaned upon a reed that has broken and pierced your heart—you have not loved, happy boy; leave love to man and sorrow !"

Lord Beaufort's eyes shot fire.

"Do you presume upon my years ?" he cried. "Dull scoffer ! The brave is a man before his years, the coward, never. Boy if I be, my playmates have been veterans, and my toy has been a sword. If I had accepted a challenge, and on the ground replied to bold defiance with random words, with folded arms, pale lip, and haggard brow, as you have, I'd never live to call myself a man. Thus says the boy, since manhood needs the lesson. Soldier and captain, do not let me strike you !"

Vyvyan moved not.

"Do it," he said, gently, "and tell your mother that I pardoned and pitied you."

"Pitied ! measureless insult."

As the fierce youth spoke, the second signal gun boomed over the waves.

"Again, and still so far," cried Vyvyan. "Out of my path ! insane one ! If there were naught else to stay me your youth and your mother's love would make you sacred to a warrior's arm. Out of my path."

Then, as Lord Beaufort only stood the more defiantly and resolutely before him, he seized his younger brother in his arms, and lifted him aside.

"Thus then, since words do not avail," he added, as he rushed up the cliff. "Oh! England—England, my second mother ! Do not reject me too—I come—I come !"

"Thrust from his pathway!" shouted Clarence, whose every vein seemed on 'fire with the insult. "You shall not escape me. Stand or die!"

On the edge of the cliff, hanging over a dark and seemingly fathomless abyss, was an old tree, shattered and withered by the lightning.

Vyvyan, who, as we know, had cast aside his sword, was helpless now, at the mercy of his brother, and rushing to this, he clung to a bough which projected far over the gloomy gulf of darkness.

"Forbear, forbear," he cried, as Lord Beaufort raised his sword.

"Your blood be upon your own head," shouted the rash boy.

And in an instant his flashing blade had descended.

Then there was a loud booming sound over the waves—the third signal-gun of the "Dreadnought"—and at the same moment a crackling, jarring noise showed that Vyvyan's frail support had given way.

One instant more and the withered bough snapped asunder, and the young Captain of the "Dreadnought" disappeared down the dark precipice.

"Good, good," said Wrecklyffe, as he crept from his hiding-place and descended the rocks; "if the deed needs completion, my steel shall do it!"

There were a few moments of undisturbed stillness.

Then down below the wild rocks two dark forms struggled in the fitful moonlight—a long and desperate struggle.

Then one of them sank lifeless on the beach, muttering strange words, while the other, after glancing above and around him, strode away hastily, and as if in dread or in anger, from the precincts of St. Kinian's Cliff.

CHAPTER XXXI.

THE TAKING OF CADIZ—THE UNKNOWN KNIGHT.

THE morning sun glinted down merrily upon the city of Cadiz on the memorable morning of the 23rd of June, 1596.

Brightly it fell upon the white pavement of the narrow streets; the broad squares; the Moorish houses, with their inner courtyards; the cupolas and minarets of the churches; the high battlemented walls and wide tree-planted promenades which stretched between them and the sea.

But the ruddy gleams fell also upon other things, which told a far different story to this seeming peacefulness.

It fell upon the swords and lances, and glistening armour of men hurrying from all parts to defend the ramparts by the sea.

Swarthy, dark-eyed, dark-haired fellows they were—stalwart and brave—the rivals of the North, the conquerors of the West, the cream of the soldiery of Andalusia.

Bells were ringing; quiet citizens and their families were escaping by the one land-gate; barricades were being thrown up in the seaward avenues; drums were beating; soldiers hurrying all ways, officers careering madly to and fro on horseback, issuing orders in voices hoarse with bawling.

Everything was excitement, alarm, and eager haste, for the earl of Essex and the English fleet had entered the harbour, and demanded the instant surrender of the town.

The alarm was only felt by the populace, and indeed only by that portion of the populace whose god was gain.

The soldiery, used to easy conquests, had no fear of defeat.

The men who had fitted out the Armada were not alarmed at the appearance of a force which they deemed insignificant.

The conquerors of the West laughed at the North, and were only eager to measure swords with those who seemed now to be their natural foes.

To the demand of Essex, an insolent answer was returned ; and as soon as the English vessels had passed by the sunken rocks, the battle commenced.

There were but few preparations necessary on board of the English fleet.

During the night no one had been idle, and the early dawn saw every man at his post and eager for action.

Both Lord Howard of Effingham and the Earl of Essex were resolved to stake their honour and the issue of the battle upon a sudden attack.

The refusal to surrender was only what they had anticipated ; and within a few minutes, as it were, England gave its answer !

This answer was a terrific broadside from the largest vessels, whose echoing thunders were the death-knell of the fair city.

I shall not here pause to describe the taking of Cadiz.

It would take chapters to tell of the heroic actions of that day ; how, in defiance of the fire from the forts and battlements, and fifteen large men-of-war, the English forced their way into the innermost harbour, and, after a fierce fight of six hours, took three of the largest ships and burnt and plundered fifty more.

When darkness fell, Essex landed part of his land forces, and waited for the dawn.

The Spaniards still held out.

Though amazed, and terrified as well, by the unexpected and resplendent successes of the English, they believed in the utter inaccessibility of their fine ramparts, and eagerly waited for morning, to pour down upon their foes—crowded in a small space—the whole force of their heavy guns.

But the result proved their mistake.

The English cared nothing for stone walls—they had laughed at them before, and they laughed at them now.

Rushing up in dense bodies, they cut down the defenders like grass, and forced their way upon the broad stone battlements.

It was some hours after dawn that the English had fought their way into the town, and were struggling bravely through the narrow streets.

Like all armies in those days, their aim now was plunder.

But there were those also fighting in the blood-stained avenues who had higher aims than this—who were cutting their way through all opposition to seize and haul down the Spanish flag which waved from the summit of St. Michael.

It was in the street of San Salvador that this terrific struggle took place.

This street was somewhat wider than the others ; and, headed by a brave leader, Don Alfonso de Spinoza, the Spaniards, seeing the design of the English upon their flag, made a bold and resolute stand.

It was a savage, determined, hand-to-hand encounter.

There was no thought, now, of plunder, or anything but the victory of the moment.

Men grappled each other in deadly grips, forced each other upon the pavements, stabbed one another in cold blood, and when weapons fell from their eager hands they throttled one another in the gutters.

In the midst of the combatants were to be seen three figures, which excited general attention even in the heat of the contest.

The one was the fine manly form of the Earl of Essex, the second Don Alphonso, the leader of the Spanish troops.

The third was an unknown knight, clad in resplendent armour, who fought always by the side of Essex.

Tall, finely proportioned, and with an arm of iron, he was the admired of all, yet unknown by all.

His connection with the army of Lord Essex was a strange one.

On the eve of the departure of his expedition, when yet the beach was dotted with white tents, the outposts brought in a man faint, wounded, and covered with terrible scars.

From what could still be seen of him, he seemed a young and handsome man of noble mien, and Essex spoke to him in gentle pity.

" You seem a soldier," he said ; " how came you in this plight ?"

The stranger put one hand over his face, while with the other he made a motion as if to put from him the recollection of some terrible scene.

"Ask me not," he said.   "I am a soldier,

yet I have no sword. Perhaps death, which has been offered to me so many times, would have been better than my useless life. Your soldiers, Lord of Essex, found me fainting and dying by the roadside; they knew me not, but pitying me as man pities man, they succoured me and brought me to you."

" What is your name ?" asked Essex.

The stranger glanced around him.

Curious eyes were bent on him.

" Frank-hearted earl," he said, " I will to your private ear alone disclose my story. Think it no insult, gentlemen," he added to those who stood around him, " there are stories which, repeated, make the heart bleed, and even make soldiers weep; and such a sight you would not *wish* to see."

The manner in which these words were spoken at once drew sympathy from all.

Essex at once dismissed his officers, and from the stranger's lips heard the story.

What this story was we need not here explain.

Suffice it to say that from that hour Essex was the unknown's friend and companion, though even to the earl he had not revealed his name.

Clad in a suit of resplendent armour, he was the admired of all: and when at the siege of Cadiz he led the storming parties, and cut down like wheat the men who swarmed on Essex, those who might have felt jealous cast aside the feeling and loved the man who risked life to preserve his leader.

It was in the street of San Salvador, however, that the scene occurred which endeared him ever to the heart of Essex.

Don Alphonso de Spinoza, as I have said, the captain of the Spaniards, seeing his men giving way threw himself upon the English leader, and endeavoured, by efforts of personal bravery, to stem the tide of the battle.

He was a good swordsman, but he found his match in Lord Essex.

The English nobleman was well known as a master in the art of swordsmanship, and a brilliant contest was the result—a contest at which even the surrounding combatants gazed with interest, and in which no one interfered.

At length, however, a crisis came.

The iron wrist of the earl began to tell on his dauntless foe.

Brave though he was, Don Alfonso could not withstand the brilliant attacks of his adversary, and began slowly to give way through sheer exhaustion.

Suddenly his foot slipped in the blood which everywhere covered the pavement, and, drawing his sword back, Essex ran it swiftly and surely through the chest of his foe.

While the Spaniard was in the act of falling back, with a yell of agony, and the earl's sword still clung in his body, Don Josè de Calvados, the second in command, leaped towards Essex, who had slipped upon the pavement, and for the moment was at his mercy.

But he was not quick enough.

Swifter eyes had seen his movements, and ere he could reach Essex, and accomplish his fell purpose, the unknown knight was upon him.

Grasping the Spaniard by the throat, he contrived, in spite of his desperate struggles, to run his sword through his body, just as nearly a dozen ruffians set upon him at once.

The Spaniards were now nearly discomfited, but they resolved to be revenged upon the two men whom they regarded as the origin of their misfortune.

These were the Earl of Essex and the mail-clad knight who had saved his life, and round these they gathered with savage howls of revenge.

While this was proceeding, another strange scene was taking place.

A youthful figure, which, from its rounded proportions, seemed to belie the male dress, that draped the elegantly-moulded limbs, was bending over the prostrate form of the young and brave Don Josè de Calvados.

Eagerly it sought a sign of life in the insensible form; and ever and anon it glanced towards the struggling foemen, who were striving in their last efforts.

Suddenly, as all hope of reviving the inanimate body faded away, the mysterious mourner rose and waited.

Then, as the English at length prevailed, and the Spaniards gave way before them, it leaned forward, so as to be heard clearly by the mail-clad knight.

" We shall meet again, Sir Knight !" it cried, " and there will be vengeance then for Don Josè de Calvados !"

The knight caught just a faint glimpse of a lovely face, white with anger ; two bright eyes, moist with sorrow, and a sylph-like, exquisite figure.

Then it sprang away, and was lost amid the shadows of a narrow avenue.

There was little more resistance now at this point.

The Spaniards, having lost their leader, began to fight wildly, and at length fled in disorder, while the Eng-lish pursued them vigorously, and the much-coveted flag was soon in their possession.

Night closed over a conquered city—over weeping wives, and mothers, and sweethearts; over sorrowing fathers and mothers.

But England's honour was avenged, and Spain's pride was humbled in the dust!

CHAPTER XXXII.

THE SECRET MISSION—THE RENEGADE—THE COMBAT IN THE STREET.

THAT evening set in dark and dreary.

The people of Cadiz had a day of terrible slaughter to dream of.

Houses burning in all quarters of the city showed ghastly heaps of mutilated corpses piled in the streets, and groans every here and there showed that the wounded and dying had in some cases become entangled with those whose dissolution was a matter of certainty.

The English soldiers, to whom, according to the brutal laws of those days, the city was given up, were running riot everywhere, and the shrieks of women, the loud imprecations of men, mingled every now and then with loud and boisterous laughter, showed how thoroughly they were giving way to the fearful license allowed them.

In the darker portions of the town, strange figures flitted hither and thither.

Men hurried to and fro with little boxes, carrying away their treasures to places of security.

Women hugging their babes to their breasts slunk along in the shadows of the ruined city, and fled away from the populous places to the dismal and tree-shadowed suburbs.

Young girls escaping from the hands of drunken brutes, fled with their lovers, whose stern faces and firmly clasped knives showed their desperate resolves.

Men and women, looking at the flames which destroyed their homes and took from them their means of subsistence, loudly cursed the invaders, never thinking how little mercy would have been shown to English homes had the Spaniards once landed on the shores of Albion.

It was in a wide square that the Earl of Essex was encamped; a square at some distance from the sea-ramparts; and it was here that for the first time he was enabled to thank the brave man who had saved his life.

"Will you not tell me your name, stranger?" he said, as he grasped the knight's hand! "you have told me your sorrowful story, why not give me a title by which to know you?"

A struggle took place for a few moments in the breast of the unknown.

Then he said—

"Mine is a name which you have heard nought of. I have fought for my country truly, but in the records of its battles mine is not enrolled. My name, most noble earl, is Vyvyan."

Essex started as Vyvyan raised the vizor of his helmet and showed his bronzed and manly face.

"Vyvyan!—captain of the "Dreadnought!'" he exclaimed. "I know you well, not only by repute, but by personal knowledge. I was in London when you were at court and received from the hands of Queen Elizabeth a diamond cross. But this is strange indeed. I heard from Faulkner that you were dead. He has

"ERE HE COULD REACH ESSEX, THE UNKNOWN KNIGHT WAS UPON HIM."

taken the command, he tells me, by your last express desire, and is now on England's coasts watching with others the doings of the Spaniards. So you were saved?"

"Alas! yes, to weary out a long and thankless life. Only in such scenes as these—in danger and in trial—can I forget the miserable past. But to our duties. I heard you but now, my lord, speak of a service that I could render you."

"In truth your services to me," said Essex, "scarcely leave me room to ask for more. I need a reinforcement. They tell me that even now the people of Cadiz are not subdued in spirit, and that to-morrow's dawn may see a renewal of the fight. I need some brave spirit to go secretly to Sir Walter Raleigh, or to Lord Howard of Effingham, to ask him to send, under cover of the night, a body of his best men. I wish this done privately that the Spaniards may not know when morning comes that my force has been increased."

"You desire a rising then?" said Vyvyan, in some surprise.

"Yes," said Essex; "but I mean no massacre. I merely mean to wrest from the Spaniards an immense ransom for their lives."

"Good," said Vyvyan. "You need a secret messenger. _I_ will go."

"I will not gainsay you," returned Essex. "To no one better could I entrust such mission. In a few moments my letter shall be ready."

He sat down at his rough table—a battered bench taken from a Spanish wine-shop—and wrote a few hurried words to Raleigh.

Then he delivered the note to Vyvyan.

"When you return," he said, "hasten to me here. Wait not for the disembarkation of the men, but hurry back at once with Raleigh's answer."

Then, with a grasp of the hand, he dismissed the young adventurer.

With one glance around him, to see if the coast was clear, set off towards the sea-ramparts.

He did not, however, take a direct route, imagining rightly enough that spies would be lurking in the shadows of the square to watch the movements of the daring enemy who had so suddenly and so unex-pectedly subjugated their fair city and humbled their pride.

Remembering a narrow and somewhat intricate route which he had noticed in the morning, he chose this in preference to the more open ways, and started quickly, loosening his sword in its scabbard, and keeping his eyes on the alert.

From the moment he started, however, he had a vague feeling that all was not right, for—whether fancifully or not he knew not—the shadows seemed to detach themselves from one another, gather in clusters, and then sneak along beside him.

Vyvyan, when he had accepted the task at the hands of the Earl of Essex, expected naturally that it would be one of danger and difficulty, but he would certainly have rather met his foes face to face than do battle with unreal forms whose presence he could feel, as it were, but whose footsteps he could not hear.

On he went more quickly, however, until at last the noise of the English encampment died away and only the stealthy steps of hurrying figures could be heard as in the plague-stricken city of London nearly a hundred years after.

It was as he gained the corner of a street—more than usually dark and gloomy it was at this point—that his enemies fell upon him.

There was a rush of feet, a shadow between him and the half-obscured sky, and then four bright blades flashed out upon him.

"Surrender!" cried a voice in English.

Vyvyan, who had instantly drawn his sword, uttered an exclamation of surprise.

"Ah!" he said; "you are English. What want you with me?"

"I _am_ English," returned the stranger; "and your enemy. Surrender!"

"I know you not, traitor!" cried the young adventurer; "but I need nothing more to tell me that you are a coward. Men, who, like me, have fought their way to manhood, surrender not to the first renegade dog that crosses their path. Let me pass."

"Die then, insane fool!" shouted the other, in a tone of fury.

As he spoke the four attacked him at once with eager haste.

Vyvyan had before this been in many such encounters, and knew well how to sustain himself under such circumstances.

Planting his back against the wall, he parried the wild attacks of his furious foemen, and kept them completely at bay, while dark spots on the white pavement proved that every now and then his lunges took deadly effect.

Led on by the English renegade, however, the Spaniards, though wounded, sustained their courage, and with cries and wild gesticulations, threw themselves upon him.

It was their haste and his coolness that so prolonged the fight; and another circumstance, in more than one case, saved the Spaniards' lives.

All his efforts were directed against the traitor.

This fellow, no matter who he might turn out to be, was a being unworthy to live.

The others might be inspired by national feeling, and so might be forgiven for all; while a renegade, fighting side by side with the enemies of his country, was unfit for existence.

Presently he saw his opportunity.

His enemies were getting presumptuous, and losing their presence of mind.

Making a sudden feint he dashed forward, and in an instant, ere his adversary could parry his stroke, his sword had passed, with a plunge and a hiss, through the body of the English traitor.

A gasping cry escaped from the villain's lips, and he fell back on the pavement just where a patch of ghostly moonlight struggled through the surrounding shadows.

There, as he lay with his hat off, Vyvyan recognised him.

It was one of his old enemies, Donald, the lieutenant of the " Black Vulture," the man who, when Wrecklyffe was struck down by Vyvyan, on his own deck, cast the young adventurer adrift on the waste of waters.

Our hero, however, had no time for speculation as to how one of his inveterate foes had tracked him over the sea to Cadiz.

The English renegade had no sooner fallen than the Spaniards again rushed to the attack, when suddenly, as Vyvyan was drawing back for a stroke, he felt his arms seized from behind, and himself dragged forcibly back.

Then, as he struggled vainly to free himself, a heavy blow was struck upon the back of his head, which, in spite of the steel casque, rendered him dizzy, and he reeled back into the arms of his unknown captors.

Then his senses left him, and he knew no more.

CHAPTER XXXIII.

THE BLACK SENTINEL—VENGEANCE FOR DON JOSE DE CALVADOS!

WHEN Vyvyan recovered his senses, he was in an elegantly furnished apartment, where, he knew not.

It had all the appearance of being a chamber in some large and palatial residence, for its dimensions were far beyond those of ordinary sized chambers, and its loftiness and elegance betokened a luxury which spoke of it as the home of some Spanish grandee.

He was so much taken up by gazing at the unwonted scene around him, that he did not at first observe a human form reclining on a couch near the window.

From where he was lying he could only see the feet and legs, which evidently belonged to a man of no ordinary size.

Resolved to see who was his companion, Vyvyan rose, and with a quick step approached the stranger, whose head was concealed by the curtains which fell across a deeply-set window.

On hearing his footstep, the man drew aside the curtain, and Vyvyan beheld the black and unpleasant countenance of a negro, who held in his hand a bright scimitar.

The black sprang up at once as Vyvyan

stood before him, and moving from the recess, retired hastily to the other end of the room, where he disappeared as if by magic.

Vyvyan now glanced down from the window upon the scene below, and recognized at once the impossibility of escape, if the apartment he at present occupied was to be his prison.

He was at the summit of a high building, whence he could see the harbour with the English fleet at anchor, and the scattered remnants of the Spanish vessels, some lying disabled, some hopeless wrecks, some half sunken, while great spars and odd pieces of timber with strange entanglements of cords, proclaimed the fate of the rest.

And he could look down too, upon the town of Cadiz, and see the English camp now swarming with life, and the people of Cadiz mustering in every direction for a renewed struggle, while the lowering of boats from the English ships and the disembarkation of men on the beach showed that some more fortunate messenger had carried the commands of Essex to Lord Howard of Effingham.

While he was gazing down at the scene before him, and, with a beating heart, listening to the hiss and hum that preceded more deadly sounds, he was startled by the opening of a door behind him; and, turning round, he beheld a lady approaching him.

She was about four and twenty years of age, and very beautiful, both in face and form.

She was rather above the middle height, with a plump, rounded figure, revealed by her tight-fitting dress and low corsage.

But it was not her form that rivetted Vyvyan's attention.

It was her face.

He knew it well again.

It was the face which he had seen the moment after his sword had plunged through the heart of Don José de Calvados.

" You know me again, senor ?" she said.

" I do, senora—that is, your face seems to me that of one whom I saw in male costume yesterday, in the street of San Salvador."

" The same, senor," replied the lady, whose manner and voice were wonderfully calm, though her eyes burned fiercely. " You remember, perhaps, my words ?"

" I do, senora."

" I was the wife," she continued, " now, alas ! the widow of Don José de Calvados. I have been but four months his bride, and when your insolent troops landed on our shores, I swore never to leave his side even in battle. I fought with him and kept my vow. He died in my arms. He lies in the adjoining chamber. I, his widow, live but to avenge him !"

Vyvyan bowed.

" I admire your love for your husband," he said ; " but, pray, senora, what punishment do you consider it just to inflict upon a soldier who has but done his duty to his country, and whose only fault is his success ? Don José would have done the same for me had he been able."

The Senora Calvados pressed her hand tightly over her bosom.

" It is enough, senor—you have killed him."

" In fair and open fight," said Vyvyan. " If you have brothers, or he has brothers whom it would please you to see me meet in deadly combat, I am willing to encounter them."

" No, no," cried the lady, interrupting him ; " it is no friend of mine whom you will have to fight, it is myself. See !" she cried, as she advanced, and pointed down towards the bustling streets of the city, " Cadiz has awakened from its lethargy. This day will see your legions hurled from our shores, and gasping in death agonies in the whirlpools of our bay ; this day will see the humiliation and disgrace of your countrymen, and here, unable to aid them, unable to tell them of their fearful error, you shall look on and see their doom. Then, when you have seen the departure of the ships in shame, you shall be taken to the lowest dungeon of my castle, and there, in silent misery, in useless hopes, in vain regrets, you shall share with me the agonies of my widowhood. Think you that I would be satisfied by seeing you die the death of a brave man ? No ; unseen by mortal eye, in utter darkness, you shall pine out long days of misery !"

" By Heavens !" cried Vyvyan, involuntarily laying his hand upon his sword.

A smile of bitter scorn and derision wreathed itself over the lips of the Senora Calvados.

" What !" she cried, " an English captain draw his sword upon a woman ! 'Tis useless, senor. If you have forgotten your knighthood, I have those here who are sworn to defend my life and honour. At one word from me a host of armed retainers—separated from us now only by yonder door—will enter and dispatch you. You are in my power. Be content!"

"Senora," replied Vyvyan, bowing, "my action was involuntary, and only drawn from me from your cruel and bitter words. I am content. I am your prisoner, and you will see with what fortitude and resolution an Englishman can bear privations and misfortunes."

As he spoke, he turned proudly from her and gazed out of the window at the city beneath, where already the fighting had commenced.

The senora gazed with unutterable anger at the handsome English captain as he stood resolutely and defiantly before her.

"Oh !" she muttered, "if he would but sue for mercy ! What would I not give to see him a suppliant at my feet ! But these English are indomitable in their resolution, and as cold as ice."

It was a strange feeling which now agitated her breast.

She almost admired the man whom she had sworn to sacrifice to revenge.

Nevertheless she was resolved to carry out her fell design.

"Adieu. senor," she said, sneeringly, as she moved towards the door.

Vyvyan merely inclined his head, and continued his observation of the town below.

The lady, white as death, and with compressed and angry lips, glanced once more upon him, and then quitted the room.

All day long Vyvyan was left alone except when the black servant entered with provisions.

He saw the surges of battle rising; he saw the fierce contests in the streets; he saw the Spaniards madly striving against the determined hosts led on by the dauntless Essex and the noble Raleigh; he saw the tide of conflict turn, and the Spanish combatants fly, and the wreathing smoke ascend from their burning homes.

And as he gazed, how he longed to be there—how he longed to prove to Essex that he had not wilfully failed in his mission !

As night drew on again, and the cries from the city grew fainter, great was his surprise that the Senora Calvados did not make her appearance.

He had fully expected to see her enter the room full of fury at the renewed defeat of her countrymen. But he saw nothing of her.

Very late in the evening, however, there was a loud tramp outside the door, and about a dozen armed men entered.

"This way," said their leader in Spanish.

Resistance was useless.

Against a dozen what could he expect—what could be the result but shameful defeat.

With a haughty bow, therefore, Vyvyan advanced into their midst, and they immediately began the descent of deep and narrow staircases.

At the basement they stopped a moment, unlocked an iron door, and then again descended into a passage whose chill air and earthly smell told that it was subterranean.

Here they again unlocked a door, and pushing him into a chamber which was enveloped in utter gloom, left him to himself.

He was not alone, however.

Scarcely had he entered when a low and dismal groan proclaimed the presence of some wretched fellow-prisoner.

CHAPTER XXXIV

THE FAIR CAPTIVE.

THE sound which greeted Vyvyan's ears when his captors departed and left him in the dismal vault, was a groan as of utter despair, coming as it were from one who had been nursing a strong hope, and had been suddenly disappointed.

Whether from man or woman he could not determine, neither could he at first tell from whence the sound proceeded.

He listened attentively.

In a few moments the person, whoever it was, spoke again in Spanish.

"Who is there; have I an unfortunate fellow prisoner?"

The voice was low and tremulous, like that of one in terrible sorrow or pain.

"Yes," replied Vyvyan, as he groped his way towards the spot whence the melancholy sounds proceeded, "yes, I *am* a prisoner."

As he was speaking he paused, for he had suddenly reached the corner of the little dungeon, and almost fallen over some person who was sitting or crouching in the corner.

His hand, as he did so, came in contact with the prisoner's head, and he felt, by the long hair, that it was a woman who was thus immured with him.

"Why are you here?" he asked, in a gentle voice, as he sat down by her side; "surely you are not the victim of the vengeful spirit of the Senora Calvados?"

"Alas! yes," returned the fair captive. "I *am* the victim of her false anger."

"Tell me your story," said Vyvyan, "it will help to pass the monotonous hours of our captivity."

"Strange that she should have given me a companion," said the lady, who was evidently young; "but she takes wild and inconceivable fits. It was the blind madness of insensate jealousy that has doomed me to this horrid captivity."

"Jealousy!" murmured Vyvyan, whose mind at once reverted to Clarence and Eveline, "it is the greatest curse mankind is plagued with. But I am interrupting you—proceed."

"I am the cousin of Senora Calvados," said the lady, "and we were brought up together from childhood like sisters.

"She always professed great love for me, but from the earliest period to which my memory carries me back, she was jealous of me.

"People said that I was more beautiful than she, and she used to look fierce and angry when they praised me; never more so than when her lover Don Josè de Calvados spoke of me in terms of admiration.

"Poor foolish girl, I knew not her wicked and revengeful temper, or I should not have suffered what I did; but thinking it no harm, and having one whom I dearly loved, I permitted him to treat me like a sister, to kiss me, and caress me, and at length I trusted him with—a secret.

"From this dates my unhappiness.

"The one whom I loved—though a friend of Don Josè's—was disliked, even hated, by my parents, and it was against their express wishes that I kept up a communication with him.

"I feared to tell Julia—that is the Senora's name—for there had gradually sprung up a coolness between us, and I dreaded least she should betray me.

"So things went on. I can see now how foolishly I acted, and how I was feeding the flame of her jealousy.

"Had she known that I was betrothed to another, I should at once have been relieved from all her savage wrath, but I feared her so greatly, suspected her so much, that I could not bring myself to make the revelation.

"At length, one evening, just as I was leaving the drawing-room, I met Don Josè.

"He was much agitated, and said in a whisper—

"'Meet me, Inez, in the beech avenue

at nine. I have news of great importance for you.'

"You may suppose (guessing as I did that the news affected my lover, Don Alfonso de Cabrida) that I waited eagerly for the hour of nine to arrive.

"I was in the avenue even before the time appointed, and wondering and pondering upon my lover's long absence and its probable cause. I started with fear almost when a hand was laid upon my shoulder.

"'Do not be alarmed, Inez,' said the voice of Don Josè, 'it is I.'

"'Are you sure we are not watched?' I asked, knowing and fearing Julia's jealous temper.

"'Oh, yes,' he said, 'there is no fear. But I will not stay long. I have bad news for you, Inez, and you must nerve yourself to bear it.'

"A chill invaded my heart.

"What could he mean! Was he about to tell me that my Alfonso was dead?

"'Oh, yes, yes,' I said, clinging to his arm, looking up into his face, 'yes, yes, I can nerve myself to bear anything but suspense. Tell me is he dead?'

"'No,' replied Don Josè, 'no, he is not dead; but he is in danger. He has been arrested for high treason, and is now in prison.'

"I knew well how terrible was such a doom, and I guessed at once that this was the work of those who desired to separate him from me.

"I knew well that when once the clanging gates of the state prison closed behind a person accused of such a crime, Heaven only knew when he would be re-released.

"This climax to my misery completely overcame me; the earth seemed to swim round with me; and had not the strong arms of Don Josè caught me round the waist, I should have fallen to the earth.

"'Poor child!' he said, kissing my cold brow, as he bent over me; 'and yet I could not, in justice to Don Alfonso, withhold the news from her.'

"It was some minutes before I recovered my senses, and all during that time I lay in his arms, with his kind voice murmuring cheering words in my ear.

"When I had quite recovered, I entreated him to give me the means of visiting my friend, but he begged of me to be prudent, and to bear a little delay.

"'Alfonso's last words to me were,' he said, 'Bid Inez, if she loves me, to be prudent. Let her not confess our love to any one. Make her promise this, by our mutual affection; for it is my passion for her which has given rise to this false accusation of treason.'

"'Can I not even send to him a message?' I asked, as I wept bitterly.

"'Yes. I shall see him. I will cheer his heart, by telling him how you love him, and how, for his sake, you will keep secret the passion for which you are now both suffering. I had better depart now, dear Inez, for I may be watched.'

"He gave me one more brotherly kiss, and then we parted.

"I did not return to the house at once with him, for I wished to be alone, and, besides, the cool breeze was pleasant as it fanned my heated brow.

"Don Josè had scarcely disappeared, however, before I had to suffer a second terror.

"A figure, clothed in white—a figure, with black hair, and a face, looking ghastly in consequence, approached me, and seized my arm.

"It was my cousin Julia!

"'Wretched girl!' she cried; 'I have seen all.'

"'Great Heavens!' I answered, thinking only of my lover and the promise his last message had exacted from me; 'did you, then, hear Don Josè's words?'

"She misunderstood me. To her my manner seemed simply an acknowledgment that Don Jose had been breathing in my ear treacherous words of love, and she tightened her grasp upon my wrist, as she whispered,

"'Beware, Inez. I heeded not his words. I saw enough. I saw you pressed to his heart. I saw his kisses. It is enough for you to have met him here alone. Now take my warning, and be guided by it. In six weeks I become the bride of Don Josè. I blame him not. He has been beguiled by your soft speeches, and your pretended childishness. Now, if I discover that in word or deed you encourage his love after I am his wife, your doom shall be a terrible one. You shall pine and languish in utter darkness for ever!'

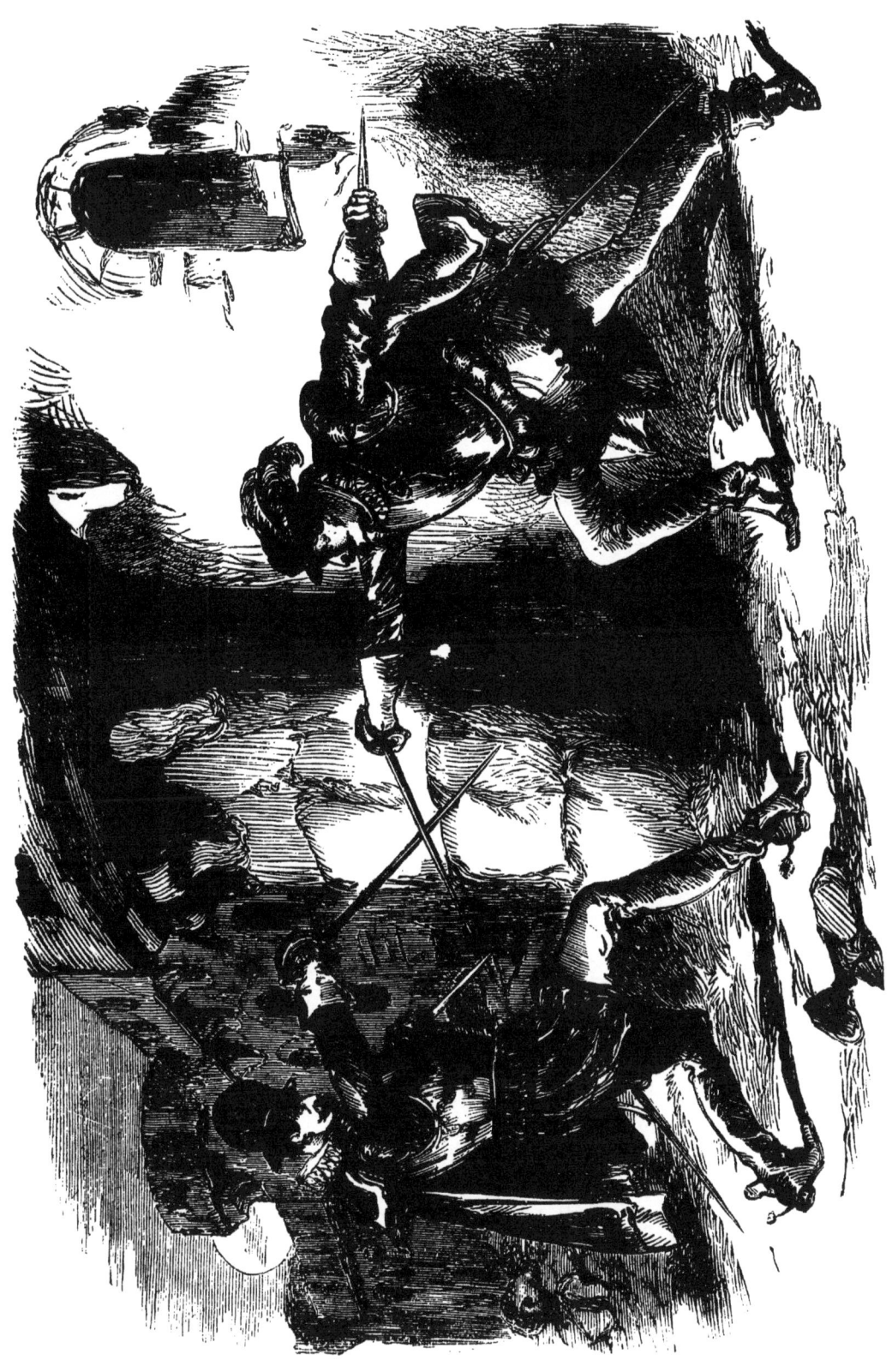

"THE NEXT MOMENT THEY WERE ENGAGED IN DEADLY STRIFE."

"I was so utterly taken aback by the passionate vehemence of my cousin, that during denunciation I could not at first speak to her, or plead my cause.

"But when I recovered the use of my tongue, I implored her to cast from her mind all idea that I loved Don Josè. I swore I had another lover who was a friend of his, and that for him Don Josè had spoken. It was all in vain, however. I could not—I dared not give his name, and she left me, bitterly reproaching me, and scoffing at what she called my weak attempt at concealment.

"Six weeks passed.

"During this time I saw Don Josè once: only once, when he brought me a message from my unfortunate Alfonso; but, after this, all access to the prisoner was denied by the authorities, and I could only live on and hope.

"I told Don Josè of Julia's unfounded suspicions, and from that time I avoided him.

"I was not even present at the marriage.

"About three months after, however, I received a letter from Don Josè, requesting me to meet him in the square of St. Michael, as he wished to speak to me of important matters in connection with Alfonso.

"As you may imagine, I did not pause to think of danger, or of my cousin's jealousy.

"During all this weary time I had heard nothing of Alfonzo, and my heart leaped at the bare idea of hearing a message from him. I was at the appointed place, therefore, exactly at the hour named; and I met Don Josè in a dark corner of the square.

"He told me, briefly, what made my bosom swell with joy.

"Alfonso had arranged everything satisfactorily for an escape from prison!

"In three nights I was to meet him at that same spot, at the same hour, and we were to fly from Spain together.

"Don Josè bade me be prepared; and, having kissed my brow, left me.

"I, too was hurrying away, when my evil genius was once more upon me. Julia had suspected her husband, for whom her love was a madness, and had followed him.

"'Traitress!' she hissed, 'you have, then, dared to deceive me. Behold your doom.'

"As she spoke, four men rushed from the dark corner and seized me.

"I had no time to cry aloud, for a handkerchief saturated in some powerful essence was pressed over my nostrils, and I lost my senses immediately.

"When I recovered I was here. I have been here ever since."

The young girl stopped.

"And has not your cousin been to see you?" asked Vyvyan, when he heard the conclusion of this strange story.

"Not once," said Inez, "Neither will she listen to any message I send. Here have I been in utter darkness since that fatal night, and Alfonso—oh, heavens! I tremble when I think of him—he either thinks me faithless, or he has waited and searched for me in this city where every step he takes is fraught with danger to him."

And, as she spoke, she bent her head and wept bitterly.

Vyvyan passed his arm round her, and drew her weary head upon his shoulder.

"Poor girl," he said gently. "We will see if escape is not possible."

As he spoke the door opened and a man entered with a lamp.

CHAPTER XXXV.

THE PROPOSAL OF A TRAITRESS.

VYVYAN, as he sprang up, was surprised to see in the hands of the rough-looking Spaniard a letter and also materials for writing.

"Here," said the man, "is a letter from the Senora Calvados. Here is paper and ink with which to send her a reply. Yonder is a bench whereon you can write.

He pointed to a stone seat in the corner of the room, placed the papers and the lamp upon it, and then left the two captives once more alone.

Eagerly Vyvyan opened the letter.

He was totally unprepared for the artfulness displayed—the treacherous appeals to his gallantry—and, at the same time, the reliance placed upon his easy yielding to dishonour.

It ran thus—

"Senor,—I write to you to let you know the only terms upon which I can be brought to release you from what will be otherwise a living tomb both for you and the lady who is confined in the same cell as yourself. Don José being dead, I have no wish to remain longer in Cadiz, and I shall, therefore, in three days quit this house. I give you this time to consider the terms I propose below. At the end of the three days, if you refuse to accede to them, I shall leave you to die. But remember that you are not alone. I appeal to your gallantry, your humanity, as well as your love of life. The lady (whose story you, doubtless, know by this time) is dependent upon you for life. If you accede to this offer of mine, you not only save yourself but her also; for if you consent to my terms, I will release her too. Don José being dead, I no longer fear her. And for you—young, brave, handsome— *you* surely have some one in England who thinks of you—who prays for you—who awaits eagerly your return—in a word, one who *loves* you! Oh, think of her— think of her sorrow if you never return; think of your own agony, loving her, yet buried in this living sepulchre!"

Vyvyan ceased reading.

Tears welled up into his manly eyes as he strode to and fro, crushing the letter in his hand.

"Oh, Eveline!" he murmured, "why should she, not knowing thee—not knowing thy beauty and thy worth, appeal to me through you? And her terms come last. What can they be? What evil does she require of me that she thus fears, as it were, to openly declare it?"

He stopped after a moment by the lamp and glanced once more at the letter.

"And now," it went on, "now for the terms. You know how I love my country. Second only was it to my husband; now it stands alone. Give me the password to the British camp; let me rid Cadiz of her invaders, and Donna Julia de Calvados will die happy and rejoin in the realms of bliss the one for whom alone she lived."

"Mad traitress!" cried Vyvyan, as he tore the letter into a hundred fragments; " and was it for this she pleaded through my sacred love? Betray my country, and for her!"

Up to this moment his fellow captive had not spoken.

She now said gently, seeing his grief and passion—

"What says my cousin?"

Vyvyan started.

He had for a moment forgotten that he had a companion in misfortune.

The remembrance now rushed painfully to his mind that the arch-traitress had included in the doom this helpless creature —had made her life dependant upon him.

He approached Inez, and sat down by her side.

"Inez," he said, "you should have read her letter. It must have been dictated to her by the arch-fiend himself."

"Tell me," she answered, smiling faintly, "what did it contain? Was it a warning against me?"

Vyvyan, as she spoke with the light of

the lamp now falling fully on her face, could see her till now concealed features.

She was very beautiful, with dark, lustrous eyes, and black curls falling over rounded shoulders, while her form was moulded in that supple and exquisite shape which makes the women of Andalusia the pride of all Spain.

The horror of her situation, the close confinement in the utter darkness, had naturally told upon her health; but a black circle round her glorious eyes, and a pallor of the skin, was all that told of the ravages of sorrow.

"No," said Vyvyan; "she has not warned me against you. It is worse, far worse than that."

He then told her the substance of Donna Julia's letter.

The young girl listened eagerly, and as he spoke of the chance of escape for her, she pressed her hand tightly over her bosom, with a convulsive motion.

When he finished speaking, she placed her hand gently on his, and gazed up wistfully into his face.

"And have you one in England whom you love?" she asked.

"Oh, yes, yes," cried Vyvyan, better than the life within me. But speak not of her. I shall never gaze upon her face again. To me England is a forbidden shore: her love an impossible boon. Death here is cruel, but it is what I seek, though death upon the wild battle-field, where England's glory claims yet my arm's best strength, would be far more to *my* taste. The Donna Julia is a traitress: she believes all others so."

"And you will refuse?" said the young girl, in a trembling voice.

"Yes. I will die for England!"

A cold shudder passed through her form.

What cared she for England?

What thought she then of honour?

What cared she about passwords and the death of chieftains and the defeat of troops, if she could return to the arms of her beloved Alfonso?

"Oh, senor," she murmured, clinging to him yet more closely, and gazing up tenderly, eagerly into his face, "oh, consider this fearful fate to which we both are doomed—death, slow, certain, horrible. Think of the hours—the days of agony for both, and think, too, if *you* have none who love you, or if *you* have one to whom you dare not return, think that *I* have one whom I love, who waits for me—whose life is mine, as mine is his."

"This is the bitter task set me by this archdemon," murmured Vyvyan.

Then he gently took her hand.

"Inez," he said, "there *is* one, as I have said, in England who loves me. What would *she* think of me if for my life, or the life of another, I betrayed my country? No, no; life is sweet to all, but it is dearly purchased by treachery. Would your Alfonso betray Spain to England for his life and the life of *my* betrothed? No. Then why ask *me*? Poor child! I pity you, and with the sword they have yet left me I will endeavour to achieve your freedom and my own. But ask me not to be a traitor. I cannot—will *not* be. Sooner would I see the moment come when you would in hungry accents beg death at my hands, and I answer you with my sword's point! Inez, I will *die* to save you, but neither for you nor myself will I be a traitor to my country!"

The poor girl's tears were falling upon her gentle bosom as he spoke.

Yet her better feelings were aroused.

"You speak as would Alfonso," she said; "we will die together."

CHAPTER XXXVI.

FACE TO FACE WITH THE TRAITRESS!

VYVYAN pressed the little hand which still lay in his, and, sitting down, wrote as follows :—

"Senora," he began, "I reject your proposal. Your appeal to my gallantry and my humanity was a disgrace to yourself—your appeal to my self-love was an absurdity. I die for England, if I am to die here ; and, mark me, no memories of friends or of loves left behind me are of avail to *me*. To *me* England is a forbidden land ; those whom I love I shall see no more.

" CAPTAIN VYVYAN."

Within half-an-hour a man appeared to demand the reply.

Within half-an-hour again he reappeared with some soldiers.

"Captain Vyvyan," he said, "your presence is required by my lady."

Vyvyan bowed, cast a look of farewell upon his fair fellow prisoner, and placing himself in the middle of the Spanish guards, quitted the cell, and ascended to the chamber of Donna Julia.

"Well, Sir Knight," she said, as Vyvyan entered, "you are obstinate."

"Say rather, lady, I am a true friend to my country," returned he.

A smile of scorn wreathed over the beautiful lips.

"Do you so love death, then ?" she said. "To you, brave, handsome, young, life ought to have many inducements."

"Madam !" cried Vyvyan, proudly, "I have no ancestors ; I have no name ; I have no home ; I have no mistress save my sword. I live to fight for England. If I die for her, it is my destiny."

"Go," she said, as she waved her guards away with an imperious gesture.

She waited a moment until they had retired, and then, approaching Vyvyan, she drew him down to a seat by her side.

"Vyvyan," she said, holding his hand and gazing earnestly into his face, while her voice assumed a tone of wondrous tenderness, "I am going to speak to you as I could speak to no other man in this world. I have offered you your life and the life of the lady who is confined with you, on one condition ; you have refused it. I have appealed to your love for some fair one in England ; you have none, or you would for *her* sake. Nay, I offer you more. Give me this password ! Stay, do not answer hastily. You have no ancestors, no home, no mistress but your sword ! I have your word for it. I offer you all, home, name, a bride. I, young (the world says beautiful), rich at any rate, will be your wife ; will forgive all—forget all—be your slave, but let me, let me be revenged for Spain !"

This extraordinary woman, as she spoke thus, vehemently pressing her hands over her bosom and gazing with her flashing eyes at Vyvyan, was a picture truly wonderful to behold.

Vyvyan, in spite of all his previous teaching, was taken aback by this proposal.

Not that for a moment he entertained it.

Young, warm, beautiful, she might be, but no woman, in *his* heart, could take the place of Eveline.

But it was such an extraordinary proposition, that he knew not for the moment how to reply.

The senora took his hesitation for acquiescence, and pressing his hand, smiled up into his face.

He soon undeceived her.

"Senora," he said, " you have astounded me. I thank you for the condescension, but—"

"You refuse !"

Vyvyan slightly inclined his head.

He knew well what revenge for Spain meant ; it meant nothing less than the assassination of the Earl of Essex.

The senora, still holding his hand, looked up sternly into his face.

"Captain," she said, " do you really understand the alternative ? Do you know that a death, slow, inevitable, terrible, awaits you if you refuse ? Do you know that you condemn, also, your fellow prisoner to this death by your refusal? Do you understand that I not only offer you and her life, but to you I give myself, my riches, and a position second to none in Spain, if you accede to my request?"

"Madam," replied Vyvyan, as he withdrew his hand, "my honour and the welfare of my country are before all. Even if I were a traitor, and were willing to yield myself to your base offer, I know well that you would not marry the man who slew your husband. But enough, no argument is required—I refuse."

The Senora Calvados took one glance only at him, and then sprang to her feet, like an infuriated tigress; her eyes ablaze —her bosom heaving violently.

"Good!" she cried, "be it so. You have sealed your own fate."

The beautiful demon then sprang towards the bell-rope, and rang loudly.

In an instant some armed men appeared.

"Conduct the captain to his cell," she said; "see that the door is well fastened, and then make preparations for instant departure. I leave Cadiz by dawn tomorrow."·

Vyvyan made no reply.

He had made up his mind to brave the worst, and he was only glad that he was enabled to carry his sword with him.

When he once more entered the cell, which was again in utter darkness, for the lamp had been removed when Vyvyan quitted it, the young girl sprang up eagerly.

"Oh! does she relent?" she cried, clutching Vyvyan's arm convulsively.

"No," said Vyvyan; "she is obdurate, as even her heart is of stone."

A shudder ran through the young girl's frame, but she did not flinch.

She had accepted her lot, and, like Vyvyan, was resolved to abide by it.

It is a strange thing, and yet, if looked into, easily comprehensible, that while a man has a sword by his side, he feels prepared for all emergencies.

Vyvyan had his sword by his side, and he could, therefore, not deem it possible that he could be lost utterly to the world.

"Courage," he whispered to the young girl. "We will yet escape. The Senora Calvados quits this place to-morrow. There will be no one to watch us. We will escape."

Dark as it was he groped about the walls, and found that around the doorway the bricks were quite loosely set in the mortar.

He smiled as he felt them, thinking how carelessly they guarded their prisoners, little imagining what a terrible ordeal they were preparing for them.

It was towards night that a red light glowed in through the chinks of the door, and as Vyvyan approached to see what it could be, he saw that the mansion was on fire!

The Senora de Calvados had resolved to punish her victims more quickly, but by a far more terrible death.

"Great God!" cried he; "this woman is but a demon in human shape. For myself I care not, but to see this poor girl tortured by the flames will be more than I can bear."

Donna Inez soon saw the extent of the calamity, but she evinced none of that extreme terror which he had so feared to witness.

"Come!" he said; "come here and help me. The heat of the flames has not yet reached the wall."

Between them they had soon succeeded in loosening several of the bricks, and dislodging them.

This, at any ordinary time, would have been discovered and stopped by the men who constantly relieved one another in the guard-room opposite; but now there was no one to interfere with their movements, and one by one the bricks were withdrawn from their places.

It was a long time, of course, before an opening was made large enough to allow of the passage of a human being; and before they had so far succeeded, the flames were roaring nearer, and the heat began to glow, and the dense smoke to curl around them!

But Vyvyan did not hesitate.

It was their only chance, and to flinch now was to lose life without an effort.

At length they stood without the door —free! but in what a position!

A wall of fire before them! A wall of fire behind!

In the face of this fearful peril, the young girl's courage gave way.

"Oh!" she cried, clinging to Vyvyan, we cannot—cannot go through those sheets of flame. Oh! merciful God! Oh! brave captain, save me!"

"Through that fire," answered Vyvyan, "is our only chance. We must dash through it bravely. We may rush to certain death, but even that is better than remaining here to linger out a slow and horrible existence. Come."

As he spoke, he threw his arm around her waist, and drew her towards the fire.

"Oh! no—in Heaven's name!" she shrieked, and, as he still drew her on, she fell fainting upon his breast.

With a prayer to Heaven for safety, he rushed forward with his heavy burden, and dashed through the wall of fire.

There was a scorching, blinding heat, a moment of madness and oblivion, and then a rush of Heaven's free, cool, blessed air, and he found himself beneath the silent stars in the cloisters of the Spanish mansion.

"Thank God!" he cried, as he hurried onwards through the stone passages which led out to the promenade beneath the ramparts, "thank God for this great mercy!"

He did not pause until he reached a spot where they were entirely out of reach of the heat and reflection of the flames, and therefore beyond the fear of recognition and interference.

Then he stopped, and placing the senseless form of the young girl upon a mound of earth, he was just about to proceed in search of water to recall her to her senses, when a tall form sprang from the shadows and approached him, sword and dagger in hand.

"Hold!" he cried, "by what name do you call yourself?"

"My name, most discourteous stranger, is Vyvyan," cried our hero. "And yours?"

"And mine is Don Alfonso de Cabrida," replied the other; "draw your sword and defend yourself."

"Don Alfonso de Cabrida!" echoed the youth, "thank Heaven, I have found you! Yonder is—"

"I desire no talk," exclaimed the other, fiercely, "Yonder is Donna Inez—once my betrothed. I need no words from you. Stand to your sword!"

"Madman!" cried Vyvyan, "I tell you I have saved her life for you!"

"I know all," exclaimed the Spaniard, who, for some reason inexplicable to Vyvyan, was mad with rage. "Defend yourself, if you do not wish me to call you coward!"

Vyvyan drew his sword, and placed himself in position.

"Come on, then, insane fool!" he said; "since you *will* fight, your fate is of your own choosing."

The stranger answered not, and the next moment they were engaged in deadly strife; while the fair girl lay still insensible upon the grassy mound near them.

CHAPTER XXXVII.

THE RESULT OF THE DUEL.—THE DISGUISED TRAITOR.

ALTHOUGH of necessity it was apparent to Vyvyan that Don Alfonso de Cabrida was acting under some mistaken feeling of jealousy, it was quite impossible in his present state of mind to convince him of his error.

He was, in fact, devoured by the most intense and burning jealousy.

A lie, invented by the Senora Julia on the moment, was the cause of all.

Alfonso, whose escape had miscarried, had now been released by the English from the State prison, and had rushed at once towards the house of Don Josè de Calvados.

There was no need now of concealment.

In the midst of the whirl and din of battle he would be unnoticed by his enemies; he would declare his passion, and with the concurrence, as he fully believed, of Julia, he would carry off his betrothed to a part of the country where he could remain in safety.

The smoke was already curling up from the mansion of Don Jose, when the eager lover arrived at the door and met the Senora Calvados hurrying forth.

In a few hurried words Alfonso explained all; his secret love; the mediation of Don Jose, and his eager desire to clasp his beloved one to his breast.

In horror Julia listened.

All was now explained; yet she dared not, even in her remorse, tell *him* how cruelly, how savagely wrong she had been.

A quick lie rose to her lips.

"She is in terrible danger, I fear," she said, "going down to visit a prisoner—my husband's assassin—whom she loves ——"

"Loves!"

"Aye, but do not interrupt me. She has, doubtless," continued Julia, "been caught by the flames."

"And is there no hope —no chance of escape?" cried Alfonso. "I must—I will see her again!"

"There is but one chance. She might reach the cloisters, and so pass underneath the battlements."

Here, as we have seen, he met Vyvyan carrying the form of Inez in his arms.

This sight, confirming as it did the false story of the Senora Julia, completely maddened him, and, as I have said, he would listen to no words of reason.

The manner in which he fought against the English captain was wild in the extreme, and it was not long before the trickling of blood down his arm proclaimed the fact that he was wounded.

Vyvyan had every desire to spare him, both on account of the fair girl who still lay insensible on the mound, and on account of his own sufferings; but the hotheaded Spaniard refused to listen to reason.

"Hold, for one moment!" shouted the young captain. "You are fighting your best friend—the man who has saved for you the being you love."

"Coward!" shouted Alfonso, and attacked him the more fiercely.

Seeing the utter uselessness of all remonstrance, Vyvyan resolved to put an end to the battle by severely wounding his adversary, and then compelling him to listen to the history of the Senora Julia's treachery.

So, regardless now of the issue of the combat, he attacked Alfonso with his skill and strength, and gradually, but certainly, the Spaniard found himself being forced back towards the walls of Cadiz.

Suddenly his foot slipped against a stone, and in an instant Vyvyan's sword had twisted itself round his adversary's blade, which flew into the air to some distance.

He was completely now at the mercy of the English captain, who grasped him firmly by the right wrist, as he fell, and prevented his using the knife.

"Madman!" he said, "I could kill you now."

"Kill, then," interrupted Alfonso.

"No, no; I tell you," said Vyvyan, "you have been deceived by some treacherous lie! I am your friend—the saviour of your betrothed bride—who for months has pined in a dungeon beneath the house of the Senora Julia, her cruel and murderous cousin! See, she awakes, sheathe your knife. Let her not see that you have drawn your weapon upon the one who swore to restore her to you!"

The Spaniard, lost in amazement, sheathed his long knife, but too late to prevent the eyes of the young girl from detecting their relative positions.

"Alfonso!" she cried, as she sprang to her feet, and rushed towards them. "Why—why is this? Oh! my beloved! it is he who saved me—for you!"

"For himself, maybe," said the Spaniard, sullenly, as he rose to the ground, and folded his arms, without offering to embrace her. "But fear not for *him*. He could have taken my life, but spared me; my life is his, and no weapon of mine shall harm him."

"Oh! cruel fate!" murmured the young girl, wringing her hands. "Listen, Alfonso! I am true—true to you as the stars are to Heaven! I swear it! It was my love for you—my reckless eagerness to see you, that caused my long—long, weary captivity. Listen! and I will explain all."

With her hand upon her lover's shoulder, and her eyes looking up with a gentle pleading in his face, Inez told her story.

Long ere she had finished speaking his eyes beamed with joy, his arm stole round her waist, and her hand was pressed in his, while more than once her words were checked by the eager kisses he imprinted on her lips.

"English captain," he said, when she had told all, "how can you forgive me? Generous enemy, strange friend, how can I reward you?"

"By making *her* happy," returned Vyvyan, as he grasped warmly the hand of the young Spaniard. "I need no reward save the consciousness of having foiled that demon who would have given her up to a hideous and cruel fate. Adieu now: hasten to some place of safety. I must away now to join the leaders, who doubtless think me dead!"

"And shall we not meet again, generous stranger?" said Inez, as, with tears in her eyes, she pressed his hand to her lips.

Vyvyan smiled.

"Perhaps, in the far future," he said. "But hark! Guns are firing; hasten, now—farewell!"

They murmured again words of heartfelt gratitude, and then, hand-in-hand, they hastened away.

Vyvyan watched them as they went; watched them until they faded away, and disappeared in the distance—just as they must now fade and disappear for ever from my story!

Conscious that he should never see them again, he passed quickly off upon his lonely way.

The sight of the reunion of the happy lovers had caused a terrible feeling of sorrow in his heart.

Where was Eveline now? Did her sweet bosom still beat with love for him —the outcast!—the discarded! whose home was anywhere but in England?

"Never for me such joy!—never for me such happiness!" he murmured, as he walked rapidly towards the square, where the tents of the English leaders still stood.

Had he been less preoccupied by his thoughts of the sweet face that had beamed upon him at Montreville; of the exquisite form he had fondly clasped to his heart; of the mother who had renounced him; of the brother who had sought his life!— he would have observed that his steps were dogged by a tall man, in the costume of an English soldier.

This man had watched with evident interest the duel between Vyvyan and the Spaniard, but had, for some reason or another, taken no part in it, although his manner was that of one who was no friend to the interests of the English captain.

He watched his movements until he reached the tent of the Earl of Essex, and was conducted within by two sentinels, and then he turned and slunk away towards the harbour.

He was evidently no Spaniard, for on his road he was several times challenged, and replied in clear and unmistakeable English.

Halfway to the harbour he turned into a little wine shop, and having ordered some wine, sought eagerly for some one.

Not finding the one he desired, however, he drank up his wine, and hurrying towards the harbour, entered a boat, which was waiting for him, with two sailors in it, near the quay, and was rowed out towards the open sea.

CHAPTER XXXVIII.

PREPARATIONS FOR DEPARTURE FOR ENGLAND—THE BUCCANEERS.

VYVYAN, of course, had been given up, and mourned as dead, for never once did the idea cross the mind of Essex, Raleigh, or Howard of Effingham, that the brave captain could be guilty of treachery to his country.

It may be imagined, therefore, that his appearance in the camp was hailed with every demonstration of delight.

"My preserver!" cried Essex, as he rose and grasped Vyvyan by the hand, "do I then see you again? I had, indeed, given you up for lost. Where have you been?"

"I have been captured by the enemy," said Vyvyan smiling. "I have been in prison—I have received an offer of marriage, and fought a battle—since I saw you. If it will not tire you, and you have the time to spare, I will narrate my strange adventures."

The idea was readily caught at, and, to an interested group of some of the finest officers that England ever saw, Vyvyan was soon narrating his story.

When he had finished, Essex gave him a slight review of all that had passed since his departure.

Cadiz was completely subdued.

The inhabitants had been laid under heavy contributions, and had been glad to pay an enormous ransom for their lives.

The booty taken was immense; and, satisfied with their victories, the English leaders had resolved to quit the place in four days.

The ships, which had been damaged in the fight, were rapidly repaired; the wounded soldiers were getting better; and, by the time named, they were expected to be quite able to be removed on board the vessels.

"You will be glad to revisit Old England under such glorious circumstances as these, Vyvyan," said Essex. "I shall introduce you to the Queen as my preserver."

"You overrate my services, my lord," returned the young sea-captain, "and as for England, if I never return, 'twere best for me and mine."

"Not if there lives and loves a heart such as you have told me of," replied Essex. "Oh! think, Vyvyan, you are not your *own* master—remember you have another heart dependent upon you —remember that long days of loneliness and wretchedness are forced by you on her who might be your happy bride."

"Fear not, my lord," replied Vyvyan, "my brother will console her."

"Ah! there speaks not your heart," said Lord Essex, shaking his head; "you know from your own soul that she loves you, and is faithful. You need not return home, but to another part of England. Doubt not, Captain Vyvyan, wheresoever *you* go *she* will gladly come. Since you have yielded up your birthright, and never wish to seek it, your presence in England can be no hurt to your brother. Do not, then, for a whim, or from false motives of pride and honour, abandon yourself and the one who loves you to misery for life."

Thus pleaded the noble-hearted Essex, as he drew Vyvyan aside.

And though he was fearful almost to confess it to himself, the brave man felt an eager desire to acquiesce in all that his companion said.

Eveline! dear, dear Eveline!

Why should he—if he must thus yield his birthright to another—yield also the one treasure—the one idol of his heart?

"I will think over your words, my lord," he said; "I see truth in them now where perhaps I should not have seen it before. My long absence from the one I loved has softened my heart, and dispelled those visions of the Golden West in which I beheld myself dying in an unknown land. I think now that death would indeed be bitter if I died not in the arms of Eveline."

"Think not of death; you will live for love and joy," said Essex, seeing that his companion's voice and manner were both becoming gloomy; "you will, then, return to England with me?"

"Yes," said Vyvyan, "I will yield to

you, and you *in* England shall fetch my treasure to me."

He little thought how soon his new-born joy was to receive a bitter check!

It was on the following evening that an event occurred which brought him once more into the power of his ancient foes.

He had just been to the beach in command of some soldiers who were re-embarking, when, as he returned from the quay towards the camp, a man accosted him.

It was the English soldier who had watched the duel, and afterwards followed him so mysteriously to the camp.

"Good night, captain," he said, "I have a favour to ask of you."

"Speak on, then," replied Vyvyan, suspecting him not, as he wore the English uniform.

Instead, however, of replying, the traitor made a sudden spring forward, and dashed something into Vyvyan's face.

The captain made an ineffectual effort to draw his sword, but, in an instant, sea, sky, and brilliant Cadiz, were swallowed up in one black chaos, and he knew no more.

When he recovered himself he was in comparative darkness, so that he could not tell where he was; but a rolling motion betrayed the fact that he was on the sea.

With a natural instinct he clapped his hand to his side, and found that his trusty sword was still there.

Then rising, he approached the table, and turned up the lamp, which before had emitted but a dull and unearthly glimmer over the dark cabin.

He saw now that he was on board a well appointed ship.

Everything in the cabin was of the most luxurious kind; while upon the walls, if so they may be termed, were hung swords and pistols, and other weapons, interspersed with pictures of domestic subjects, battle scenes, and voluptuous beauties.

Walking to the door, he tried to unfasten it, but the effort was useless.

It was firmly bolted, and would have resisted far more strenuous attempts than he made to open it.

Before creating any disturbance, or allowing any one to be aware of the fact that he was awake, he resolved to look out over the sea, and discover, if possible, whereabouts on the wide ocean he was.

Peering out through the port-holes, he discovered that his sleep must have been a long one, for he was far out upon the Mediterranean, and the coast of Spain was rapidly lessening in the distance.

No other vessels were to be seen anywhere, except some that appeared like tiny specks upon the horizon.

Resolved now no longer to delay the knowledge of whether he was with friends or foes, he again approached the cabin door, and thundered loudly at it with the hilt of his sword.

For some time no answer came.

He could hear men walking to and fro on the deck; he could hear the creaking of timbers and ropes, and the flapping of sails.

But no human voices were near him.

He knocked again loudly, and shouted also.

Then, after a pause, steps were heard approaching, and being resolved, in the event of treachery, to sell his life dearly, he drew back to the opposite side of the cabin, and drew his sword.

When the cabin door opened, there entered a tall man, young, and of commanding aspect, dressed in a somewhat fantastic garb, while in his belt were pistols of an immense size.

A sword of Turkish fashion was stuck in his girdle, and in his hand was a pistol.

Behind him were a crowd of ferocious ruffians—a set of villains such as Vyvyan had never set eyes on since the days when he was compelled to witness the butcheries perpetrated by the crew of the "Black Vulture."

The pirate, for as such Vyvyan at once regarded him, removed his hat, and bowed mockingly as he entered, while Vyvyan stood fiercely before him with his sword drawn.

"I trust Captain Vyvyan is well," said the buccaneer, with a grim smile.

"Tell me where I am, and why I am here!" answered Vyvyan, fiercely.

"My name is Captain Morgan, at your service," returned the buccaneer. "This ship is named the 'Black Vulture,' being christened after the unfortunate vessel which once was commanded by the brave and famous Captain Wrecklyffe. We are now *en route* for the West Indies."

Vyvyan's heart sank within him.

En route for the West Indies, when he had so lately consented to return to England with the Earl of Essex to see Eveline again, to cast off pride and false ideas of honour, and seek happiness with her!

And now all was changed.

"You give no answer to my question!" he cried, fiercely. "Why am I here?"

"For revenge," returned the buccaneer. "Both Wrecklyffe and Donald failed to act as your kind kinsmen would have wished. I shall adopt a better method. In the West Indies, as a slave to a Spanish master, you will have little chance of escape."

"Heaven will yet aid me," answered Vyvyan. "I fear not your threats."

"Attempt no escape from this ship," added the pirate, "or instant death will be the result. On your word of honour not to do so we will permit you to roam at will."

It took no long time for consideration in such a case as this.

To attempt resistance against such odds would be simple madness; to remain a prisoner in the cabin was like a living death.

"I accept your terms," said Vyvyan. "To escape in daylight would be impossible. As for the night, I say nothing."

Once on deck he saw how vain would be any effort at escape.

On the wide ocean which everywhere surrounded them not a single sail was to be seen, except in the far, far distance, and as far as it was possible to tell these vessels were proceeding in an opposite direction to that taken by the "Black Vulture."

The ship upon whose deck he stood was a beautifully built and rigged schooner of many tons burden; her planking was clean scraped, her sails new, everything exquisitely finished.

Everything was all that could be desired, except the crew, who were, as I have said, some of the most villanous specimens of humanity that could well be found.

They regarded him with fierce scowls as he made his appearance.

Gladly, had they had their own way, would they have hurled him overboard, but a strange feeling induced the buccaneer to spare his life.

It appeared to this man as if Vyvyan had a charmed existence, which it was useless to attempt to destroy, and it was his liberty, therefore, he now attacked.

He might be successfully retained in slavery—he could not be killed except by cold-blooded murder, which was against the creed of mariners, however wild.

Vyvyan paid no heed, however, to their muttered curses, or taunts, or their evil looks, but paced to and fro until, seeing Morgan leaning over the taffrail, he approached him.

"For this service you expect payment from Sir Grey de Malpas, I presume?" said he.

The pirate smiled and glanced, with a not unfriendly glance, at the noble figure of the adventurer.

"Most assuredly Sir Grey will pay me," he said, "for he is a man who dreams wild dreams of titles and estates, and would have them for himself though a path of blood must be trodden to achieve them. But I have a strange notion that the fate of Wrecklyffe lies at your door."

Vyvyan eyed him sternly.

"Such men as Wrecklyffe die always sudden deaths," he answered, "and all men who follow in his footsteps can hope for little more."

A sinister smile crossed the bronzed face of the buccaneer.

"I see your drift," he said; "but why should we be foes? Why not return to England together, claim your birthright and defeat your cowardly foes? Promise two thousand pounds, and I will land you safely on the shores of Cornwall."

"I refuse," answered Vyvyan. "I will make no bargain with you; life is not so sweet that I should pay a price for liberty to a pirate, and may be an assassin."

The pirate's brows lowered darkly.

"Have a care," he said, "or I may break my vow, and besmear my deck with your blood."

As if desiring to restrain his passion, he then moved away, and left Vyvyan to himself.

CHAPTER XXXIX.

THE STORM—THE WRECK.

As night fell over the sea the wind rose, and the pitching and rolling of the vessel plainly told Vyvyan that she was becoming somewhat unmanageable.

Loud, and as it seemed angry, orders were given, and men's feet scurried hither and thither along the deck as if in eager haste to obey commands, shouted to them in a hoarse and discordant voice.

Now and then a crash and a sharp whizz told of the snapping asunder of some rope, while the masts groaned and the great waves dashed angrily against the vessel's sides as if eager to break through and devour their human prey within.

Vyvyan was sitting in his chair and musing, when a slight scraping noise near at hand attracted his notice.

As he turned towards the spot the panel behind him suddenly opened and a man entered.

Naturally imagining that he was about to be the victim of some attempt at assassination, Vyvyan leaped to his feet and partly drew his sword.

The strange man, who was attired in the costume of a common sailor, smiled as he fastened the door behind him.

"Fear not," he said, "I am a friend, although a stranger to you. I come to give you timely warning."

"Of what?"

"Of the coming of a friend."

Vyvyan glanced at him suspiciously.

He had been so accustomed to being made the victim of deception that he could scarcely bring himself to believe that this man was in reality the bearer of good tidings.

"I have learned prudence in my time," said Vyvyan. "Before I trust you, I must know what you have to tell, and who you are."

"You are right," returned the man. "I am here by force; I am compelled by poverty to work for them. I know well your home, your story, and I know Alton the priest, who, in my youthful days, often led me into the right path, and strove to guide me from error. I was a wild fellow,

however, and paid little attention to his teaching. Yet I would gladly aid you. The storm is driving us far out of our course, and on our track is an English vessel."

"Ah!" cried Vyvyan; "This sounds well. But how know you that it has friends of mine within it?"

The man smiled.

"Its name is enough to tell you that—its name, borne to us over the seething waves. The 'Invincible,' whose captain is the Earl of Essex!"

"This is good news, indeed," said Vyvyan. "Forgive me for my suspicions. But how will Lord Essex know of my presence here?"

"It will not matter. He is even now in pursuit. Evidently he knows well the character of this vessel, and designs to attack it. Give no longer to Morgan your word of honour not to escape. When the attack is made, in the heat of battle I will open the cabin door, and release you; and now farewell."

At this instant the ship gave a tremendous lurch, so sudden, that it caused the man to stagger back and clutch at something for support.

"This will alter matters most strangely," said he; "my help will avail little against the ragings of such a storm as this. Your friends will scarcely be able to bring up their ship to attack us."

"The tempest will perhaps save your captain the trouble of carrying out the revenge of Sir Grey de Malpas," said Vyvyan, bitterly, "cooped up in this cabin, how can I battle with men or with the elements."

"True," cried the man, "but you shall not be cooped up to die a death which no brave man would wish for. I know I can trust to your honour; and I shall leave your door unlocked now. Quit not this cabin until you hear my voice crying—'Vyvyan; it is time!'"

Vyvyan grasped the hand of his unknown friend.

"My word upon it," he cried; 'fear

not that I shall betray you. Were the angry waves to be dashing in upon me, I would not move to cause you trouble. But one word more and you can go—what is your name?"

The man smiled bitterly.

"Alas! I know not what my name may be," he answered; "they call me William de Grey, but of that anon. When we have escaped the common danger, then may we have more time for speech; and then you shall know more of my strange story. For the present, farewell; and remember the token—'Vyvyan; it is time!'"

He left the door unlocked, and Vyvyan was once more left to his thoughts.

Sad thoughts they were, indeed.

In days gone by, when he had pressed on amid the storm of battle, or had been helpless, at the mercy of the waves, he had had sweet thoughts of home to keep up his courage and soothe the anguish of his mind.

Hopes of a meeting with a mother who would clasp him to her breast, and bless him; hopes of a reunion with another, loved more dearly still!

Now he had lost all hope save of Eveline.

He had for a long time, as we know, resolved never again to place foot upon the shores of England.

But the adventures and perils he had gone through in Spain had changed his mind.

The words which Dona Inez had spoken had influenced him for good.

Assuredly he would not break his vow to his mother, but he could claim still the hand of the one he loved; and who was doubtless pining for him even now.

It was unjust to let her waste her young life in regretting and sighing for one who was wilfully keeping from her.

Yet Beaufort!

What of him?

Had he succeeded in persuading his beloved one to be faithless to her trust?

Vyvyan glanced out of the narrow window at the storm.

He could see every now and then the huge waves lit up by the violet lightning, which was all that served to illumine the gloom of the fast approaching night.

The loophole was so small that he could see very little.

But what he *did* see was grand in the extreme.

The billows advanced like rolling mountains, large enough as it seemed to overwhelm the vessel, which rose, however, like a thing of life and floated buoyantly on their summits.

Amid the raging of the tempest he seemed to hear strange voices—to hear the sweet tones of Eveline, as she had leaned over the balustrades of the terrace at Montreville, singing her weird song to the tossing waves.

In the lulls of the storm the words came to him—

"Bud from the blossom
    And leaf from the tree,
Guess why in weaving
    I sing, 'Woe is me!'
'Tis that I mean you
    To drift on the sea,
And say when you find him,
    Who sang, 'Woe is me!'"

"Oh! woe is me! indeed," murmured Vyvyan; "the earth has changed for me since then! When I clasped her waist in the happy sunshine of Montreville, little did I dream that the clouds would come so soon. Hard fate, indeed, to find a mother merely to know the pleasure of discovering her, and then to be thrown hopeless on the world again!"

He ceased gazing out of the loophole and flung himself down upon the couch.

"Why did I live to learn the secret of my birth?" he continued, speaking aloud; "why was I told at all? Why was the dreadful mystery revealed to me? Why could not Alton have permitted me to live on in doubt? And yet would not my instinct have told me that that proud Countess was my mother?

The storm now was increasing rapidly

The ship laboured heavily, almost helplessly, in the trough of the sea, and every now and then came crashing sounds as if the spars were falling on the deck.

He could hear the hoarse shouts of men: and the curses of the officers as they issued their orders, amid the gloom alternated with the glare of the lightning.

He became strangely impatient.

How intensely maddening was it to be a prisoner at such a time!

But never for an instant did he dream of breaking his word to William de Grey.

A strange sympathy seemed to link him to this man.

He, too, was without name, save that which had been given to him by strangers: he, too, had no mother : had never known one: had never known either the strength of a father's affection!

But had he experienced also the horrible reality which *he* had ?

These thoughts surged wildly through his heart.

The time seemed to pass with terrible slowness.

Suddenly a huge wave struck the vessel amidships, and it heeled half over quivering in every plank.

At the same moment there was a terrific crash: and in the midst of the thunderous noise he heard a voice exclaim :

"Vyvyan—it is time !"

He lost not a moment.

Springing up he leaped to the door and opened it.

There was no chance of his being discovered, for it was so dark that he did not perceive the man who had aided him until, as he ascended the ladder, he heard a voice say—

"Come on deck quietly, and speak not. Amid the turmoil and the dismay no one will observe you."

As they reached the deck they found that the crew were endeavouring to launch the boats.

By the cries which were heard on all sides he could tell that some great disaster had happened—that in fact the vessel was stove in, and that the water was pouring into the hold.

The utmost confusion prevailed.

A dozen orders were shouted out at once, and not one of them obeyed.

Every man, in fact, was for himself, and in the struggling and tumbling and the rolling of the ship many fell overboard into the wildly-raging sea, while two of the boats were dropped over likewise.

It was no wonder that such consternation and confusion prevailed, for it was as dark as Erebus, and it was only possible to note the huge waves as they poured in, by their white crests.

William de Grey kept close to the side of Vyvyan.

"Captain," he said, as they steadied themselves by holding on to the bulwarks, "will you be guided by me ?"

"On such a night as this one needs a guide, in truth,' said Vyvyan ; "but whither would you lead me ? "

"Nay, jest not, gentle sir," said De Grey. "I mean in advice I desire to guide you. Go not in those boats—if indeed they can be launched. It will be better to trust to the ship or to a floating spar than among such a reckless crew."

"You are right," said Vyvyan. "It would be wilfully casting myself into the arms of my enemies. I will wait here with you."

The storm now increased in violence, and the spars fell crashing to the deck: the rigging making a hopeless tangle everywhere.

Cries of agony from men struck down by the heavy spars, mingled with the curses of those who were foiled in their efforts to launch the boats.

And over all boomed the thunder and flashed the lightning; while the hissing sea swept ever and anon across the decks.

At length the wind became terrible in its noise and violence.

The ship was rapidly filling, and was hurled hither and thither like a cockleshell.

The boats had long since disappeared with their occupants into the depths of the raging main, when suddenly one gust more fierce than the rest struck the mainmast at the same time as a large wave, and it went by the board.

Simultaneously with this last accident, Vyvyan found himself swung into the sea, amid an entanglement of rigging and spars.

He was half stunned of course; with a roar of surging waters in his ears, and a crash as of a thousand rending beams.

And then for a time his senses left him, and he knew no more.

When he awoke again the storm had passed away, leaving a heavy roll and swell of the sea.

The dawn was just breaking; and the sea was everywhere illumined by a silver light.

His limbs were numbed, and his senses dulled by the fearful tempest; but the first thought which flashed across his mind was of Eveline.

The memory of that song came to him over the rolling billows, even before he was well awakened to the scene around him.

"HE ENTERED THE ROOM PISTOL IN HAND."

And then a sweet hope stole into his breast.

Fate was with him.

Fate was fighting for him.

Here out on the open sea, in the hands of reckless murderous men who sought his life, the very tempest had saved him!

Was it not a warning that he was to return to England, to greet again the sweet face which he had seen last so sorrowfully raised to his?

He shook off the pleasant dream, however, and glanced around him.

He was floating, he saw at once, on a huge pile of mast, to which two other men were clinging—holding on like grim death to the tangled mass of cordage—the sea rolling its fierce waves right over them.

It was difficult, of course, at first to recognise the companions which the storm had given him.

But, presently, as the light grew stronger, he saw that the men were Morgan the buccaneer, and William de Grey.

He raised his voice high.

" Ha! my friends," he said, " we meet on better terms now! In the hold of your ship, Captain Morgan, I was your prisoner. The sea has freed us all. The ocean is like the grave, it shows no favor to any."

The buccaneer uttered a loud curse.

" Ha!" he cried, " we started at a wrong time. Rather would I have met the Earl of Essex and his war ship, than this terrible storm."

Vyvyan laughed.

" Ha!" he cried, " both would have been the same to me! The tempest and the Earl were both my friends. But, at least, if I am to die out on this ocean, *you* will bear me company."

The buccaneer answered with a loud curse, but made no other remark.

William de Grey was between the two enemies.

" Well, my friend," he said, " you have escaped after all."

He feared not now to confess that he was on the side of Vyvyan.

" Yes, for what?" cried our hero; " to float as I have done before, out on the vasty deep, with nothing to look forward to but destruction."

" Ha!" said de Grey, " you have better prospects than that; believe me, we are close to the Barbary coast, and ere long, when the sun has risen higher, you will see the long sandy coast stretching out for miles and miles. There, at least, will be *terra firma*, if it is but useful to give us time for thought."

The sea now was restless in the extreme, as if it was rolling its great waves inland, and they were being flung back again in anger.

It was evident they were approaching the coast; and, presently, as the sun broke gloriously from behind the last of the storm clouds, Vyvyan saw that the prophecy of De Grey was correct.

He beheld the long, low line of sand, with here and there, in the distance, a shadowy tree.

Towards this the mast was rapidly drifting, raising itself on end ever and anon like a living thing.

Presently they felt it strike the bottom, and stop.

Then, after a shivering motion, it once more went plunging on, until presently, by a blow, as it were, from a wave, much larger than the others, it was flung upon a mound of sand, where it stuck fast.

" Grounded!" said De Grey. " We have gone as far as we can expect to be taken we must wade the rest."

Vyvyan at once disengaged himself, and prepared to fight his way to shore, through the boiling surf.

De Grey followed his example.

But Morgan the buccaneer held back.

He seemed indeed paralysed.

When the other two were ready to start, he was still hopelessly clinging to the rigging and the mast, with a scowl on his brow; a glaring defiance in his starting eyes; a look altogether as if he was cursing the whole of mankind.

" Now, Captain Morgan," said Vyvyan, " pray follow us. We are going ashore; and unless you want to feed the fishes, come quickly also."

" I cannot," said Morgan, with an oath; " I cannot. I am numbed; my head swims; my limbs are stiff; I am entangled so in the rigging that I cannot move."

Vyvyan placed his hand to his belt, and drew forth a flask of spirit which he had brought from Cadiz.

" Here! drink some of this," he said, " it will revive you. As for the ropes, my knife will separate them; and I will aid you ashore. When men are in peril at sea, Providence would look ill upon them if they quarrelled."

He stooped down, cut some of the ropes with his dagger; and then having helped Morgan to rise to his feet, he gave him the flask.

But he could not take it.

Cold, or fear, seemed for the moment to have paralysed him; and Vyvyan was compelled at last to pour it down his throat.

This at once produced its effect.

Spirits in those days, even to a pirate, were not things of common use, and the effect was instantaneous.

He recovered his nerves, the hopelessness and abject sullenness left his face, and he began to move with them towards the shore.

CHAPTER XL.

ON THE COAST OF BARBARY.

THE difficulties of the three shipwrecked men were not yet over.

The wide expanse of sand was anything but firm, and ever and anon they sank deeply.

But they were not destined at present for more misfortune.

Stumbling and floundering about for a long time, they at length reached shore, where they all three sank exhausted upon the sand.

Vyvyan had kept up his courage and his energy to the last.

But even *he* now felt exhausted.

Morgan was sullen again for some time after they landed in safety.

He looked round him as if to measure the possibilities of some further villany; and then suddenly, as Vyvyan lay at full length upon the soft sand, he brightened up.

"Well, comrades," he said, "now that we are thrown together on this desert shore we must help one another."

"Just so," said De Grey; "we should be but poor adventurers if we thought of spite and wrong, when dangers on sea and land surround us. But as not one of us know our way, what are we to do?"

"The best we can," said Vyvyan; "the best can do no more! We had better as soon as we are able make our way inland. We *must* eat; and on this sandy shore Heaven's bounty will be scant."

"True," said Morgan, who had by a visible effort thrown off his lethargy, "true—I am hungry and thirsty, and am ready to start at once."

Vyvyan rose.

"Let it not be said I delay you," he cried; "I am ready."

"And *I*, too," said de Grey.

And over the waste of sand they started in the direction of a clump of date-palms which seemed to grow upon a hill.

Little was said by Morgan on the way.

His scowl was gone, but he mixed not much in their conversation.

In fact, in spite of the loss of his ship and his men and his treasure, he seemed to keep in his inmost heart some thought which gave him pleasure.

So Vyvyan and De Grey were left for a time together.

"So, De Grey," said Vyvyan, "you are an orphan?"

De Grey glanced round at him with a look which expressed a great deal.

"An orphan," he said; "No! Call it not by that word. I am one who knows neither mother nor father, though I suspect the name of one and know the name of the other. Left as a babe in the care of an honest fisherman, I was brought up by Alton, the hermit priest; and only upon condition that I would never betray him did he consent to explain all."

Vyvyan listened eagerly.

This was a strange revelation.

Alton, the priest, mixed up again with a mystery of birth!

Who could this De Grey be?

Suspense was useless.

In such a position—amid such dangers and on a continent from which it was so unlikely they would escape—why should this man keep back his secret?

"De Grey," he said, "why not tell me your secret?"

"I cannot do more than say one name," replied the other; "you know I am styled William de Grey. Think of the latter name, which Alton the priest has given me, and then listen to this"—

And he whispered in Vyvyan's ear a name as if he feared that the very winds of the desert would hear him; and cast the news abroad.

Vyvyan grasped the hand of his companion, but for a moment he spoke not.

In fact, the intelligence which had been given him had been almost overwhelming.

Suddenly, however, as Captain Vyvyan pressed on ahead, he said—

"De Grey, the name which you have whispered in my ear, has roused strange memories in my heart! It links our chain—the chain we both must bear. I, too, an orphan, left to Alton's care, will whisper to you a name which will prove my words."

He leaned forward and whispered.

His companion, although suspecting much, was startled by the information conveyed in one brief sentence.

"We are more than friends," he cried, as he grasped Vyvyan's hand in a firm grip; "Providence has sent us together to work out the good end."

"Against your father!" questioned Vyvyan, sharply.

"Aye," said De Grey, with flashing eyes, "aye! truly! Is he not my worst enemy? Is he not—but let it be for a time! Let us escape first, and then we will plan for the future."

Then, as if suddenly nerved by memories of a terrible past, to speak more freely he said—

"There is one thing more I wish to tell if you will listen to me."

"Listen! aye! readily will I listen," said Vyvyan. "The story you tell me makes strange echoes in my heart, and I am eager to listen."

"Alton the priest," said De Grey, "had no hand in my undoing! It was all the work of my father.

"I was told strange stories of the sea and its treasures, and the golden mines of far away foreign lands.

"And I was caught by them as many a young adventurer had been caught before.

"But it was not until I was twenty years of age that I was induced to cast my bread upon the waters.

"I was introduced to the captain of a noble ship—a man whom I respected at once from his appearance.

"How sadly wrong I was!

"But I will not detain you long with a record of my folly and its punishment.

"Suffice it to say, that I shipped with this man, and had scarcely been two days at sea when his real character came out.

"I was in my cabin one evening when he entered the room pistol in hand, and followed by a mob of men with drawn swords.

"I knew not of course what this meant, but I was aware that I was in danger.

"My sword flew at once from the scabbard.

"And yet how foolish was this exhibition of anger!

"What could I do against such a gang of reckless thieves?

"What want you, gentlemen?" I cried, starting forward.

"We wish to convey to you some information," said the captain, hat in one hand, pistol in the other, speaking with a kind of mock humility.

"Be quick with it then," I said.

"It is very brief," said he. "I wish your sword to be delivered up to me, as henceforward you are a prisoner."

"And why?" I asked.

"We give no reasons," he said; "it is enough that I am captain of this vessel, and that I command it."

"I grasped my sword firmly, and glanced at my foes.

"My heart bounded wildly.

"Of course my first impulse was to leap forward and endeavour to fight my way through them.

"But that I saw soon was utterly useless.

"My helplessness flashed across me in a moment.

"In the face of such odds," I said to the captain, "it would be madness to talk of fighting. But pray condescend to tell me why this thing is done."

He shrugged his shoulders.

"How can *I* tell," he said. "I am only acting under orders."

"Whose?"

"He waved his men back, and, approaching me, whispered in my ear.

"It was *his* name, and then, knowing what I did, I gave up my sword willingly.

"From that time, in very truth, life has had no charm for *me*.

"I gave myself up to the life set forth to me in that ship, and here I am.

"I am scarcely ashamed of the past, because my life was shaped for me!"

He paused.

"The name of this captain?" said Vyvyan. "Pray tell me!"

"He who walks before us—*he* is the man—Captain Morgan," replied De Grey.

"Ha!" exclaimed Vyvyan, "this, then, inks our chain still further. I see *now* the cause of my last misfortune. Fool to think that love and devotion to Wrecklyffe caused this man to pursue me to my ruin! His orders came from England!"

During this conversation they had been nearing the hill upon which the palm trees grew.

They saw now that it was not a mound of sand, but evidently a mass of broken masonry, over which the sand of the desert had drifted, forming it into an apparently round hill.

As they approached there seemed upon it signs of human life.

De Grey paused a moment as he beheld the forms of living beings.

"I suppose we *must* advance," said he to Vyvyan; "to remain upon this arid plain would be to starve hopelessly. With those men we may be in danger; but we may certainly find the means of escape."

"We choose between two evils," said Vyvyan with a smile, "therefore we must accept the less. Let us advance."

Morgan, the buccaneer, had now joined him.

"Yes," he said, "it will be best to proceed. These men may accept a bribe from us, and place us on board one of their vessels. Anything, as De Grey says would be better than starving on the shore without a chance of attracting the notice of a passing vessel."

And so they journeyed on.

The sun was now pouring down with terrible heat upon the burning sands.

Even the sea they had left behind them looked hot.

They were glad, indeed, therefore, when —as they neared the place—they saw high trees of the palm tribe, looking bright and green, and showing therefore the presence of water.

It was of this they were most in want.

Their throats were fairly parched by their long abstinence from drink; and as they neared the high ground they broke into a run.

Vyvyan, who was the strongest, and most high-spirited of the three, rushed on in advance, and encouraged them by cheery words.

He was the first to reach the path which led up over the rocky wall that separated the sandy waste from the oasis.

"Come, my friends," he said, "come, I scent the fresh air! As the war-horse scents the battle from afar, so I scent the regions of fresh life, and this horrid desert. Come on, my companions, there is at least hope here for us."

Thus adjuring them, seeming indeed to forget the terrible injuries which had been inflicted upon him by Morgan, our hero led the way towards the oasis, and as he climbed to the summit of the hill, or rather at the top of the rocky wall, he saw that they had in reality approached the regions of human habitation.

It was a most mixed scene that he contemplated.

There were huts and tents mingled together in strange confusion.

People were moving about busily, engaged in a variety of occupations; but as soon as they perceived Vyvyan and his companions they threw aside their tools and rushed in a body towards the strangers.

It was not the purpose of the three shipwrecked men to run away and make their escape, though under other circumstances they might have been tempted to do so.

The men who so quickly surrounded

them were quite black and savage, wearing only a white waistcloth which served only to give a darker tint to their skins.

They waved the weapons which they had caught up at random wildly in the air, while they uttered continually a rhodomontade which was utterly unintelligible to Vyvyan and his companions.

The latter kept making gestures which plainly explained the fact that they were in want of water—a something wherewithal to assuage their thirst.

The strangers, however, seemed either unable or unwilling to comprehend them.

One of them—after a moment—went rushing down the hill in the direction of a tall man, who was standing by himself at the bottom of the declivity.

Seizing him in somewhat a rude manner he hurried up him the ascent, and brought him to the spot where Vyvyan and his friends were standing.

The man seemed to all appearance a Spaniard, and his first words proved this conception to be correct.

"Ha! Senors," he said, "you look English to all appearance!"

"We are," cried Vyvyan; "we have been shipwrecked on this coast, and we ask for hospitality."

A strange smile flitted over the lips of the Spaniard at this word.

"Hospitality," he said; "a strange word indeed to mention in this country. The hospitality that *you* will receive will be the same meted out to *me*—slavery—the brutality of a master—the worst brutality of his chief hireling."

"We must submit to that," said Vyvyan, "but there will be soon some chance of escape. Or since these men of Barbary are such slaves to gold, surely they can be bribed."

"That remains to be seen," replied the stranger, "but I will explain more at another time. At present to talk to you without the sanction of this demon of mischief would be to cause your destruction as well as my own."

At this moment, as if to prove the correctness of his words, he was addressed by the man who had run down the hill so anxiously to fetch him.

"What is it they say?" he cried.

"I cannot well understand them," replied the Spaniard, warily. "What questions shall I ask them, your excellency?"

The "excellency," whose attire was almost as scanty as the others, looked somewhat suspicious.

But he answered—

"Whence come they?"

"From England."

"Why are they here?"

"They have been shipwrecked on this coast replied the interpreter.

"Ha!" exclaimed the African, "that proves their ship was coming hither; why were they bound to this shore? Why was that?"

Vyvyan was at a loss to reply.

He glanced at Morgan, who understood well the Spanish spoken by the interpreter.

"Fear not, tell the truth," said Morgan, who in this had a hidden purpose of his own; "say that you were my prisoner."

"This captain, here," replied Vyvyan, accordingly, "had me a prisoner on board his vessel. Another time I will explain the reason; but this is of little moment to your master. What we wish for is food and drink, for which we will gladly pay."

"Say nothing of money, most noble sir," replied the Spaniard, "that would be a signal for your murder. Leave this to me."

"The stranger who speaks to me," he added, addressing the African, "was a prisoner on board the ship of that one of his companions. Another time he will explain all; but now they ask for drink and food."

The man glanced at the three suspiciously again.

Only for a moment he thought.

Then he said, as if suddenly forming a resolution—

"Well ask them no more questions now. Bring them down to the palace, and let them have food and drink. Then we will speak to them again."

This speech, as it was translated to Vyvyan and his companions, gave to them the utmost satisfaction.

They simply testified their gratitude in a few words, and then followed their conductor down the hill and through the tents and huts.

The crowd followed them with countenances which evidently proved that they were disappointed of some treat.

They had expected, in fact, nothing

else but the destruction of the white men, or their being dragged ignominiously, with lashes on their backs, to the market place, where they would be proclaimed the slaves of the king.

They even testified their disappointment by sullen looks, and by strangely sounding cries.

But the king took no notice of them in any way.

Evidently he was quite used to, and quite prepared for, such ebullitions of temper, and he stalked along in a stately manner, preceded by the one who had acted as intrepreter, and followed by Vyvyan and his companions.

Their way led them at first, as I have said, through the tents, and the miserable huts of the natives.

But presently a change came for which they were unprepared.

On turning suddenly an angle in the wall which stood on the left side of the encampment, they came upon a scene of great beauty.

A large building had been raised of bamboos and date palms; a building which had, in its rude way, a kind of architectural beauty.

In front of it were gardens of lemon and citron, and orange trees, and grand old palms, which, rising in clusters, cast around them a luxurious shade.

The gardens were laid out in a manner which would have done credit to any European gardener.

Fountains flung up their pleasant spray, which fell back in a myriad diamond drops, as the rays of the sun fell upon them.

All around was shade, and comfort, and luxury; such flowers, magnificent in size and colour, as Vyvyan had never seen.

The intrepreter took them to a table, which stood beneath the shade of a cluster of date-palms, and here they were soon served with a goodly repast; their torn and sea-sodden clothes being beforehand replaced by dry and sound ones.

When this had been completed, time was appointed them to rest; and the interpreter informed them that after this they would learn from the king—Abdoolah Ben Nazum—the fate that would be assigned them."

"The fate," said Vyvyan; "that is a strange word! Cast by the sea upon the shore of an unknown land, we have a right to claim hospitality, and to ask to be sent homeward in the first vessel that hails for England or for Spain."

"I, too, was shipwrecked," returned the Spaniard, "and you see me now!"

"Well," said Vyvyan, "I should be glad, indeed, to hear your history. I have no desire to sleep. In fact, my thoughts are too busy to give me much chance of slumber. Sit here, I pray, and tell to us your history."

The Spaniard took one rapid glance up at the windows of the palace.

Then he said—

"Well, if I do, I must be brief, though, perhaps, even a few words from me may prove good as a warning to you. If I am discovered to be telling you anything, I shall be shot at once, or hanged to the nearest tree."

"Depend upon it, I will keep good watch," said Vyvyan; "no one shall approach without your having good notice. Proceed, therefore, without fear."

"My story, as I said before," proceeded the Spaniard, "will be a short one."

"I have been on this continent, among these savages, for over two years, and during that time I have had only one chance of escape.

"A chance, be it said, which nearly caused my death.

"I was shipwrecked with a number of others, but I was the only one who survived.

"With me I had a quantity of gold in a belt, and so had my fellow sufferers.

"They are all dead now, and I know nothing of them, or of their friends.

"Why," thought I, "should I not help myself to the good things which Providence has sent me?

"It was assuredly no harm, and so I helped myself to the contents of their belts, and making it up in a large packet, I hid it among some rocks and sand where I should be able to find it again.

"During this performance I had been repeatedly interrupted by strange noises, and at last, as I started at one sound louder than the rest, I saw a black form dashing away at headlong speed across the sandy waste.

"I guessed at once that I had been watched, and accordingly I made a feint of following him.

"This of course made him fly all the faster.

"As soon as he was fairly out of sight, I hurried back to the spot where I had deposited my treasure, and dug it up again.

"Then I looked for and soon found a second place where it would be safe; and I had not long placed it in a secure concealment when a large body of men appeared, coming suddenly upon me from the rocky wall.

"I can speak their language as you see, and consequently I had no difficulty in explaining my position.

"I told them I had been shipwrecked and needed help, and they listened patiently.

"But I observed that they eyed me askance, and said very little to me."

When I had told my story, the head man among them said—

"We will now go to the king.

"And so without further comment or explanation I was marched off to this palace.

"The King Abdoolah listened patiently to my story."

Then he said—

"The Spaniard is doubtless rich!"

"I have not in my possession one single gold piece," I said truthfully.

He smiled grimly.

"I know that," he said, "because you have hidden your treasure."

"If I have hidden a treasure," I replied, "and you know it, then your majesty, or one of your majesty's servants can find it."

"Let it be so," he said.

"I was given then a fine repast, and while I was enjoying it, a black (the one I suppose whom I had caught watching me) left the palace with several others to seek for the treasure.

"I ate and drank contentedly, for I knew what the result of his expedition would be; that, in fact, he would not find the treasure.

"He returned with a blank face enough.

"Of course he had not discovered anything.

"He quickly told the king what he was pleased to call his 'misfortune,' and Abdoolah's face grew as black as night.

"What means this, stranger?" he asked. "You are shipwrecked upon our shores. Allah is great, and Mahomet it his prophet! Do you think you are not sent hither for some purpose?"

"The ways of Providence are inscrutable," I said. "I may be here for some purpose: but certainly not to enrich you! I have no treasure."

"You were seen to hide it, Spaniard," he cried, "hide it on this shore, which belongs to me. So tell me quickly where is it?"

"Of course I had not much time to think.

"But I remembered this.

"I was alone on a foreign shore; if I gave up this money to the savage who demanded it, I should be in no way the better off.

"He would simply destroy me, that no trace should exist in regard to the robbery of my money.

"The notion that I had money concealed from him would doubtless be the means of preserving my life until such time as I had a chance of escape.

"I have no money," I answered, "that I can deliver to your majesty."

"You refuse, then, to tell me where you have deposited this treasure," he said furiously.

"I did not like to tell a direct falsehood, and accordingly I continued to give him evasive answers.

"Your majesty has been misled," I said. "I can say no more."

"Then by the beard of the Prophet!" he cried, "you shall remain here until you do tell; aye, until you point out the exact spot where you have hidden this treasure. If you had acted honestly and shown me the hiding-place of this money, I would have hailed the first ship and sent you home to your native land. As it is, you shall be my slave."

"I made no remark except a bow, and murmured 'I must yield to thy will.'

"From that hour to this I have been his slave.

"Again and again from that time I have been asked, on pain of death, to reveal the secret of this treasure.

"But I have refused always.

"To him the money shall never be given, for when once I yield it my fate is sealed.

"I hope yet to return to Spain with

it, to enjoy it in my own native land.
And yet even while I say this I know
not how to do it."

"With the sword," said Vyvyan; "but
tell me, why did your attempt at escape
nearly cause your ruin?"

"Hush! speak not so loud," exclaimed
the man, looking about him anxiously,
"even though they do not understand
the language I speak, I dread to speak
too loud.

"I will explain," he added in a lower
tone. "The King Abdoolah has among
his wives a Circassian, whom he bought
from one of the pirates and slavers who
infest this shore.

"She is a Christian—a woman of some
five-and-twenty years of age—a woman
of firm resolves.

"A woman, too, of handsome form
and face; one too, who hates the king.

"In her own country she was betrothed
to a Circassian of her own age and faith,
and her horror at being forced to become
the wife of this Abdoolah was indescribable.

"By dint of all manner of devices she
contrived at length to have speech with
me.

"It would take too long to tell you how
this was managed; but at any rate, we
met by appointment in the gardens of
the palace.

"Here she proposed to me a plan of
escape—one which she had long ma-
tured—which struck me as being capable
of accomplishment if carried out properly.

"But there was a condition attached
to it which at once caused me to refuse
all participation in it.

"It was that on a certain night she or
one of her attendants whom she could
trust, should enable me to enter the
palace, where I should murder the king
in cold blood.

"Nothing but this act of revenge for
the wrong done her would satisfy her.

"Of course I declined.

"She begged. she implored, she offered
me her love—she threatened.

"But in vain.

"Sword to sword and man to man I
would not mind even now risking my
life with his.

"But not in cold blood would I destroy him to secure my liberty and that
of a hundred others.

"I have not betrayed her, however.

"It was discovered that I met her;
and I believe that she was flogged.

"As for myself, I was flung into a
dungeon, and had it not been that I
knew their language, and that I was
useful to Abdoolah, I should have been
tortured to death.

"However, my knowledge of their
tongue and the faint hope that I would
yet reveal the whereabouts of my treasure saved my life.

"I tell you this as a warning.

"When she knows that you are here,
she will be certain to try the same with
you. Have nothing to do with her. You
have no treasure, and know not the language of this savage; you would be destroyed at once."

"Fear not," said Vyvyan, "the beauty
of no woman would induce me for one
instant to swerve from the right. My
heart is buried is England: no fear is
there that it will meet its resurrection
here or elsewhere. We will wait awhile
and see if the wreck of the pirate ship
comes ashore. There may be things
washed in by which we may be able to
bribe these savages."

"Unless, indeed, they take all for
themselves," said the Spaniard.

"There may be things of which they
know not the use," said Vyvyan; "but
at any rate, there is another way of
escape—and that is force. We are four,
and no doubt the power of gold will
enable us to bribe some of the blacks to
aid us."

"That is doubtful," cried the Spaniard;
"but, come whatever danger there may,
I am one with you. My life here is one
long misery."

"I would rather die than risk such
another," said Vyvyan; "but now that
I have told you my name let me hear
yours."

"My name," replied the Spaniard, "is
Don Henriquez de Calvados, and I hail
from Cadiz."

Vyvyan could not repress a cry of surprise.

"Calvados," he said, "that brings
strange memories to me; and as such is
your name, I think it is but my duty to
tell you a recent incident in my history."

Quickly, without any reservation, Vyvyan told the story of his adventure in

Cadiz with Don José de Calvados, which resulted in the death of the latter.

He expected, naturally, a storm of anger—if Don Henriquez turned out to be a relation of Don José.

It happened very differently to what he had anticipated.

"Captain Vyvyan," said Don Henriquez, "the man whom you killed in fair fight is my cousin, and was my rival. I shall be all the more eager to return to Cadiz, for Julia will be mine."

"You love her even now," said Vyvyan, in surprise.

"Yes," said Don Henriquez, smiling, "what she did, or rather wished to do, was for the good of Spain. It was mad patriotism. But, hush! here comes our masters."

And with a grim smile the Spaniard rose from his seat.

CHAPTER XLI.

THE WRECK ASHORE.

THERE was still a burning heat in the air, when the king came out from the palace.

But he was impatient to hear more.

Abdoolah, in fact, had a terrible greed for gold.

He would wade knee deep in blood to obtain treasure, and he had a fixed idea in his mind that all Spaniards and Englishmen were laden with treasure.

"Well, most noble travellers," he said (of course through his interpreter), "are you refreshed after your rest and your meal?"

"Much, I thank your Majesty," replied Vyvyan: "and as soon as it is cooler we are going down to the sea shore, to see if we can discover any sign of the wreck."

The idea of Vyvyan and his friends going down to the sea-shore alone in such an independent manner was not at all to the liking of the African King Abdoolah.

But still he kept his objections to himself.

He thought it, in fact, better to watch than to give vent to any outbursts of fury.

Perhaps if he allowed them to have their own way, they might be the means of his discovering an abundance of things which otherwise might be lost to him.

But not on this account would Vyvyan and his friends be spared.

They would be used as instruments to discover wealth, and then they would be destroyed, where Henriquez de Calvados, owing to his knowledge of the language, would be spared.

So he made no objection.

As soon, therefore, as the heat of the day was over, he and Morgan the buccaneer and William de Grey took their way towards the beach.

To their surprise they were not watched or followed by any one.

They were allowed to roam whithersoever they listed, and they accordingly, seeing that apparently no danger, pressed out as far over the sandy beach as they could go in order to obtain some trace of the wreck of the pirate ship.

It was only a dim idea which had presented itself to Vyvyan's mind when he spoke of the chance of finding the pirate vessel.

But it was realised in the strangest of ways.

Suddenly, as they turned a point where a huge heap of sand had been piled up, he came suddenly upon a sight which raised the utmost wonderment in his mind.

The pirate ship was there.

High and dry on the sand, driven into the drift of a sand bank, and lying with its broken bowsprit upraised towards the sky, as if threatening the land on which it was stranded.

Of course it was bashed, and indented, and knocked out of shape.

But there it was.

The very ship in which he had watched and waited for help from De Grey when Morgan the buccaneer had prayed so earnestly for vengeance against him.

It was not the ship which Vyvyan had so longed to see.

It was the large boat of the ship—the only one which had not been capsized or stove in.

This was his hope.

If they could only contrive to bring this boat a short distance inland up the creek, they would be enabled to so conceal it that they might defy the utmost scrutiny of the King Abdoolah.

And Morgan the buccaneer entered fully into the scheme.

At the first landing on the Barbary coast he had made up his mind to betray Vyvyan and William de Grey: the latter simply for the reason that he had helped our hero.

But now his opinions had changed.

He had seen no chance of obtaining favour with the savage king, and he thought that after all it would be better for him to throw in his chance with his late prisoner and his friend than to run the risk of the friendship of a treacherous black.

So Morgan now turned out of extreme use.

He knew the coast well.

He had been shipwrecked there; he had sold goods and slaves there; he had, in fact, traded there with everything.

And so without any searching and ferreting about he was enabled to point out to them a spot where, as I have said before, a small boat could be hidden away easily.

The boat on which Vyvyan had so much relied for the escape of himself and his comrades was able to carry a good sized sail, and would have been able to have shown a good pair of heels to any of the Barbary cruisers—at any rate for a time.

The only chance of ever its being discovered if they were enabled to place it in its hiding place, was that the King Abdoolah or some of his blacks might come to visit the wreck.

How was this to be got over?

It was a knotty question.

But it was settled by Morgan the buccaneer.

"Captain Vyvyan," he said, "you will allow *one* thing, and that is, that *I* am best acquainted with my own ship. In the hold of the vessel there are barrels of gunpowder, which we can easily blow up. I will send the vessel towards the skies, and all *visitors* who may happen to be on board."

As he said this, he looked significantly at his companions.

They both understood him to a certain extent, though not completely.

"What is it you allude to—explain Morgan," cried Vyvyan, "for if it be murder I am not one with you. Life is too short to take away except it be in fair fight."

Captain Morgan muttered a curse.

"I understand you not," he said angrily. "I know this, however, that, by fair means or foul, I mean to escape from this Barbary coast. It is not, as I have said, the first time that I have been on shore here; and I know, therefore, their barbarous cruelty. If the King Abdoolah or any of his courtiers were to come on board the ship, I would blow them to Mohammed's Paradise much more swiftly than ever the prophet went in his dream!"

"Even a savage I would not see slain in cold blood," said our hero; "if he attempted any treachery, however, then would mine be the hand to send him to his reckoning."

Morgan smiled.

"You little know this Abdoolah," he said, "or you would never think about him without coupling treachery with his name. However, let us get this boat out, or we shall have a drove of these savages upon us."

He lost no time in scrambling towards the point where they could most easily remove the boat; and, having shown them what to do, it was not long before the long-boat and its sail and mast had been recovered safe and sound and run up the little cove.

Here it was grounded, filled and covered with sand, and there left; not even so much as a mound remaining to indicate the spot where it was buried.

They had hardly done this when Abdoolah and several of his men, including Henriquez de Calvados, made their appearance on the sandy beach.

They came on leisurely enough.

In fact there seemed so little likelihood of a feasible escape that Abdoolah made no haste to prevent it, preferring, in fact, to find them busy with the stranded ship, which the artful old savage knew well, from his spies, had been thrown high up on the sandy shore.

Vyvyan and his companions, as I have said, saw him coming.

But they did not desist from their work.

Without taking any notice of the approaching crowd of blacks, they walked about the deck examining everything, and then—one and all—disappeared into the hold to search for the barrels of gunpowder.

These seemed of more especial account to Morgan than all the treasures of which the old Arab dreamed so much.

"Ha! ha!" he cried, bursting into one of those uproarious laughs with which he had been accustomed to rouse the quarter deck of his ship, when she was merrily scudding before the wind, "ha! ha! here is the treasure which would do good to the King of the Barbary Coast. Let him take a few barrels into his palace, and place us near them, and then see how long it would be before he would pay a visit to the stars!"

Vyvyan caught him by the arm.

And when he looked round he was astounded at the glance in the face of the Heir of Montreville.

"Come, Captain Morgan," said Vyvyan, "I'll have no more of this.

"From youth upwards I've fought against all treachery.

"I will be with you in any fight, open and honest; and if I were confined in a dungeon I would blow up the place, reckless of all I might incur.

"But when I am free—with the free air to breathe, the free sky above me, the free earth beneath my feet, the free sea to gaze upon—I cannot see reason for treachery."

He glanced along the shore as he spoke, and saw that it would be some little time before Abdoolah and his host could reach the ship.

Then he turned once more towards Morgan.

"I have a few moments to speak," he said, "and I will briefly tell you something, which, even pirate as you are, should make you more honest towards those you deal with.

"Some years since I was in Spain; and I was out beneath the battlements of the town, when I heard a cry for help.

"It was evidently the cry of a woman, and rushing to the spot, I saw that a young girl was lying on the ground, and that a man was slinking away.

"I was just behind him.

"I saw at once that he had not observed me, and I could have run him through if I had chosen.

"But no!

"I had never done a treacherous action, and I was not going to do so now.

"I placed my hand on his shoulder; he started round, and soon we were at it—sword and dagger.

"But the fight did not last long.

"He was a splendid swordsman, for as his dress denoted, he was one of the Spanish guard.

"But he seemed to desire no fight; and when he found breathing time, he cried—

"Stay, stranger, why are we fighting?"

"That I may know," I replied, "what you have done to that young girl, who lies helpless yonder."

"He drew back, and lowered his gleaming sword.

"Why did you not kill me?" he cried; "you were behind me, and could have stabbed me in the back."

"I am a soldier," I answered, "and never do such things as that. No matter how great a villian a man may be, I would never act the traitor to him. Tell me, why is that girl lying senseless yonder."

"The cause is simple," he said; "she had money and jewels, and I robbed her."

And as he spoke he put up his sword.

"And now," he said, "I am going to restore them. You have given me a lesson in nobility."

"Yes," added Vyvyan, still addressing Morgan, as the African Abdoolah came pressing up hurriedly; "Yes, that man kept his word.

"He returned every jewel and coin that he had taken from her, and during my stay in Spain that man was the most faithful retainer I had.

"He wished, indeed, to follow me all together.

"But that I would not allow.

"He would have had to fight against his own country, and that I would not be the means of securing.

"I parted with him at Cadiz, and he was a changed man."

"And how no you think this applies to my plan for putting out of the way this hideous African despot?" said Morgan, with a sneer.

"I think," said Vyvyan, "that it proves that even in the blackest hearts there must be *some* chord of sympathy which honesty of purpose and kindness can touch. And more than that, why should we destroy innocent lives? Why should we kill his wives, his children, and his men, because we desire to be rid of him?"

"Bnt here he comes," added Vyvyan; "we must do our best to propitiate him."

CHAPTER XLII.

THE AFRICAN MONARCH SHOWS HIS TEETH—A PLAN OF ESCAPE.

WHEN Abdoolah made his appearance at the side of the wreck, Vyvyan was leaning over the broken bulwarks.

"Welcome, most noble king," he said.

The king smiled.

That is to say, that he grinned so as to show his huge white ivories.

"Have you found what you desired to find?" he asked.

"No, not all; but much that will be pleasant to your majesty," replied our hero, readily.

"And what is that," asked Abdoolah.

"*This*," said Vyvyan; "there is an abundance of gunpowder, and many muskets. That will be grateful to you, I know."

"Truly it will, oh! noble stranger," said Abdoolah; "but is there no gold?"

"No; at least I have found none," said Vyvyan.

At this moment Morgan thought it full time to speak.

"Most gracious king," he said, "*I* was captain of this ship, and *I* can tell you that no gold was in it."

The African shook his head.

"Ah!" he cried, "I know well the strangers who roam through the world in search of treasure. They always say, ' I have none.'"

"But this is true," exclaimed Morgan; "I swear it. I am a pirate. I acknowledge it. I am a free rover of the wild ocean, and I was in search of plunder. But I did not find it. I should not have scrupled to have taken anything which came in my way, no matter how hard I should have had to fight for it. But I did *not*, because I was overtaken by the storm, and flung helpless on the mercy of the waves."

"Come, your majesty," he added; "come and examine the ship for yourself; and see where could I have hidden anything."

The black king took him at his word.

He left his men, where they were crowding on the sandy beech, and crawled up the rigging.

Then he said—

"Pirate—if so you choose to call yourself—if you prove yourself to be true, you and your friend shall be admitted to a high post of honour."

"In what position?" said Morgan, with a strange eagerness.

Traitor as he was to the backbone, he saw in this a chance of venting his spleen upon Vyvyan.

"That we will talk of another time," said Abdoolah; "in the meantime let us look over this ship."

The African monarch was evidently greatly pleased with the free manner in which he was taken over the shipwrecked vessel of the famous pirate.

And he found that Morgan had spoken the truth.

At any rate, to all appearances, it seemed to be so.

There was not a hole of any kind where he could have stowed away anything in the shape of treasure.

Abdoolah came out satisfied.

Vyvyan and his companions followed him back most unwillingly to the palace.

All would have preferred remaining where they were.

But as it was they had no choice.

And, each having different reasons to desire to remain, they did not confide their opinions to one another.

At length the palace was reached.

Here a place was assigned to Vyvyan, with William de Grey, while Morgan the buccaneer was summoned to a private confidence with Abdoolah.

CHAPTER XLIII.

THE AFRICAN KING HAS A BRIGHT IDEA.

The chamber assigned to our hero was a pleasant one enough.

It was, in fact, in no respect a prison, although they knew well that they were not free agents.

" What think you of this, De Grey ? " asked Vyvyan, after he had surveyed from the window the light and pleasant garden.

" I think, now, that there are more dangers than one."

" How so ? "

" I think that Morgan and this African king will plan your destruction between them. I feel certain."

" What makes you believe that," said Vyvyan.

" Because I saw it in his look to-day. One glance was enough to assure me that we were both in peril," said De Grey, " and *you*, perhaps, more than myself."

" When did you think this ? "

" When we were on board the wreck, said the other ; " when the black king promised him a high position."

" Good ! " cried Vyvyan ; " linked as we are by fate, it is strange indeed that our thoughts should flow so thoroughly in one channel. At that very moment the same idea rushed through my brain. Yes ; he will betray us."

And as he said the last words as if to himself, he walked to the window which overlooked the grounds.

His mind once more was in a strange turmoil.

Now that he was in danger—face to face with a peril, from which it seemed difficult to escape, he felt a home sickness—a longing to see the face of Eveline, and clasp her loved form to his heart.

And now and then another vision came to him.

A vision, which he endeavoured with all his strength of mind to cast from him.

A vision of a mother, forced by absence to long for the son she had discarded !

What he saw in the garden was something which was certainly ill calculated to repress any such emotions as these.

A mother was seated under the shadow of some stately palms, with a baby at her breast.

The mother was gazing down in love at her infant, while the child's hand was toying with her bosom.

" Ha ! " he muttered, " why did I see this ? Oh ! why did my mother discard me ? Should I have been standing here, a prisoner and in peril, if my mother had not disowned me ? "

And he sank on an ottoman near the window, and buried his face in his hands.

Meanwhile, Captain Morgan had sought the presence of the African king.

The latter had evidently conceived what he thought a wondrous idea.

He grinned to the extent of his capacious mouth as he saw the captain of the pirate vessel.

" Welcome," he cried ; " sit down beside me here."

And he pointed to a place on the ottoman near him.

Morgan sat down.

His evil mind saw at once that he was about to be taken into favour.

"Well, your majesty," he said, "speak on. I am your patient listener."

The African, after a slight pause, said—

"You are a good sailor?"

Morgan laughed.

"I know every sea, and every rock it holds," he cried; "is that enough?"

"Yes," said the king; "but tell me can your ship be repaired? Can it be made again to sail upon the wide ocean?"

The pirate's heart leaped at this.

He saw before him now the chance of escaping with life and treasure, and of repairing, to a certain extent, the loss he had sustained.

Even as regarded Vyvyan—whom for such a paltry motive he had resolved to destroy—there was now open to him a good opportunity of carrying out his evil purpose.

"Yes," he said; "with what remains of the ship we can fashion a bark that can well sail on the sea. But tell me for what purpose do you want it?"

The African rubbed his hands, as if he was so enjoying his inward thoughts that he was unable to answer for a time.

"I cannot explain now exactly what I do want it for," he said; "but can you guarantee to me that you can make a ship of any kind that will ride upon the sea, and bring to me a treasure from a foreign land?"

Morgan was a clever man.

He knew well that this African savage had in his mind some thievish purpose, some plundering of an enemy, or some seeking for another man's treasure.

And so he—knowing well what profit he would get from the transaction, and what chances of revenge, too, he might have, answered—

"Yes; though of course it depends upon what amount of treasure I am supposed to bring in it."

"It is only a small treasure," replied the African king, "but we may have to fight a large force to obtain it. Can you make the ship strong enough to enable me to fight an enemy?"

"Oh! yes," said Morgan, eagerly.

"And you have gunpowder?"

"Yes."

"And cannon?"

"Yes; four."

The king rubbed his hands again.

"Ha!" he said, "that is what I have longed for; that is what I have hoped for so long. If you will only do as I wish you, you shall be my head man; you shall never want to return to England any more, or to roam the seas. You shall be my commander-in-chief."

Morgan knew well that the best thing was to accede to the wishes of the king.

So he accepted the matter in a serious light at once.

"I accept the post, mighty excellency," he said, "but you must be aware that there are great dangers connected with it. In the first place, if I fail I shall incur the displeasure of your majesty."

"Fail in what?" said the African king suspiciously.

"Supposing that I were to fail in making the ship?"

"Then I should consider that you were a fool," said Abdoolah.

"Why?"

"Because you have told me that you *could* make it."

"Providing I had the men."

"You shall have them."

"Very well," said Morgan, "I will go on. But there is another thing."

"And that is?"

"Suppose that even with the great assistance that your majesty can vouchsafe to me, I was unable to fight the enemy and defeat him?"

"I should know from my people whether you did your best," replied the king; "and then you must remember that you will have good assistance from the white men who are with you."

Morgan shook his head.

"No, no," he said; "do not believe in that. They are not my friends."

"How came they with you, then," asked the king.

This of course was only asked for the sake of seeing whether either Vyvyan or William de Grey had told a falsehood.

For an instant Morgan was inclined to betray them.

But then his cunning nature recoiled from such an idea.

If he betrayed his English friends—whom could he call on to aid him in the building of the ship, which was to convey him—not as Abdoolah had said—in

"VYVYAN'S SWORD FLASHED THROUGH THE PIRATE'S CHEST."

search of treasure, but in search of the shores of old England ?

So he said at once—the thought I have named having flashed through his mind in an instant—though it was difficult after his first speech to alter what he had said—

"How are they with me, you ask. Then I will tell you. One—that is Captain Vyvyan—was given to me as a prisoner; the other is only one of my sailors."

"And yet you say," said the African, "that they are not your friends, after they have been shipwrecked with you, and escaped with you."

Morgan shrugged his shoulders.

"You want me," he said, "to do you a service ?"

"Yes."

"Does it require any prowess ?"

"Yes."

"Then leave it all to me," returned Morgan, insolently; "your people are not of our people, and know nothing about fighting."

"They do !"

"You think so, but they do not," returned Morgan; "now will you listen to my plan."

The voice of Morgan was becoming more commanding. He saw that the negro king was thinking better of him, and so he began to be bombastic.

"Yes! I will listen to your plan," said the African king.

His voice expressed anxiety.

But he did not express it in words.

"Well then," said Morgan, the buccaneer, "you know that we have two Englishmen—or rather Europeans here."

"Yes."

"Leave the commanding to me, and to my friends," said Morgan, "and within a month we will have a ship ready that will bring you treasures from everywhere. We will bind ourselves to you

for a year, but there *must* be conditions."

Morgan said this advisedly.

He knew well that it would not be right to let the king see that he was too eager to accede to his wishes.

"And what are the conditions ?" said the king, gloomily.

"That at the end of one year we shall be allowed to visit our own native land."

"And return to me ?"

"Yes, of course," said Morgan. "I have your promise to make me commander of your forces; but there is some one in England whom I should wish to bring out with me."

"Certainly," replied the king, beginning to be convinced, "and out in my kingdom, I know that there are many fair maidens who would be willing to become your wives."

"I thank you for your hospitality and your kindness," replied Morgan with affected annoyance, "but in our country one wife is considered enough. However, that is not the question. If you will not interrupt me I will explain all."

"Speak on, I listen," said the king.

"You must let me have the assistance of as many men as possible," said Morgan, "for we shall have to fell timber and saw planks."

"Saw !" exclaimed the king. "What is that ?"

Morgan smiled.

"That is just it," replied he. "You know nothing about shipbuilding, and when this ship is built I shall have taught your people the art, so that they will be able to build vessels for you themselves. For this I ask freedom of action for myself and friends."

"Certainly," said the king, "you can go and come as you please. I will come and see you build the ship, so that I shall some day be able to direct them myself."

CHAPTER XLIV.

THE BUILDING OF THE SHIP.

No time was lost.

The African king having conceived this wondrous idea of building a ship, at once he was eager to see its fulfilment.

So a quantity of the best men in the colony were detailed to aid the Europeans in their task.

Never had the scantily-clad colony been so busy before.

There was heard everywhere the felling of timber in the palm groves.

Men and women, too, were employed incessantly in carrying the trees.

The carpenter's tools had come ashore with the ship, and consequently there was not any difficulty.

The natives had abundance of axes, and were soon taught the use of the saw.

And so the long, low line of shore was soon the scene of such business and work, as had never before been seen there.

Vyvyan looked on at the workers with great pleasure.

"What a pity," said he to De Grey, "that we cannot teach them more of our civilized ways. It would put an end to many of their savage ways."

"Ah!" exclaimed De Grey, "but it will not be so. It will never be so. How can you expect to make anything of such savages as these."

"They can work, if they are taught," replied Vyvyan. "You see for yourself. Why should they not be able to do everything? See what a beautiful land it is."

De Grey smiled.

"Beautiful! do you call it," he said.

"Yes."

"Does it equal the shores of Old England? Does it equal our own neighbourhood—the coast near the Castle of Montreville?" asked De Grey.

"Nay; then why speak of that?" asked Vyvyan; "the glorious fields. the lovely lakes, the evergreen landscapes. Oh! where is there a land like England?"

Vyvyan paced to and fro for an instant as he said this.

Then, as if he were overwhelmed by those memories, which included Eveline and that mother of whom he had so painfully been reminded by the woman with her baby at her breast, he cried, as he seized De Grey by the arm—

"England! Why talk to me of England! Oh! for her green fields and beauty now! I can see now in my mind's eye her lovely landscapes—her rivers—her streams! her hills and dalés.

"Why was I driven from her?

"Why was I ever asked to quit her lovely shores?

"Why am I here, an outcast and a wanderer?"

De Grey smiled bitterly.

"Ha!" he said, "ha! you make me smile. You talk to the winds. Why do you not talk to your own thews and sinews? Why do you not think to yourself—if we are brave we will win?"

Vyvyan almost resented this.

He looked angrily at the speaker.

"There is no England for me now!

"Why did you ask me to think of her?

"In England there is the only one I ever loved.

"I am an outcast, you know.

"Outcast from love—outcast from the place of my birth—outcast from all that I hold dear.

"Well, well, let us leave it alone," added Vyvyan; shall I tell you one thing?"

"Aye, what is that?" asked De Grey, dreamily.

"This," said Vyvyan. "I was once on the deck of my ship the 'Falcon.'

"I was looking round and fancying to myself how foolish it was to wish to live

"I was thinking, here we are out on the rolling sea, and we know not for a moment whether those whom we have left behind care whether we ever arrive home or not.

"But this is why I ask you to be

brave. I saw coming along a foreign ship.

"Didn't I know then that I wished for home?

"Didn't I think to myself, 'put aside those idle dreams, here is a battle coming, and you must fight for home and liberty.'

"And there *was* a battle.

"A terrible one too.

"It was a Spanish corsair, and, though many mouths on board our ship watered for the gold she contained, she attacked *us* first.

"It was just what my men wanted.

"We fought, all of us.

"And well too.

"I brought my ship up; we closed and we sprang upon the deck of the pirate.

"The pirate chief's sword flashed as I rushed towards him.

"Ha!" he cried, "another traitor.

"I staggered.

"A traitor!" I cried; "why?

"Why?"

"Because, my friend," he said, as he prepared to give me my quietus, "because *you* are an Englishman; and so am *I*. And *you* are a traitor, if—

"I waited for no more.

"The men were closing round me.

"My sword flashed through the pirate's chest.

"And as he fell back, with uplifted arms—the cry was 'Surrender.'

"And they did surrender.

"My men took the ship. The shouts were 'hurrah! hurrah!'

"Of what avail was it?"

He paused.

De Grey looked enquiringly round.

"I do not see what this has to do with it," he said.

"No; I suppose not," replied Vyvyan; "but I will explain. I believe in our triumph. I believe we shall win. But, *then*, what have we to live for?"

"You say 'we'" returned De Grey.

"Yes."

"Why so?"

"Because," cried Vyvyan, "I know that we have nothing much to go home for. And another thing—no matter what we do—we *must* recall the past."

De Grey shrugged his shoulders.

"We are building a ship," he said, "when it is built we shall be on the wide sea once more. Wait till then. There is yet a deal to be done."

The ship went on apace.

The Africans worked manfully.

No one suspected the hidden boat, for Morgan took good heed of what he was doing, and was careful that no one went near the creek, where it was concealed.

The ship, day by day, approached larger dimensions.

Under the directions of Morgan and the others, the vessel was fashioned with extra thick decks and so forth.

And when it was completed the old king was invited to be on its deck, when first it glided out upon the radiant waves.

Merrily the ship sped as she was launched upon that summer sea.

The king, as he stood on its deck, was radiant with smiles.

"This is glorious," he cried; "for *this* you shall all have freedom."

Vyvyan's heart leaped at this.

He was no coward.

But still he longed for home.

Warnings had so repeatedly come to him; visions of his mother and Eveline, his sweet promised bride, had been so frequent that he felt called towards home.

Freedom, therefore, was a great word to him.

"It is worth freedom to have taught you such a trade as this," said he; "*you*, cooped up in your kingdom, knowing nothing of the glories of the sea, are nothing to what you *can* be, owning a number of ships, and the dominion of your seas with it."

"Ah!" replied the king, grinning at the interpreter as he said his words, and shaking his head at Vyvyan in a strangely comical way; "it *will* be grand! Then I can carry my men to the shores of my enemy, king Ka-lulu, and have my revenge for old scores."

Morgan the buccaneer heard these words with intense satisfaction.

They, in fact, told him that his hateful plan had succeeded.

He approached the king and Vyvyan.

"The king has need of more men," he said.

He said this respectfully.

Abdoolah was quite deceived.

"Yes, yes," he cried eagerly: "I know well that I do want more men. To-morrow we will embark, and then, perhaps, I shall be able to repay you in golden treasure for what you have done."

Far out on the billowy ocean the sun was glittering merrily.

But there was a little cloud, as it were, on the sea, almost resembling an island.

Vyvyan, as he leaned over the bulwarks, glanced at this, and it reminded him of England.

"Golden treasure," he thought; "what is golden treasure to the one that I expect when I reach that other shore.

The building of the ship was over.

The sailing was to come.

Morgan now threw off his old reserve.

He saw that his plan was on the eve of accomplishment; and he was traitor enough to keep silent while he perfected the scheme which was to bring triumph and glory to himself and ruin to his fellow adventurers.

"My king," he said, "if you will be guided by *me*, you will find yourself not only king of the country that you are now governing, but miles and miles away on a prettier and a more golden coast."

"I *will* be guided by you," said Abdoolah, who was now enthusiastically in favour of the men, whom the day before he would have hung.

"To-morrow, then, I will ask you to bring your ministers and your men on board, and I will take you to the island of Cedars."

Abdoolah was suspicious at this.

"Island!" he cried; "there is no island on this coast."

"Yes," said Morgan, "there *is*. That only proves the necessity of your having a fleet. You know not the power you could have if you had ships to scour the coast, and bring you the gold and silver that can be dug up in the island of Cedars and at other points far away on this coast."

"*You* will be the captain," said Abdoolah.

"Yes, *I* am the captain," replied Morgan, "and my two friends here are first and second lieutenants. But *you* will be commander."

He knew well how to flatter the pride of the African king.

When they landed Morgan took Vyvyan apart.

"Captain Vyvyan," he said, "shall we work together in this?"

"Certainly," replied Vyvyan, "it is my place to work with you."

"Then," said Morgan with a strange smile, "I tell you this. To morrow we shall not only be free, but princes of Barbary if you choose."

Vyvyan would have spoken to him at this.

He would have made some remonstrances.

But it was of no avail.

The pirate was too artful.

He passed away suddenly as if he was anxious for something.

And the king not understanding him, did not follow him along the deck.

He was too eager for the morrow.

⮑⚬⮐

CHAPTER XLV.

THE SAILING OF THE SHIP.

NATURE seemed specially to have accommodated itself to this venture in which the Heir of Montreville was so much concerned.

The morning broke bright and beautiful.

The sun shed its golden glory over myriads of wavelets, which seemed as if they were gold-crested under the kiss of the day-god.

Over this pleasant ocean, which seemed to invite the launching of many a brave ship, there was not to be seen a single sail.

And into this silence of the sea the African king sent his first ship.

With him went his ministers and his men, fifty of them fully armed and equipped.

De Grey took Vyvyan aside.

Such a scene as this had never been beheld on that coast before.

At the appointed time the king and all the great men of his tribe came down to the beach, and embarked on board the vessel.

At this moment Morgan the buccaneer seemed to lose his head.

He gave orders as if *he* were the king instead of being a slave.

And when the ship sailed at last he found himself master.

Neither Vyvyan nor William de Grey took any part in the proceedings.

There was a silent feeling between them that there was something wrong.

There was a good reason for this.

Morgan had been seen in too close conversation with one of the black chiefs, and when they were fairly out at sea, De Grey, approaching our hero, said—

"Captain Vyvyan, beware!"

"Of what, cousin," said Vyvyan, "for such you are?"

"Of Morgan," replied De Grey, in an undertone; "he has some how or another obtained command of the blacks—at least, those who are the head of the band."

The words had scarcely left his lips when a sudden wind swept over the ocean.

The little waves broke into billows, and the ship began to roll violently.

"Now," cried de Grey, "see for yourself."

Vyvyan glanced in the direction pointed out.

Morgan, springing up the rigging, issued his orders as if he had been the captain and Abdoolah was no one.

The ship was now making for the open sea.

The black king gazed wonderingly as he beheld the long narrow line of coast disappearing as it were and mingling with the ocean.

He had, in fact, never been so far from home before.

He had been into the interior of the country: had seen vast plains of sand, only interrupted by groups of date palms.

He had seen villages—if so they could be called—in oases in these deserts.

But he had never been in the presence of the mighty ocean, grand with its wind-swept billows, rising gold-crested as they were kissed by the sun of the morning.

Suddenly, Morgan gave an order quickly, which brought the ship up.

Then he sprang upon a barrel.

"Now, my men," he cried, "to your duty."

It was evident from the way that he spoke that he knew well that he could depend upon those to whom he spoke.

Instantly about twenty of the blacks sprang towards Vyvyan, De Grey, and the black king.

Morgan knew well that anything in the way of treachery was not in the heart of Captain Vyvyan.

He had expected, therefore, that he would help the black king.

But he had forgotten that both Vyvyan and De Grey were armed.

Lost on the sea, left to the mercy of the waves, driven by the storm without a helping hand, they at last landed on a shore where such things as a good strong English sword was unknown. But the wreck had supplied what the sea had taken from him.

The pirate vessel had in its hold an abundance of weapons of all kinds; and so when Vyvyan and De Grey passed on to the deck of the pirate vessel they had swords and pistols too.

When the blacks sprang towards King Abdoolah, therefore, two swords flashed in the sunlight.

Vyvyan knew well that his real plan now was to stand by the African king.

He had always suspected Morgan, but he had not thought that he would so soon throw off the mask.

"Back, villain," exclaimed Vyvyan, as he stood before Abdoolah, "traitor and outcast, what mean you?"

"This," exclaimed Morgan, as he aimed a terrific blow at his head. "This, for Wrecklyffe."

"Even Wrecklyffe was not such a coward as *you*," exclaimed Vyvyan, "who will speak for me to this king?"

He had forgotten that the Spaniard was there.

The Spaniard who acted as interpreter.

"*I*," he cried, "can speak to the king."

"Tell him quickly," said Vyvyan, as he aimed a tremendous blow at his enemy, "tell him that there is treason aboard. This is a planned matter between Morgan and some of his ministers, and he must rouse his crew at once."

Don Henriquez translated literally the words, quickly too, to the African monarch.

Abdoolah's eyes lit up as it were with fire as he heard the news.

It was indeed news to him.

Snatching a pistol from Vyvyan's willing hand he fired recklessly and madly at Morgan.

As he did so he shouted aloud—

"Men of Serai Town, be awake! We are betrayed by the northern sailor! Think of your homes and your wives and your little ones, and do not listen to the words of strangers."

Of what use was this appeal?

There was only one white man to oppose all this host of blacks.

Yet Morgan had succeeded.

He had so estranged the feelings of the blacks that they had consented to leave their king and roam the wild seas with him.

At a sign from Morgan they made a dash at Abdoolah.

Crash went a shot from Vyvyan's other pistol through the brain of a huge black, who seemed to be Morgan's chief coadjutor.

A huge negro, who apparently had been bribed by Morgan to betray his master.

Morgan uttered a loud curse as he saw his best man fall upon the deck.

But although this was a partial victory for Vyvyan, it was in reality his downfall.

With a terrible yell, the other blacks dashed forward, and in a moment Vyvyan and his party were surrounded.

They fought well, but how could they hope for success.

The king's party had no weapons of a better nature than broken muskets, sold to them by piratical bands; bad rusty swords, and so forth.

The blacks who had been enrolled on the side of Morgan were armed with good weapons, given to them out of the wreck by Morgan, and they knew how to use them too.

During the building of the ship he had lost no opportunity of teaching them the use of the guns which had made his crew so powerful upon the sea.

And so when a few of the blacks joined with Vyvyan to aid the king, they turned the cannon upon them.

The battle was soon over.

Fight as Vyvyan would, he could not battle against dozens and dozens: and so at length — disarmed and helpless, bound with cords—he stood face to face again with *his* foe, and Wrecklyffe's friend.

"Why is this?" cried Vyvyan, "what hideous treachery is this?"

"It is no treachery," replied Morgan, "nothing of the kind. You were my prisoner before; you are my prisoner again. This time you shall not escape me. Down with them."

These last words were spoken in the language of the country.

And the effect was instantaneous.

Vyvyan and De Grey were seized and dragged down into the hold of the vessel.

The negro king was brained and thrown overboard; and the only blacks that stuck to the remnant of royal dignity were so terrified by the success of the daring man from the north, that they knelt on the deck, bowing their heads, and saluting him as if he were a god.

Morgan, the pirate, laughed aloud, as he saw the humbled crew.

"Ha! ha!" he cried, "the Fates hurled me out upon the world as a reckless— maddened man: a man who had lost everything in life—even hope, which is the sweetest of all.

"What had life to offer *me*, whose father and mother were murdered before my eyes: whose bride was snatched from me at the very hour of our wedding.

"When that happened, life itself was before me: but all the light was gone from it. What was it to me, but a barren waste."

"And so—my lads—hey! for our island home."

In another moment Vyvyan and his companions were battened down in the hold.

"What, now," said Vyvyan, "is to be done" (addressing De Grey); "do you wonder now at my feeling in bad spirits

—hopeless—despairing. The fates seem to have declared against me."

"Against *me* they have always done so," replied De Grey; "it is nothing new. But this time we are in such a dilemma that I cannot see my way out of it."

"Nor *I*," replied Vyvyan; "I fear that this will close our career on this coast, and for ever! This man Morgan is resolved to destroy me. He has some insane idea of chivalry in his memory of the dead pirate Wrecklyffe. He promised him to destroy me, and he has done his best to keep his word."

"What think you is his plan?" asked De Grey.

"I feel sure I understand his aim," replied Vyvyan: "he will sell us into slavery. He knows that will be more terrible to our minds than death."

"To *me* it will be," replied De Grey.

"And to *me* it will be a horrible terror, for I have so much to live for, if I *can* but have my freedom," said Vyvyan; "my love, whom I have left in England; my enemies to punish also."

"It would not matter so much if we could fight hand to hand and sword to sword," said De Grey; "but battened down here with this wretched crew we have no hope."

The Spaniard who had acted as interpreter between the negro king and his guests was among the prisoners in the hold of the ship.

"This is only as I have suspected," he said, addressing Vyvyan and De Grey; "I have all along known that there was some conspiracy against you and the king."

"Why not have said so?" said Vyvyan.

"I have warned you against this pirate," replied Don Henriquez de Calvados; "I have told you again and again that you were in danger."

"But what could I do?" said Vyvyan.

"You need not have embarked."

"Why, then, did *you*?"

The Spaniard shrugged his shoulders.

"How could I avoid it?" he said; "I have been a slave so long, that even if I had known that it was my duty to refuse, for my own sake and the sake of those I love, I should very likely have acquiesced."

"We have nothing to do but wait and hope," said Vyvyan.

Meanwhile the ship sped merrily over the sea.

As I have before hinted, the Island of Cedars was a place existing only in the imagination of Morgan the buccaneer.

It was not to any such place that he intended to direct his ship's course.

He was in search of the dominion of king Ka-lulu, whom king Abdoolah had mentioned to him.

He knew well the spot to which he alluded.

It was a district where a wide river rolled its lazy way towards the ocean.

And in the bed of this great stream were stores of gold—which, as in the realms of Lazistan, could be raised by the fleece.

The natives of this place knew well this secret of wealth.

Not for sale or barter was this yellow ever sought for dross used.

They had no communication with the white conquerors of the east.

On their heads it was placed in wreaths.

Children used it for necklets; young warriors used it to circle the arms and legs of their brides.

Young and old, high and low, wore it: and Morgan the buccaneer laughed as he thought what an indiscriminate slaughter would bring him in the way of plunder.

Morgan had with him men who were in no way ignorant of the coast.

They had been before overland to the territory of these people.

Under the command of Abdoolah, they had descended upon these peaceful blacks, and by murder had accumulated large stores of gold.

But Morgan proposed nothing of this kind now.

He had filled the heads of these men with other ideas.

He had promised them a grand future.

Under *his* leadership they would sail triumphant over the sea.

He would teach them how to meet the Spanish galleons in fair fight, and win from them rich stores of plunder.

So while Vyvyan and De Grey were lost in memories of the past, and thinking only of the way in which they could escape and turn the tables on the villainous pirate: Morgan and his men sailed over the sea triumphantly; and the ocean was loud with their wild songs of glory.

CHAPTER XLVI.

IN ENGLAND AGAIN.

Sir Grey de Malpas one bright morning quitted his house, and made his way eagerly up the steep ascent which led to St Kinian's cliff.

He and the landscape around seemed strangely out of place.

The sun was bright over land and sea.

The waves of the reckless ocean were just stirred by a gentle breeze: a breeze that toyed too with the branches of the trees—that grew up high on the cliff.

The golden light fell on the tiny crests of the billows: and kissed the bosom of the inland lake that lay nestling in the shadow of the castle of Montreville.

Everything looked so green, and gay, and pleasant, that Sir Grey looked quite out of place.

His parchmenty face; his queer smile; his evil eyes; his walk, leaning on his stick seemed so utterly at variance with the lovely aspect of nature, that anyone standing on St. Kinian's cliff, and seeing him climbing up the steep ascent would not have failed to notice the strange anomaly.

And yet there was a gleam of joy in his eyes as he went up the rugged side of the hill.

Evidently he was overwhelmed by some inward evil joy; and was eager to try the result of the accomplishment of some new plan of villainy.

What a different scene was there on the summit of the hill that he was approaching.

There, on the crest of the rock, stood a man, whose white hair fluttered in the wind.

A man, whose calm blue eyes gazed upon the sea as if he were thinking of an unblemished past, and could look confidently to his future.

This was Alton the priest.

Years had pressed their weight upon his brow.

But they had left few lines upon his face.

He had had his troubles—he had a lost love—-he had been hunted by enemies.

But he had the possession of all others which is the best.

A clear conscience.

And so his features were beautiful—refined—grand—as compared with those of the man, who, with compressed lips and clouded eyes, struggled towards him up the side of the rugged hill.

" I give you good day, Alton," said Sir Grey de Malpas, as he neared the priest; " it is a morning on which all the world should smile "

Alton seemed as if he were about to say something suddenly.

But he restrained himself.

" Yes," he said, " it is indeed a lovely day; a morning on which blessed thoughts alone should enter the mind of men. But pray tell me what brings you to my home so early."

A glance of evil meaning was in the eyes of Sir Grey de Malpas as the priest spoke.

" I am here because you have betrayed me," he said.

The priest started.

" Betrayed you ? " he cried.

" Yes ; betrayed me," replied Sir Grey ; " you know the charge I left you."

" What! have you come here to speak of Vyvyan again?" said the priest, sternly. Has he not already suffered enough at your hands ? Let him rest now, for, if my heart tells me truly, he is but a memory, for his crushed and weary life has passed away ! "

Sir Grey started at this, and forgetting himself in his eager villainy, clutched the priest by the arm.

" Dead ! " he cried, " dead ! it is not possible. He will live yet to see me triumph

" Nay, then," cried Alton, sternly, " he will not live to see that, because that will never be."

Sir Grey de Malpas recoiled at this.

He had always, as he had thought, found Alton a willing instrument.

But he was wrong.

Alton was apparently an instrument, because he desired to further the ends of justice.

He knew, perhaps, unfortunately for himself, the secrets of all the Montrevilles.

And now confronted with Sir Grey de Malpas, what could he say but the truth?

The truth that welled up from the depths of his true heart.

Sir Grey's eyes flashed as if he could for a moment have roused up some of the pluck of his youth, and struck the priest to the earth.

In fact, his nervous, half-palsied hand, that was so eager to grasp the crown of office, to touch the insignia that appertained to the Montreville Estate, was raised as if to strike the hermit.

" What mean you?" he cried.

He spoke in savage accents.

But Alton, apparently, did not fear him.

" Do not use intemperate language to *me*," he said; " the world is wide enough for you and for *me*. Tell me, at once, what you want. Tell me unreservedly —because I wish to hear all you have to say at once, and then never to look upon your evil face again."

" I wish," said De Malpas, who almost feared the energy of the hermit priest, " I wish to say, as I said before, that you have betrayed me. You know well that I left you a certain charge, and *that* you could not see to."

The priest looked at him loftily.

" What!" he cried, " do you allude to William de Grey?"

" I do."

" And what of him?"

" Did I not deliver him entirely to your charge?"

" Yes."

" Where is he?"

The priest faltered a little at this.

He was a good man.

He had no wish to do wrong to anyone.

But he had an earnest desire to do right, and when he found terrible family troubles, he tried, as far as possible, to smooth the road for those who were more sinned against than sinning.

" How do I know?" he cried. " How can you ask me to know?"

Sir Grey de Malpas stamped upon the ground angrily.

" What mean you, Alton," he cried, " you are the only one of whom I can ask anything. I demand an account of the one whom I left in your charge."

" And *I*," said Alton, " can say nothing except what I have said before, and what, perhaps, will only serve to exasperate you."

Sir Grey De Malpas leant calmly upon his stick.

Yet this calmness meant anger.

" It will not exasperate me more than I have been exasperated before," he said.

" Then," said Alton, boldly, " I will tell you what you seem to have forgotten, because it is so many years ago.

" You told me a secret then.

" How long ago it seems!

" You told me of a secret love—of a being whom you worshipped and of one whom yet you dared not name as your own."

" What then?"

" Do you remember how you begged of me that I would not reveal your words?"

" I do."

He said these words sternly

Apparently they meant but little.

But they were intended to convey a great deal.

Sir Grey did not reply for a time.

" Ha!" he said, " you are unjust."

This was after a while as he gazed out over the wide ocean.

" There was no injustice," said Alton the priest.

" No injustice! Prove it then!" replied Sir Grey.

" I will," said the hermit, placing his hand upon his arm. " You once loved a maiden far beneath you, as I have said before. You then had a son, and fearing the anger of the great people of Montreville you rushed to *me*—me, the unfortunate priest who has to learn and advise upon all these great people's wrong doings.

" Well, as in the case of Vyvyan—your master!—the Rightful Heir of Montreville—I took charge of this child for you.

"I knew well that he was never able to claim his rights.

"You promised many things.

"You said—but no matter, why prolong it? Shall I whisper something? No! But I *will*. Grey de Malpas! You have done wrong, and you will suffer. He lives, and is coming home!"

This was too much even for Sir Grey.

He seized the priest fiercely by the arm.

"Ha!" he cried, "you lie, as well as prophecy! I tell you that I know well that you knew from the first that I never wished to see that brat any more, and yet I have information that he is even now alive, a man, willing to fight me for my inheritance because I was fool enough to marry in secret and give my name where it need never have been."

The priest for a moment seemed disinclined to speak.

But he did at last.

"Ha!" he said, "the sins of the Montrevilles follow them everywhere. The son which you wished so much to disguise is not dead, as you say, and why?"

Sir Grey replied not.

"*I* will answer you," said Alton, "because I refused to have a hand in his murder. Is that enough."

"Enough for *me*," replied Sir Grey. "I knew, as I have told you repeatedly, that you are my enemy. and that is sufficient. By Heavens! a bitter retribution shall be yours."

"Why?" exclaimed Alton.

And he smiled bitterly.

Although there was still something triumphant in his smile as he thought of his far off Vyvyan.

"Why?"

"Do you ask me why? I will tell you, because you were trusted by me to save me from a disgrace, and you have not done it."

Aud then he gathered something up of his old dignity and walked away.

Without even a word.

Alton looked after him regarding him closely.

"Ah!" he murmured, "bad relic of an old race! You have brought disgrace and—yes, it is true—infamy upon the race of Montreville! And yet I father your wish. May the wretched boy die, so long as Vyvyan, the real Heir of Montreville, lives to claim his own."

He stood watching the lame old Heir of Montreville (the real earl as he hoped each moment of his life to be) as he descended the steps of the rock.

And then, good old man as he was, he turned aside, saying—

"Heaven help me! How can I say else? When is Vyvyan coming to set this all right?"

CHAPTER XLVII.

THE SEA FIGHT.

WILD were the cries of joy, as I have said, as Morgan and his men went sailing away.

The blacks were delirious with the emotion of the moment.

They knew well, some by sight some by report, the realms of King Ka-lulu.

The "Golden Fleece" to them was no novelty.

And so away they sailed, pressing onward, according to the wishes of their new leader, until they had gone far beyond the coast from which they started.

Naturally the object of their voyage was something which roused to the utmost the energies of the blacks.

Gold!

Gold!

What could be more beautiful to them?

But in the midst of their dreams they were disturbed.

On the first evening they saw approaching them a large ship.

A ship armed with heavy ordnance, and flying the Spanish flag.

The latter seemed to know that Morgan's ship was wrong.

The rig and so on was outlandish.

Of course, under the circumstances this idea was ungenerous.

But how could their opponents pause to think of this?

They could not think that the ship had been put together on the shores of Africa.

And so they demanded its surrender.

The answer was Morgan's usual battle cry.

"Death or Glory."

And then the fight began.

Loudly the battle cries rang through the air.

On deck and below.

It was with a feeling akin to mad joy that Vyvyan and his companions heard the news that an enemy was approaching, and that there was a chance of having a real brush with them.

Whatever enemy Morgan the buccaneer had, must of necessity be a friend to them.

So it was with eagerness indeed that they listened to the roar of cannon, and the hurried trampling of feet overhead.

Of course there was terrible danger.

At any moment a cannon ball might come crashing through the timbers of the ship, and destroy them.

But of this they did not think, though of course the idea could not help occuring to their minds.

"I wonder what ship this is," said Vyvyan; "whoever they may be they are attacking with great spirit and vigour."

"We shall soon have a chance of seeing the fight," replied De Grey, with a grim smile; "it will not be long, I fancy, before a cannon ball makes a peep hole for us."

The words were scarcely out of his mouth when a ball came crashing through the timbers not far above their heads.

Vyvyan at once sprang up, and thrusting his head through the opening, saw that the attacking party were composed of Spaniards, who had brought up to the attack a splendid vessel, bright with fresh paint and gold.

She looked like a fairy thing almost, in spite of her size, with her swelling white canvas, and her graceful hull dipping at every swell of the waves.

"She is a friend at any rate," said Vyvyan, "because the Spanish flag, though raised against the English, are enemies to the Africans. See! see how they fight! Oh! how I wish I were with them."

De Grey held his arm, as he thrust his head and nearly his shoulders through the aperture and dragged him back.

"So we will be presently."

His eyes were lit up by a strange light.

"What do you mean?" cried Vyvyan.

"Look there," said De Grey.

Vyvyan glanced in the direction which had been pointed out to him.

He saw through the broken place riven by the cannon ball, something which gave him really courage.

A huge axe and other weapons.

He knew De Grey's meaning at once, and sprang forward.

At once a huge axe was wielded in his hands.

One crash and the intervening door was assaulted.

A second and it was broken down.

Vyvyan and his companions were free to ascend.

They were armed, for in the hurry and confusion nothing had been said about weapons.

And so they went on deck with weapons ready for action.

The pirate Morgan was certainly not prepared for this.

With the European chiefs battened down in the hold he of course imagined himself to have a fair field.

However, he had never expected this attack at all.

When he sailed over that bright ocean after his prisoners had been properly secured, he had turned the prow of his ship towards that region where King Ka-lulu revelled in his golden streams.

King Ka-lulu was a savage like King Abdoolah.

But he was of a different type.

He was a man who delighted in accumulating riches round him of every kind.

Riches that he could look at.

If his subjects dug up the proceeds of the golden streams, he had them made into beautiful armlets, and necklets or vases.

Grottoes near his palace were adorned with the golden store.

Amid lumps of quartz and granite and so forth, glittered huge pieces of gold.

Gold paved his palace yard mingled with other metals.

Gold mingled with the adornments of every portion of his palace.

To this real El Dorado, therefore, it was that the buccaneer Morgan directed his ship.

The gold that these savages knew not how to use, he knew well how to spend.

So away he was speeding in all haste, when to his astonishment and fear he heard the booming of a far off gun; and turning in the direction saw a big ship coming down upon him.

I say fear.

And it was really fear that animated him.

Such a feeling had, indeed, been foreign to him for many a long day.

But with such a crazy ship as he had what could he hope to do.

The vessel, as we know, had been framed out of any timbers that could be scraped together.

The old planks had been linked up as best they could with the palm planks.

And a crazy affair it was that the African king was so proud of.

He had never seen, belonging to himself, any vessel of any kind.

So, to see a ship in full sail, no matter how crazy it might be, so long as it belonged to himself, was so grand a thing to him, that he lost sight entirely of the fact of how badly it was built.

Bad as it was, he would in his mad exultation have sailed all over the world in it.

But Morgan knew better.

He was well aware that the craft he sailed on was a desperately risky affair.

That, in fact, it would be dangerous to trust to it, except on a quiet summer sea, when the waves were still, and the wind was quiet.

Still more dangerous was it when an enemy was in sight ready for action with guns, which, if properly directed, would blow the newly-built ship out of the sea.

However, Morgan, buccaneer and pirate as he was, was as brave as a lion.

He did not care how or when he was assailed.

On the open sea he would have attacked a Spanish galleon, if he had had only enough men to board it.

And so, when he saw the enemy approaching, and knew that his prisoners were safely battened down in the hold, he had the decks cleared for action.

Of course my readers have not forgotten that he had no white sailors on board.

His crew consisted purely of blacks.

And, though blacks have before this been good sailors, these blacks were perfectly innocent of everything nautical.

And so it was a terrible job this marshalling of newly-enlisted sailors, who did not know a jib-boom from a broomstick.

However, by dint of constant and persistent exertions, he at length obtained sufficient mastery over his crew, and by the time that the enemy closed with him, they were under sufficient control to be able to be commanded upon any occasion.

The fight I need not describe.

It was a miserable scramble.

Yet a brave one.

The blacks were as brave as if the salt sea air had given them fresh courage and strength.

They swarmed up the rigging, and when the enemy were alongside, they dropped from it upon the deck.

It was a strange fight.

The attacking vessel was a Spanish one.

Well freighted, and ready to go home.

But still, seeing this unsightly vessel rolling in the trough of the sea, and seeing the black objects which swarmed in its rigging, the captain of the "Cadiz Treasure" made at once towards it, and attacked it naturally as a prize.

And thus, therefore, the fight began

CHAPTER XLVIII.

VYVYAN IN A NEW ADVENTURE.

AT the moment, when Vyvyan and his new friends rushed upon the deck, swords in hand, the Spanish seamen had begun to be in the ascendant.

The blacks, who so madly and so courageously had plunged as it were upon the deck of the " Cadiz Treasure," were gradually driven back.

One by one they were slaughtered, and flung overboard to feed the fishes.

As they deserved—having been traitors to their king.

But when Vyvyan and his friends appeared on deck, Morgan and his men gazed for an instant in wonder at them as if they were discussing in their minds whether the three (the king's minister and his companions), would join in the affray in their favour.

They were soon undeceived if such was their idea.

Henriquez was no coward.

And, as he saw Vyvyan and De Grey raise their weapons and dash at the crowd of negroes, he joined them.

The apparition was so sudden and so unexpected that they were utterly confounded.

Like all the men of the same race, they had an absurd veneration for royalty; and to see the favourite of their late king, leaping up when he was never thought of, to attack their enemies was more than they could understand.

They were fighting for treasure and attacked by an enemy.

Why should the favourite of the king, who had been imprisoned by his own people, try to aid them?

The question was soon solved for them.

Henriquez, they saw, was not on their side.

His sword flashed like that of Vyvyan and of De Grey, from its sheath ; and, as the two white men dashed forward, he fought with them.

" For Spain and liberty ! " shouted Vyvyan, loudly.

" For Spain and liberty ! " shouted Don Henriquez de Calvados.

" For England ! " cried De Grey, with a mocking laugh.

" For the black flag ! now or never ! " cried Morgan.

But the cries had had their effect.

The crew of the Spanish vessel knew at once that the little band of armed men, who had issued from below decks, were their friends.

" Hurrah for England ! "

" Down with the black pirates."

" This way ! this way ! "

Such cries as these greeted the ears of our hero and his strangely assorted companions as they fought their way from the spot where they had so suddenly emerged into light.

And Vyvyan, seeing how matters were, and that the crazy old hulk on which he stood would soon collapse, knew easily what to do.

To talk was useless.

All that was left to him was to take the initiative.

" This way, my friends," he cried, and he leaped towards a point where the brave Spaniards were endeavouring to force their way upon the deck of the African ship.

De Grey, with the Senor Henriquez de Calvados, knew at once what he meant and followed him.

As the Spaniard's knowing now that they had friends on board redoubled their efforts, Vyvyan drew near to Morgan.

This was nothing to displease the buccaneer.

Vyvyan, the enemy of Wrecklyffe, the one whom the latter reckless ruffian had left Morgan to destroy, was before him now sword to sword and man to man.

" Ha, traitor ! " cried he, " you turn now upon your own countryman ? "

Mad words these from a pirate and an assassin !

But he meant them in his own heart.

He dashed at Vyvyan eagerly.

For a moment they were engaged alone, and both were so engrossed in the hate and vengeance which actuated their hearts that they almost forgot where they were.

But this did not last long.

The Spaniards, seeing that they had allies on board their enemy, pressed onward still more rapidly.

They rushed upon the deck of the foe; and when Vyvyan was hard pressed by Morgan and some of his blacks, the captain of the Spanish ship was side by side with him.

"Ha!" he cried; "we have come to the rescue of brave men, I see."

Vyvyan laughed aloud, as his sword sought another black's heart.

"Brave, I hope; but certainly your friends," he said; "*we* are prisoners, and remember this black, who fights by my side, is true also! He is Don Henriquez, of Cadiz, here only through treachery, and my friend."

They knew nothing of the death of King Abdoolah, but they trembled for the future.

What if this African king should bargain with the others to sell these men into slavery?

Yet what could he do?

It was better even now than he had expected.

The Spanish cruiser had won the day; and they were soon *en route* for Spain.

━━◦◦✕◦◦━━

CHAPTER XLIX.

THERE IS MANY A SLIP BETWEEN THE CUP AND THE LIP.

BUT there were circumstances over which Vyvyan had no control.

The officers of the "Cadiz Treasure" had heard a whisper in regard to the plunder which was to be obtained from King Ka-lulu.

The plunder, in fact, which had been the mutual object of King Abdoolah's minister and Morgan the buccaneer.

And, as they had had by no means a successful voyage hitherto, they regarded this as a splendid opportunity of filling their pockets.

And so, just as Vyvyan was making up his mind that he was going to return to Spain, and thence to England, he found himself once more drifting along the African shore, in the direction of the realms of King Ka-lulu.

The only one to whom Vyvyan could tell his secrets was William de Grey.

They were together on the morning after the fight, where no one was observing them.

"De Grey," said Vyvyan, "at what position are we now?"

"Worse than before; at least, in your case," said De Grey, "if you desire to return to England."

"Why?"

"Because these Spaniards, grateful though they may be to you for your sudden and unexpected aid, and for your assistance to their captain, will not turn out of their course for you."

"What, then, is to be done?" said Vyvyan.

"We must either abide by the wishes of the officers of this ship, or we must do a desperate deed."

Vyvyan started, and gazed in astonishment at his companion.

"A desperate deed!" he cried.

De Grey smiled.

"Nay, then, I mean no murder," he said; "I mean desperate as regards ourselves."

"What is it that you propose?" said Vyvyan, in a low tone.

"You see yonder pinnace."

"Yes."

"Well, then, what I propose is this,"

THE RELICS OF THE DEAD REVEALED.

said De Grey: "We will go boldly to the captain and tell him that our object is not plunder. What we desire is to return home quickly. Ask him to allow us to launch that pinnace and take our chance upon the open sea. The ocean is in a kindly mood; the summer sun shines bright. We shall risk a thousand perils; but so we do when we venture into the kingdom of King Ka-lulu."

"True," said Vyvyan, "I have sailed these seas before, and know them well."

"Then you think my plan is good?" said De Grey.

"I do."

"Then do *you* go and speak to the captain," said De Grey; "you have more courage than *I* have in such matters as these. Go, and may good fortune attend you."

Vyvyan accepted the office at once.

He was never one for procrastination.

Turning from De Grey he went at once in search of the head officer, whom he found lazily looking over the bulwarks gazing at the summer sea.

"Well, most noble Englishman," said he, as Vyvyan approached. "In what can I serve you?"

"Greatly," said Vyvyan.

"Then name your desire, and it is granted," replied the Spanish officer.

"You must know, then, my friend," said Vyvyan, "the object of my life at present is to return to England. I wish for no plunder. I have a voice calling me to make my way at once to my native land."

The Spaniard smiled as he gazed at the speaker.

This handsome adventurer, who desired only to see his native shore, and cast aside the temptations which were offered to him of gold to be had for the taking.

"Come down into my cabin," he said, "we can speak there in private."

He led the way, and in a few moments Vyvyan found himself in a luxuriously furnished cabin.

A cabin that was in unison with the splendour of the rest of the ship.

It was more like a splendid apartment in some Spanish Don's house than anything else.

"Be seated," said the officer; "speak your mind freely to *me*, for I am a Spanish gentleman, although fortune has caused me to roam the seas."

"I will speak freely," said Vyvyan, and with reservations he told his story.

He suppressed much; but the Spaniard saw even what Vyvyan did not see.

"If you wish for my advice," he said, "I will give it."

"This, then, is my advice," said the Spaniard; "go home."

Vyvyan pressed his hand to his brow.

"I cannot bear to think of the future," he said, "if the future in England, if my life—my Eveline—is not there! My love I ever dreamed of in those days at Montreville. I had no right there! I came there as a rough sailor, not as one who knew anything of that grand old place! And yet I knew it in my dreams, when as a boy I floated over those summer seas, under the very cliffs that were mine! To my companion, Don Henriquez, I do not fear to tell the truth. We have been in so many dangers together that I think it would be un-christian almost to keep back even a secret."

"Nay," said the captain, "it would not be un-christian, but it would be foolish."

At the moment that the captain and Vyvyan were talking no one was listening.

The sailors were attending in a lazy manner to their duties.

On everything there was a summer haze.

"Will you believe in me, then?" said Vyvyan.

"Yes."

"Then give me the pinnace, and with the help of my friend we will soon make our way home. We do not desire wealth or anything of that kind. All we desire is freedom."

"You cannot be long in that desire," returned the captain.

And in a short time it was done.

The pinnace, which Vyvyan and De Grey had asked for was floated out on to the sea, and away they sped in the direction of the Spanish coast.

"Hey! for England once more," cried Vyvyan.

CHAPTER L.

ST. KINIAN'S CLIFF ONCE MORE.

A TWELVE-MONTH had passed away since the night when Vyvyan and Clarence Beaufort met on the gloomy summit of St. Kinian's Cliff; a twelve-month, during which the roses had paled on Eveline's cheek, the light had dimmed in Beaufort's eye, and the heart of Lady Montreville—eaten into itself, as it were—racked by strange and bitter fears, yet knowing not what it feared.

Sir Grey de Malpas had not yet triumphed.

All was uncertain still; there was no proof to fix on Clarence the guilt of murder; and the coronet and the fortune were as far as ever from the brow of the dastard kinsman.

It was bright noon, as, on this day—about the anniversary of Vyvyan's departure—Sir Grey, scarcely looking older than he had on that fatal night, walked up the rugged path towards St. Kinian's, and leaned upon his staff, on the summit, to commune with himself.

"A year," he murmured to himself, "and Wrecklyffe still is mute and absent, even as Vyvyan is. I can understand it now. He saw, and haply shared, the murderous deed of Beaufort, and *his* wealth has bribed the pirate to desert me in my poverty. That Clarence slew his brother, I have no doubt. He shuts me from his presence; but I have watched him wandering alone. He is, I am certain, haunted by some secret terror! I have marked the white lip and glassy eyes of one for whom the grave has ghosts, and silent horrors."

Yet with this knowledge, Sir Grey's mind was still racked with uncertainty.

"The Lady Montreville," he muttered, after a pause, "excludes me from her sight, on a vague pretext that I sold her first-born to the pirate. She sends me alms still, lest the world should say, 'See! her poor cousin starves!'—but does she guess Beaufort's guilt? No, no, she lives, and death would be her portion if she knew it. This deed of Clarence

known unto the world would make me heir of Montreville. Oh! mockery! how can I proceed without proof? How charge him without a witness? How cry, 'Here is murder,' and produce no corpse? And yet there is something within me which tells me that the end is not far distant. Ah! here comes Alton. He has been wondrous close of late, and seemed to shun me. Good morrow, Alton."

"Sir Grey de Malpas!" exclaimed the priest, advancing along the rocks as quickly as his tottering steps would bear him. "I was on my way to your house."

"Can I then serve you, good Alton?" said Sir Grey.

"You can, even if it be but in listening to me and counselling me in my difficulty. The boy I took from you—you will remember—returned a man twelve months ago."

"It is true."

"I was then absolved from my oath," continued the priest, "and upon this very spot I hailed him the Rightful Heir of Montreville. From my arms he rushed to claim his birthright and his mother."

"She never told me this," muttered Sir Grey, a new light dawning on him.

"That night," proceeded Alton, "his war-ship sailed to our fleet, and I thought him with the battle. Time went by; heaven's breath had scattered the Armada, and I hoped to welcome him again. He came not, and I thought 'his mother has abjured him and law detains him, while he arms for justice.' Hope sustained my patience until to-day."

Sir Grey started.

"And why to-day?" he asked.

"The very friend who led me to his breast when first he came to England returns, and—"

"Well?"

"He fought not with his country," said Alton, the tears standing in his eyes, and his head drooping on his chest.

"And this cold friend," said De

Malpas, "has suffered all question to sleep for a year?"

"He was not in fault," said Alton. "His bark too rashly chased the flying foe, was wrecked on hostile shores, and he was taken prisoner. He has hurried with his first steps to tell the fatal news."

"Lean on me," cried Sir Grey, soothingly, "you are faint."

The priest recoiled.

He had not forgotten if De Malpas had, the last interview between them.

"Nay, I need no help," he said. "Oh! Grey de Malpas, can men so vanish except in murderous graves? You turn away. What think you?"

"What murder is there without motive?" answered the wily villain, who now saw plainly before him the path of treachery which he had to follow, "and who had motive here?"

"His unnatural kindred," returned the priest, solemnly.

"Kindred!" exclaimed Sir Grey, starting away with well-assumed dismay. "Ensnare me not! My kindred, too, you speak of. Old man, beware how you asperse Lord Beaufort!"

The priest clutched him by the arm.

"Beaufort! Oh! horror!" he cried, "how the instinctive truth starts from your lips."

"From mine, priest?"

"Ask no pardon of man," pursued Alton, sternly, "if in this hideous crime you were accomplice, for——"

Sir Grey rudely shook off his grasp and drew himself up to his full height.

"I accomplice!" he exclaimed, with simulated anger. "Nay, then, since it is *my* good name you call in question, this is my answer. Prove, examine, search, and call on Justice to belie your slander. Go seek the aid of Sir Godfrey Seymour—a dauntless magistrate, strict and upright."

"Aye," thought he, with grim satisfaction, "at heart a Puritan, and hates a lord!"

His apparent zeal acquitted him in the eyes of the priest.

"You may be right," said he. "I will take your counsel. Sir Godfrey bears with all the character you give him. I will go and seek his aid."

"And remember," said Sir Grey,

"while you acquit *me* that *I* lay the charge on none."

The priest shook his head as he prepared to depart.

"Heaven reads the heart," he said, "man can but track the deed. My task is a stern one, but mark you, I'll fulfil it."

Sir Grey rubbed his hands, and his evil eyes glistened as the priest departed.

"Scent lies now," he murmured, "suspicion begins to fall. I must await Falkner here, he will be my ready tool."

He had not long to wait, for within a few minutes Falkner entered with some sailors, to whom he was giving instructions, not noticing at first the presence of Sir Grey.

"Learn all you can," said the young rover, to them; "when he was latest and where. Meanwhile I seek yonder towers."

"Doutless, fair sir, I speak to Vyvyan's friend," said Sir Grey, stepping forward, as Falkner was about to pass him. "My name is Malpas. Can it be true, as Alton informs me, that you suspect your comrade died by murder?"

"Murder!" repeated Falkner.

"And by a rival's hand? What! are you amazed!" pursued the treacherous kinsman, "surely I so understood the priest."

"Murder—a rival!" repeated Falkner. "Truly he loved a maiden?"

"In yonder halls, indeed," said Sir Grey.

"Oh, despair!" murmured Falkner, "am I too late for all but vengeance? Speak, sir; who was this rival?"

Sir Grey raised his hand deprecatingly.

"Vengeance!" he cried; "fie. Seek yonder towers and learn compassion. Sad change, indeed, is there since here, in the silent night, your Vyvyan met the challenge of Lord Beaufort."

"A challange, say you?" exclaimed the young sea-rover; "here, and at night, too? This increases suspicion."

"Yes, this is the place," said Sir Grey, who saw now that he could speak more openly; "see how sheer the edge; see the crags, caves, and chasms below! If the foot slipped—let us suppose heedlessly—or if some weak, wounded man were plunged headlong into such an abyss, what burial place could be more secret?"

"Come with me," said Falkner, who had stepped aside, and wandered near the edge, "look, where far down the horrible descent the waves rush through some subterraneous cleft, how the sea-gulls swoop their ghastly wings!"

"They swoop so before a storm," said Sir Grey.

"No," returned Falkner, still gazing down below, "The Heavens are clear! The storm *they* speak of is that which shall overwhelm the guilty. Thus I have seen the foul birds in lone creeks sporting round the bones of shipwrecked mariners. There is no use in delay—I will at once descend—my heart tells me there is here something to be learned."

So saying he waved his hand to Sir Grey, and began the perilous descent of the cliff.

With a heart full of hateful triumph De Malpas drew near, and leaning on his stick glanced down at the venturesome seaman.

From bough to bough of the weird trees he swung, dwindling down as he leaped from peak to slippery peak.

The loose stones rattled—but staggering, half falling, from ledge to ledge, he kept on his perilous way towards the spot where still the sea-gulls wheeled.

Then the crags closed around him—he disappeared, and all there was once more still.

"Oh! diver for the dead!" murmured Sir Grey de Malpas, "bring up but bones, and around the skull I'll wreathe my coronet!"

Little did Sir Grey de Malpas dream what Vyvyan was then doing.

Little did he imagine that he was plunging across the wide ocean in a tiny boat with another being, who, of all others in the world, he desired least to see.

If he had, perhaps his evil thoughts would have been less triumphant in their nature.

CHAPTER LI.

WHAT DE GREY TOLD IN THE STORM.

WHEN Vyvyan had been advised by De Grey to risk a voyage on the open sea, in the little boat, there had been a calm and gentle ocean.

But the ocean is well known for its treachery; and long before the night fell, there were symptoms of an approaching storm.

The pinnace was a splendid sailer.

She leaped over the waves like a thing of life.

Her sails bellied out, and she rushed on at a pace which bade fair to run them soon to their destination.

But there were elements of great danger around them.

The wind began to rise.

The waves began to be foam-crested; and the boat to pitch and toss in a perilous manner.

"I fear we have made a mistake, De Grey," said Vyvyan; "this pinnace is scarcely suited for such a sea as this."

"Nay, then, we must not be too hasty in our judgment," said De Grey; "this boat rides well. She will be able to stem a greater storm than this."

He spoke too hopefully.

At this moment the wind rent the sail, and away went a part of it torn into ribbons.

Vyvyan saw the danger now.

But he was a man, as we have seen, who never met peril half way.

His mind at once took in the situation.

"We are wrecked once more," he said; "it is our fate to be so, I fancy. We must keep as still as possible. See here, as I grasp the corner of the sail, we speed along again. This peril suits me, De Grey."

De Grey smiled.

"*I* do not mind it either," replied he, "for I feel that my life is only a drifted waif upon the ocean. I feel, in fact, as if I had no right to live; and when I see these perilous waves around me, I experience a sensation as if death was always near me, and that I should accept its embrace as I should that of a loved mistress."

Vyvyan seized his hand and pressed it.

"My friend," he said, "you must not give way to such thoughts. You can never have known love or you would never speak as you do."

Vyvyan felt a shudder pass through his friend's form as he spoke.

"Nay; say not so, Vyvyan," said De Grey, in a hoarse voice. "I have loved, and I have lost; that is why I know that there is no future before me."

Vyvyan, still holding the torn sail, round the gathered end of which he had bound a rope, thought a moment.

The Montrevilles seemed to have fortune strangely against them.

Here was another hopeless one.

What if he lost him now?

What, if in a mad fit of desperation, he were to leap into the boiling waves.

It was better to comfort him.

"You are young yet," he said. "Why should you indulge in such mad dreams! You have a bright future before you. Tell me of the past. It cannot be worse than mine."

"Ah! say not so," said De Grey. "Listen and know."

"I will."

And this is what De Grey told in the storm.

In Spain he had accidentally become acquainted with a lady—the Donna Inez D'Almira.

Young—handsome—rich—she was a glorious prize to win.

And yet, meeting De Grey at the house of one of the Spanish Dons whose friend he was, she was at once smitten with him, and permitted him, without any declaration as to who he was, to be her suitor.

De Grey had won money.

But very little.

He, in fact, had been like Vyvyan a tempest-tossed man.

But he did not think of this.

He was in love.

That explains a great deal.

As it blinds persons to a great deal.

He allowed his love entirely to overcome his judgment.

Without remembering that *she* was rich, and of noble family, he offered her his hand and heart.

She listened smilingly.

"I am not a man of wealth," he said, "but by the influence of my friends I can rise to a good position.

"I can do anything for such a one as *you*," he said, as he laid his hand upon his heart; "my love will conquer all."

"I care not for wealth," she said.

He was at her feet in a moment.

"Then you are mine," he said passionately.

He seized her hand.

But she withdrew it quickly.

"Rise," she said, "there is one other thing."

Her voice was very cold.

It chilled him thoroughly.

He rose and resumed his seat.

"What is this *one* thing?" he said, in a voice which trembled with emotion.

"Tell me that you are of noble birth!"

This was his answer.

Of course De Grey's countenance changed.

"Of noble birth," he said, "yes; but—"

He hesitated.

"It is right that I should know," she said; "speak on."

And De Grey told her all.

As he did so, he feared the result.

The story seemed to freeze her into a stone.

When he had finished she rose.

"Senor," she said, "you have completely deceived me."

The words were said in such a voice that it prevented him speaking for a moment.

And *then*—she was gone.

After this all efforts to see her were in vain.

He tried every method that he could invent.

But to no avail.

She was obdurate.

The curse cast on him by his father was upon him.

And his heart from this moment was broken.

Such was the story he told in the storm.

Vyvyan listened earnestly.

But he was unable to give much comfort.

At the moment that he was about to speak, the wind rose still higher than before—the waves began to mount fearfully, and suddenly the sail was swept completely away.

They were once more at the mercy of the waves.

Drifting they knew not whither.

It was a terrible time for these unfortunate adventurers.

No one but themselves could imagine what torture they were enduring.

Apart from the fact that they were heart broken in regard to the dearest ties of earth, it must be remembered that they had been so often shipwrecked, that it produced in them a terrible sensation of loneliness.

At one moment hope was in the ascendant in their hearts.

Then in an instant they were hurled into the uttermost depths of despair.

No one who has not been thus out upon the lonely and voiceful sea, can imagine how terrible is the feeling of knowing that you are out on that vast waste of waters —alone—utterly alone as these two men were—without the possibility of claiming help anywhere.

They glared out over the restless sea, even in the deep darkness of that terrible storm, in eager hope, though in their inmost hearts they could hardly expect aid.

Suddenly, however, to their astonishment, they saw near them a ship's light.

Loudly they shouted.

Could it be true ?

Yes, they were answered, and presently a huge dark mass was near them.

Then a rope was flung out, and they were not long in being hauled on deck.

In an instant they recognized the mixed crew upon it.

It was the "Cadiz Treasure" driven out of its course by the storm.

❧

CHAPTER LII.

A TERRIBLE SURPRISE.

LITTLE was Vyvyan prepared for what came next.

Suddenly a tall figure loomed up before him.

A mocking laugh rang in his ears.

The laugh of Morgan the buccaneer.

It will be remembered that when the Spaniards saved Vyvyan on the deck of the black pirate ship, our hero and De Grey took no notice of what became of Morgan.

He had been placed down in the hold with some of his men.

But bribery ruined all, and hardly had night fallen when a terrible massacre took place.

It was a scene worth describing, but hurrying as we are homewards towards the Towers of Montreville, we must give it in brief.

Morgan and his chief men rushed upon deck, and within half an hour the command was again in his hands.

Now, when he saw Vyvyan he laughed aloud.

"Ha!" he cried, "caught once more. Down with him into the cabin. After the storm he shall dangle at the yard arm."

Resistance was useless.

They were seized by a dozen hands, and borne below.

But there was aid and hope for Vyvyan yet.

Hardly had he been seized and carried down than a panel in the cabin wall was opened and a black man appeared.

A man whom Vyvyan had befriended during the building of the ship.

"Fear not," he cried, "I will save *you* and your friend too."

"What mean you," asked Vyvyan, hardly able to conceive the idea that he had found a friend in so unexpected a quarter. "What makes you believe that you have this power to aid me?"

"There is an English ship," said the man, "bearing down upon us, and on the deck I heard the words, 'Heavens! we are foiled now—that is the ship of Essex, the English admiral!'"

"Essex!" exclaimed Vyvyan, in utter surprise, "can it be possible?"

"I know not this Essex as you call him," said the black, "but I know *this*. You saved my life once during the building of the ship when they would have brained me; and I swear I heard the name. If it gives you hope, I thank Allah for it. To a friend, be a friend I say."

Vyvyan seized him by the hand.

Black as he was, he was still a man of honest heart.

"How will you do this, my friend?" he said, "I cannot see it."

"You must be still and wait," said the black.

And then he moved hurriedly back to the spot whence he had come, and disappeared again through the panel, leaving Vyvyan in a state of strange bewilderment.

Here was a friend, sprung up suddenly, to aid him in his extremity.

The approach of Essex in pursuit of the pirate vessel promised a speedy combat, in which it would be a matter of no difficulty for him to join and fight his way to his own friends.

Anxiously now he watched and waited.

The vision of Eveline was once more uppermost in his mind, and he resolved that not without a severe struggle would he relinquish the hope of once more clasping her to his breast, and claiming her as his own sweet bride for ever.

The storm for some time raged with unabated fury.

The wind howled like some mad creature amid the rigging.

Voices of men were drowned amid the voices of the tempest; masts creaked, ropes cracked, sails fluttered and flapped, waves rolled and plunged; yet still onwards the "Cadiz Treasure" rushed, for behind it was a remorseless enemy that cared neither for wind nor wave.

The Earl of Essex had recognised an enemy in the "Cadiz Treasure," when Morgan had run up the black flag.

And he was determined at all hazards to capture it.

Towards the morning the wind lulled a little, and the waves had settled into a wide swell, which rolled the vessel from side to side in spite of the counteracting influence of the sails.

Just as dawn cast its gentle halo over the ocean a ball came whizzing through the timbers of the "Cadiz Treasure."

Then a broadside crashed in, and after a few moments the pirates answered with a cannonade that made every timber in the vessel creak and tremble.

Vyvyan rushed to the door and tried it, but it was firmly secured.

"Essex will kill me like a rat in his hole," he murmured; "unless I can force my way on deck, all will be useless."

As he spoke the panel was pushed away and the black stepped in.

"Be not impatient," he cried, as Vyvyan advanced eagerly towards him, "the 'Invincible' is bearing up towards us. Then is your time—but not till then. To rush on deck now would be to court death, for you would be at once cut down."

Vyvyan, though burning to join in the affray, could not but see the truth of these words, and he waited, therefore, sword in hand, by the side of the black, who stood with eager face, anxiously listening.

At length the sea seemed to rise and plunge madly against the cabin windows.

Then came a bump which proved that the "Invincible" was alongside, while a loud and prolonged cheer showed that the brave boarders were ready for their work.

"Now, then," cried the black, "now follow me on deck, and we will cut our way through these cut-throats."

With these words he led the way up a steep ladder, and in a few minutes they were standing together on the slippery and blood-stained deck of the vessel.

The "Invincible" was now close up to the pirate ship, and the men, eager for action, were already beginning to swarm over the bulwarks and up the rigging.

The pirates had not bargained for such a fight as this.

To attack helpless merchantmen, no matter of what nation they were, was *one* thing.

It was another thing altogether to be assailed by a fully equipped English man-of-war, full of men flushed with victory and reckless of consequences.

Nevertheless, there was no flinching on the part of Morgan's sailors.

Devils as they were they were yet brave, and loud cheers were their responses to his loudly shouted words of command.

Engaged though he was, his eye nevertheless continually swept the deck, and Vyvyan had no sooner reached it, than the quick eye of Morgan the buccaneer caught sight of him.

"Ah !" he cried, foaming with rage at the probable issue of the fight, " you shall not escape me. In this hour of bloodshed the life of one more victim will matter not to me."

And with a bitter curse, he bounded towards Vyvyan and attacked him with the wild and insensate fury of a madman.

It seemed truly now as if Vyvyan was compelled to fight his way against unceasingly magnifying hosts of enemies ere he could reach any haven of rest.

It appeared, in fact, as if he was now punished for casting his bread upon the wild waters, and choosing the desperate life of a rover in lieu of the peaceful one which Fate had well nigh placed in his hands.

Yet he could not regret the course he had taken.

He knew nothing of his mother's bitter anguish—nothing of the wild entreaties which the night wind had wafted towards him from the battlements of Montreville.

So he only looked upon himself as the saviour of his mother's cherished idol, and the aider of her destiny.

Now, however, that old memories, and old hopes had been revived in his mind by the words of the Earl of Essex, new vigour seemed instilled into his arm, and

as he faced the infuriated pirate who had rushed so madly at him, his eyes glittered with undaunted fire.

The buccaneer soon saw that he had one to deal with whom, in the heat of such a fray, when his services were required elsewhere, it would have been better for him to have left alone.

It was not now the stripling whom Wrecklyffe had cast adrift upon the waves.

It was the bold-eyed, strong-armed, daring man who stood before him.

The battle raged round fiercely.

Morgan's first-lieutenant, seeing his captain engaged, took command of the men, and with a dashing bravery worthy of a better cause, led them on against the sailors under Essex.

For a long time the issue of the two contests was doubtful.

Both Vyvyan and Morgan were brilliant swordsmen, and the swords flashed and gleamed between the two antagonists so that those who, in the desperate fight could watch them, could scarcely tell from whom came the parries or the lunges.

So it was with the fight between the pirates and the men under Essex for some time.

Swarming crowds of struggling, fighting, swearing, shouting sailors thronged everywhere, hacking and hewing at one another like demons, but for a long time remaining in one compact body, as it were, neither making progress one way or the other.

They had the usual incentive to exertion—the cheering presence of good leaders.

The fall of these is generally the signal for disaster ; and at them, therefore, the worst of the fight is directed.

At length Morgan began to yield ground.

He had, inadvertently, glanced behind him to see the progress of the battle, and during that moment he had received a violent wound from Vyvyan's sword.

Loss of blood began now to tell upon him, and though fighting with the same ardour and courage, he yet found himself driven irresistibly inch by inch towards the extreme end of the deck.

His gait was now unsteady, and his actions wilder, and in his own heart he could not but foresee the dismal issue of the conflict, unless some fortunate accident occurred to save him.

Vyvyan, on his part, perceiving the advantage he had gained, roused his flagging strength, and attacked the pirate more fiercely.

It was not now a duel such as he had fought with the young Spaniard, whose life he had wished to save.

It was a contest with a bloodthirsty buccaneer—the scourge of the seas, whom it was his duty, as it was his wish also, to kill.

Presently his opportunity came.

The pirate's sword was held but loosely, but with a kind of expiring effort he dashed at the young captain.

Vyvyan drew back his weapon, turned aside the point of the sword, which would have drunk his heart's blood, and, in another instant, his bright blade went plunging through the chest of the buccaneer.

Morgan gave one despairing yell; one glance of terrible hate he cast upon his slayer, and then his sword dropped from his grasp and he fell heavily upon the deck.

A loud cheer from the sailors of the Earl of Essex proclaimed the fact that they had been watching with interest the desperate fight.

This, however, was not the only demonstration which followed the fall of the bold and savage buccaneer.

His men also had seen it, and, as I have before said, a feeling of disheartenment at once invaded their souls.

Their first-lieutenant, truly, was a bold and energetic man, and led them on bravely to the charge.

But he was not Morgan.

They had been used to regard this man as one of the invincibles, and when *he* fell it was like a proclamation of defeat.

Their discomfiture was still more complete when the Earl of Essex, leading on his boarders, leaped to the side of Vyvyan; and the two lieutenants soon shared the fate of the principal leader.

They had no chance now, and seeing that all hope was gone, they cried as with one mutual voice—

"Surrender!"

In a few moments the carnage was stopped, and in an incredibly short space of time there was peace and a wondrous stillness, where lately had been heard the clashing of swords, the shouts of combatants, the groans of the dying, and the explosion of muskets.

The first person whom Vyvyan sought for when he had thanked and welcomed his preserver Essex, was the man to whom he owed his escape from the cabin at the commencement of the fight.

He found him at last lying dead upon a heap of others, grasping by the throat one of the pirate crew.

He had died fighting for the good cause.

A prize crew was at once put on board the pirate ship, the command given to Vyvyan, and with a fair wind and a calm sea he set sail for England.

To meet a stranger fate than had ever yet befallen him.

CHAPTER LIII.

THE FIRST BREATH OF FEAR.

IT was on the day of Alton's last visit to the priest that Lady Montreville was sitting in her room, with the casement opening on a balcony, overhanging the sea.

Time had dealt, perhaps, more gently with her than might have been imagined; but there were still evidences in her whole bearing that she had suffered deeply.

Her form had lost much of its roundness, and her eyes had in them a strained and weary look, as if she were for ever watching and hoping against hope.

Always thinking of Vyvyan, the discarded son, whose noble heart she had discovered and prized too late—always thinking of Clarence, whose strange and wild behaviour was the talk of all—always thinking of Eveline, and the sorrow she had brought upon her—always thinking of stern Spirit Eyes watching her, and a Spirit Heart blaming her—what was her life but one long misery?

She was gazing out vacantly on the sea, when Marsden, the old seneschal entered.

"Lord Beaufort will neither hunt nor hawk, my lady," he said.

"Neither hunt nor hawk!" cried his mother. "What means this constant gloom? Can you not guess the cause? He *was* so joyous."

"Young plants need air and sun," said the old man, "man's youth needs the world. Young men pine for action. Yet find comfort, madam; if you recall the date the cause is clear."

"You have marked the date then?"

"Yes; since that bold seaman's visit," he returned.

"Your tongue runs riot, man!" exclaimed Lady Montreville, sternly. "How should that stranger—I say a stranger—strike dismay in Beaufort?"

"Dismay, madam!" said Marsden. "I say not that, but emulation."

"Aye, good Marsden," returned she, "you speak my thoughts; and I have already prayed our queen to rank your young lord with her chivalry. This very day I expect the return of my envoy."

"This day, madam! I will go forth to meet him."

And with a profound bow the old seneschal quitted her.

"It is true," murmured the wretched woman, pressing her hand over her aching bosom, "such *was* the date. Has Clarence guessed the secret?—guessed that a first born lives? I dread to question him, and yet I would gladly know. Oh, my son, my noble Edmond, where wander you? Not one word to say you live. Your very bride forsaken, as if love, frozen at the parent well-spring, had left every channel dry."

She started suddenly.

"Ah!" she cried, listening, "what tread is that, heavy and weary? Can that be the step that used to tread the earth as if in scorn? Yes, it is Clarence."

Sad change indeed in Beaufort.

His dress was neglected, and he entered shivering, though a mantle of fur was wrapped round him.

"How fares my precious one?" demanded Lady Montreville, advancing and laying her hand tenderly upon his shoulder.

"Cold, cold," he said, "and yet but now I saw a beggar doff his frieze, warm in his rags, while I shiver under ermine. For me 'tis never summer, never, never! Ho, there without, bring wine."

In a few moments a servant entered, bearing a goblet of rich workmanship set in jewels.

"Oh! how your hand burns, Clarence," cried his mother, "this is fever."

"That hand!" exclaimed Lord Beaufort, withdrawing it with a shudder, "*that* hand always burns! See here, my mother," he added, pointing to the cup, "the cup, the wondrous Tuscan jeweller, Cellini, made for a king! A king's gift to your father! Why serve such gauds to me?"

"Foolish boy," said Lady Montreville, "you yourself ordered that it should be so in one of your proud whims."

"Ah!" said Clarence, sadly, "it seems impossible I could ever have been proud. What is this wine?"

"The Malvoisie," returned the servant, "which your lordship's friends last year esteemed your rarest."

"One year seems then to have soured it into nausea," cried Clarence. "Take it away, it is rank."

"Oh! how wild he seems," murmured Lady Montreville to the servant. "Go, send for the physician; quick, go. Oh! Clarence, Clarence!" she added, turning to her son, "is this the body's sickness or the soul's? Is it life's youngest sorrow, love misplaced? You do not still love Eveline?"

"I have forgotten that I loved her," said Beaufort.

"Perhaps, then," continued his mother, "you love one whose birth might more offend my pride. Well, I *am* proud; but I could hail as a daughter the meanest maiden from whose smile your lip caught smiles again."

"Fear not, poor mother," said Clarence; "never had a hermit gazing on skulls in his lone cell a heart so proof against woman's smiles as I have."

As he spoke, the old seneschal entered again with a letter.

"It is from the queen, my lady," he said, as he handed it to the countess; then he added, turning to Beaufort, "my dear young lord, be gay. Lord Essex, the noblest of all noble knights, is on his road from conquered Cadiz, with the armed suite that won his laurels. He has sent before to greet you, and prays you will meet him in London."

"The flower of England's gentry, spotless Essex!" exclaimed Beaufort. "Sully him not, old man; bid him expect me not."

".Joy, Beaufort, joy!" cried his mother, as she concluded the letter. "August Elizabeth owns you her knight, and bids you wear her colours and break your maiden lance for England's lady."

"I will not go," said Beaufort; "barbed steeds and knightly honours are not for such as I am."

"They should be glorious to the young my lord," said Marsden.

"Aye, to the young!" cried Clarence, passionately. "*I* am not young. Youth is a poet's dream—I have dreamed it long ago. Look on my soul, old man— is it not more grey than your blanched hairs? Yet in London and its tournaments there is a chance of death; let me go."

CHAPTER LIV.

TERRIBLE EMOTIONS.

LADY Montreville was distracted by Beaufort's words.

"Oh, he raves!" she cried. "Heed not his words. Send quickly for the leech."

"I know these signs," she murmured to herself, as Marsden departed. "By my own soul I know them. This is not love, this is not honour's eagerness for action, or even natural suffering; *this is guilt.*"

"Clarence," she added, aloud, as she turned to Beaufort, "come sit by me; put your arms around me and lean upon my breast; so, that is well. Now, whisper low. *What is your crime?*"

Lord Beaufort burst into tears.

"Oh! mother!" he cried, vehemently, "would you had never borne me! Nay, deem me not ungrateful. For *your* sake I speak. You—justly proud, because you are pure—you, on whose name there is *no* soil, do you say 'crime' unto your son, and is his answer tears? Hark!"

Softly, gently without, the voice of Eveline was heard singing, as she had done a year before—

"Blossoms I weave ye,
To drift on the sea;
Say, when you find him,
Who sang, 'Woe is me!'"

"Have you no news?" she asked mournfully, as she entered from the terrace, and approached Beaufort.

"Of whom?"

"Of Vyvyan."

"That name!" murmured Lord Beaufort. "Her reason wanders, and so, mother, does mine, when that name is uttered. Hush, hush it!"

The young girl seemed not to hear their words.

She gazed mournfully at both for a moment.

Then she approached Lady Montreville, and kneeling, kissed her hand.

Then, as she rose, she said in a voice, whose extreme melancholy was very touching—

"We spoke of Vyvyan. Know you nothing of him?"

Lady Montreville pressed her lips to her brow—bending down and dropping tears upon the young girl's heaving breast.

"Nay," she said; "we know nothing of him. Would that we did, dear Eveline."

"And yet I cannot think him dead," said Eveline. "I dream of him even now in my slumbers."

"Last night I saw him—well, and in

all the strength of his manly vigour—standing before me."

"His face was radiant with kindness; and in his old gentle voice he said—

"Courage, Eveline; we shall meet again."

And then as she said this, she took both hands of the Countess, and looked wistfully up into her face.

"But then, dear child," said the unhappy lady of Montreville, "this was but a dream."

"I know it, gentle lady," said Eveline; "but you of all others ought to know how *he* fares; he whom *you* love, too, so dearly! I know not who he is, but he has in his eye your happy look—your haughty bearing."

"You are right," said the wretched mother, whose heart was oppressed by such a new and terrible sorrow. "Mayhap even now your dream may prove a true one. I pray it does so."

"Oh! it will do so!" said Eveline, "if we *do* but pray for it; and if we love Vyvyan as we ought. You always were like a mother to him, and spoke as one."

And so she moved away.

"Kill me at once!" said Lady Montreville, in a voice of agonised entreaty, as Eveline left them, and flung her garland into the sea. "Kill me at once, and when I ask again 'What is your crime?' reply 'No harm to Vyvyan!'"

"Unhand me! let me go!" cried Beaufort, and breaking from his mother's tender grasp, he fled from the room.

"Oh! heaven!" said Lady Montreville. "My punishment begins most terribly. Ah! Marsden, what news now? You seem disheartened."

"Forgive my haste," said the old man as he entered. "Amid St. Kinian's Cliff a stranger venturing has found bleached human bones, and to your Hall—which is nearest at hand, and has ever been famed for justice—he is leading on the crowd, and says the dead was Vyvyan."

"Ha! who named Vyvyan," exclaimed Eveline, as she returned from the terrace, "has he then come back?"

"No, fair mistress," answered Marsden.

"If on this terrible earth pity lives still, lead her away," said Lady Montreville.

'I promised him to love you as a mother," said Eveline, clinging to her. "Kiss me and trust in heaven—he will return!"

And then she went.

As Eveline departed, Lady Montreville sank down upon her chair.

The horrors around her truly seemed unreal, and her brain throbbed and pulsed with fear and anguish.

But she was not long left alone.

Within what seemed but a few moments the door again opened, and Marsden and a servant entered.

"Noble mistress," said the latter. "Sir Godfrey Seymour, summoned here in haste, begs your presence in the Justice Hall.

"Mine? Where go you now?"

"Sir Godfrey bade me seek my young lord," said the man.

"Stir not, my son is ill," returned Lady Montreville, quickly. "You yourself can attest it. Oh, Marsden, in his state a rumour of what is passing here might overturn his reason. Go, lure him away. If he resists, use force—as to a maniac. Good old man, you love him; his innocent childhood played around your knees. I know I can trust you. Quick—speak not, but go!"

Then, turning to the servant as Marsden sped away, she said, in a firm voice,

"Announce my coming! Oh, heaven, grant me strength," she murmured, "to shield the living son! Death with the dead to-morrow will be my welcome portion!"

She knew not, of course, what was even then passing in the precincts of the castle.

Clarence Beaufort had, as we know, received the invitation of the Queen herself to come to London.

At first he had rebelled against the idea of leaving the Ancient Halls of Montreville.

But now it was different.

He did not fly because of the arrival of Sir Godfrey Seymour, for the reason that he knew nothing of it.

Why he left was, that after that brief interview with his mother, his brain was in so terrible a whirl that he could not rest at home.

Of all others in the world his mother was the one whom he desired not to know the terrible doubt which existed in his heart.

And so, when he rushed from her presence, it was to the stables that he at once made his way.

There, of course, no question was made, when he asked for his favourite steed; and leaping on its back, went dashing away without any attendant.

It had been his custom to do so for many a long day.

Those who saw him, could not know that just as he was he had started for London.

Started without even a word of adieu either to Eveline or his mother.

There was something in the long wild ride before him which suited his present humour.

And, in fact, when he dashed along that road—on the top of the rocks—with the sea-breezes blowing upon him, the scent of the briny waves seemed to drive from him for a time all thoughts of that terrible scene so long ago—on the summit of St. Kinian's Cliff.

CHAPTER LV.

THE LONDON OF ELIZABETH.

THE sun was very bright on the morning when, leaving behind us the stately halls of Montreville, we ask the reader to accompany us to London, as it was in the time of good Queen Bess.

Over the street, known as the street of the Golden Fleece from the inn which stood at its corner, though, indeed, its real name was Carlton Street, the sunny glitter was specially noticeable.

For it was a very pretty street.

Pretty in the shape of its houses, in the peculiar style of many of its buildings—pretty in the cleanliness, which was the characteristic of street and buildings too.

It was a street much frequented by a certain class of " bloods " not of the first class, but still men of some substance and standing in their way.

On the morning on which we speak the street was at its laziest.

Women lounged over the pretty green balustrades of houses, or over the railings in front.

Children played on doorsteps or in the tiny courtyards.

And at the " Golden Fleece " a goodly business was doing, for the sun was hot—the day was a dusty one—and the people around were thirsty.

Sitting on one of the benches outside, which were placed there for the accommodation of the public, were two men, who, by their dress, their swarthy faces, and their manner, were evidently recently returned from an expedition—men who had that half-military, half-nautical look which was characteristic of the wild adventurers of those days.

One was a man of some forty-five years of age.

The other was much younger, but both seemed as if they would be awkward customers in a combat hand to hand.

" Well, Righton," said the one as he clapped his hand upon his companion's shoulder. " I am glad we met this morn. This London is so big a place that we might have missed each other in our rambles."

" Aye, it is rather larger than the deck of the ' Invincible,' " cried the other; " but as sure as my name is Ashburn, I am glad to see the old place again. We might surely have often been forgiven if we had expected never to have set eyes on England again."

" Aye, we have seen many brushes with the foe in our time," said the one named Righton, " yet still our leaders seem to like hard knocks better than peace."

" What mean you? " asked Ashburn.

" What mean I, man," repeated the other; " why, I mean this, that instead of taking rest my lord of Essex and his men are to join in the gay tournaments which our good Queen Bess has ordered to be held in honour of the defeats of the Spaniards. Such a thing as the taking of Cadiz could not be overlooked by our Queen."

Ashburn laughed.

"No; you are right," he said, "though she is one who will not marry, she likes well to have men about her, and see their valiant actions. When are the jousts to come off?"

"In three days."

"And where?"

"At the place known as Freeman's Fields, though better known as the Crooked Fields," replied Righton.

"Well, well, we must be there," said Ashburn. "It would not do to be absent when our noble leaders are present at such a scene as that."

"Our leaders, you say," replied the other, "but there is *one* to be present whom we respect almost as much as we do them."

"And who is that?"

"The mysterious knight."

"What he of the closed helm?"

"Yes."

"Then by St. George I would not miss the sight for the world," replied his companion, "for where *he* is, then there will be some good fighting."

They paused for a moment as this was said to take a draught of ale.

As they did so a third man joined their party; a rough and storm-beaten man, much as Wrecklyffe had seemed when he sat upon the table outside the inn near Alton's dwelling, and told Vyvyan wild stories of the sea.

This one, however, was not so well attired or so wrecklessly joyous as that wild sailor.

He had a wild and eager look about his eyes as if he was searching constantly for some one, or as if there was something which was on his mind—a dread idea of revenge or some sorrow—too nameless to speak off.

He sat down before the two rough companions, and with a grim smile, said—

"I heard you speaking of Essex and his men; are you of his crew?"

"Yes," said Ashburn, "we sailed with him in the 'Invincible.'"

"Ah! then by the stars you shall drink with me," cried the stranger; "brave men deserve to drink with the brave. What ho there! drawer."

The drawer, who was leaning against the door regarding the group somewhat curiously at once hastened forward.

He was by no means a well-favoured man.

In fact he was decidedly ill-favoured.

His eyes were too near together; his nose was too narrow at the bridge and too big at the bulge; his head had a way of protruding; and his gait had in it a kind of oiliness.

But he could be very civil, and though he glanced at the stranger as if he recognised in him some kindred spirit he bowed with infinite servility to those whom he had served first and who had given him a gratuity.

"Let us have some fresh ale, and of your best," said the stranger; "plenty of it too, for *I*, too, have come from off the sea, and am glad to hear again my own language, and taste again some right good ale instead of listening to the jabber of foreigners and drinking sour wine."

The two sailors, Righton and Ashburn, were somewhat at a loss what to make of this strange being.

But they were themselves rough men, used to wild scenes and so forth; and so casting off the momentary unpleasant feeling which had come over them, they tried to make themselves friendly with their unexpected companion.

"Well, it *is* pleasant," said Ashburn, "to think that we have once more reached our native land. Here's health to you, my friend. Where do you hail from?"

"That is a question easily answered," said he. "My name is Ellersleigh, and I was seaman on board the 'Queen's Victory,' that ship that sailed with Essex."

"I know it well," said Righton, as he quaffed some ale; "its commander was Captain Wetherton—a great favourite with Elizabeth."

"Yes, that was he," said the man who had called himself Ellersleigh, "and a fine commander he was, though stern and resolute. We fought in that engagement at Cadiz, as you know."

"Yes, it *was* a fight," said Ashburn,

"THEN, BENDING LOW, CLARENCE PRESSED THE QUEEN'S HAND TO HIS LIPS."

with some enthusiasm, "it will be long before I forget it. Didn't they fight, those Spaniards! They deserved to win! though I'm glad 'fore heaven they did not."

"What has become of that knight—that mysterious knight who fought so well with Essex?" asked the stranger.

The two sailors were off their guard now.

"What knight?" said they. "Do you mean the one whom the crew of the 'Invincible' saved from the pirate ship?"

"Yes," replied Ellersleigh, "that is he."

"He came to England with us," said Righton, "and he is even now with the Earl of Essex. But do you want him?"

The man brought his hand heavily down upon the table.

"Aye," he cried, "I *do* want him. I owe him a—thanks, I mean."

From this there was a coldness between him and the sailors who sat there.

They were friends of Vyvyan, to whom he alluded as the mysterious knight.

"Then you will find him, as I say, with Essex," replied Ashburn.

"And at the tourney?"

"Yes," said Righton.

"Then I will be there, too," said the man; "he will know me at once when I tell him my name, and show him my face."

"But," he added, "are you not coming with *me* to Ludgate Hill?"

"Why there my friend?" asked Ashburn, with a semblance of jollity.

"Because," replied Ellersleigh, "the Queen is going in State to St. Paul's to give thanks for her victories over Spain, and there will be there Sir Walter Raleigh and the Earl of Essex, and I doubt not also that the sweet-voiced bard, who has so charmed our senses."

"What! Will Shakespeare!" said Ashburn, eagerly.

"Aye, Will Shakespeare!" replied the other, "it is of him I speak. He is no seaman, I know; but they tell me he knows well how to tell us of the roar of the tempest and the tuneful voices of the sea! He talks of the ocean as if it were his friend as it is to us. Depend on it I go if he be there."

"When does this take place?" said Righton.

"Within the hour," said Ellersleigh; "in fact I am off there now."

And he sprang up.

As in doing this he turned his back, the two men exchanged glances.

They had read the character of the man.

They knew that harm lurked in his jaunty manner, and his boisterous mirth which accorded so ill with his lowering evil eyes.

But they said nothing.

It was best they thought to be on the watch.

So the three set out together in the direction of St. Paul's.

It was a gay sight there.

Though the edifice which then reared its head over the hill of Ludgate was not so imposing as the one which now stands towering over London, it was a handsome church; and the houses around—strangely formed as they were—were extremely picturesque in their position and their shape.

Gay crowds thronged the streets.

Men and women in their best attire walked along what in those days served for pavements, and even in the middle of the roads; for as in the present day on occasions of public celebrations, vehicles were not allow to pass along the streets, except, indeed, those which were in some way connected with the royal procession.

Flags hung from poles thrust out from windows, and from ropes running from one side of the street to the other.

Music made the air everywhere redolent of sweet sounds.

Everywhere there was loud laughter and gaiety, and every now and then the voice of some happy maiden (whose heart was overflowing because it was holiday time), broke forth into some pleasant song.

There was no mistake about *this* being a holiday, and about everyone intending it to be one.

Not a shop, except those which were in some way connected with enjoyment, were open.

The cake-shops and the taverns, and the shops of the sellers of little flags and patriotic emblems and so forth were open, and doing a roaring trade.

But business, so to speak, was suspended.

Presently there was a grand flourish of trumpets.

People on high points of vantage waved their kerchiefs, and cheered loudly.

Musketeers in brightly gleaming helmets and half armour came galloping up the hill.

The people drew back upon the side walks.

Crowds in those days were not such crowds as they are now.

They were fewer in number, and, more than that, far more controllable.

So the musketeers were welcomed with loud cheers, and the crowd pressed back to make room, and then a gay cavalcade appeared, conspicuous in which was a personage on a white horse.

This personage was not slow in being recognised and saluted by the people.

It was good Queen Bess!

CHAPTER LVI.

THE PROCESSION—THE STRANGE KNIGHT.

GAY, indeed, looked the procession as it advanced up the hill.

First came a band playing a gay tune.

Then came musketeers, and men-at-arms of all kinds.

Then came gentlemen-at-arms, and knights in armour, and gay horsemen of all kinds.

For it was not a military spectacle, though it spoke of England's glory and victory.

Cannon came thundering up the steep ascent; lances and pikes glittered; pennons waved gaily.

But it was essentially a gala, and every one treated it as such.

By the side of the Queen rose two knights—the one Essex, the other a knight in black armour, with his vizor down so as to completely conceal his face.

Near at hand, too, was another, a much younger knight, whose face was unfamiliar to any.

On his features there was a strange look.

A look as of triumph, and yet a wild distracted hunted look as if his thoughts were far away.

There was a manner about him too as if he had escaped from some great terror and peril, and knew that he for the time was safe.

Need I say that this was Clarence Beaufort.

Arrived in London he had lost no time in presenting himself at Court.

He had no credentials with him, but his name was enough.

He was already well known to the Queen by name, and when, therefore, he mentioned that he was Clarence de Beaufort, Earl of Montreville, it needed no introduction to obtain him audience of Her Majesty.

The Queen received him alone in one of the stately chambers of the palace.

She was a connoisseur in manly beauty, and recognized at once the vigorous grace of Beaufort.

But she was a reader of human nature too, and saw that, young as he was, with all the world before him, he had something on his mind.

"I am glad, my Lord of Beaufort," said Elizabeth, "that you so gladly accepted my invitation."

A smile somewhat of the old style illumined his face as the Queen addressed him.

"Who would not accept the invitation of so noble a lady," he said, "even if she were not a queen? My mother told me of your wish that I should come to London, and gladly did I hie to do your gracious bidding.

"I waited for no retainers or attendants," he continued, "but leaping on my horse's back, I galloped away to this city.

"But careless as I came, and with no retinue, I shall none the less be a true and valiant knight. I only seek service. By my sword I swear it."

And—on the sword which he drew from its scabbard—he imprinted a passionate kiss.

Then bending low he pressed the Queen's hand to his lips.

She looked down compassionately upon him.

"Put up your sword, my Lord of Beaufort," she said, with a gentle smile; "it is treason to draw your sword in the presence of your Queen! Nay, look not so dismayed; you are forgiven. Sit by me here, and answer me truly. Have you a private sorrow?"

As she said these words she sat down upon a velvet cushioned couch, and motioned him to sit beside her.

He did as he was directed.

Almost mechanically, be it said.

For her words had touched a strange chord in his heart, and he saw before him, in his mind's eye, the scene on St. Kinian's Cliff.

The Queen saw his agitation, and guessed, as a woman would, that love was at the bottom of his sorrow.

"Say," she cried, as she placed her hand upon his arm, "say, do you love one who has slighted you?"

"Nay, I love no one, but my Queen and my country," he said, moodily; "it is the desire to serve them that brings me hither. I come to beg some service where peril is, that I may seek it."

It was evident to Elizabeth now that there was something more on the mind of Clarence than he cared to speak of.

So, as he was there at her wish, and was not likely to make a quick return to the Castle of Montreville, she said, calmly, in a gentle voice, which soothed his troubled spirit—

"Well, well, I will not question you further now. But as you ask for peril, I will give you a chance of mimic peril to commence with. I allude to the jousts which are soon coming off in Freeman's Fields."

"Ha!" thought Clarence de Beaufort, as he had thought at Montreville, "there is a chance of death even there!"

"Most noble lady, I accept the chance with eagerness," he cried, "and I shall do so with more pleasure if I may be on that occasion your special knight, and break a lance in your honour."

"It shall be so," said the Queen, seeing a bright light springing to his eyes, and mistaking its nature and cause, "on the day of the jousts you shall wear my favours. And now I will commend you to the special care of Essex."

She rang a bell as she spoke, and an attendant at once appeared.

"Bid the Earl of Essex attend me," said the Queen.

The man bowed lowly.

"The Earl is even now in the antechamber, awaiting the order of your Majesty," he said. "I will hasten to inform him of your pleasure."

In a few moments the Earl had entered.

He made a low obeisance to the Queen, and kneeling, kissed her hand.

Then, turning to Clarence de Beaufort, he bowed, saying:

"My lord of Beaufort, I am happy to greet you in the presence of England's royal mistress. I have heard of you before."

He gazed somewhat curiously at Clarence as he spoke.

A shudder ran through the frame of Clarence.

"Ah," he thought, "can it be possible he knows my crime."

But the thought fled at once.

He bowed low, though his smile, influenced as it was by the ideas which had so recently rushed through his brain, was a somewhat ghastly one.

"I am proud, indeed, to meet thus," he said, "the flower of England's chivalry—matchless Essex."

Essex smiled as he grasped his hand.

"Glad, indeed, am I that you think well of my deeds if it will induce you to emulate them. Then shall I think I have not worked in vain."

He turned then to the Queen.

"And now, most noble lady," he said, "what commands have you for me."

"I wish, my lord of Essex," she said, "to deliver over to you the charge of this young earl, who has come to London by our command, and who was so eager to reach our city, that he came alone from Montreville, without attendants."

She beckoned Essex apart.

"See to him well, Essex," she said, in a low tone; "the look of madness itself is in his eyes, and I wish to guard him well for the sake of his gentle mother."

"Or for his own," said Essex, with a sly smile.

Elizabeth tapped him with her fan.

"Ah! jealous one," she said; "thou art always full of such whims. But for my sake, Essex, see to him. Methinks he has some deadly sorrow on his heart, weighing heavily there. A little life in London will do him good—more than a whole existence spent amid the gloomy halls of Montreville."

"You say truly," said the earl; "depend upon it, I will take great care of him."

"And as to the procession to-morrow," said Queen Elizabeth; "he must ride by my side."

"Your orders shall be obeyed, most gracious madam," said the earl; and so having taken his leave, Clarence was led away by Essex.

Thus came it that, on that day of gala in the city, he rode by the side of the Queen.

And so on they went together to the great cathedral, where, amid the roll of sacred music, the Queen gave thanks to Heaven for her victory.

And outside the multitude swayed and surged, and talked of their "brave" Queen and of "matchless" Essex, and wondered who that knight was whose vizor was kept so persistently down.

And then, presently, forth they came again; and as the Queen passed down the hill, William Shakespeare, leaning against a post, attracted her attention.

She turned to Essex.

"See yonder," she said; "is not that Will Shakespeare who leans so dreamily against that post, gazing on this scene?"

"Yes, my gracious lady."

"Then I will stop and speak to him," said the Queen; "he writes most noble verses."

The procession paused as the Queen stopped her white charger in front of the spot where stood England's greatest poet—then only in the bud of future glory.

She sent an attendant to him, and the poet, who was as graceful in his person and his walk, as in his verse, advanced. hat in hand, to meet her.

She extended her hand to him, which he raised to his lips, and pressed on it a kiss which told of his real wish for her patronage.

"William Shakespeare," she said, "I have read much of your verses, and heard more. You have my royal wishes for your success. You must see us at our Court."

Elizabeth was nothing if not royal.

She had done what she considered to be her duty—she had conferred patronage publicly on a poet.

So when Shakespeare said—

"I thank you, noble lady, for your kindness—"

She bowed with graceful hauteur; and by a gesture, showed that she desired to advance.

So Will Shakespeare retired again to his post.

But his heart was bounding with a new emotion; and his face flushed with pleasure.

He knew that he had advanced one step further up the ladder of fortune.

Meanwhile, Righton, Ashburn, and Ellersleigh had watched eagerly the whole scene.

The former two gazed on in real pleasure.

Triumph was in their eyes, and in their bronzed visages.

But Ellersleigh gazed on with an evil eye.

He scarcely answered a word addressed to him; and when his companions cheered lustily, he was silent.

They observed it, of course; but in the excitement, they did not care to speak to him of it.

But when the procession had passed by, and the mob, too, was flowing Strandward to catch a last glimpse of

"The fair virgin,
Throned in the west"

(as Shakespeare said afterwards), they turned to him—

"What is the matter, Ellersleigh,"

said Righton; "you look as if something had gone ill with you to-day."

"Aye; it has."

"Pray what is the matter."

"Much; but *there*, you are Essexmen, and cannot understand my feeling."

"We may," returned Ashburn; "we may; so why not tell us?"

"I will," he said, having taken time to consider what falsehood he should perpetrate; "you saw you those noble leaders?"

"We did; and hurrahed them to the top of our bent."

"Well," said Ellersleigh, "that is it. The leaders, who do nothing, get all the glory; and the strong arm and the brave hearts, who do all the work, get no praise or glory at all."

"But, come," he added; "come; let us drink. And then my passion may be allayed."

And so they went on together.

They soon reached a tavern on Eastcheap, call the "Goldbeater's Arms."

By this time Ellersleigh's gloom had by some means or another vanished, and when they entered they were all in the same good humour.

And so they sat down in a pleasant room which overlooked the street still gay with people, and there indulged in good roast beef and flagons of foaming ale,

As they drank they of course became communicative, and many a thing was extracted from Ashburn and Righton in regard to the mysterious knight.

Ellersleigh was an adept in dissimulation, and he managed consequently to obtain from them what information he required without exciting any suspicions on their parts.

At length they separated.

Mutual promises of future meetings were made, and then, while Righton and Ashburn went in the direction of the West End of the city, Ellersleigh betook himself to the East End.

No sooner had he left his companions than his old scowl came upon him again.

His countenance expressed again all the evilness of his passions, and he muttered to himself as he went on—

"Ah! my time is even now coming. It is he. I know that it is he."

Who could this new foe be?

CHAPTER LVII.

THE COUNCIL AT MONTREVILLE.

WHILE these events were happening in London in preparation for Clarence Beaufort's first appearance at a royal joust, events at Montreville had not stood still.

The words of Marsden had not been wrong.

As, in fact, he hastened away in search of Beaufort, in obedience to the commands of the distracted mother, there was a loud flourish of trumpets in the courtyard, and as Lady Montreville hastened to the window she saw a solemn cavalcade.

First came two men on horseback clad in black velvet trimmed with gold.

Then came a gentleman alone on horseback in velvet and ermine.

Then followed several other solemn looking individuals who had as much merriment and gaiety in their appearance as mutes at a funeral.

As they paused near the inner gates, one of the men in advance raised his trumpet and blew a shrill blast.

What this was for when they had already announced their coming it would indeed be difficult to say.

However, it was apparently some formula, for the party now at once dismounted and entered the hall ushered in by Marsden and others.

The real business of the visit was not slow in being commenced.

In a vast feudal hall, Sir Godfrey Seymour, a reverend old magistrate was soon seated at a large table where a clerk was employed in writing.

He had been summoned at a moment's notice, by the impetuous friend of Vyvyan, and had lost not a moment's time, as we have seen.

Falkner, Vyvyan's friend, was standing near Sir Godfrey, while a retainer held back the curtain of a recess, where, on a tressel, and covered by a cloak, lay the bleached bones that Falkner had discovered beneath St. Kinian's Cliff.

"See," cried Falkner, "the relics of the dead are revealed at last. I claim these bones as those of my murdered friend!"

His manner was greatly excited.

He, of course, knew little and cared less in regard to the forms which ought to be observed before a court of justice.

All he thought of was that he was there as Vyvyan's friend and avenger; to tell all he knew, and to claim justice.

He stood, therefore, with head proudly erect, his right hand upon the hilt of his sword, his left hand extended in the direction of the bones which lay in the recess.

"Be not unnecessarily excited," said the judge, in no way displeased by the show of anger and eager sorrow shown by the young sailor; "explain calmly, if you can, your reasons for these thoughts."

"Sir Godfrey," said Falkner, "at the time when we were ordered to sail against the Spanish Armada, Vyvyan was one of those who were called to the war.

"But our vessel, after all, had to sail without him.

"I know well that no cowardice kept him back.

"He was a soldier, good and true, I will swear; and left in the castle here one whom he dearly loved that he might join our force against the Spaniards.

"We fought without him then, and I being taken by the enemy, was kept a long time a prisoner.

"When I could find means of returning to England, I hastened hither, and by what I learned was induced to search beneath the rocks.

"What I found there lie yonder; they are all that remains of Vyvyan," he exclaimed, "they cry for justice."

"Be patient, sir," said Sir Godfrey, "and give us ampler proofs that yonder undistinguishable bones are relics of your friend."

"Sir," cried Falkner, impetuously, as he pointed to Sir Grey de Malpas, who had come forward at these words, "that gentleman can back my oath that these —the plume and gem—are those that Vyvyan wore. I found them beneath the rocks."

"It this so?" asked Sir Godfrey.

Sir Grey de Malpas bowed low.

"Since law compels me—yes. I must vouch for it," said he, with assumed reluctance. "But let me fetch my lady, and while I am absent draw that curtain —let not that sight appal her and her son!"

Sir Godfrey Seymour bowed sadly as Lady Montreville presently entered, and seated herself.

"Your pardon, madam," he said, in a tone of deep respect; "you know my imperious duties and my dismal task."

"Yes, sir, I have been informed what terrible errand brings you to my halls. I pray you be brief," she said, scarcely raising her eyes from the ground.

"Was there a guest in your house— one Vyvyan, captain of a war ship—this time a year ago?"

"Yes, but one short day. He came to Montreville to see my ward, whom he had saved from pirates."

"I pray you, madam," continued Sir Godfrey, "did he in his converse with you speak of any foe, concealed or open, whom he had cause to fear?"

"He spoke of none," said Lady Montreville, firmly.

"Nor know you any such?"

Lady Montreville hesitated but a moment, and then answered—

"I do not."

"Would you further question this lady?" said Sir Godfrey, in a low voice, to Falkner.

"No," cried the young seaman. "She is a mother, so let her go. I await Lord Beaufort."

As he spoke there entered Sir Grey de Malpas.

He was in a state of intense excitement—an excitement which to a great extent seemed caused by triumph.

"Who called Lord Beaufort?" he said, in a voice which was intended to be full of anxiety and emotion.

"This gentleman," said the judge, "desires to see Lord Beaufort before he continues his statement."

"Is it necessary—quite necessary?" asked Sir Grey, glancing with unnecessary significance at Lady Montreville.

"It is," answered Falkner, fiercely. "I demand to see Lord Beaufort."

"Then I am bound to say," replied Sir Grey in a low tone of apparent sorrow, "you cannot. He is not within the castle."

Lady Montreville herself started in wonder.

"Not within the castle?" said the judge sternly. "I have reason to think that when we were within but a moment's walk of the gates he was here."

Sir Grey was silent.

But his silence was more significant than words would have been.

The judge conferred with one who sat near him.

Then turning to Sir Grey he said—

"Sir Grey de Malpas, I am certain that you know more than you feel inclined to say. I command you in the name of law and of justice to say—where is Lord Beaufort."

"Then, my lord, since you force me to speak," said Sir Grey, avoiding now the gaze of Lady Montreville, "I cannot say where Lord Beaufort is, for by this time he is far away. It seems that when you were announced he hastened to the stables, and saddling himself the swiftest horse there, he mounted it, and without even an attendant fled away on the road to London."

"Sir Godfrey, believe him not," cried the wretched mother. "He knew not of your coming. He received this day a message from the Queen, in which she desired his instant attendance at court. He did not wish to go, and only went at last because I pressed him to. He must have been at the stables as you came up, I swear. I pray you, sir, believe him not."

"It may be true, my lady," said Sir Godfrey, "and yet it all seems strange. Why should a man summoned by the Queen proceed to London alone, and not attended by a proper retinue?"

"I know not, sir," replied Lady Montreville, "unless it be that he was in anger with me. We quarreled slightly, I confess."

The judge again for a moment conferred with his companion.

Then, after a moment, he said—

"This is a most sad and heart-rending affair for every one concerned. But it is necessary to sift it to the bottom We must therefore defer the enquiry until such time as Lord Beaufort can be brought back from London. Sir Grey de Malpas, to you I give the task of bringing back to this place your fugitive kinsman."

Sir Grey de Malpas bowed.

"Your commands shall be obeyed," replied ne, "I will start for London at once.

"And I," said Lady Montreville, eyeing him sternly, "will accompany you. When my son is in danger, it is my duty to be near him."

"You, madam!' cried Sir Grey in surprise and ill-concealed vexation, "consider the journey's length and its dangers."

"I cannot think of danger,' she said, "in such a case as this.'

"We will go together, sir," she added, turning to Sir Godfrey Seymour, "and you may depend upon my returning as quickly as possible."

Sir Godfrey bowed respectfully.

"I have no doubt of what you say," he answered, "but I can allow no one to defeat the end of justice. I am grieved, indeed, to see a lady in your position in society placed in so sad a case. But I am bound to administer justice to both high and low, and I must send with you one who will have power to arrest Lord Beaufort should he offer to escape."

Lady Montreville bowed.

She could say nothing.

In fact, her heart was too full for words.

"And now," said Sir Godfrey, rising, "this council is dismissed. Until such time as Lord Beaufort is brought back to Montreville, I ask of all present to hold their peace. This matter is one likely to cause grave scandal, and justice demands silence until the real culprit be found."

Then as Lady Montreville passed out

amid men, whose heads were all uncovered, the council broke up.

Margaret of Montreville retired to her chamber, not even pausing to speak to Eveline.

She flung herself on her knees beside her bed.

"Oh! Heaven, be merciful!" she said. "Heaven, be merciful! This, then, is my punishment. One son discarded, one son accused of murder."

She shuddered, and her tears fell fast as she murmured these words.

"Murder!" she added, after a moment, "aye! that is the awful memory! He trembled and turned pale when I asked him what ailed him and spoke to him of guilt. Oh! it is heavy indeed to bear. Edmond! Edmond! thou art indeed amply avenged!"

Meanwhile, Sir Godfrey Seymour had a private word with Sir Grey de Malpas ere he departed.

"Think you, Sir Grey," he said, when they were alone, "that Lord Beaufort will return, or will his mother contrive for him some means of escape to some foreign country?"

Sir Grey shook his head.

"It is not a pleasant subject for me to speak of," he said; "but, still, a mother's love—"

Sir Godfrey's face grew sterner than ever.

"True, true. I will dispatch a special envoy to the Court to warn the Queen," he said: "I will have no lack of justice where I am concerned. An earl is nothing more than any other!"

"What mean you?" asked Sir Grey. "Your words would seem to imply that you think him guilty! Remember, Sir Godfrey, he is not yet tried."

"True; but there seems evidence of guilt. However, we will say no more now," said the stern knight; "look to it that you do your best to bring him back. If it be possible, it would be better for him to be brought hither without knowing why he is summoned home. There is a great deal to be learned from the face of a man when he is first told that he is accused of a crime."

Sir Grey bowed.

"You are a great observer of human nature, Sir Godfrey; I will do my best to do as you desire me, for then you will be able to read innocence in his face, I trust. I cannot answer, of course, for what Lady Montreville will do. As I said before, a mother's feelings are not to be repressed; but I will endeavour to persuade her as far as I can to do as you wish."

And so they parted.

As soon as Sir Godfrey had gone beyond the precincts of the castle, he spoke to one of his men, who set off at full speed towards London.

The net was drawing closer and closer round Lord Beaufort.

The sins of the mother were to be visited upon the youngest son.

CHAPTER LVIII.

PREPARING FOR THE JOUSTS.

GREAT were the preparations in Freeman's fields on the morning after the procession.

On the day before, during the time that the gay procession had been making its way in the direction of Ludgate, some of the workmen had escaped for the purpose of snatching a glimpse of the Queen.

But, except during this short period, they had all been incessantly at work.

First, a large space was cleared and filled with sand.

Around this were erected barriers of great strength, so as to withstand the accidental shock of horses.

These barriers were formed of huge uncouth beams, and fixed with immense bolts; but, as one set of artificers finished off the rough work, another set fitted on elegant trappings of crimson and gold.

At certain intervals were tall masts, with flags, surmounted by a variety of figures of all kinds.

Here a bird, in silver, seemed as if about to take wing.

Here some animal, of no special kind, crouched as if to spring.

Each mast had its own peculiar animal, and, no doubt, its own significance; and as for the flags, they seemed to have been chosen more for the sake of their gaudy appearance than for any special meaning.

Crowds of people pressed round to see the preparations; and so popular was good Queen Bess in those days, that loud shouts of applause rent the air, as they fixed up the throne, as it were, on which Queen Elizabeth was to take her seat to witness the jousts.

It was a splendid affair; formed, of course, of huge beams beneath, but covered above with crimson velvet, covered with gold bands and gold lace.

In the centre was a high seat, the arms of which represented two lions' heads; while on either side were lower seats to accommodate two favourite ladies.

And overhead was a gorgeous canopy, —a protection alike from the sun and the rain.

Among those who gathered round the workmen at their labours, was Ellersleigh—the scowling ruffian, who had made friends with Ashburn and Righton.

He stood against one of the posts, with folded arms, watching eagerly the proceedings, until, presently, one tall burly workman paused a moment in his labours to wipe his heated brow.

"Well, my friend," said Ellersleigh, assuming, as far as he could, a gay and pleasant demeanour, "you are hard at it for the pleasure of others."

The man glanced at his companion in surprise.

"What do you mean, my friend," he said; I think these jousts are for the pleasure of every one who loves England and her glory."

"Yes, and those who like shows," said Ellersleigh; "for my part, I think they are selfish matters."

"How so?"

"They are only given to flatter the leaders," replied Ellersleigh; "who will be here to represent those who really fought and bled for England?"

The man laughed.

"Oh! it would only be folly to think like *that*," replied he; "there must be leaders in everything, or what difference would there be between the skilled workman and his labourer."

"But there will be here to-morrow," he added, "the brave sailors and soldiers who fought for England against the Spaniards, and when the people cheer the leaders they will cheer also the men."

"No doubt it will be a brave sight," said Ellersleigh; "I should like to have a good view; cannot you contrive it for me, my friend?"

"For my part you can have my place," said the man, "I care not for it. I'd better like to be among the general crowd, with my wife and children. They will be pleased enough to think that I have time to spare to them."

Ellersleigh's eyes sparkled at this.

This was just what seemed to suit his evil purpose, whatever that was.

"And what is your place?" he asked, in as calm a voice as he could command.

"Simply to stand here and open this gate to admit the champions, as they enter the lists from the covered place yonder where they dress and are aided to mount their horses," replied the workman; "any one can do this, and I am allowed to find a substitute."

"Very well, it is agreed," said Ellersleigh, with a leaping heart; "let us go at once and have a drink, and then you can explain all to me: the time I am to arrive and so forth."

The man hesitated only a moment.

"Well, he cried, "I see no reason why I should not. I am thirsty, and yonder at the sign of the "Golden Apple" we can obtain as good a glass of ale as can be got in the whole of "Merrie Englande.""

So the two went across to the well-known tavern together.

The honest workman and the treacherous foe!

Here, over a foaming tankard of the best ale, they talked over matters; and in half-an-hour, Ellersleigh had learned all he required in regard to the proceedings of next day.

He was to be at the lists exactly at six o'clock in the morning to aid the men in their last touchings-up of the place, in company with the man Shelton, as he was named.

Then the latter was to indue him in the clothes which he was to wear (a kind of red and blue suit, trimmed with gold), and introduce him, as his substitute, to the Marshal of the Lists.

After this he would be left entirely to his own devices.

He left Shelton, with his heart full of eager malice.

He saw, at length, a chance of accomplishing his vengeance.

"Ha!" he muttered, as he passed away, "this time, at least, Vyvyan shall not escape my vengeance. I have good proof it is he now. First Wrecklyffe, and now Morgan, have fallen by his sword. In the moment of his triumph I will kill him, if my own life pays the forfeit. Both my friends gone; my sister's hopes blighted by her husband's death! These things would urge me on if nothing else would! But, *then*, there is left as another incentive, the oath which we buccaneers have taken—to follow up the destroyers of one another. To-morrow will settle all scores."

CHAPTER LIX.

THE TOURNEY.

THE next morning broke bright and beautiful.

The sun rose in a sky almost undimmed by a single cloud.

Nothing in nature, or in any of its surroundings, was there to show that any evil spirit in man was plotting to mar the glories of that day.

London was astir betimes.

From all quarters there began to arrive gaily dressed people, of both sexes and all ages, for the news of the grand tournament, in honour of England's successes at sea, had spread everywhere.

It was a more general holiday, in fact, than it had been even on the day of the procession to St. Paul's, to celebrate the grand successes of the English arms, and to give thanks for them.

Then it was only a moving spectacle, passing up a certain street.

A place now was found where the people could see their Queen at leisure.

And so Freeman's Fields (or the Crooked Fields, as they were called), became suddenly popular.

And now all London, as I have said, flocked towards them.

Long before good Queen Bess and her cavaliers reached the place it was surrounded by an eager though not a tumultuous crowd.

Every one was dressed in his best.

And this, in those days of bright colours, meant a great deal.

So when good Queen Bess and her cavaliers came upon the scene they saw a brilliant assemblage.

An assemblage which, one and all, rose to greet and welcome them.

Such a roar of voices, perhaps, had never welcomed the Queen of England before.

Even her iron heart was touched by such a show of grateful loyalty.

She was always one to answer her people with a smile and a bow.

But it was always easy also to tell when the smile was real and when it was not.

This time every one could see that the smile was genuine, and from her heart.

She bowed again, and again, to the great crowds which surged around her.

"Really, Essex," she said, as she turned to the favourite of the day, "this makes one glad to be a Queen."

Essex bowed deeply.

He was nothing if not a courtier.

"It is worth being an Englishman to have such a Queen," he said.

"Flattery again! What can I believe when all men say the same," replied the vain Queen.

So, talking, they made their way towards the dais.

Here they dismounted.

The Queen seated, Essex retired to take his station behind the throne.

On either side of Elizabeth sat a lady.

The one the Countess of Somerset, the other the Duchess of Devonshire.

And all around were lesser luminaries; among whom, however, could be found more brilliant eyes—more rosy cheeks—more pearly teeth — more creamy shoulders—than among the higher ones.

At length all were seated.

The whole of the Court had gathered round good Queen Bess.

The rest of the populace formed one vast tumultuous crowd around them.

But they soon settled down.

And then the trumpets blew loudly, and all was hushed.

From opposite sides of the lists there rushed in two knights-in-armour.

They were both seated on splendid steeds, and both seemed magnificent horsemen.

So, though it was only a mimic fight, the excitement of the people was roused to the highest pitch.

One of these knights had a white horse and was dressed in black armour, which of course gave him a most conspicuous appearance.

The other had a black horse, and was habited in light steel.

The black knight had a black plume, the other a white and red one.

They were thus, of course, easily to be distinguished, even in the melée.

The Queen watched the black knight with considerable interest.

Presently she turned to Essex.

"Is that," she said, "the knight of whom you spoke to me so much?"

"Yes; that is my mysterious knight," said Essex, smiling.

"I am eager, indeed, to see him couch a lance," replied the Queen; "you have spoken of him so highly."

"You will see him do as I have told you, most royal lady," said Essex; "unless, indeed, his right arm has lost his cunning. See how splendidly he sits his horse, and canters round the lists."

"And yet you say he is a sailor," said the Queen; "what knows *he* of horses?"

Essex smiled.

"Your coasts, Madame, would not be so well protected as they are if we were *only* sailors," said Essex. "We must learn to fight anywhere; against anything! Even ladies' smiles."

The two Duchesses looked sweetly conscious.

The Queen leaned back and tapped him on the face with her fan.

But a loud fanfaronade at this moment put an end to all the folly.

Every eye was now directed towards the arena.

The two knights were marshalled in their places; their lances, blunt, of course, as was the rule at these peaceful tourneys, were couched, then they started their horses at full speed, and met with a crash in the centre of the list.

It was a terrific onset.

The Black Knight was still in his saddle when the shock was over.

The other fared very differently.

Both horse and rider were hurled to the ground amid a blinding cloud of dust.

The Queen started almost from her throne at this sight.

"Your friend seems, indeed, to be a strong knight," she said. "I trust it is not the custom in the country whence he comes to kill people in jest."

Essex smiled.

"Most gracious madam," he said, "you are doing him a most gross injustice."

The Queen bridled up at this.

"What mean you, Essex?" she cried; "methinks you give your tongue too great a license."

"I mean, indeed, no harm, my Queen," he said, "I cannot betray my friend's secret, but this I *can* say, he is an Englishman, and as brave and true as any in your service. But he wishes for a time to be unknown."

"Then *I* will not be the one who will break through his incognito," said Elizabeth; "but see, the knight who fell is badly wounded. He cannot walk."

"Stunned merely, I should fancy," replied Essex, "his armour is heavy, remember, my lady, and that would make it difficult for him to move even were he quite well."

There was no further time for conversation.

Another knight came galloping into the lists.

He was a French knight, the Chevalier Roland de Crespigny, and a gallant cavalier he looked.

He rode round the lists gaily waving his sword, and as he came opposite the Queen's dais, he brought his horse up with a sudden reining in, which nearly brought him on his haunches.

Here he bowed deeply, and then he raised his lance on high and shouted—

"Long live Good Queen Bess!"

He said the words in excellent English, and so loudly that they reached far and wide among the multitude.

It was answered by such a roar as never, perhaps, had been heard in the Crooked Fields.

It was like the thunderous roar of a stormy sea.

The Queen's face flushed with pleasure, and she eagerly glanced now at the lists to see how fared this knight, who, Frenchman as he was, seemed to have enrolled himself of his own accord as her champion.

But he shared the fate of the other.

The Black Knight seemed to carry all before him.

The Chevalier Roland de Crespigny was a tall and heavily built knight.

But before the lance of the Black Knight he went down like chaff before the wind.

The Queen bit her lip.

Even in this mimic fight she liked not the idea of her self-made champion being thrown to the ground by one she knew not.

"Methinks your friend is not a loyal knight, Essex," she said, "or he would at least have made a semblance of being defeated."

"Nay, then," said Essex, who was secretly irritated by the captious whims of this most exacting of Queens, "you place knightly honour at a very low ebb, most gracious lady. Neither my friend nor any other knight would care to sham defeat. It is the good fortune of my friend to be a splendid rider and a magnificent soldier. He has fought well for your majesty, and has never deemed it too much to plunge in among a storm of bullets and a raging maddened crew of desperadoes to plant the flag of England upon the mast of an enemy. Why, then, should he now be the one to mimic defeat?"

"True, true," said the Queen, whom Essex knew so well how to guide; "true, true. I did but give way to a woman's fancy, which should never rule a Queen. But who comes here?"

The French knight had been helped out of the lists, and another champion, mounted on a coal black horse, appeared.

"Ha!" cried Essex, excitedly, "this is not what I wished!"

The Queen scanned eagerly the features of the new champion.

He had his face exposed, and the Queen recognised him at once.

She clapped her hands together gleefully.

"Ha!" she cried, "this is my young champion, Clarence de Beaufort. See, he wears the royal colours!"

"Why look you so pale?" asked the Queen; "one would think you had special reasons indeed to befriend this unknown knight."

"Aye! that have I," said Essex, whose face was white now with some strange emotion. "This fight ought not to take place. I pray you, madam, let me forbid it."

The Queen's face now expressed the greatest anger.

"Essex," she cried, "remain where you are. I command you. There must be some treason in all this that you are so anxious to spare this stranger."

Essex saw from the face of the Queen that she was in no humour to be played with.

So with a sigh he drew slightly back to watch the jousts.

The Black Knight sat on his horse like a statue—like one turned to stone, when his eyes fell upon the opponent who now came into the lists.

He for a moment appeared as if he were meditating in his own mind what to do, whether he should receive the attack of his new adversary or fly from the arena.

Clarence, on the other hand, wore upon his face a smile of perfect beatitude.

Oppressed by the weight of a woe inexpressible, it seemed now truly as if he had found a haven of rest.

To his weary soul death seemed the only acceptable boon.

And as he pranced round upon his splendid horse and, pausing opposite the Queen's dais, raised his lance adorned with the royal colours, his face, as he bowed deeply, was beaming with a joy indescribable.

A joy which seemed to spring from the realisation of the fatal hope which he had boldly expressed to the Queen.

Ellersleigh had up to this moment been unable to carry out or even attempt to carry out his deadly plan.

His heart was bounding with savage anger at this.

The man Shelton had certainly performed all he had promised.

It was, in fact, only opportunity that he lacked.

But for this he abused the man who had placed him innocently in his place.

Shelton, of course, knew nothing of the diabolical purpose for which Ellersleigh desired to be doorkeeper of the arena.

And yet the villain abused him as if he had purposely thwarted him.

" The devil fly away with him for a deceiving rascal," he cried, as the Black Knight once more took up his position on the side of the arena opposite to them. " I shall have no chance whatever against my enemy even now. If I had but Shelton here, and the opportunity of doing as I liked with him, I would wring the very nose off his face."

But the manœuvres of the strange knight was soon such as to surprise him.

He seemed, in fact, to have lost all his activity and resolution.

He galloped slowly round the lists, and seemed as if he was for some reason or another avoiding an encounter.

Clarence moved slowly to and fro uneasily.

His proud spirit once aroused began to chafe under the notion of being made appear ridiculous before the Queen on the occasion of the first tournament in which he had been engaged.

He knew well the use of arms for he had been well trained at Montreville; but he had never yet attempted to show his prowess in public.

The notion that this strange knight who had so easily vanquished others was avoiding him for some reason or another, made him angry, and he paused at last, saying in a loud voice—

" Now, sir knight of the black helm, waste not the Queen's time. The people will think your heart has failed you."

Thus adjured, the Black Knight rode into his place.

" I did but rest my horse," he said, in a loud voice; " after two such victories he had need of it."

Clarence bowed.

Then they couched their lances and ran full tilt at one another.

The combat which ensued was an extremely interesting one.

One that called forth loud applause, and yet puzzled a great many.

The mysterious knight turned off, by an adroit use of his blunt lance, every effort of his adversary to thrust at his breastplate.

Again and again Clarence de Beaufort rushed furiously at him.

It was all in vain.

At any rate, for a long time.

The Black Knight seemed in no hurry to attack his adversary.

He seemed, in fact, anxious to amuse the public with a little display.

Then came an unexpected event.

Both the combatants retired to the extreme edge of the lists, and then at a given signal they dashed forward furiously.

They met in mid career.

The shock was great, but it was apparent to nearly every one that the Black Knight made no effort.

To those experienced in the tourney, and who had seen his brilliant performances before, it seemed certain that he could if he had liked have turned off every one of Clarence's strokes.

But he was caught full in the chest.

His horse fell *or was pulled* on to its haunches, and the Black Knight nearly rolled over into the dust.

The people gazed at the scene in astonishment.

They saw that evidently the Black Knight had some reason for not wishing to win the day.

The marshal of the lists, however, had no idea of letting things end in this way.

He at once rushed up to the spot where the Black Knight had leaped from his saddle.

"Here is a sword, most noble sir," he cried, "as you are not flung from your horse into the dust, you and your antagonist must try the ordeal of the sword."

"Most willingly would I obey your commands, most worshipful sir," replied the Black Knight, "but in very truth I cannot. My right arm has received such a shock that I cannot well hold a sword. I must even confess myself beaten."

There was no preventing this refusal to proceed, and consequently the Black Knight, after a low bow to the Queen, took his way from the lists.

Elizabeth turned to Essex with a sly laugh.

"Ha," she said, "your champion, then, is not invincible."

"Nay, then, your Majesty," said the Earl, who had an expression of pain upon his face. "I never said he was invincible. But I have reason to believe that he had a motive in his defeat."

The Queen thought a moment.

"Will not this strange knight disclose himself to me?" said she. "Will you ask him, Essex?"

"I will ask him this very day," said Essex; "he would act as you wish to no one but yourself; but he will no doubt trust to a Queen's honour."

The tourney now went on as before.

But to many the sight had lost much of its charm.

The strange knight had been expected by all to be the hero of the day.

And now that *he* was out of it, there seemed no one to take his place.

CHAPTER LX.

THE END OF THE JOUSTS—THE ATTEMPTED ASSASSINATION—AN UNEXPECTED RESCUE.

So that the jousts should not flag for want of support, Essex and others of the nobles went into the lists after Clarence de Beaufort had gone through several successful encounters, and loud and tumultuous were the shouts of welcome as they recognised the leaders who had led the English on to victory on many a hard-fought field.

It was a grand day for Elizabeth.

She was at this time in the zenith of her glory.

And well she knew what all this enthusiasm meant.

She knew that every cheer was another rivet in the support of her throne.

At length the jousts came to an end.

The bands struck up a loud-resounding melody.

Amid roars of applause Essex aided the Queen to mount her white palfrey,

and once more the merry assemblage moved towards the royal palace.

It was a gayer cavalcade now, however, than it had been in the morning.

All those who had taken part in the jousts were now present in armour.

Many were those who wore emblems of their victories and signs that they had been there, from those who were ready to show their appreciation of their courage.

Little bouquets of flowers, and little knots of ribbons had been fastened to helm and breastplate by fair hands, and the Black Knight and Clarence de Beaufort had emblems of royal favour.

The people all manifested their joy in a hundred ways.

But there was one there who did not join in the general joy.

This one was Ellersleigh.

He had hoped in the position in which

"HORSE AND RIDER WENT HEADLONG TO THE GROUND."

he had been placed by the man Shelton, to be able to do some injury to the horse of the Black Knight, so that he would not prove competent to win a single encounter ; and in a general melée he had intended to stab him in the back, if he could find a chance of doing it unseen.

But he had never had even the ghost of an opportunity of carrying out his evil intenton.

And as the day went on his potations were deep, and his brow grew darker, his murderous eyes more inflamed, and he uttered horrible threats to himself.

A chance occurred to him at last that he little thought of.

Just at a moment when he least expected it.

Not, be it said, a chance of doing the cruel act unseen.

That idea had long since been driven out of him by the drink.

He was, in fact, nothing but a furious madman by the time the jousts were over.

The very worst of madness was his.

He was a madman keeping down his furious anger.

He had resolved in his drunken rage to sacrifice himself rather than not carry out his murderous design.

So he planted himself in such a position that he could see the whole eavalcade defile before him.

As luck would have it, or rather let me say ill-luck, the Black Knight was on that side of the procession which passed nearest the would-be assassin.

Ellersleigh clutched his dagger eagerly.

His plan was to rush forward, run his long knife into the horse's stomach, and then, as the wretched animal fell, to leap at its rider, and stab him in some vulnerable point.

He made one desperate plunge as the strange knight came near.

Having given himself up entirely, he made no hesitation.

His rush was a well premeditated one, and the stab he gave to the unfortunate horse struck home.

The animal reared up in its excessive agony.

Then it gave vent to a short neigh, and fell.

Its rider fell too.

It was exactly as the murderous wretch had anticipated.

The Black Knight had no time to leap to the ground before his enemy was upon him, stabbing madly at him at every point where he deemed it possible to find a vulnerable part.

But rescue was at hand.

Rescue from a quarter little expected by the Black Champion.

Clarence de Beaufort happened to be riding just behind him.

And when he saw the cowardly and unprovoked attack upon the brave, though unknown knight, whom he had met in the lists, he leaped at once to the ground.

Others saw the deed.

But they were not in time.

Clarence leaped so quickly and lightly over, that he was before them all.

His sword at once flashed from its sheath.

Not that he had any idea of fighting the wretch.

He was there for vengeance.

Not knowing who it was whom he was befriending, he dashed upon the assassin.

"Vile wretch!" he cried, "turn on me, not on the helpless!"

The answer was a volley of blows delivered at the back of the knight, who had been partially stunned, but was partially recovering himself.

There was an end of it all soon, however.

The villain, fancying that he at length had his enemy in his power, had lost all reason, and the first knowledge that came to him that he had failed in his object, was a wound from Clarence's sword.

He had only time to realise his disappointment.

Not an instant was given him to speak.

Without hesitation, without thinking of the presence of the surrounding nobles or the Queen, Clarence had struck again, and his sword leaped through the assassin's body.

Without a groan he fell back dead, and in an instant after the strange knight sprang to his feet.

"Kind sir," he said, as he grasped the hand of Beaufort, "I owe to you my life. At some future time, when most you have need of help, may I be there to aid you."

Clarence could not reply.

His excitement now was over, and the

words of the strange knight had brought once more to his mind the woes and miseries of his life—the terrors which had driven him to London from his ancient home of Montreville.

But the emotion, visible on his features, was enough thanks.

He saw the face pale, the lips quiver, a moisture invade the eyes, and he guessed the reply which was still unsaid.

The Queen had been purposely surrounded by her courtiers to prevent her from seeing the ghastly scene which was passing so near her.

She could not, however, fail to know that something unusual was happening.

"What is the matter? What has happened?" she asked of Essex, as he came up to her flushed and excited.

"A ruffian leaping from the crowd attempted to assassinate my friend, the Black Knight," he said; "your nobles closed around you for fear some other villain might have designs upon your Majesty."

"I thank you, my lord of Essex," said the Queen, haughtily, her temper changing, "but if you would keep my good opinion do not treat me as some silly maiden who is afraid of the sight of blood. I am a Queen, and desire to be treated as such."

"Your Majesty mistakes me," replied Essex; "but I will explain. It is only the extreme loyalty of your subjects which caused them to have this idea. Where would England be if it lost *you?*"

The Queen smiled.

She loved flattery, but this was so grossly patent that she could not avoid feeling amused.

"It is very well to flatter," she said, "but still it does not away with the fact that you have treated me like a silly child. Let us hasten on to the palace, and there I wish to see and speak with this mysterious stranger."

"Very good, your Majesty," said Essex, "I will give orders to hasten on the procession."

"But tell me, how did this happen?" said the Queen, as Essex once more returned to her side.

Essex briefly explained all.

"So it was my youthful knight that saved him," she said.

"Yes, I am glad, indeed, to say so,"

said the noble captain, "it could not have happened better had it all been planned."

On reaching the palace the Queen retired at once to her private boudoir.

Here in a few minutes she was joined by the Black Knight.

His face was still concealed, but he knelt before the Queen humbly to show that it was no disrespect—no lack of courtesy which made him act thus.

"My most noble lady," said he, "forgive me that I appear before you without showing my face. I have resolved until a certain date never to allow my features to be seen."

"Could you not take the word of a Queen that she would not betray you," said Elizabeth.

The words were said in a true and earnest voice.

Elizabeth, in fact, was at her best.

She meant the words she uttered.

How could he refuse her?

"My Queen," he said, "I will trust you so far as to show you my face; but even now I cannot give my name. That is my greatest secret."

He rose and raised his visor.

The Queen started as her eyes fell upon his noble features.

"So like, and yet so much more stern and handsome," she murmured.

Then she said, aloud—

"Enough, brave knight, I have seen your prowess in the tourney, and I respect you for it. But I respect you more because I fancy that I can fathom your secret. Go on and prosper, and, believe me, you have a Queen's best wishes with you."

"Which is something to remember and give me courage," he said. "Farewell, madam, and may Heaven bless and preserve your Majesty."

He then retired, leaving the Queen deep in meditation.

The evening following the jousts, Clarence de Beaufort was just thinking about retiring to rest, when visitors were announced.

To his surprise he found that they were his mother and Sir Grey de Malpas.

His astonishment, as may be supposed, was utter and complete.

He would as soon have thought of seeing the ghost of Henry VIII., as Lady Montreville and Sir Grey.

His thoughts naturally reverted to the terrors he had endured at home, and, of course, they were connected in his mind with their coming.

"What is the matter, dear mother?" he said, when he had embraced her, and coldly received Sir Grey.

"You must return at once to Montreville, my son," said Lady Montreville.

"Return!" he cried.

"Aye, my son, it is a necessity."

"But I cannot! I dare not!"

"Nay, then, Clarence, I must appeal to your love," said his mother; "it is for my sake that I ask you this. It is to settle something, which cannot be settled without you."

"What is it then?" asked Clarence.

"That I cannot explain now," said his mother; "you must wait until we reach Montreville."

"Then," said Clarence, with unaccustomed firmness, "I refuse to go!"

Lady Montreville looked earnestly at De Malpas.

Her lips quivered, and her features were deadly pale.

"Let it be so," said Sir Grey.

"Let it be so!" exclaimed Lady Montreville. "Court my own ruin!"

"If to his former sins your unnatural son wishes to add matricide, how can I prevent it?" said De Malpas. "Let us go. This is no place for *you*. Madam, you must fly to France, and let the crumbling old Towers of Montreville, in after ages, tell the story of an undutiful son."

During these speeches, Clarence de Beaufort had been pacing rapidly to and fro.

Suddenly, as Sir Grey finished speaking, he said, abruptly—

"Say no more. I will go. Perhaps this act will atone somewhat for the past."

That very night Clarence had sent his dutiful respects to the Queen, and the party had set out for home.

Home!

What a home it was to seek!

CHAPTER LXI.

THE STRANGE ACCUSER.

As soon as it was known that Lord Beaufort with Sir Grey de Malpas and the countess had reached once more the Towers of Montreville, Sir Godfrey Seymour was at once informed of it by the treacherous kinsman.

The solemn array again entered the court-yard of the castle, without the knowledge of the young lord.

He was indignant when he heard from Marsden that Sir Godfrey was there, and that his mother knew it.

"What means this, Marsden?" he cried. "Am I not master here, that I am told nothing of these things before they happen? 'Fore heaven, I'll bid them begone!"

As he spoke thus, Beaufort, pale and angry, and followed by Marsden and other attendants, burst furiously into the Hall of Justice.

It was evident from the surprise which Lord Beaufort evinced, as he entered it, that he knew nothing of the cause of the proceedings.

Sir Grey de Malpas had carried out well the wishes of Sir Godfrey Seymour, and even Lady Montreville, as we have seen, had yielded to the wishes of others, and had kept from her son the knowledge that he was to return to the Halls of Montreville to meet his trial.

"Off, dotard, off!" cried Clarence, as he flung from him the arm of Marsden, who was striving to repress his violent anger. "Guests in our hall! This is a surprise."

"He is ill!" exclaimed his mother, as she quitted her seat, and advanced towards him; "he is sore ill. A fierce fever has possession of him; I will lead him forth. Come, Clarence, darling, come."

Lord Beaufort heard not her words.

His eyes were fixed curiously upon Lieutenant Falkner, who again came forward as accuser.

"Who is this man?" he asked.

"I am the friend of Vyvyan, whose pale bones plead yonder," replied Falkner. "We have met before!"

In an instant a change came over the face of Clarence Beaufort.

His complexion turned to an ashen grey colour, and he took the arm of Lady Montreville.

"I—I will go," he said, losing all presence of mind; "let's steal away, mother."

For an instant then she felt angry with herself to think that she had brought him from London; that she had not, in fact, contrived some means by which he could have escaped to some foreign country, and there remained until this matter had blown over, or had been explained in some manner favourable to Clarence.

Her mother's heart, of course, was distracted by a thousand doubts and fears.

She had been convinced before that the best way for her son to meet this accusation was to boldly face it.

But now she felt as if she had treacherously betrayed him to his enemies.

The more strong was this feeling in her heart as her son added in a low whisper—

"Oh! mother! how could you thus deliver me over to my enemies? Let us go."

There was one there, however, whose purpose would have been quite baulked by this.

It was now or never with him.

This one was Sir Grey de Malpas.

Upon the issue of this judicial contest all his high hopes were staked.

Murder once fixed on Beaufort—and that the murder of the Rightful Heir—then who but Sir Grey remained sole Lord of Montreville?

Sir Grey, therefore, as he saw the desire of Beaufort to quit the council-chamber, hurried forward and intercepted him.

"Stay, my lord," he said, in a whisper, "and you, too, my fair cousin. This is but madness. This wild rover has already questioned you before your visit to London, and demands to question your son. To steal away is to avow a crime. For such refusal of all reply illness is no excuse. Lord Beaufort, if you do not remain, you accuse yourself. Madam, if you force him hence, you condemn your son."

"True—true! Clarence, let us remain and face them," said Lady Montreville, as they neared the table at which the clerk was writing.

"Lost friend!" murmured Falkner. "How often, in war, was thy word, 'spare!' Methinks I hear thee now!"

Then he added, turning to Beaufort, "Young lord, I came into these halls demanding blood for blood; but your remorse—for this *is* remorse—disarms me. Speak boldly—I am young myself, and know how hot youth is—do but say, 'After warm words, offspring of jealous fury, quick swords were drawn—man's open strife with man—passion, not murder.' Say this, and may law pardon you as a soldier does!"

As Falkner spoke, Marsden, the seneschal, was called aside by Sir Grey,

"Call Eveline," said De Malpas; "she can attest our young lord's innocence."

Beaufort, meanwhile, seemed struck dumb with horror, while Falkner eyed him now with a less kindly glance.

"He will not speak, Sir Godfrey," he said, turning to the magistrate; "let my charge proceed."

Lady Montreville saw now that the critical moment was coming.

She pressed her son's arm closely.

"Clarence," she said, in a stern undertone, "whatever the truth may be, of that hereafter. Remember now nothing but your birth—your name. Your mother's heart beats beside you; take strength from that."

"Keep close then, mother," replied her unhappy son, "and for *your* sake I will *not* cry—'twas passion, yet still murder!"

During these few words of private colloquy, Sir Grey had been conversing aside with Sir Godfrey, and pouring now more boldly into his ear his venomous suggestions.

"Jealous love, then, was the motive?" said the magistrate, as Eveline and Marsden were seen approaching. "Likelier that, indeed, than Alton's wilder story. Sweet young maiden, if I am blunt, forgive me. We are met here on solemn matters, which relate to one who, it was said, was your betrothed."

"To Vyvyan!" exclaimed Eveline, clasping her hands in fear.

"The same. It is also said that Lord Beaufort crossed his suit, and that your betrothed resented it."

"Unarmed!"

"His very words," murmured Eveline.

"Oh! vile assassin!" exclaimed the young sea-rover, fiercely.

Sir Godfrey raised his hand deprecatingly.

"Accuser, peace!" he cried. "This is most grave. Lord Beaufort, upon such signs as, with your own strange bearing, demand an appeal to a more august tribunal, you stand accused of the wilful murder of one Vyvyan, Captain of the

"STAND FORTH, SIR GREY DE MALPAS!" CRIED THE KNIGHT; "THOU ART THE MAN!"

"No, forgave——"

"Yes," interrupted Sir Grey de Malpas, now speaking openly for the first time, "yes; when you feared some challenge from Lord Beaufort, did not Vyvyan cast down his sword, and say, 'Both will be safe, for one will be unarmed?'"

A hurried murmur passed through the hall, and men looked one another fearfully in the face, while both Falkner and Sir Godfrey Seymour repeated as with one breath—

'Dreadnought.' Will you say anything against this solemn charge?"

"Murdered!" interrupted Eveline. "He, Vyvyan! and you his murderer, Clarence, in whose rash heat my hero saw frank valour? I, to whom his life is as the sun is to the world, before Heaven will swear you innocent!"

"Be firm—deny, and live!" murmured Lady Montreville to her pale and sorrow-stricken son.

Lord Beaufort drew himself up.

He recognised the all-important task before him, and with a vacillating attempt at his former haughtiness, he said—

"You call my bearing strange, Sir Godfrey. What marvel, sir, when I am stunned by having brought to my charge a crime so dread as this? What proof is there against me?"

As he said this, Sir Grey de Malpas stole gently behind the curtain, while Lady Montreville took up her son's speech.

"Words deposed by whom?" she said. "A man unknown—a girl's vague fear of quarrel—his motive what? A jealous anger! Phantoms! Is not my son mine all? and yet this maid I plighted to another! Had I done so if loved by him and at the risk of life? Again I ask all present—what is the motive?"

"Rank, fortune, birthright! miserable woman!" came the answer like an echo, as Alton stepped forward from the recess.

All present started in surprise.

"Whence come you, pale accuser?" muttered the countess, with pale lips.

"From the dead!" returned the priest, solemnly. "Which of ye two will take the post I leave? Which of ye two will draw aside that veil—look on the bones and cry, 'I'm guiltless!' Have you, my lady, conspired with him to slay your first-born, or knows he not that Vyvyan was his brother?"

Like the fall of a thunderbolt came these words upon all present.

With a gasping cry, Lady Montreville pressed her hand over her bosom, and, after an ineffectual effort at speech, swooned away, while Eveline, who, until now had held to Beaufort's arm, hurried to the side of the countess.

Beaufort stared wildly at Alton, and then, seizing Sir Grey's arm, he cried in a tone of agony—

"My brother! No—no—no! Say kinsman, he lies!"

"Alas!" said Sir Grey, bowing his head, as if in the depth of great sorrow, "it was even so!"

"Oh! wake, mother, wake!" cried Clarence, wildly. "I ask not speech. Lift but your brow—one flash of your proud eyes would strike these liars dumb!"

"Read but her looks," said Alton, solemnly, "to know that you are——"

"Cain!" cried Lord Beaufort. "Out with your sword, brave Falkner—hew off this hand! You called me 'assassin.' Too mild a word for me! Say rather 'fratricide!' Oh, Vyvyan—Vyvyan!"

Then, overwhelmed with shame, agony, and remorse, he clasped together his hands, and fell insensible on the floor.

"This cannot be," said Eveline boldly. "No. Oh, wondrous Mercy! that from the pirate's knife, the terrible seas, and all their shapes of death, did save the lone one to prove how vainly man on earth despairs while God is in the Heavens! I cling still to thee, as Faith unto its anchor! Back—back, false kinsman!" she added, to Sir Grey. "I tell you Vyvyan lives. The boy is guiltless!"

"Poor, noble maid," murmured the brave young rover, "how my heart bleeds for her!"

Lady Montreville at this moment started from her swoon, casting back from her brow the tresses which had escaped from their fastenings.

Her mother's heart was now charged with a terrible feeling.

She would sacrifice herself—cast in the teeth of the world its condemnation, and save Clarence at the expense of her own dignity—her own honour—her own life!"

"Sentence us both!" she exclaimed; "or stay, would the law condemn a child so young if I had urged him to it?"

A frown crossed the face of the judge as this strange woman, torn by conflicting emotions, uttered these wild words.

"Unnatural mother!" he cried "hush! To such words as these I will not—cannot listen. To another tribunal you may state these reasons, which, in the eyes of all, will condemn you as an unheard-of wrong-doer, but not to me. Sir Grey de Malpas, approach!"

This was the moment of triumph for De Malpas.

The poor cousin was already recognised chief power in Montreville.

Once more before his eyes, not now visionary, as before, but real, solid, close to his grasping hands, the titles and honours, the wealth and all the pleasur it could bring, that had been denied to his ardent youth.

Already he saw fawning lacqueys and wondering crowds, and heard himself spoken to as "my most gracious lord," and listened to whispers of the strange freaks of fortune—of hopes long deferred and now fulfilled.

Content already sat in his heart—already he was standing as it were in his own halls—already he could look from the battlements on fair lands and say:

"These, all these are mine!"

He advanced, however, towards Sir Godfrey Seymour with a look of affected sorrow upon his face.

"Sir Grey," said the magistrate, "to you I entrust these prisoners—you, who ere long, perchance, will be raised to the earldom by the just forfeiture of felon lives."

As he spoke he motioned to the halberdiers, who advanced to arrest Lord Beaufort and his mother.

"Make way for us," cried Sir Grey de Malpas, in a loud tone of newly-acquired authority.

At the moment that Sir Grey spoke he appeared as if suddenly his stature had increased.

He drew himself up as it were by supernatural strength; the lines of his face seemed to disappear as his face became filled out by the rush of blood caused by his triumphant pride.

One haughty glance he gave around upon those who were assembled.

Then with a bow, which, although formal, had in it a kind of simulated kindness, he said—

"And now, Lady Montreville, and my Lord Beaufort, it is my unpleasant duty to request you to follow me, since I am commanded by Sir Godfrey Seymour to hold you in safe custody."

Both Lady Montreville and her son knew well the character of Sir Grey.

They were, therefore, in no way deceived by any show of kindness on his part.

They merely bowed consequently, and placed themselves between the two bodies of halberdiers, none of whom could avoid displaying the sorrow which they felt at the disaster which had befallen the house of Montreville.

Sir Godfrey Seymour, stern judge though he was, knew that he was in the presence of a terrible family catastrophe, and as mother and son passed out he slightly inclined his head.

There was a halt as they reached the outer hall.

Here Lady Montreville and Clarence had to separate.

Whither they had to go they knew not.

There was an abundance of rooms in the old Castle of Montreville which were unoccupied.

But they were certainly not prepared for the choice of chambers which Sir Grey de Malpas had made.

"Martin Dacre," said the latter, "conduct Lady Montreville to the grey chamber."

The man addressed bowed deeply.

"Madam," he said, "will you follow me?"

"Lead on!" said the unhappy lady.

And then she cast a wistful look at Clarence.

This look was enough.

In another moment he had sprang forward.

"Mother," he cried, "they separate us in body, but they cannot separate us in mind. Take no thought of me, mother—run no risks for me. Whatever wrong has been done has been mine, and mine only!"

"Hush! say no more before thy worst foe!" said Lady Montreville.

"Aye, truly, my worst foe and yours, mother," said Clarence; "it is for that I say, live to thwart him. If I am sacrificed for the evil I wrought in my mad haste and wicked vengeance, at least do you live so that the honour of the name shall not be in the keeping of such a man as De Malpas."

"Come!" said the poor kinsman, "time presses. I should not hasten you, but Sir Godfrey Seymour awaits my return."

Lady Montreville made no direct reply to this.

"Whither lead you my son?" she asked.

"Whither?" replied Sir Grey, "indeed, but to the Eagle's Tower."

Lady Montreville started.

"Oh! why thither, Sir Grey?" she cried, losing for a moment her presence of mind.

The poor kinsman smiled.

It was a smile so evil that all present saw the wicked triumph which lurked beneath it.

"You know well the legend of the Eagle's Tower," he said; "this is no time to repeat it. Come, Lord Beaufort, the worthy magistrate will not wait."

Lady Montreville at the mention of the legend pressed her hand to her breast.

"Wretch! then it is premeditated!" cried she, "may Heaven reward *you*, as *you* are treating *us*."

Then with a last fond embrace mother and son parted.

"This way, my lord," said Sir Grey.

And Beaufort with a haughty gesture bade him lead on.

CHAPTER LXII.

THE EAGLE'S TOWER—THE REVEL ON THE WILD SEA-SHORE.

THE Eagle's Tower was on the extreme left of the old castle—the tower which had proved fatal to the brave page who sacrificed himself so many years before to save the honour of the young bride he loved so well.

But this was not the legend to which Sir Grey had alluded.

It was a far older one.

One which had reference to an ancestor, who had been accused of doing, if he did not do, a desperate and wicked deed.

For this he had been, as Beaufort was, imprisoned in his own castle, and to avoid the iron hand of justice he had hanged himself in the room which had been given to him as a cell.

The rooms which he had occupied had never after been used.

They were, in fact, kept apart in order to be rendered available if on some future occasion one of the race should do an evil deed again.

Until Clarence de Beaufort, none had been accused.

He knew nothing, of course, of the sad memories which preyed upon his mother's brain.

He knew nothing of the father of Vyvyan who had given his life to save the honour of the bride he loved so well.

"This is a gloomy place that you have brought me to, Sir Grey," he said, as he entered the chamber with its heavy curtains and furniture, which, though in reality *not* mouldy, seemed so with age.

Sir Grey started.

The voice in which the words were said was one so different to that which was usually adopted by Clarence, that it was no wonder that he was surprised.

It was nothing like the voice which was wont to wake up the echoes of the old corridors of Montreville.

It was firm—stern—sedate.

Years seemed to have been added to his age suddenly.

"Yes," said Sir Grey de Malpas, "it *is* a gloomy place."

"And why, then, has it been chosen for *me*?" asked Beaufort.

"It is a fitting place for malefactors," replied the other.

Clarence turned upon him with a savage flush of anger.

"And you, Sir Grey," he cried, "standing there before me, dare to tell me that I am a malefactor when you know that your whole wish and aim in life has been to destroy me and my mother."

His hand was on his sword hilt as he spoke.

Sir Grey gave a sneering smile.

"Ha!" he cried, "fresh for murder again? It comes natural to you it seems."

Clarence, who had half drawn his sword by this time, thrust it back angrily into its sheath.

"Bah!" he cried, "you are not worth staining a good sword for!"

And turning, he passed to the window, he looked out over the fair landscape, o'er which Vyvyan's father had so often looked upon the rocks, too, on which his young life had been wrecked.

Sir Grey said no more.

He turned to the halberdiers.

"Lead back to the Justice Hall," he said, in a loud tone of authority.

And then, turning the key in the lock of Clarence's room, he followed them.

He was now in his element.

At length, if it was only for a time, he was master of Montreville.

His old golden dreams were realised.

He was,—if this terrible ruin overtook the mother and son—Heir of Montreville; and as his lean limbs tottered along with all the newly inspired strength of authority, he glanced round him in a manner which was intended to prove how he would act in case he was to obtain possession of the estates for good.

His interview with Sir Godfrey Seymour was not a long one.

A few formal remarks were passed, and then the trial was adjourned until three days had gone by.

Willingly would Sir Grey de Malpas have held high revel in the castle that night.

But he dared not.

What would the retainers and others have said if he had openly expressed his joy when the ruin of the family was imminent?

However, there was that joyous spirit within him that he was unable entirely to restrain himself.

Under pretence of going away on business, he left the castle under the care of Marsden—with such strict orders as were sufficient to show his newly-constituted authority, and quitted the castle for the night.

He went straight to his own lone hut on the sea shore.

We have mentioned it before although we have not described it.

A wretched lonely dwelling, on the verge of the ocean, where the great billows made hoarse melody through day and night.

Here he knew well that he could keep high revel with his companions without being afraid of discovery.

On reaching the hut where he had spent so many hours of lonely misery and silent brooding, he dispatched to the neighbouring inn a man whom he kept to take care of the place in his absence, and also to help in obtaining the rude meals which the poor kinsman indulged in.

He was an object which would have alarmed some people, and only came to the aid of the poor cousin, because no one else would give him food or shelter.

Had he endeavoured to obtain it elsewhere, he would have been met with ridicule and scorn; and there was something, too, in the morose nature of the poor kinsman which suited him.

The wild crew which Sir Grey de Malpas soon gathered round him, was one which cared neither for decency nor anything else.

What cared they that the Lady of Montreville and Clarence de Beaufort were in durance, or that Vyvyan was dead.

Their only cause for remark was the fact that they were able, through this terrible misfortune, to revel in all that fed their evil passions.

Loud songs were wafted out upon the night air.

Songs, and laughter, and cheers, which were answered by the roaring of the billows at first, but which was presently mingled with the awful roarings of the thunder.

The day had been terribly hot.

In fact, since early dawn it had been promising a storm.

And now it was a fearful one.

While the tankards chinked, and the wine was poured out in rich red gushes,—spilled on the floor by eager hands; while the song and the joke passed around, and everything that was said and done was outrageous and out of place, the thunder boomed so as to rock the very foundations of the cabin, and the lightning playing against the casements, which were broken here and there in places, illumined ever and anon the faces of the revellers with ghastly distinctness.

Presently the wine began to take effect upon the drinkers.

For there was an abundance of good cheer.

The poor cousin had wasted on this occasion all the store which his miserliness had been able to collect for emergencies.

He had, as far as he could do so, stinted nothing; and so it was not long before those whom he had invited, lay rolling under the table.

He cared not for this.

It was the commencement of what he considered would be his life at Montreville.

Already from the lips of these drunken brawlers he had received the adulation which he so loved.

What would it be?

How would it give balm to his heart when he was Earl of Montreville; when he trod as master through those stately halls; when those who fawned upon him and congratulated him upon the strange freaks of fortune were of a higher class; men and women, too, were in the same category as himself.

The wine which he had imbibed seemed not to take the same effect upon him as it did upon the others.

In fact, his nerves were too overstrung to enable the drink to have any power over him.

He was simply nerved up now by his potations of wine to any amount of courage.

He did not like the atmosphere of that room, however.

It was hot and disagreeable, and those who were in it made it appear infinitely worse.

However, it was easy to escape.

He approached the door and opened it.

The storm was just approaching its end.

The thunder still rolled, and the lightning played over the ocean.

But there was no wind, and the waves rolled merely to and fro in quiet billows.

"It is something like the ending of *my* miseries," said Sir Grey de Malpas; "the storm is over: and though still the thunder of discontent is booming, and the lightning of wrath is flashing, there is the sea calm, which tells me of my future restful life."

At this instant he saw approaching him, a figure.

It appeared like the figure of a man, but it approached so silently, and so glidingly, that as he gazed upon it, a strange fear invaded the mind of Sir Grey de Malpas.

A shudder passed through the frame of the poor kinsman.

He turned his head, and then suddenly gazed again.

The figure seemed to grow larger as it advanced.

Sir Grey could stand no more.

He turned hastily and passed into the little cottage.

Still the drunken slumberers slept on.

As he closed the door, however, the storm seemed to return.

The thunder boomed again more fiercely than ever: the lightning flashed as noisily.

And then suddenly, in the midst of the strange light, there appeared at the window a face!

A face that in that storm and night seemed white and ghastly.

One look was enough for Sir Grey.

He gave a gasping cry and fell senseless among the wine-liking crew that everywhere cumbered the floor.

CHAPTER LXIII.

APPROACHING THE END.

IT was dawn when Sir Grey de Malpas awoke from his swoon.

He roused his wretched boon com- panions — gave them some wine and dismissed them — and then, after dressing himself as scrupulously as he could be, he bent his way to Montreville.

At twelve that day Sir Godfrey Seymour arrived again.

He had, he said, heard news of something which necessitated the immediate renewal of the trial.

Accordingly once more Clarence de Beaufort and his mother were brought into the presence of an anxious crowd and arraigned.

Scarcely, however, had the old evidence been gone through when an unexpected incident occurred.

At this moment the loud braying of a trumpet was heard without the walls of the castle, and in another instant a servant burst hurriedly into the hall, saying—

"My Lord of Essex has just passed the gates, and even now he waits at no long distance. But an armed knight, that rode beside the earl—when he heard, from the crowd without, the reason of the tumult—sprang from his steed, and against all odds forced hither his way."

He had scarcely delivered himself of this speech, when a knight in half armour, with his vizor down, and wrapped in his horseman's cloak, burst into the hall.

"Forgiveness of all present," he said, bowing to Sir Godfrey, and the others around.

"Who art thou?" asked the magistrate, somewhat sternly.

"A soldier knighted by the hand of Essex upon the breach of Cadiz," replied the stranger.

"And what is thy business?" asked Sir Godfrey.

"To speak the truth. Who is the man accused of Vyvyan's murder?" replied the stranger.

"You behold him yonder," said Sir Grey, pointing to Beaufort, who had now been raised from the ground and stood near his mother.

"'Tis false!" exclaimed the mail-clad stranger.

"His own lips have confessed his crime," said De Malpas.

The knight turned fiercely.

He drew his gauntlet from his hand and threw it on the ground with an angry gesture.

"That!" he cried, "that to the man whose crushing lie bows down that young and innocent head upon his mother's bosom. Dare you say to me that he confessed this crime?"

"Aye, confessed," said Sir Grey de Malpas.

"Oh, tender conscience!" pursued the knight. "I have heard from those without the object and the result of the trial. I will tell the story, for I know it well myself.

"They met, truly, on the summit of St. Kinian's Cliff.

"Vyvyan, rough sailor as he was, galled and provoked Lord Beaufort, who raised his hand.

"To the sharp verge of the rocks Vyvyan recoiled, backed by an outstretched bough,

"The bough gave way, and Vyvyan fell; but not to perish.

"Saved by a bush-grown ledge, that broke his fall, he lay a long time stunned, and when at length he opened his eyes, he beheld upon a grey crag, between him and the abyss, the face and form of an old pirate foe.

"He saw the villain raise his flashing sword, and then he sprang to his feet, just in time.

"A long while, down among the rocky darkness, they contested for life, but Providence watched o'er Vyvyan, and it was *his* steel that entered the recreant bosom —steel that he snatched from his coward foeman's belt.

"Stung by late remorse, his enemy, as his conqueror bent over him, gasped forth a dread confession, whose every word Vyvyan remembered.

"The bones you found beneath the cliffs are those of Murder's Agent!

"You will ask me who was the arch-schemer—Murder's inventor? I will tell you.

Ho! Grey de Malpas! Stand forth!

"THOU ART THE MAN!!"

The words rang through the Hall of Justice, and echoed in every heart.

There was a ring of truth in them, which no one could avoid recognising.

CHAPTER LXIV.

IN WHICH THE CURTAIN DESCENDS.

SIR GREY DE MALPAS, though wonder-stricken at the words and the demeanour of the bold knight, saw all his future staked upon his bold demeanour.

Swiftly, as with the hand of youth, he drew his sword from its scabbard, and stood upright and defiantly before his strange foe.

"Hemmed round with toils," he cried. "Crouch no more, my soul! Base hireling, doff thy mask, and my good sword will write the lie upon thy front. By Beaufort's hand died Vyvyan."

"As the spell shatters the sorcerer when his fiends desert him," shouted the knight, "let thine own words bring doom upon thyself. Now face the front on which to write the lie."

As he spoke, he cast off his helmet and showed to the astonished crowd the noble features of the long absent Vyvyan.

For an instant there was an utter silence throughout the Great Hall.

There was only one feeling throughout the assemblage.

To see Vyvyan himself, standing there full of health and strength, was more than they could well believe.

But it was soon proved to be the truth.

As Sir Grey de Malpas beheld the well-known lineaments of the man whose death he had sought to compass, his sword fell from his hand, and he staggered back into the arms of the retainers.

"Air, air! My staff!" he cried, as he pressed his hand to his heart; "some chord seems broken here. Marsden, your lord shot his poor cousin's dog. In the dog's grave, mark, bury the poor cousin."

As he spoke, he sank exhausted into the arms of the servants, and was borne away unregretted from the scene.

In fact no one noticed him after the first outburst of feeling was over.

"You live, you live!" cried Eveline, advancing with a rush to her mail-clad lover.

"Yes," said Vyvyan, as he pressed her to his bosom; "is life worth something still? Mine all on earth, if I may call you mine."

"Yours, yours through life, through death," she murmured; "one heart, one grave! I knew you would return, for I have lived in you so utterly; you could not die and I live still. The dial needs the sun; but love reflects the image of the loved, though every beam be absent! Yes—yes—I am yours—all yours, dear Vyvyan!"

"My place," said Lady Montreville, pointing to Beaufort, "is forfeit on your breast, not his. Clarence, embrace your brother, and my first-born. His rights are clear; my love for you suppressed them. He may forgive me yet; will you forgive me also, my unfortunate son?"

"Forgive you!" exclaimed Beaufort. "Oh, mother, what is rank to him who has stood banished from out the social pale of men, bowed like a slave, and trembling as a felon? Heaven gives me back mine ermine—innocence; and my lost dignity of manhood—honour. I miss nothing else. Room there for me, my brother, on your breast. I claim it from you."

"Mother, come first; love is as large as Heaven," cried Vyvyan, and as he spoke, the long-tried woman rushed forward, and was clasped to her son's bosom.

"But why so long did you delay—why so long did you keep your safety from our knowledge?" asked Captain Falkner.

"What! could I face you, my friend," said Vyvyan, "or claim my bride till I had won back honour?

"The fleet had sailed, the foemen were defeated, and on the earth I lay me down to die.

"The Prince of England's youth, frank-hearted Essex, passed by; but later I will tell you how pity woke question—soldier felt for soldier.

"Essex then, nobly envying Drake's renown, conceived a scheme kept secret, till our clarions, startling the towers of Spain, told earth and time how England answers the boast of her invader.

"Clarence, you see I have won the golden spurs of knighthood!"

"But, my son," asked Lady Montreville, "why did you not disclose yourself to us when we were in London. So much then would have been saved to all of us."

"And lost," said Vyvyan. "I knew I should be in time to rescue my brother, and therefore delayed until I could confront and defeat that murderous archschemer, Sir Grey de Malpas, whose plan was to destroy us all that he might reach the earldom himself, no matter through whose ruin."

"But," he added, "there is another thing I would ask my brother."

"What is that, Edmond," said Clarence. "I will answer anything"

"Well, then, do you remember the tourney at the Crooked Fields, in London?"

"I do."

"You remember the knight whom you conquered in the lists?"

"Aye; but he seemed to *me* to wish to lose."

"But do you also recollect that you saved his life."

"I do," said Clarence, smiling.

It was, indeed, a pleasant smile, for a sweet hope had entered his breast.

"Is it possible," he added, "that that knight was you, my brother?"

"Aye! *I* was that knight," cried Vyvyan; "and to *you* I owe my existence. I have to thank you for my being here now!"

As he spoke, and laid his hand with an affectionate smile upon the shoulder of his brother, there was a loud blast of trumpets without the castle, and in another moment a man in armour entered the room.

He bowed to all present.

"My Lord of Essex sends you all greeting," he cried, as he raised the vizor of his helmet; "and as the weather threatens to be tempestuous, he asks for shelter."

"Welcome, most welcome will my brave lord be here," said Lady Montreville.

Then blushing faintly, as she turned to Vyvyan, remembering something suddenly, she added,

"Edmond, invite him to *your* castle. All, all is yours now."

"Sweet mother," said Vyvyan, "as for worldly gifts, we'll share them. Nay, then, my brother, hush! Love me, and your gift is as large as mine. Fortune stints gold to some—impartial Nature shames her in proffering more than gold to all; joy in the sunshine, beauty on the earth, and love—sweet love, brighter still than all.

"Are these so mean?

"Place grief and greed beside them —even though decked in a sultan's splendour—and then compare them. The world's most royal heritage is that man's who most enjoys, most loves, and most forgives. We are all Lords of Montreville; therefore, in the name of all, invite the Earl of Essex to our hearth."

The mail-clad retainer, who had brought the news, departed at these words; and, in the space of a few minutes, as it were, a splendid cavalcade filed into the grand old hall.

Forgotten, then, as if never existing, were the thoughts of Vyvyan's death, the cloud on the noble escutcheon, the grief and shame of Beaufort, the agony and fears of Lady Montreville.

All eyes were turned upon the brilliant array of knights, and a loud and echoing cheer rang through the lofty hall as the Earl of Essex doffed his glittering helmet, and raising the hand of Lady Montreville, pressed it to his lips.

That day was a day of general feasting at the old castle.

Never since the old, old days had so much wine been consumed, or such splendid joints roasted, or such a jovial scene been witnessed.

It was a thorough day of thanksgiving, rejoicing, and forgiveness, and the dawn of the next morning saw every one in Montreville happier far than for many a year gone by.

And that day, moreover, was the dawning of happiness still greater.

The marriage of Vyvyan and Eveline, postponed through so many years, took place amid the acclamations and smiles of as gay an assemblage as ever graced the old Castle with their presence.

Lord Essex himself gave the bride away, and never, perhaps, had a happier or a more handsome couple graced the marriage altar.

Gone now were all the jealous thoughts of Lord Beaufort.

Happy in the love of his brother—in the renewed hopefulness of life, he learned to love another, who in time became his wife, and shared with him the grand old home, from which he had once imagined he would have been dragged in shame.

Sir Grey de Malpas survived but a few days the utter destruction of his hopes, and died without the regret or respectful sorrow of any.

Lady Montreville lived a long, and calmly happy life with her two sons, as did also Alton, the priest, as chaplain to the Castle, never regretting the aid he had afforded in the past to him, who through all dangers—through sea storms, and perils by land—had yet by manly courage and devotion proved his position against malice and hate, as RIGHTFUL HEIR OF MONTREVILLE.

THE END

9 781535 814348